Of Time and Place

Of Time and Place

B. R. Freemont

Two Harbors Press
212 3rd Avenue North, Suite 290
Minneapolis, MN 55401
612.455.2293
www.TwoHarborsPress.com

ISBN-13: 978-1-937928-72-8
LCCN: 2012936875

Distributed by Itasca Books

Cover Design and Typeset by Wendy Baker

Printed in the United States of America

For Ruffie

I

Savannah, 2060

I WAS RETURNING FROM ONE of my distasteful, although fortunately infrequent, visits to Washington. In order to justify the payments I received, I needed to perform a bit of consulting work, and from time to time be in contact with a continually changing nonentity in the Federal Energy Department. I had taken the train to save money. As usual, it was running late, taking nine hours to make a six-hour trip. We did encounter a one-hour power-down in North Carolina, but, still, a three-hour delay is a three-hour delay.

Elsewhere, trains could travel at four hundred kilometers an hour. In this country, even on the faster intercity routes, two hundred was a top speed. Our trips tended to be longer; all the more reason for trains to be faster. Why had we not invested in the necessary infrastructure? Worst of all, through our outmoded rail system we were wasting energy—and this particularly bothered me.

In Savannah, the train station was located a few kilometers from downtown in a rundown area of scrub brush and litter. A poorly maintained bus carted passengers from the inter-city train station to downtown locations. I got off at Drayton Street where I needed another vehicle—a street tram—to take me south, out of the historic district.

So there I sat on a plastic bench. I might have entered the waiting tram, but it probably wouldn't leave for another thirty minutes. The bench was uncomfortable; however, it was no doubt cooler than the tram. At seven in the evening it was still hot, probably around thirty degrees, definitely warmer than normal for October in Savannah.

Thus far, there were only three people waiting for the tram. If we could get to ten people, it would leave. Otherwise, we needed to wait for the seven thirty scheduled departure time. That was the rule. The rule had been instituted a number of years earlier in order to save energy. There were many rules, which needed to be followed in order to deal with the chronic energy shortage, and I knew them all too well.

Two more people arrived. Another head poked out of the corner café to check the progress on obtaining a quorum. I figured about six people were now waiting. Slowly, I sauntered to the red and white tram and took the two steps one at a time. Not desirous of conversation, I sat in the middle of the compartment two seats away from any other occupant. A stout, middle-aged woman followed me aboard and sat in the seat across the aisle.

"Sure is a warm day." Her remark was directed at me.

"Yes," I replied succinctly, but I knew that even my monosyllabic reply was not likely to end the exchange. The Southerner, especially a southern woman, is talkative and extroverted when compared with a Northerner, and very much willing to share his or her opinions with a total stranger. I know this may not always be true, but it is a generalization that applies more often than not.

"Shame we have to sit on this infernal tram and wait for more people or for seven thirty. Can't stand all these oppressive rules we live by. More oppressive than an August day in our fair city. Well, at least it *was* a fair city. I remember when y'all could see hundreds of visitors walking through the squares and on River Street. So many of us were involved with the tourist industry. A paltry few visitors we see now. We used to have horse-drawn carriages taking people around. Sure they'd leave a scent of manure mingling with the tea olives, but that added a degree of pungency to the atmosphere." Taking into account her flowery language and choice of subject, my companion had possibly been a tour guide and perhaps was now unemployed or at least under-employed.

"Yes, ma'am." Although only a recent transplant to Savannah, I knew enough to say "ma'am" to a woman of age thirty or more. And this woman was clearly in the "or more" category.

"But I suppose y'all are too young to recall this."

"I only moved to Savannah six months ago." I rounded up my period of residency. "But I used to come here when I was young. My parents rented a condo on Hilton Head for vacations." I realized my multi-sentence reply would prolong the conversation until one of three things happened: I exited the tram, she exited the tram, or she found a more congenial person to talk to.

"But y'all are really too young to know how things were earlier in the century when Savannah was a bustling, expanding city. Florida had had its heyday, and then people were arriving here in droves. Savannah's self-imposed isolation was over. And look at poor Hilton Head, now. I'm sure you'd see all those condos empty. People just can't get there, or afford it. Pay all our money in taxes. You see, young man, I'm sixty-seven years old. I bet you're barely thirty."

"Closer to forty," I replied with a tinge of guilt in my tone, not that I should have felt guilty about my age.

"Still a youngster, as far as I'm concerned. Anyway, Savannah was much better back then, and we didn't have these absurd rules. Of course, I used to have my own car. Last one was a nice Honda. Bought it new out on Abercorn. Must have been a dozen dealerships out there. No such thing as a car dealership anymore. A few people have those electric thingamajigs, but real cars are few and far between. I recollect . . ." My new-found acquaintance stopped in mid-sentence. "Well, Lance Pritchard, haven't seen you in ages." I was quickly forgotten, as she began a conversation with an old friend, who had just entered the tram.

A few minutes later, the tram began to move south on Drayton Street. Twenty-five years earlier, Drayton Street was one-way in the opposite direction, but it was commandeered to serve as the main North/South light tramline thoroughfare. Drayton was not as alluring as Bull or Abercorn, and it went through none of the unique and irreplaceable squares.

As internal combustion engine vehicles declined in availability, the LTL, light tram line, became popular in modest-sized cities, which previously had no subway infrastructure. Savannah, for all its fame and notoriety, was still a rather small city. Its suburbs had extended much farther in all directions. Even most of the inhabitable land between Savannah and Hilton Head Island to the northeast had seen extensive development. But now some of the more outlying suburbs had been abandoned in the process of re-urbanization.

In the downtown historic district, the tram stops came every few blocks—Broughton, President, Oglethorpe, Liberty. Then the spacing widened. Savannahians, like most Americans, learned to do more walking as cars were abandoned. In twenty minutes we reached Victory Drive, and my stop would soon arrive.

From the tram stop, my walk to Mrs. Pinckney's house took only three minutes. The home was large and imposing, much too large for an elderly widow. As a consequence, a number of years earlier, she divided the house into four apartments. The largest one was Mrs. Pinckney's. Two others consisted of two rooms each. I occupied one of these, and Mrs. Humphreys, a widow like Mrs. Pinckney, rented the other. The last was smaller, amounting to no more than a bedroom, bathroom, and a small alcove, which—as far as I could tell—served no purpose. With this limited space, the room was generally rented by a student at the Savannah College of Art and Design, or "SCAD," as it was known locally.

One of the special arrangements Mrs. Pinckney provided, at least to Mrs. Humphreys and me, was a home-cooked meal each Monday and Wednesday evening. As I arrived this particular Wednesday, I saw that the dining room table was set for one, and Mrs. Pinckney was busily at work in the kitchen.

She spotted me and beckoned to me. "James, I'm glad I saw

you. I'm going out this evening to help at the temple."

"The Jewish temple?"

"Yes, Temple Mickve Israel," Mrs. Pinckney replied with arched eyebrows indicating that I should realize a temple would serve Jews, just like a church would cater to Christians.

"But I thought you were a Presbyterian?" I pursued stupidly.

"Of course I am. And you're probably wondering why I'm involved with Temple Mickve Israel. If you were a true Savannahian, you'd understand. For the moment, let's just chalk it up to our local history and eccentricity." With that lack of an explanation, I realized that I would have to wait to have the mystery solved. "At any event, Mrs. Humphreys and I ate. Y'all's can be reheated whenever you're ready to eat."

Most likely, Charlene Pinckney expected me to leave the kitchen at that point. But I lingered, watching the petite, sixty-five-year-old woman finish putting some dishes away. She noticed that I was watching. "Do I remind you of your mama?"

My mother was taller, and she had let her hair turn gray. Charlene Pinckney's hair was dyed a coppery blond. But I lied. "Yes, a bit."

"Is she still living?"

"Oh, yes. Very much alive—in New Jersey."

"Then you can visit with her any time you like."

"I'm staying put in Savannah for the time being."

"Why did you come here anyway?"

"To work."

"But I don't see you working."

"I do some consulting."

"You consult here in Savannah?"

"With all of our communication modes you can conduct business with anyone in the world."

"That still doesn't explain why you came to Savannah," Mrs. Pinckney persisted.

"How about to be warm in winter?"

"Okay, I'll accept that. But I think you're escaping from more than a cold winter."

"You're a clever woman, Mrs. Pinckney."

"Are you going to give me an explanation?"

"When we have much more time."

Charlene Pinckney smiled. "Be secretive, then, but I'm sure a woman is involved."

I smiled in return, but said nothing.

II

Washington, 2053

KATE HASTINGS WAS A WOMAN no man would forget no matter how hard he tried. I had met her on a few occasions before 2053, but these encounters had always occurred in large Federal Energy Department gatherings. In March of 2053, I had my first face-to-face conversation with her.

I had worked at the Department of Energy, now called the "Federal Energy Department" to differentiate it from state counterparts, for four years after getting my master's degree in energy resource management. For the most part, my first four years at the department were a monumental bore. I was first assigned to a unit that assembled a variety of statistics, some on a weekly, some on a monthly, basis. Of course, the initial numbers were generally inaccurate, so revisions had to be made. This was not exciting work, nor the sort of work I had anticipated when I graduated. I endured it because I had faith that something better would emerge in the future.

In 2051, my initial period of tedium was temporarily alleviated by a six-month assignment in the New York regional office. I was able to share an apartment with a fraternity brother, Steve Durham. In addition to college, I knew Steve from having grown up in adjacent towns in northern New Jersey and having competed against him in track. Although different in personalities and outlook—Steve was much more outgoing and more of a risk taker than I—our paths seemed to cross on multiple occasions and were destined to cross again.

While in New York, we spent little time together. Steve also worked for the government—in the State Department—and although he was attached to the staff at the United Nations, he was frequently absent on foreign trips. Thus I often had a very comfortable two-bedroom, Upper East Side apartment to myself. Unfortunately, New York was only an interlude. Within six months, I was back in Washington, assigned to a different unit but still wrestling with tedious statistics.

With great forbearance I quietly endured the assignment for nearly a year. Then, one day, I found myself almost involuntarily heading for Mr. Lemmingsby's office. Mr. Lemmingsby, who was never referred to by his first name, was more interested in the perks of his office than in his employees. He was also my boss's boss, and going outside the strict chain of command was a somewhat daring act, given the tight, suffocating structure of our unit. With a combination of timidity and temerity I asked permission to enter his office.

"Okay, Lendeman, I'll give you five minutes." Mr. Lemmingsby had one sheet of printed paper in the center of an otherwise immaculate desk. I sat down and hesitated. "Go ahead, then. State your purpose."

"I guess it comes down to this, Mr. Lemmingsby, I'd like a transfer to a unit that does policy development work."

"You're very direct, Lendeman. Do you have some gripe with this unit?"

I replied tactfully, I thought. "It's not the unit or the people. It's the work. I've been doing statistical work for most of my four years in the Department. My training is in energy policy. I'd like to use that background."

Lemmingsby seemed to scowl. He drew an amber-handled letter opener, which resembled a dagger, from a desk drawer. The antique served little purpose, since only an occasional government document came in a sealed envelope. Most likely, it simply provided tactile comfort to the handler and a degree of intimidation to the observer. "Policy, eh? I've been in the Department for nearly thirty years, have done precious little policy work. Of course, you probably consider me a mere paper-pusher."

"No, sir, not at all," I interjected quickly.

"You know, the type of work we do is vital for this country. May not be glamorous, but it's the nuts and bolts of the Department. Can't develop policy without the facts. We're the facts. We provide knowledge."

"I appreciate that." Warming to my argument, I added, "I'd simply like to do work more in line with my training. I think I'd enjoy it more."

"Enjoy? Are we supposed to enjoy our work? Work is work. It is honorable and valued. But you want the glitz."

"I think I stated my reason for the change, and glitz isn't part of it."

Lemmingsby twirled the letter-opener and pondered his next move. "Yes, you've made yourself clear. I'm going to think about your request. I might do a little checking to see what's available. Just don't expect a miracle. You know, many people would be happy to have a good, secure job in the government these days."

"I appreciate that. I'd also appreciate your pursuing my request."

Lemmingsby simply nodded, and I knew my time had expired.

Two months went by, and in that time I don't believe I received so much as a "good morning" from Lemmingsby. Of course, his three direct subordinates probably did not receive such a greeting, either. I told myself I needed to approach Lemmingsby again and find out if anything was being done about my request. I gave myself until the end of the month to make my move. It was then the tenth.

One morning, the office was unusually quiet. For some reason, half the staff was away from their desks. Lemmingsby sat in his office with a solitary memo in front of him. I got up from my chair and took a number of steps in his direction. I think he detected my approach. He took the memo, swiveled in his chair, and turned his back to me. I figured the time was not yet propitious.

The following week was not favorable, either. It was the week when the unit crunched most of the monthly statistics and was the only time of the month in which I was truly busy. Monday, Tuesday, and Wednesday I sat at my computer, assembling incoming information and adding it to appropriate spreadsheets. Thursday began the same way, and then, about ten o'clock, I felt a tap on my shoulder. It was Lemmingsby.

"Lendeman, you're coming with me," he stated brusquely. "And put your jacket on."

We descended to the basement, and I realized we were heading to the tunnel that led to the other Federal Energy Department building across the street. It was a perfectly nice day, and we could have crossed the street, but I sensed that Lemmingsby preferred the confines of government office space—even subterranean—to the infinite expanse of sky and fresh air. We continued along the dim passage, lit with highly energy-efficient diodes. The harsh light made Lemmingsby look even older than he was. The lighting was likely no more flattering for me, but there were no mirrors.

Midway along the tunnel, he asked, "Do you know where we're going?"

"To the other Energy Department building across the street."

"But where, specifically?"

"I have no idea," I readily confessed.

"Well, you'll find out soon enough."

We took the elevator to the fifth floor and headed to a suite of offices intended for higher-ranking people within the department. The floors were thickly carpeted, and the walls were paneled. After a fairly lengthy walk, Lemmingsby opened a door on which a small plaque read:

K. Hastings
Assistant Secretary

The name Kate Hastings certainly meant something to me. Although not the secretary or one of the two deputy secretaries, she was generally thought of as one of the most influential people in the department—and certainly the most audacious.

Upon entering, we were in a fairly large reception area. An administrative assistant was hunched over a keyboard and computer screen. After a few moments, she looked up and asked if she could help us.

"Yes, we're here to see Ms. Hastings."

The admin assistant smiled sweetly. "And could I have your names?"

"Lendeman," I replied promptly before Lemmingsby could answer for me. He, too, gave his name.

We were encouraged to take seats and told that Ms. Hastings should be with us shortly. Lemmingsby looked unhappy being out of his own element, having to cool his heels in someone else's waiting area.

I tried to recollect when I had met Kate Hastings. It was only a brief encounter. The assistant secretaries were trying to have lunch once a month with the new advanced hires. I sat at her table along with four other newcomers. She was gracious, asked us a few questions about ourselves, and then ended up dominating the conversation. I was impressed with her far-ranging knowledge and unconventional ideas. She had entered government several years earlier after rising quickly in business, and she let it be known that she was not about to fit graciously into the civil servant mode.

After that, I saw her give several presentations via closed circuit broadcast, but we had not met again face to face. And hers was certainly a face to remember. It was lean and pale with penetrating gray eyes and framed by blond, almost white, straight hair. Her forehead was expansive and wrinkle-free, except when she was working through a difficult issue—or angry. Thin lips surrounded a small mouth filled with perfectly even, pearly teeth. Her neck was long and elegant, much like her overall stature. Her thin frame and carriage along with a head being a bit small in proportion to her body enhanced the impression of height.

This image was going through my mind when the admin assistant returned to us, indicating that Ms. Hastings was ready to see us. Kate Hastings's appearance coincided with my memory, except her hair was pulled back into an abbreviated pony tail and secured by a silver clip. She asked us to be seated.

"Good of you two gentleman to come over here." As if we had had a choice. "Mr. Lemmingsby knows the purpose of this visit. James—I've heard you prefer to be called 'James'—I want to talk to you about a job in my office." I tried to conceal my joy. "I understand you've been interested in a position involving policy development."

"Yes, definitely." I thought my brief reply struck a balance between wanton exuberance and indifference.

"Good, then we have some talking to do. And, Mr. Lemmingsby," Kate stood up, "I appreciate your bringing James over here." I stood, too, and mumbled a "thank you" to Mr. Lemmingsby, thinking he had something to do with this fortuitous course of events.

Lemmingsby did not expect to be dismissed so quickly, nor in this manner. But he recognized he had no choice in the matter, said a brief "good-bye" and left.

Kate settled back in her chair. "So, James, tell me why you'd prefer policy work to statistics."

"Frankly, I thought the choice would be obvious. Certainly, the data are essential to understanding our energy position, but policy analysis and determination require creativity."

Kate smiled. "So creativity is important to you. You see, some people are happy collecting and massaging the data—and that's important, too. A person like Mr. Lemmingsby might be happy spending his entire career doing just that, and I suspect he is happy in his own way. It's also something that's relatively safe. Certainly mistakes can be made. But when you're dealing with policy, you're tackling myriad contradictory forces, such as politics, unintended consequences, and just plain fucking up."

The last phrase, coming out of Kate's sweet, feminine mouth, jarred me out of a sense of complacency. She did not want me to feel comfortable, not at this point. "But even in a unit that's devoted to data collection and dissemination, I'm sure you've found some things to interest you." It wasn't a question, but I was expected to respond.

"On rare occasions." I was thinking about the unit's football pool, but thought better of replying in that fashion.

"Tell me, you must have done something aside from cranking statistics."

"Yes, I can think of one thing."

"And what's that?" she prompted.

"I lobbied to get out of the area."

Kate smiled. I suspected she had a sense of humor and appreciated my reply. "So you did. But, certainly, you don't think my area provides twenty-four hours of excitement each day."

"I couldn't take that, either. I hope you don't think I'm looking at this matter simplistically. But I've done some work in a field office and have good academic credentials. I know there's more to the F.E.D. than Mr. Lemmingsby's statistical unit." Even as I spoke these words, I could sense their inadequacy.

"I can see you're a very determined person, and I'm aware of your background. That's why you're here." Kate smiled briefly.

I wondered if I was getting off on the wrong foot and ruining my chances. "I know it's difficult to convey the depth of my interest in this area, or what abilities I can bring to the job."

"I suppose it's up to me to assess your abilities and how you can fit into a job in my area. But, frankly, I don't have the time to do that at the moment. Meet me later in the day, and we'll discuss it further. Do you know the Café Golliwog?"

"On K Street?"

"That's the one. Meet me there at six."

III

Savannah, 2061

SOMEHOW THE MONTHS IN SAVANNAH were gliding by. I did some consulting work and continued to collect pay from the government. In my own terms, I was doing okay.

It was late March. The weather was warming. Azaleas were in bloom. The change in the weather encouraged locals to don short-sleeve shirts. Some wore shorts.

After a late breakfast, I took a half mug of coffee and a laptop into the garden behind Mrs. Pinckney's house. A high hedge and a number of ornamental plantings provided ample privacy. Three chairs, a chaise lounge, and a small glass-topped table sat on a concrete patio. I took a chair next to the table, opened my laptop, and spread out some work papers.

I was not alone for long. The SCAD student, who rented the smallest apartment at Mrs. P's house, called out, "Hey, Mr. Lenman, great morning." Since my back was to the door, I had not seen her approach. I cringed at the interruption to my privacy— and also at her practice of leaving a syllable out of my last name.

"Oh, hello, Jacqueline." I knew she preferred the use of her full first name, rather than the diminutive "Jackie." I did not, however, know much else about her, since she had only moved into the Pinckney homestead in February after another SCAD student left.

"Thanks for leaving the lounge chair for me. I want to get some sun. I hope I won't bother you."

"No, go right ahead. I'm just trying to do a little writing."

In truth, I felt that she would inhibit my work, and I doubted she would keep silent. She proved my point when she immediately tried to converse with me.

"You do a lot of writing," Jacqueline observed as she took her sweatshirt and jeans off, leaving only a skimpy two-piece bathing suit to maintain propriety. "Are you working on anything interesting?"

"I'm trying to record some information I researched while I was working for the government." I was satisfied that my reply was a reasonable blend of truth and obfuscation. It was intended to stifle further discussion along that line. I looked in Jacqueline's direction to see if she would react to my reply. As she turned her head toward me, I was reminded strangely of Kate Hastings. I noted that Jacqueline's body was rather thin and taut like Kate's, although Kate was several centimeters taller. Jacqueline's hair was a reddish blond and short with an inclination to curl—nothing like Kate's wispy, shoulder-length silver blond. Jacqueline's facial features were quite regular but less angular, and her chin was less assertive than Kate's. But her eyes, like Kate's, were that mysterious shade of gray.

Jacqueline was less interested in my reply than in my attentive gaze. "Do you think I'd look better if I gained some weight? I'm one point seven meters tall—well, almost—and I weigh a little over forty-five kilos."

"Aren't you happy with the way you look?" I tried to avoid a direct answer on a sensitive subject.

"No fair. I asked you."

"I think you look fine. You might be a little thin, but better that than fat. Don't you think?"

This time Jacqueline was willing to reply. "That's what I think. Anyway, I don't really have the opportunity to put on weight. With school and two part-time jobs, I'm generally running in one direction or another. On Thursday and Friday nights I wait tables at Francesco. You'd think I'd get fat from their pasta, but they're only willing to let me have a few leftovers. When I'm at school, I only get snacks. But you don't have that problem."

"Do you mean I'm overweight?" I asked, a bit irked.

"No." She emitted a girlish giggle. "I mean you must be pretty rich. You can afford to have Mrs. Pinckney's meals. You don't really have a job, and you're much too young to collect a pension."

"Thanks for the 'young' part."

"So are you rich?"

"You're not shy about asking questions. No, I just get by on some pay I still get from the government." I tried to reply simply and avoid the term "disability pay."

"Sounds like a good deal to a struggling art student like me. I've been working on a BA for five years, and who knows where it will lead when I finally get it."

I might have been encouraging. I should have uttered some gratuitous, optimistic remark about the future. However, my opinion of the future was muddied by my view of the past. Both were decidedly negative. It was easier to remain silent rather than lie. Jacqueline turned away, resting her head on her forearm. I hoped the conversation was finished.

Two minutes later, when I had just returned to my writing, Jacqueline again broke the silence. "Do you mind if I call you Jim?"

"I really prefer James, and family members call me Jamie."

"I'll call you James. Maybe I should continue to call you Mr. Lenman. But I bet you're not that much older than me."

"Bet I am."

"Bet I'm older than you think," she countered.

"You're probably twenty-three, since you mentioned that you've been in college for five years."

Jacqueline grinned. "That's good detective work, but what you don't know is that I didn't start college immediately after high school."

"So you're twenty-four or so. I must confess I thought you

were a bit younger."

"Like nineteen or twenty. Most people make that mistake. And how old are you? Probably too old to be called Jamie." She smiled again—a funny smile that crinkled the corners of her eyes too much.

"Why don't you guess? You made me guess."

"I don't want to guess. If you're younger than I guess, you'll be insulted that I thought you were so old. And if you're older than I guess, you'll be embarrassed to tell me your real age."

I was momentarily impressed by her analysis of human nature and her consideration for my feelings. But she spoiled my illusion by impulsively saying, "Okay, I'll guess. Thirty-five."

"You're close. I'm just past thirty-five."

"Then that's not so old. You're certainly not old enough to be my father. Just a somewhat older friend." Suddenly I was Jacqueline's friend. She shifted position on the chaise lounge, and her bikini top needed to be adjusted. She looked at me as I watched her reposition her breasts. "You need to come and see me at work some time."

"I don't know if I'd have occasion to eat at Francesco."

"No, I mean my other job. I work at the Durango on Wednesday and Saturday nights."

I realized that Jacqueline was quite a busy young woman, even if her class load was light. "Where's this 'Durango'?"

"Oh, you don't know the Durango?" The eyes crinkled again.

"No."

"James, you have been living a sheltered life in Savannah."

"Is it a bar?"

"Well, yes, in part. It's just over the state line in South Carolina. I dance there."

I was beginning to get the picture. "Topless?"

"Does that shock you?" Her expression was now serious, and she was looking directly into my eyes. I sensed she wanted an honest answer.

"No, not at all. Do you enjoy that kind of work?" I wondered whether my tone was still casual.

"It doesn't bother me. I don't mind men looking at me. Even if I'm not very large on top, I think they find me attractive. And if you don't mind, I'm going to take my top off for a few minutes. In my profession it's better not to have a bra line interfere with a nice tan."

What could I say in return? Would it be more chivalrous to refuse her request or accept it? "Go right ahead. I need to return to my work."

"Could you do one thing for me? Would you kind of keep your eye on the back door?"

"Sure. Of course." I probably blushed. "Don't want to invade your privacy."

"No, it's not about you. I'd like you to be on the lookout for Mrs. Pinckney. I don't want to give the old dear a heart attack." Her eyes crinkled again. "But I don't mind you seeing my tits. I'm used to guys doing that."

IV

I ARRIVED AT THE GOLLIWOG promptly at six. I looked around for Kate Hastings but sensed she would keep me waiting. There were several empty seats at the bar. I took one and ordered a tonic, without gin. Kate Hastings would not find me at any more of a disadvantage than I was bound to be.

I waited and, after twenty minutes, needed to order another tonic water. The bartender asked if I was waiting for someone. "It's obvious, I suppose."

"Look, people don't come here to swill tonic water by themselves."

After I started on the third tonic, my phone rang. It was Kate. "Are you still at Golliwog's?"

"Yes, of course." I suppose I would have stayed there until closing time awaiting Kate or her instructions.

"Give me ten more minutes. I got tied up in a terribly important meeting. See you in ten." She didn't wait for my reply.

I took another sip of my tonic, figuring it would have to last another half hour and not ten minutes. But Kate Hastings surprised me, and she arrived almost exactly ten minutes after our call ended.

"I see you have a drink already. I'll need to catch up." She got the bartender's attention and ordered a Scotch and water. The drink arrived promptly. Kate took a healthy swig and indicated that we should move to a table. She seemed to be well known at Golliwog's. We were immediately given a choice table, tucked into a private corner.

"Here's what I want you to do," she asserted, while leaning over the table and putting her face within a half-meter of mine. "Tell me about yourself."

"About myself?" I was somewhat confused.

"Yes. I want to know a lot more about you."

"Where do you want me to start?"

"As far back as you want."

"Okay. I was born in New Jersey. My family was very normal. My father worked for a large insurance brokerage company. My mother was a housewife and a part-time bookkeeper. I have a sister." I wondered whether I was already starting to bore Kate. "Is this really what you want to hear?"

"Yes, but I'm sure you'll get to the more important part shortly."

"I went to public grade schools and a high school. I was a good student." I tried to study Kate's face to see if she was following this banality. "I did well enough to get into Stanford. Even at that point I was interested in the problem of dealing with our diminished energy resources. As you know, Stanford has an excellent energy management program.

"After getting my bachelor's degree, I pursued my master's degree at the University of Georgia. Again, I chose one of the top-notch energy programs. But you know all this. You've no doubt read my résumé."

"Of course, but tell me why you were interested in the energy problem." Kate took another drink of Scotch and leaned forward again. Her gray eyes drilled into mine.

I thought for a few moments before beginning my reply. "I grew up when the energy shortage, really the petroleum shortage, was producing the most profound changes in the way we lived. For example, before I reached my teens, my family was able to take summer vacation trips. Several times we went to Hilton Head Island. Once we went to Canada, twice to Cape Cod. By the time I was finishing high school, we could not go on a motor trip. In fact, it didn't even make sense for us to own a car anymore. Of course, that's just one example. But everyone went through a similar experience in the thirties and forties."

"Yes, but not everyone chose to go into energy management." Kate smiled sweetly, but I detected a hint of condescension. "Why did you?"

I paused in order to re-collect my thoughts. In truth I had a number of reasons, but I chose to concentrate on a single aspect. "I grew up in northern New Jersey, about seventy kilometers west of New York City. Until the time I was thirteen, my father worked in a suburban office of his company. In the thirties, many of these suburban offices were declared nonviable, not being accessible by public transportation. My father was reassigned to an office in New York City, and his position allowed him to telecommute only one day a week. He needed to take a tram to a train, then transfer to another train taking him into the city. The commute was two hours each way. He did this for four years before having a heart attack. It didn't kill him, but it forced him to retire at age fifty-five. He found nothing to do in retirement. He puttered around the house. He read a little, and watched a little TV. But, mostly, he sat in an easy chair, thought about his lost productive life, and vegetated. A few years later, he died. The doctor said it was congestive heart failure. I think my father willed it.

"I knew that draconian steps had to be taken to allocate the remaining petroleum energy in the world, but I wasn't sure the rules were necessarily fair or workable. I was determined to find out more about how the policies were developed and applied. In short, I wanted to find out if my father's death was a necessary casualty of energy dependency or a . . ."

"Needless sacrifice." Kate finished my statement.

"Exactly."

"And what have you concluded?"

"I'm still searching for answers."

"So that's why you want to work for me?"

"Not exactly. I search for the answers in my spare time. I want to work in your area, so that I'll have some part in creating policies that are necessary and fair."

"And what would you do if we develop rules that don't meet your standards?" Kate's question was appropriate, and one I hadn't considered before.

"Good question. I guess, if necessary, I'll need to adapt. But I suspect there would be a limit."

"Well, I suppose we all need some ideals. But just realize that most policies are a compromise. They're subject to the political process, and politics is the art of the possible. It rarely leads . . . no I'll modify that, it *never* leads to perfection. I'd say our work is more political than scientific." Kate looked at me in an appraising way. "Think you can handle that?"

"Yes, I'm sure I can."

"In light of your admitted idealism, why should I believe you?"

I had to think quick and hard. I knew I couldn't say that I'd pursue the ideal while others could concentrate on the politics. "Hopefully I'll be in a position to develop policies that are the fairest ones that can get through the political process."

Kate grinned. "You slithered out of that corner. You know, I thought you'd be interested in developing a comprehensive national energy policy, not just rules for allocation."

I replied instinctively, without much thought. "Have we ever had a comprehensive policy? The time for that was fifty years ago."

Kate said nothing for a few seconds. I figured my brash assessment blew my chances of working in her area. She had been staring at me but, when she replied, she averted her gaze. "Unfortunately, you may be right."

She went on to talk about the projects currently active in her area. I was certain she omitted the more confidential ones. At the end of her discourse, I was bold enough to state that I would love to tackle some of that work.

Kate replied quickly. "Don't worry. You're in."

V

Savannah, 2061

MRS. PINCKNEY SAT AT THE dinner table, carefully doling out the evening meal to me. On this occasion, and it was a rare occurrence, Mrs. Humphreys was not present for dinner. She was visiting a cousin who lived in Statesboro. Mrs. Pinckney granted no credit for a missed meal and, as a consequence, Mrs. Humphreys made certain to take full advantage of the board she paid for. Only grave illness or a free meal elsewhere could prevent her from enjoying Mrs. Pinckney's hospitality.

"I don't believe I've made this chicken dish for a while. It was a favorite of Mr. Pinckney's, but it does take a little more time than the normal baked or fried variety." Charlene Pinckney wanted to make sure that I appreciated the effort she had expended.

"It's excellent," I obligingly replied.

"My dear departed husband insisted that I prepare it every two or three weeks. He called it my 'Georgia pecan chicken.' But I frequently made it with walnuts as opposed to pecans, and I sincerely doubt if it's a Georgia recipe at all. Of course, Mr. Pinckney couldn't really tell a true Georgia dish from, let's say, a Cajun one."

"Some people just aren't very knowledgeable about food." Somehow I felt the need to try to defend the dear departed Mr. Pinckney.

"That was rather true of my husband. But also he was not a native Savannahian, not even a native Georgian." Based on this statement and Mrs. Pinckney's far off expression, I expected to hear that the late Mr. Pinckney hailed from some remote part of the country, if not the world. "No, my husband's family came from South Carolina. He spent the first twenty-five years of his life in Beaufort."

"I see," I replied, but since Beaufort was only about a hundred kilometers from Savannah, I did not really appreciate the fine distinction.

"'Pinckney' is definitely a South Carolina family name. My family—I'm a Bulloch—definitely did come from Savannah, and I was born at the Mary Telfair." I assumed this was crucial to solidifying Mrs. Pinckney's Savannah heritage. "The Bulloch name has long been associated with Savannah. You can see Bulloch graves in Colonial Park Cemetery. Have you visited the cemetery?"

I shook my head "no," as Charlene Pinckney continued. "One of my ancestors was Jimmy Bulloch, who was a captain in the Confederate navy. He spent a good part of the war in England, obtaining ships for the Confederate cause. And do you know who his nephew was?"

"I have no idea," I replied quickly, perhaps revealing my lack of interest in the family history of Mrs. Pinckney, née Bulloch.

"Well, his nephew was no less than a president of the United States. And I bet you can't guess which one."

Now that Charlene had progressed beyond her family to American history, my interest increased. I thought about her question and about late nineteenth and early twentieth century presidents. From the recesses of my memory I recalled that Woodrow Wilson grew up in the South. So I verbalized this speculation.

"Not a bad guess, but Thomas Woodrow Wilson was raised in Augusta. I'll give you a clue. You'd probably think of this president as a quintessential Northerner."

I thought for a few moments, but no reasonable idea came to mind. "You'll have to tell me."

"Well, I'm a distant relation of Teddy Roosevelt. You see,

Teddy's father married a Bulloch girl."

As I digested this surprising information, along with the remainder of my dinner, the doorbell rang. In this day and age it was unusual for an evening caller to arrive unannounced, since public transportation was infrequent after seven o'clock and few people had access to a private vehicle. Perhaps the caller was a neighbor, although Mrs. Pinckney's neighbors rarely visited her in the evening.

I remained at the dining room table while she went to the front door. I was surprised when she returned and indicated that two visitors wanted to speak with me. I had been in Savannah for about a year. Except for the occupants of the Pinckney residence, a few librarians at the Bull Street library, and some shopkeepers, no one knew me. Had I accumulated some unpaid bills or lost track of an egregiously overdue book?

My visitors awaited me in the front parlor. Two gentlemen, neither of whom I recognized, were standing in the middle of the room. A large man with a big, pudgy hand greeted me first. "My name is Joe Porter, and this is Aaron Smith." Porter's colleague was a black man, rather large in his own right, but small in comparison to Porter.

"Hi. I'm James Lendeman."

"Good to meet you. You're not in the phone directory."

"No," I replied simply, not wishing to reveal that I wanted to be difficult to locate.

We sat down. I said nothing, so either Porter or Smith had to begin. Hesitatingly, Porter began. "You probably wonder who we are and why we came to talk with you."

I nodded my head, awaiting with a bit of trepidation the explanation to follow.

"Aaron and I are with the regional energy council." So that was it—energy again. "I assume, given your background, Mr. Lendeman, that you know what a regional energy council does."

I had worked extensively with such organizations in California and New York, so I was well aware of their responsibilities. But how did these people in Savannah come to know about me? "Yes, I know what you do. But I don't know how your work concerns me."

This time, Mr. Smith spoke up. "To come to the point, we're not operating very effectively at the moment. We particularly need someone who has a professional background. Most of us are local people who have picked up a little knowledge here and there about the energy issues that affect our community. When we make our decisions we tend to do so by the seat of our pants. We find that we're frequently challenged and criticized. It's difficult for us to defend our positions. We greatly need a person with your professional expertise to add to our local perspective."

"How would you expect me to help you out?"

"We'd like you to take one of the spots on the council."

I was surprised by the offer, and concerned, as well. My government status was complicated and formulated specifically for me. Allegedly, I was on part disability pay and was also on call to do *ad hoc* consulting, although I had not been called upon to do much consulting since I left Washington. True, the work on the energy council was only part time, and the pay was modest. But it would require me to make decisions about energy issues, and I was not sure that I was prepared to return to that type of work.

"I need to check with my former boss to see if I can do this," I stated, figuring that as I explored the possibility of joining the council, I would be able to find a better excuse for declining the offer.

Porter spoke up. "We understand that you're cleared to take this job."

"You spoke to Washington?"

"No, we got your name from Atlanta. They got your name from Washington. We assume it's been okayed."

I fumbled for a response. "Well, I still feel that I need to check for myself. There are some points . . . Let's just say I need to verify that this is permitted."

Porter looked at Smith and gave a slight shrug. "We understand."

Smith handed me a business card. "Please let us know as soon as possible."

I thought of an additional issue. "Shouldn't I be a permanent resident of this area in order to serve on the council?"

Smith did not hesitate. "You did register to vote."

Damn poor decision, I thought to myself.

VI

Washington, 2053

WORKING FOR KATE HASTINGS WAS nothing like working for Mr. Lemmingsby. Despite her rank, Kate was not the least bit remote or formal. Immediately I felt comfortable calling her "Kate." During the first month I was infrequently in her office, but I did not feel that it was off limits. Most of our contacts were through her administrative assistant.

Her admin would deliver work for me. Sometimes it was a report Kate wanted me to read and comment on. Sometimes she wanted me to analyze news coverage of our area. These little items seemed almost like make-work assignments. I knew Kate had asked for my security clearance to be raised, so I could work on more critical matters. But, all told, my first month on the job was genuinely disappointing.

One day—a rather gloomy, chilly morning, as I recall—I gave some trivial commentary on an internet story tangentially involving the department, to Kate's administrative assistant. My faint hope was that Kate would eventually take a glance at my work and want to discuss it.

Kate's admin assistant took a quick look at what I was delivering and tossed it in a pile that was one step away from the trash basket. "Oh, by the way, James, Ms. Hastings would like to see you at three o'clock."

"She wants to give me a reading assignment herself?"

"Pardon?"

"Never mind. I'll be back at three."

"Please don't be late."

"Am I ever?" I smiled. The admin assistant did not.

The hours went by exceedingly slowly. I thought about the meeting to come and tried to prepare myself for another disappointment. I arrived outside of Kate's office promptly at three. The admin assistant looked at me with perhaps a hint of disgust. What did I ever do to piss her off? "Please take a seat. Ms. Hastings will be with you in a few minutes."

Five minutes went by. I expected the five minutes to stretch into ten and then into twenty. However, within another minute a rather distinguished-looking man burst from Kate's office, gave me a quick glance which bore some hint of malice, and darted out the door. Kate came part-way out of her office. Her face bore a half-smile, as her eyes followed the gray-haired gentleman's departure.

She quickly turned to me. "Come on in, James." Her tone was bright.

She led me to a corner of her office which contained a couch, a low table, and a comfortable chair. She took the chair. I headed for the couch. I watched her lithe figure settle slowly into the chair and reminded myself that I needed to think of her as my boss and not as a woman.

Kate began with a comment that was probably designed to be small talk. "I've read your reports and commentaries. I think they were well done, very even-handed and cogent. Your conclusions appeared logical."

I had hoped that my conclusions were logical in *fact* and not just in appearance, but I was not prepared to fence with her. "Thank you for the compliments."

"But I didn't call you in here to talk about what's gone before."

Promising, I thought.

"No. First of all, your security clearance has been raised to level four. I'll be able to get you involved in a wider range of work—sensitive stuff."

"Great." I was sincere.

She paused before beginning again. "What do you know about the Merton Committee?"

"A few things—it mainly focuses on full resource utilization, and it . . ."

Kate interrupted. She hadn't really wanted an answer. She only wanted to get my attention. "The committee is currently looking at our use of oil shale reserves. Merton's an old bastard, trying to generate some publicity for his reelection. He doesn't really give a shit about oil shale reserves. He only cares about Lewis Merton. He's been getting around the term limit law by taking his two terms in Congress, going back to state office for a few years, and then returning to Congress. Of course, that's typical for his type."

"And what type is that?"

"A politician." Kate's face reddened. She no doubt knew that most people felt she was a skilled politician in her own right. "Anyway, I need to appear before his committee in a few days. He might go off in any direction, trying to dig up any old crap. We have to be ready. You'll be accompanying me. So will Frobisch. Do you know him?"

Hastings was intent on her own train of thought. She didn't notice my negative gesture. "Well, Frobisch knows the geological part. He knows what we've done and where we've done it. I think this time Merton will get into the economics of oil shale usage. That's where you come in."

She got up and walked toward her desk as she continued. "I have to know where the waste is, where the inefficiency is, where we've screwed up. Have we granted preferential treatment to anyone? I'm sure you get the picture."

She carried a moderate stack of reports and books over to the couch. "Read these by the day after tomorrow. These two," Kate indicated the two top reports, "should be the first you read. We'll discuss them tomorrow."

I felt that I was being dismissed, and I made a movement to

take the pile of material and get up. Kate placed a restraining hand on my arm. The touch of her hand felt like an electrical charge going through my body. Her tone became more personal. "James, this is important. It is of utmost importance. After the hearing, Merton has to know that he's met his match. He needs to know he better keep his nose out of our business. He'll only lose political capital if he fucks with us. We can't get sidetracked, spending our time fending off a has-been congressman. We have better things to do. James, I'm sure I can count on you."

She looked down at her hand, which was still on my arm, and withdrew it slowly. "I'll see you tomorrow at ten," she said almost in a whisper. Now it was time to go.

I took the pile of materials back to my cubicle and began to read the one Kate had put on top. To a person who had focused on energy matters, the reports held some interest. On the other hand, much was devoted to dry statistics and an even drier discussion of their meaning. I managed to plow through the first report by six thirty and decided I would be better off continuing at my apartment after a light dinner and several cups of coffee.

That evening, through a prodigious effort, I managed to tackle the second-highest-priority report, another that was deemed to be of lesser priority (although I knew not why), and a quick skim through a book on oil shale production, which was less valuable than others I had previously read. I tentatively concluded that Kate underestimated the extent and quality of my education, perhaps because her formal education in the economics of energy production was scanty. Her practical experience served as her education in these matters, and, in general, it served her very well. This observation made me realize that I could definitely be useful to her. My knowledge and analytical abilities would complement her keen instincts.

I looked at the pile of information Kate had given me. The one-foot-high stack told me something else—that Kate was not technologically savvy. For most of the material, she could have given me the titles of the items, and I could have accessed them via my computer. The reports were probably security controlled, but certainly the books and pamphlets could be accessed online. As a test, I turned on my computer and accessed the multinet. The book that I had just skimmed was found in fifteen seconds. I used Prango to find a book I had read years earlier on the same subject. This, too, was accessed quickly. With the new tome now on my screen, I forwarded it to my page palette so I could read in my recliner. I skimmed through several chapters and decided my initial impression was correct. The book was better than the one Kate had given to me.

Perhaps Kate never got used to a page palette and therefore relied on printed materials. That would also explain the foot-high pile. Or perhaps she intentionally cultivated a twentieth-century image. But, no, her clothes did not fit that conjecture. I would have to learn more about my boss.

At ten o'clock the next morning, I was called to Kate's office. Another man, a few years older than I, was already present and seated in one of the two chairs drawn up in front of Kate's desk. "James, I'm not sure if you know Jeff Frobisch. Jeff, this is James Lendeman." I extended my hand.

Instead of extending his hand, Frobisch informed me, "I just got over a cold, and I don't want to pass it on."

I hesitated before responding, "Well, I appreciate that, Jeff." Were we off to a good start?

Kate was ready to begin, already drumming a pen on her desk. "Okay, now that we've gotten the pleasantries out of the way, I'll give you an idea of how I want to approach this problem."

Inwardly, I smiled for two reasons. First, I did not feel that Frobisch and I had exchanged any pleasantries, merely introductions. Second, Kate clearly viewed these upcoming hearings as a problem and not representative government carrying out its constitutional duties.

"So, here's what I want to do. We'll need to examine what we've done with oil shale reserves over the past five years. I know that's longer than I've had any responsibility for the issue, but Merton won't respect any such timeframe. We have to see where the weak points have been in our strategy or execution. Obviously Merton intends to attack us, not praise us. He needs to score some political points. He wants to get some feathers in his cap for the fifty-four elections. Unfortunately, these bastards have to run for office every few years.

"There's been little legislation touching this area in the past five years, so most of the things we need to look at are FEC decisions and administrative rules. We should also look at the type of contracts formulated in the private sector. Our perceived mistakes can be those of omission as well as commission. If Merton thinks we've been lax in our oversight of what companies are doing with the reserves they're exploiting, we'll be on the firing line for that, too.

"I have some meetings today that I can't get out of. But I'm trying to clear my calendar for tomorrow. The two of you should put your heads together today." Irrespective of Frobisch's cold, I thought. "Compare your impressions on where we might be attacked. Think about how we can defend our positions. Tomorrow we'll get together at nine and spend the rest of the day going over this stuff. The next afternoon I'm scheduled to go before the committee. That will give us a morning in between to finalize our thinking and hone our approach. You two will be with me at the hearing, but I need to know this stuff cold in advance. I won't be able to get too much input from you while it's in progress. Is it clear where we're heading?"

Without saying a word, Frobisch and I nodded our assent.

"Okay, get to work."

Before Frobisch and I parted, he had told me that he could probably reserve a conference room near his office, and we met there just before lunch. Both of us were carrying mini-computers, some relevant reports in hard copy, and writing paper. The accumulated materials looked almost identical. We took seats on opposite sides of a plain table which could seat up to eight.

Frobisch had sandy-colored hair and blue eyes only slightly obscured by large glasses with an evidently weak prescription. I learned that he had been in the Department for about ten years, coming right after completing his bachelor's degree. Like me, he was single.

We began by sharing some general impressions about oil shale policy and administration. Frobisch started and quickly demonstrated the knowledge he had acquired during his tenure. Essentially, he outlined a chronology of geological issues the Department had confronted regarding shale oil in the past decade. The list was comprehensive, and I had no doubt that it was accurate. What Frobisch did not cover in his fifteen-minute recitation was his evaluation of these actions.

In return, I communicated what I felt were the economic effects of these policies, who they favored, and how government could be criticized for what we did. Obviously our tacks were quite different. That was the reason why Kate put us together.

After starting to discuss our vulnerabilities, Jeff and I went to lunch in the Department cafeteria. Frobisch ordered a salad. I got a hamburger and fries. In the midst of a busy cafeteria we chose not to discuss our current project. We talked about our earlier experiences in the Department, about where we grew up, and what sports we followed.

Frobisch finished his salad rapidly, and I noticed he was eying my French fries.

"You on a diet?"

"Kind of. If I don't watch what I eat, my weight can get out of hand. I see you're not eating your fries."

"I will be eating them. I have a funny way of eating. I finish one thing first and then go on to the next. But if you want a few fries…"

Frobisch leaned over and spiked three fries in one swoop.

"Hey, I thought you had a cold."

"No, not really. But I didn't know if you had a cold. So I thought I'd be sure before shaking hands."

"You're very cautious. Aren't you?"

"You bet." Frobisch smiled, obviously thinking that I had complimented him.

After lunch, Frobisch and I worked another five hours before we felt prepared enough to field Kate's questions the next day. At home, I spend another hour reviewing my notes and some key reports before turning the TV on to catch up on the news. I watched for only a few minutes before realizing how tired I was, so I got ready for bed and fell asleep promptly.

I had not set the alarm, but that was unimportant, since I always had a strong internal clock. Sure enough, I awoke at six thirty, about the same as I normally did. I quickly showered, shaved, and put on a clean shirt and my best-pressed suit. I got a bagel and coffee at the office cafeteria and ate at my desk while scanning additional background material on oil shale laws and regulations.

At nine o'clock, I headed to Kate's office. Frobisch was already waiting outside. Kate's admin assistant had her head buried in front of her computer screen. Through some unfathomable method, she would know when Kate was ready for us. Besides asking each other how we were doing, Frobisch and I found it difficult to carry on a normal conversation. After five minutes, without a call coming from Kate's office, the admin assistant announced that Kate was now ready to see us.

Kate wore cream-colored slacks and a black blouse. Her silver-blond hair was piled high on her head. "Good morning, gentlemen. Ready to get to work?"

Jeff and I nodded in unison. Kate motioned for us to take seats at the circular table in one corner of her office. With no formalities, we began to address the issues that Kate had outlined the day before. We were particularly looking for vulnerable areas where Merton could attack the work of the Federal Energy Department, knowing that Merton's only goal was to create some favorable publicity for himself.

We began to toss out some of the points Frobisch and I had listed. After several were mentioned, Kate said, "Let's try to bring a little more organization to our approach. We'll cover legislation first, then administrative decisions, relations with the private sector, and, finally, interdepartmental relationships."

By noon we had only covered the legislation and had barely begun to tackle the administrative decisions. Kate ordered some sandwiches and soft drinks to be brought in. We took a fifteen-minute break and then simultaneously attacked roast beef, turkey, and administrative decisions of the F.E.D.

By four o'clock we had gotten through administrative decisions and had just begun on private sector relationships. Kate's admin assistant stuck her head in the door. "Merton's office is on the phone. He's moving the session from the afternoon to nine a.m. He hopes to finish the session by twelve thirty."

Kate's reaction was quick and violent. She slammed her fist on the table, but her thin hand was incapable of making a loud sound. She should have used one of her books. For this purpose, it would have been even better than a page palette. "The bastard's doing this on purpose. What can we do? We have to show up." Turning back to the messenger, she said, "Tell him we'll be there."

Kate turned back to Jeff and me, "I had hoped for us to wrap things up by six tonight and then reconvene in the morning. In view of the circumstances, I think we'll likely go into the evening. We can work through dinner. Okay?"

I figured Kate's question was rhetorical, but I responded anyway, "Yes." Frobisch fidgeted.

"Jeff?" Kate turned to Frobisch, looking for his affirmative reply.

"I'll make some changes in my plans. I need to make a telephone call." He was clearly irked and left the office to make his call, as Kate was saying, "Go ahead."

Kate drummed her fingers on the table and bit her lower lip. After a minute, she said, "Let's go ahead. He can catch up whenever he returns."

Kate and I began to pick up where we had stopped. Frobisch returned and took his seat without saying a word. Kate did not inquire if he had cleared his calendar for the evening. After a few minutes of strained conversation, we all settled back into the pattern which had taken us through the earlier part of the day.

At a quarter to six, Jane, Kate's admin assistant, knocked on the door and entered. "Kate, if you don't have anything else for me, I'll be leaving."

"Just one thing. Make a reservation for the three of us at Rodolfo's at six thirty. Try to get my usual table in the back corner."

Frobisch broke in, "I couldn't get out of my appointment. I need to leave at six thirty."

Without looking at Frobisch, Kate turned back to Jane. "Then make it a reservation for two. Thank you."

For another twenty minutes, we tried to continue our exploration of questions we expected to get from the Merton Committee. Rather, Kate and I continued. Frobisch neither contributed, nor was asked to contribute. He knew he was going to pay a price for his absence at dinner, but he had made his decision.

A little after six thirty, Kate and I were in Rodolfo's, seated at a secluded table, which had had a "reserved" notice on it before the card was whisked away. The atmosphere improved with Frobisch's departure.

"What do you want to drink?"

Not knowing if Kate expected us to be teetotalers while working through dinner, I replied, "Oh, anything's fine with me."

Kate smiled in return. "Well, do you like wine?"

"That would be great."

Kate ordered a bottle of Maremma, an Italian wine that I had never heard of before. We began to study the dinner selections. Kate interjected, "The veal is always good here."

A tall, dark-haired man in his early forties arrived at our table. "Signora Kate, always good to see you here."

"And it's always good to see you, Enzo." Kate introduced me as a colleague, and told me that Enzo was Rodolfo's son. Enzo informed us that gnocchi gorgonzola was the special and could be served as either an appetizer or main course. I could tell from a wrinkle that formed on Kate's brow that she would eschew the gnocchi. Enzo offered to take our orders if we were ready. Kate promptly chose a salad and veal saltimbocca. Following suit, I ordered a salad and veal Marsala, although I would have loved to try the gnocchi.

As we settled into our first glass of wine and salads, the atmosphere eased, but not until Kate dispensed with one point. "James, I hope you will never do what Jeff did this afternoon."

"I'll try not to." Then I made a half-hearted attempt to defend Frobisch. "Maybe he really has something critical to do this evening. Maybe he has a sick parent . . ."

"His parents live in Florida. No, he has a date with some bimbo and is hoping to get laid."

I was surprised at Kate's bluntness and hoped that I hadn't blushed. I tried to think of a reply that would both defend Frobisch and not alienate Kate. Nothing came to mind. To sum up, Kate added, "Well, I hope he screws her because he certainly screwed himself."

With that final jab at Frobisch, Kate returned to dinner and business. We accomplished a considerable amount during the meal and during another hour back at the office. In my estimation we did not miss Frobisch in the least. At nine, Kate wrapped up, saying, "It's best not to pull an all-nighter. Let's try to be fresh in the morning." I turned to leave. "By the way, I'm taking an electrocar from the motor pool. Do you happen to live in Arlington?"

"No, I'm up north-west."

"At least let me take you to the Metro stop."

"Great. Thanks."

Before I could exit the electrocar, Kate squeezed my forearm. "Thanks for sticking with me tonight. I think we're going to be fine tomorrow."

When I arrived at my apartment, I knew I was tired, but I also knew I'd have trouble getting to sleep. Not only was I thinking about what had happened that evening, but also I was anticipating the next day's challenges. In addition I knew that I would be Kate's main resource at the upcoming committee hearing. Frobisch was to be pushed aside.

I tossed in the bed, rearranged the pillow every few minutes, sat up, turned on the light several times, and pulled some Energy Department memos to read. If they wouldn't put me to sleep, what would? They didn't. I set the alarm, despite my good internal clock, as it approached two in the morning.

All too quickly the alarm rang. Even though I had plenty of time, I rushed to shower and shave. I arrived at the office at a quarter to eight, stopping to get a doughnut and coffee to take to my desk. I unpacked my briefcase as I took a bite of the doughnut and a sip of the coffee. During my second bite, the phone rang.

"James, you're here. Good. Come to my office. I want to review a few points before we appear before the committee."

"Sure," I mumbled in return, trying to prevent the wad of doughnut still in my mouth from affecting my speech.

Kate and I rehashed some of the key points we had covered the day before. Kate knew the information perfectly, but she was obviously nervous. At half past eight, she said, "Would you call Jeff Frobisch and tell him to meet us in the committee hearing room?"

"Will he know where it is?"

"Well, let's see if he's resourceful enough to find out." She smiled a bit wickedly.

The pecking order was clearly established. I was Kate's key aide, at least for the moment. But I realized that Frobisch's fall could be repeated by James Lendeman's the next day.

I had viewed committee hearings before, but as an outsider. The course of this one surprised me. Merton called the hearing to order and stated that oil shale utilization was going awry, in his opinion. Therefore, this hearing was critical. Then he announced that he was going to have to miss a portion of the questioning due to an urgent matter. He turned the meeting over to the next senior congressman and left.

Congressman Tennant was as surprised by this rapid shift in plans as any of us. He slowly found the words to get himself started. From the look on his face, as well as from the expression of other committee members, they were all a bit put out. They also probably did not share Merton's objective of grandstanding on this rather technical and esoteric subject.

The questioning began in a desultory fashion with congressmen and -women searching for meaningful questions to ask. Many surrendered a portion of their fifteen-minute question periods. They figured there were more points to be lost than won on such a dry subject. All questions were answered with ease, and Kate was not challenged with follow-up questions. Several of the reporters who were present walked out. A little after ten, Merton re-entered the chamber. His second in command quickly handed the gavel back to him.

"With the indulgence of the committee and if there are no objections, I would like to take my turn at questioning rather than waiting for the end." There were no objections.

Merton warmed up with a few questions about the staff available within the F.E.D. to administer oil shale issues. These softball questions might have been designed to make Kate feel complacent. Then he got to the crux of the issue.

"Miss Hastings." Kate, of course always preferred to be called "Ms." "Miss Hastings," he reemphasized, "are you aware of Cooper-MacDonald?"

"Yes, they hold many oil shale land leases." Kate replied. I knew we were both trying to figure out where this was leading.

"Have you read Cooper-MacDonald's annual report?"

"No. I'm not in the habit of reading annual reports." I scribbled a note to myself reading: huge profits.

"Maybe you should make it a practice. Are you aware that Cooper-MacDonald cleared twenty-two billion dollars in after-tax profits last year?"

"I believe I've heard of a figure in that range," Kate replied with a tinge of hesitancy in her voice. I began to dig furiously through relevant files on my laptop. Frobisch, who was sitting a row behind Kate and me, remained quiescent, probably secretly hoping that Kate would be taken down a peg.

"Miss Hastings, are you further aware that seventy percent of those profits came from oil shale leases granted by your department?"

Kate looked quickly in my direction. I could render no immediate help. I glanced at Frobisch; he turned away. "If you say so, I'm certainly prepared to take your word for it," Kate replied with all the control she could muster.

"That's definitely the case," Merton reaffirmed. "Other companies were no doubt bidding for those leases, but Cooper-MacDonald ended up with the majority and particularly those which proved to be the most lucrative." By now I was on the trail of the history of Cooper-MacDonald's leases. I slipped Kate a note: "only two leases granted to C-M in the past six years."

Merton was ready to continue, but Kate interjected, "My information is that only two leases have been granted to that company in the past six years."

Merton had been ready to pursue his original line of questioning, but he decided to depart from his plan and give Kate a brief lecture. "My dear Miss Hastings, I realize you've only been in your current position for three or four years. And perhaps many of these leases were granted to Cooper-MacDonald before you assumed control of your segment of the F.E.D. However, you're still obliged to look after the interests of the American people. If they are being taken advantage of by a monopolistic company, you should be looking at how these leases were obtained and whether unfair profits are accruing to any company, whether it is Cooper-MacDonald or any other company."

During Merton's harangue, my computer was accessing more information. Fifteen leases were granted to Cooper-MacDonald before 2043. These were the largest and, no doubt, the most profitable. I slipped Kate a note to this effect. For a second she turned away from Merton and smiled in my direction. She and I knew the significance of that date. Perhaps Merton forgot.

Merton was continuing to talk about government's responsibility to serve the American people from whom its power was derived, and how the private sector's greed must be guarded against. At one point, when Merton paused to take a breath, Kate interjected boldly, "Congressman Merton, may I ask you a question?" She did not wait for a reply. "Are you aware that Cooper-MacDonald was granted fifteen out of its nineteen leases prior to 2043? These are, by far, their largest oil shale leases."

Merton again began to lecture Kate, the committee and the audience, in general, about the responsibility of government and, particularly, the executive branch. Suddenly, he stopped in mid-sentence. The significance of the year 2043 must have struck him. He cleared his throat, looked around the room for inspiration, and then turned to an aide behind him. "Excuse me, I've just received information that my presence is required elsewhere. Unless there are objections, I will adjourn this hearing." No objections were heard. In fact, the room seemed to exude a sense of relief.

"Ms. Hastings, I'll let you know when we're prepared to resume this hearing."

"I shall await your word, Congressman."

Kate turned to me. "Let's get out of here." She strode from the room. I followed, and Frobisch followed me.

Frobisch caught up with me. "I don't get it."

"You don't recall Lipton-Stroud, the law that was enacted in 2042 and took effect January 1, 2043?"

"Sure, that's the law that sets the standards for granting oil shale and new offshore petroleum leases. We refer to that law quite often."

"But before that, the F.E.D. was required to grant leases under the Simpson-Lovelace Act."

Frobisch's brow furrowed. "Yes, so?"

"Simpson-Lovelace was almost called 'Simpson-Merton.' Congressman Merton was a co-sponsor and obviously a key supporter of the legislation."

"So the F.E.D. was just following the dictates of the Simpson-Lovelace Act in granting those leases to Cooper-McDonald."

"You got it."

Kate had gotten twenty paces in front of me, as I was talking to Jeff. "James, are you coming?"

I shrugged in Jeff's direction. He knew that I was obliged to follow Kate, while he was obliged to get lost. I sensed his humiliation, but I was not prepared to share it. Momentary glory awaited me.

Kate slammed the door behind us. "Grand slam home run. It will be a long while before Merton will want to tangle with me, with us. You stick with me, and you'll do very well."

"And you'll do even better."

"Now, don't let success go to your head," she replied with a rare laugh.

"There's one thing I don't understand," I added with some boldness. "Why did Merton step into such a minefield?"

"Essentially, Merton is lazy. He doesn't do his homework."

"But he has a staff to keep him out of trouble."

"They're lazy, too. Since the institution of term limits, congressmen come and go. But the staff tends to stay behind. New congressmen may bring in a few outsiders, like people who helped on their campaigns, but they need some experienced hands to get them up to speed quickly in Washington. So the experienced staff is just passed on, and they tend to get complacent and lazy. That, I suppose, is one of the downsides of term limits. Whenever you put something new in place, there are unintended consequences."

"I guess that applies to our work, too."

"That's why I need bright people like you—to figure out all the consequences." Kate smiled. I appreciated having my ego stroked, but I also felt the weight of expectations being placed on my shoulders.

VII

BY THE END OF MAY, Savannah was beginning to provide a substantial dose of its summer weather. Whereas in winter the middle of the night power downs were rare, in the hot weather they occurred two or three times a week. More energy was expended to cool than to heat, and the usage had to be restrained. Savannah did not warrant the same priority for energy allocation as did Washington or New York. Residents knew that only a battery-operated alarm clock could be relied upon. And when I awoke with the sheet soaked with sweat, I knew that the air-conditioning had been off during the night.

I liked working outside in the garden behind Mrs. Pinckney's house, but by eleven o'clock I needed to retreat into the air-conditioning. This particular morning was comfortable, and I had a number of papers spread out on the glass-topped table. At my elbow was the remainder of my breakfast coffee.

From the corner of my eye, I noticed Jacqueline in shorts and a tee shirt entering the garden. "Good morning, sir." She announced herself coyly.

"Good morning, Jacqueline," I replied blandly.

I looked down at my papers, but also noticed that Jacqueline was considering carefully how to arrange the chaise. Did she want to get sun or be in a position to chat with me? She adjusted it twice and still was not satisfied. "What are you working on?"

"Just some paperwork."

"I can see that."

"Then why did you ask?"

"Oh, you're in a fine mood this morning. Sorry to have interrupted you."

"And I'm sorry for being curt with you. I don't particularly enjoy the work I'm doing."

Jacqueline was now draped over my shoulder, looking more carefully at the papers on the table—or at least pretending to do so. "Then why do it?"

"I made a commitment to serve on the regional energy council. I have to review these construction proposals. Plus I can use the extra pay."

"Except for the money, it does sound pretty dull." Jacqueline walked back to her chaise, sat upright on the front edge, arched her back, and fell silent. She seemed to be considering her next move. After a minute, she stretched out, face down. I glanced in her direction every minute or so.

"Damn, it's getting hot," she exclaimed. "I'm going to take my top off, if it won't bother you."

"I've seen you without your top on."

"So you remember. I think it bothered you on that occasion," she said, as she slipped her tee shirt off. She was facing me, so I would be sure to notice her bare breasts again. "How come you've never visited the club to see me dance? Don't I appeal to you just a little bit?"

"You're very appealing, but I can see you here. Why take a difficult trip to the club? I don't have a private car."

"I don't have one, either, but I get there."

"So you do," I replied simply.

"That's a comment, not an answer," she noted cleverly.

"What was the question again?"

"When are you going to come to the club and see me dance?"

"You must have an enthusiastic, admiring audience. Why do you need me?"

"It's not a matter of my need. It's yours."

"My need?"

"Yes, it can't be very exciting for you, cooped up with our landlady and Mrs. Humphreys, unless you prefer their company to mine." Jacqueline's teasing was all too obvious. By now she was lying on her stomach.

I was prepared to tease her in return. "Mrs. Pinckney is a very charming woman."

"I'm sure she is, and probably a lot more your speed."

"Mrs. Pinckney is very gracious in the way she educates me about Savannah."

"And though I'm young, I might be able to educate you . . ."

Jacqueline stopped in mid-sentence, and I heard steps behind me. "Did I hear my name mentioned?" Mrs. Pinckney asked.

"Mr. Lendeman was just telling me how you were educating him about Savannah," Jacqueline replied with aplomb.

"How sweet of him. And I hope you realize that our sun is excellent for sunbathing, but you can get burned quite quickly."

I wouldn't have been surprised if Mrs. Pinckney had intentionally composed the double entendre. From the smirk on Jacqueline's face, I knew she had not missed it. "Mrs. Pinckney, if my papers are in the way, I can move inside."

"That's a gracious offer, James, but I'm only here to water a few plants. Then I'll be out of y'all's way."

Mrs. Pinckney's presence, although brief, broke the flow of banter between Jacqueline and me. I returned to my paperwork, but the heat was becoming unpleasant. I gathered up my materials and took a few steps toward the back door.

Jacqueline called after me, "James, please be gracious enough to come to the club some evening, and I'll make certain you get a complimentary lap dance."

VIII

THERE WAS A PERIOD OF a month or so after the Merton Committee recessed when boredom returned. Kate was traveling to regional offices, and she did not choose to have me join her. Some work was left for me, but several of these small projects had the appearance of make-work assignments.

Two or three times a week, I received a call from Kate's admin assistant beckoning me to her desk to pick up information about some new task. I couldn't understand why Kate didn't directly contact me with the details of the assignments. After picking up the fifth or sixth such message in this indirect fashion, I asked her admin assistant, "Ms. Sorel, I have three questions for you."

Jane Sorel, who felt her authority was derived directly from her proximity to Kate, was somewhat taken aback by the impertinence of my questioning something coming from Ms. Hastings. "Yes," she replied warily.

"First, why doesn't Kate call me directly regarding these assignments? It would seem a simpler route."

I could see Jane bristle. Now she was sure I was being impertinent. "Very simply, Mr. Lendeman, when Ms. Hastings calls me, she communicates many items, including tasks for any number of her staff. She feels it's more efficient than placing calls to each of you. I agree with her logic."

"But if I have some questions regarding what Kate wants, I'd have to get back to you. That would not be highly efficient. But, let's say I concede your point. Then my next question is 'Why don't you visit me on occasion, rather than having me come here each time?'"

"Mr. Lendeman, in that case I might miss a call from Ms. Hastings."

I did not have the audacity to ask Jane what she did when she needed a potty break. I wouldn't have put it past her to take the phone into the john.

"Ms. Sorel, one more question. After work someday, would it be possible for you to join me for a drink?"

Jane Sorel's brow furrowed. "That might not be proper, considering we're in the same unit, but I'll consider it."

"Then how about considering it for tomorrow afternoon?"

"Mr. Lendeman, that was your fourth question. You are only allowed three."

For the first time, Jane Sorel smiled at me.

That night I had a dream about having sex with Jane Sorel. It was an enjoyable dream. I awoke and couldn't get her out of my mind.

I didn't know much about her. Kate appreciated her for being efficient, well organized, reasonably intelligent, and trustworthy. She was single. That much I knew, otherwise I wouldn't have invited her for a drink. I had picked up the information from somewhere that she had worked in the F.E.D. for about six years and was a college graduate. Therefore, I assumed she was close to my age.

Other than that, I could only judge her by actions and appearance. She was inclined to be very serious, at least around people from the F.E.D. and particularly when Kate was present. She was average height and was more curvaceous than Kate. Her hair was brown, and her eyes were blue. On occasion she wore glasses when working but didn't seem to need them for most purposes. Without being beautiful, she had an attractive face with a short nose and small mouth. Her hair was likely medium length, but, thus far, it had always been pulled back into a bun. She would easily fit the image of a librarian, albeit an attractive one. It was worth a drink or two to get to know her better.

After lunch that day, I received a message to pick up an assignment from Jane, as Kate was still on her nationwide tour. I listened politely as Jane related the details of the task and then handed me a typed version to make sure there would be no misunderstanding.

"Seems clear enough, but I have one or four questions."

"One or four?" My statement seemed to confuse Jane.

"Yes, it depends on your answer to the first."

"And what's the first?"

"Did you consider my offer from yesterday?"

"Yes, I did, Mr. Lendeman."

"And what's your answer?"

"Maybe."

"That's somewhat encouraging. How about today?

"Could we make it tomorrow?"

"That's even more encouraging. Since tomorrow's Friday, let's make it drinks and a dinner. I would think on a Friday, we should both be finished here by five thirty."

"Five thirty sounds fine."

"Then tomorrow at five thirty. Naturally, I'll come to your office."

Jane had a troubled look on her face. "Could we meet at the restaurant?"

"If that appeals to your sense of decorum, we certainly can. I'll pick a place and call you tomorrow." I turned as if to leave.

"Oh, Mr. Lendeman, I was counting. You only asked three questions."

"So I did, and I have one left. Do you think you can call me 'James'?"

"I suppose so." Again I left Jane with a smile on her face.

The restaurant I chose was close to the office, yet not

frequented by the F.E.D. staff. I arrived first and asked for a booth in the corner. I told the hostess that an attractive brunette would be joining me. She had the presence of mind to flatter me, saying, "Lucky girl."

I ordered a glass of red wine. Jane arrived about ten minutes after me, full of apologies.

"No need to apologize. I was somewhat early."

"I would have been here on time if I hadn't gotten a call from Kate. She's in San Francisco now."

"Nice place to spend the weekend."

"Last weekend she was in Dallas."

"Not bad, but I'd take San Francisco."

"Did you ever live there?"

"No, but I visited a number of times when I was in college, and enjoyed some good California wine. Speaking of wine, do you want one?"

Jane hesitated. "If you don't mind, I think I'll have a rum and Coke."

"I don't mind."

"I never quite developed the taste for wine. Never lived in a wine-growing region."

"New Jersey is not exactly a mecca for vino, either."

"So that's where you grew up." That led to Jane telling me about being raised in Vermont. Her father was a manager of a ski resort. When that business declined because the energy shortage prevented the vast majority of people from traveling, her father stayed on and had a succession of odd jobs. None of them paid enough to enable the family to maintain its prior standard of living. Jane's mother helped with part-time employment.

With the help of some scholarship money, a student loan, and campus employment, Jane attended Susquehanna University in Selinsgrove, Pennsylvania. But due to the energy crunch schools in the hinterlands, without access to good public transportation, had problems with declining enrollment. Susquehanna closed its doors after Jane's sophomore year. Jane moved to Washington, taking a job with the Federal Energy Department.

"I began to think that failure would follow me throughout my life. My father had failed. I chose to go to a college that failed. I was afraid that I'd fail at the F.E.D. But I completed my bachelor's degree online. Sure, it's not equivalent to what I would have gotten from Susquehanna. But many people have been forced into online education.

"I first worked in an admin pool, then for a pretty competent section head, then Kate took notice of me, and I've been working for her for the last two . . . well, almost three, years. I think she has confidence in me. That gives me confidence in myself.

"She's an amazing person—brains, ability, looks. She has it all. I work hard at not letting her down. In some ways, this is the best time of my life."

"It's not in other ways?" I asked.

"The job is demanding. When I get involved in government policy or economics or any technical subject, I'm afraid of screwing up. Frequently, Kate assumes I know more than I really do. I only had one science course and one economics course in college. I'm an English major. I guess I'm good at making sure the written reports contain proper grammar, but I have no idea if they're factually correct."

"One can't do it all," I commented diplomatically.

"Kate seems to, and I think she thinks you can, too."

"She's commented about me?" I was a bit surprised, but why wouldn't she share opinions with her own admin assistant?

Jane hesitated, thinking she might be violating a confidence. "She's made a comment or two, but I do get to assemble her personnel notes."

"That's understandable."

"I figured if Kate is beginning to place her trust in you, I can at least have a drink with you." Jane blushed. "I don't think that came out right."

"I understand. You feel I'm trustworthy. You won't get in trouble with me."

"Not on a first date, at least." I couldn't conclude whether Jane was being coy or innocent. I didn't particularly like being thought of as a safe date.

But Jane had gone off in another direction. "Now that I told you my life story, tell me yours."

I gave Jane a brief rundown of growing up in New Jersey, about how my father was impacted by the energy shortage, leading to his early retirement and early demise, and how that led to my interest in energy resource management. I quickly outlined the basic facts about my education at Stanford and UGA, but I suspected she knew some of that from my file, which she no doubt maintained. I told her my mother was still alive and that I had one sister. I rarely got to see them.

For the first time, Jane interjected a comment, a rueful comment, "Yes, that's how it is these days. If a family becomes separated by geography, they never get back together. We live in isolation, don't we?" It was a common comment on life in mid-twenty-first century America.

Our first date was typical, unexciting but satisfactory. The conversation flowed easily. We ate our dinners without spilling drink or dropping food on ourselves. Since Jane lived in PG County, near the university, and I lived in northwest Washington, we said goodbye at the Metro station. Before departing, Jane planted a brief kiss on my cheek. A mother, sister, or daughter might have done the same.

Through Jane, I continued to get modest assignments and questions from Kate, as she progressed on her countrywide tour. She was in Minneapolis and soon heading for Chicago. Another week and she would be back in the office.

After picking up a request from Kate, I asked Jane if we would be following up on our first date. "Why not?" was her seemingly indifferent reply. However, the next day she called me. "Could you stop by my desk?"

"Sure," was my succinct response. The strange thing was that this was not Jane's normal mode of summoning me. Usually she would simply say that I needed to pick up an assignment from Kate.

When I arrived at Jane's desk, she began talking in a low voice, although no one else was around. "I didn't want to talk over the phone."

"Something hush-hush from Kate?"

"No, something hush-hush from me." Before I could insert a witty rejoinder, she blurted out. "Tomorrow night my roommate is going to be out. How about coming over for a home-cooked meal?"

"Sounds great. Can I bring some rum for you and wine for me?"

"Sounds equally great."

After getting her address and directions, I asked, "So nothing from Kate?"

"Nope. Sorry to disappoint you."

"You didn't disappoint me. You made my day." I tried to sound chivalrous.

Jane's apartment was located about a kilometer from the University of Maryland campus. The area was populated with a mix of college students and young professionals. The housing had been spruced up over the past twenty years as people moved back to the inner suburbs. Her apartment consisted of a living room, kitchen, dining nook, two bedrooms, and a bath.

I looked around quickly and said, "Very attractive."

"You talking about me or the apartment?"

"How about both?"

"Then I thank you, my apartment thanks you, and my roommate thanks you."

"What does you roommate have to do with it? Is she very attractive, too?"

"She pays half the expenses—and I think you'd find her attractive. Unfortunately, you won't be able to meet her tonight."

I could have picked up on the last comment and continued the banter, but I decided some change of direction was required. "Something smells really good."

"My perfume?"

"I didn't get close enough, yet, to smell your perfume."

"I sense you have some hopes, or are they expectations?"

"Gee, you're making this difficult. I was talking about your cooking. What's in that big pot?"

"Coq au vin. Did you bring some other *vin* for dinner?"

"You bet—an Oregon pinot noir."

"I guess that will go well with the chicken."

"It sounds like you have a little expertise in these matters. Picked it up from your boss?"

"Kate? Does she like to cook? We've never discussed the subject." Jane's response led me to believe that her relationship with Kate was focused on work.

"She seems to enjoy dining at good restaurants, and she seems to know something about wine."

"Good for her," Jane responded tersely. I made a mental note to omit Kate from our discussion. "No, there are other ways to pick up this information. If you recollect, my father used to run a ski resort. We had some pretty good chefs. I used to hang around the kitchen when I was a youngster. Picked up some pointers and also collected some recipes. And how did you pick up your knowledge?"

"My parents enjoyed wine with dinner, at least when things were better and they could afford decent wine."

"Did you have to sneak the wine?"

"No, when I was a teenager they'd let me have samples. They didn't think I'd become an alcoholic from tasting a few centiliters of wine."

"A very commendable attitude—almost European."

"I suspect that if you go to any wine-producing area, you'll find the same notion."

"As in the Willamette Valley?" Jane asked as she looked at the bottle of pinot noir.

"I suppose so. Unfortunately I've never visited the Oregon or California wine regions so I can't speak from personal experience."

Jane handed me a corkscrew. "Dinner should be ready in a few minutes. Will you do the honors?"

She was busy at the stove, but glanced at me while I sized up her old-fashioned waiter's corkscrew. I cut the capsule, screwed the auger into the cork, and then properly used the flange for leverage. "You've done that before," Jane observed.

"Guilty as charged."

"You know, I think I'll try some wine tonight. Have to try to find out why Kate and my roommate like this stuff."

With me filling the wine glasses and Jane carrying the coq au vin to the table, we began our dinner. I complimented Jane on her cooking. She complimented me on the wine, despite her lack of knowledge. The dinner conversation wandered through discussions of working at the F.E.D., during which Jane skirted any issue which would divulge confidential information, our friends from college, the high cost of living (including ways of stretching our incomes), and the sad state of government in the United States and the world in general. Although the conversation was spirited, it was also negative in tone. After a while we sensed that we, in essence, were dumping our complaints on each other, and concluded that our grandparents lived in the best of times.

I helped Jane clear the table. "How about watching a movie? I subscribe to A Million and One Movies."

"I used to, but I never seemed to have the chance to watch enough to justify the expense. What kind of movies do you like?"

Jane hesitated for only a second. "I think the adventure films from the end of the last century were the best. I don't think many films made in the last fifty years can top them. My favorites are the *Indiana Jones* pictures. Have you seen them?"

"Yes, but not for a long while. If you want to watch one, that's fine with me."

"*Raiders of the Lost Ark?*"

"*Raiders of the Lost Ark* it is."

Jane switched the entertainment center on, did a search for the movie, found it in a few seconds, and a few seconds later it began. "I guess this is one thing we have that our grandparents didn't—instant access to thousands of films."

"A million and one," I countered.

"Whatever. Since we can't go anywhere and vacations are meaningless, they keep us from going crazy."

I sat on the sofa, and Jane took a seat next to me. After a few minutes, she was leaning against me. I put my arm around her shoulder. She snuggled closer. I wondered whether she planned to watch the picture through to its conclusion.

After a while, I realized that my arm had gone to sleep. I whispered to Jane that I needed to switch position. We readjusted ourselves. Jane put a pillow on my lap and put her head on it. I deduced that Jane was intent on watching the film to its end, which didn't bother me, since it was good and I hadn't seen it for years.

It was a long film. At the conclusion we arose from the sofa and stretched, I commented that I should be leaving. If I waited longer, I would have trouble getting a Metro train.

"I guess all good things must come to an end," Jane observed.

"Yes, I enjoyed this evening, too."

"Certainly you can stay a little while longer," Jane urged.

"To help you clean the dishes."

"No, silly man. We're on our second date, and we shouldn't part with only a handshake."

"Are you proposing to kiss me?"

"Yes, that's very appropriate for a second date. Do you agree?"

I responded through my actions rather than words. We quickly fell back onto the sofa with Jane on top of me. I remember thinking how much I enjoyed her breasts pressing against my chest. Then I managed to cup my left hand on her right breast. She did not resist. Her lips, especially the lower one, were full. There was a pleasurable sensuality in moving my lips and then my tongue over and through them, and then having her respond.

After a few minutes my hand went lower. Her buttocks were generous but firm. Then my hand went to her thigh.

Jane pulled away just a bit. "You know that feels good. But this is our second date, not our third."

"You really have a schedule for everything."

"I told you. I'm very organized."

We had begun disengaging our bodies. "Is there going to be a third date?" I asked.

"Do you want there to be?"

"No fair. I asked my question first."

"Yes, I'd like that."

With that response, I took her hand and shook it, figuring a second date only warranted the one passionate kiss already shared.

"No, damn it. I want a goodbye kiss."

I obliged.

IX

I WAS NOT ENJOYING THE summer in Savannah. The heat was oppressive and the air-conditioning was minimal. The work on the regional energy council was beginning to put a strain on me—not physical, of course, but psychological. I was not as strong as I used to be, and I knew I was being manipulated.

I was now hearing from Joe Porter and Aaron Smith, my two key colleagues on the council, all too frequently. Since they now had an expert from Washington within their midst, they saw little need to make decisions on their own. It seemed as if every document that came their way was forwarded to me for my opinion. After a month of experiencing this behavior, I tried to turn the tables on my associates. Several proposals to expand facilities were forwarded to me attached to one multinet note which simply said: "Your input, please. Joe and Aaron."

I waited a day before sending my terse reply. "F.E.D. regulations call for regional council principals to make decisions regarding proposals that will impact energy usage. James."

Quite quickly, I received a reply. "We will make final decision but want your consulting opinion first. Joe and Aaron." So much for my tactical gambit.

A week after our exchange of notes, Joe and Aaron took their reliance on me one step further. They asked me to attend a meeting with a developer who was proposing an expansion of a freight transfer station. Earlier, the proposal had been sent to me for my input. I had pointed out that the energy usage analysis was flawed and even at that the projected usage was unsatisfactory by government standards. Joe and Aaron, as they explained to me, "wanted me to communicate the technicalities of the rejection to the developer."

I countered by pointing out that they must have handled this job on their own a score of times. "Sure we've done it," they replied, "but we're not sure we've done it particularly well. We want to observe a master at work, so we can learn to do it better in the future. You know these rejections are the most difficult thing for us, not having the expertise that you have."

How could I resist such unctuous reasoning? I relented. "Okay, I assume you'll pick me up on your way to the developer."

"We sure will."

I decided that, in return for performing these additional duties, I would find a way to extract some extra benefits from the regional energy council. And I knew what form the major benefit would take.

As planned, Joe and Aaron picked me up fifteen minutes before our meeting with the developer. One of the features of an energy-starved society was that we didn't have to worry about being held up by traffic. We knew that it would take ten minutes for the trip from Mrs. Pinckney's house to the office of the developer's lawyer on McDonough Street.

In the meeting, Joe and Aaron quickly turned to me to explain the basis of the plan's rejection. I gave a complete and somewhat pedantic explanation of how the developer's plan did not meet government regulations, citing the specific rules for their enlightenment.

The developer did not dispute my evaluation, realizing that my expertise was clearly superior. What he did ask was how the plan could be modified to comply. I gave a brief idea as to how this could be done, but pointed out that such changes might make the plan economically unfeasible. I advised the developer to hire a consultant if he chose to pursue the plan.

After a few more questions, all in the room sensed the meeting was coming to a conclusion. Joe attempted to summarize. "I think this was very productive since James was able to so accurately point out where your plan was coming up short. Even if we approved it at the local level, he saved you the trouble of getting it knocked down in Washington." What Joe failed to point out was that few plans of this scale were ever reviewed in Washington. But we shook hands and pretended that we were all happy with the conclusion.

When we got out of the office, Joe asked if I could return home on the tram line, since he and Aaron needed to head toward Pooler. "Sure," I replied amicably. "Oh, there's one way you could help me out from time to time."

"What's that?" asked Aaron, a bit suspiciously.

"You gentlemen are able to take the electrocar home every night. I'd like to borrow it from time to time. I doubt if it would be more than two or three times a month. I figure now that I'm going beyond the scope of simply consulting, I should get to use the council's electrocar on occasion."

Joe and Aaron looked at each other. "Yeah, I guess that would be alright. But you'll have to keep it to a minimum."

"And let us know as far in advance as possible," the other added.

The next day I received a telephone call. "This is Len Dailey . . ." For a second I was stumped. "I'm the developer you met with yesterday."

"Oh, sure, Mr. Dailey. Sorry I didn't recognize your name quicker. Haven't had my morning coffee, yet." A lie.

"Quite alright. Listen I have a little business proposition for you." I could see what was coming. "How would you like to be my consultant on modifying this proposal so it will pass muster with the government?"

"I'm not sure that would be exactly ethical, since I could be asked to review any revisions."

"But couldn't you clear it with Aaron and Joe, so you'd be out of the loop on any later review?"

"I don't know . . ."

"Look, no need to make any decision now. Why don't we have lunch together, tomorrow, and we'll discuss it some more?"

"Guess we can do that."

At twelve thirty the next day, I arrived at a café that Len had suggested. He was already seated at a corner table. "This is very attractive," I commented, looking around at the Tiffany-style lamps and decorations.

"I'm sure some of this stuff is a hundred and fifty years old. Strangely enough, the place is run by SCAD. The food's okay, and some of the waitresses are real cute—SCAD students."

Before I picked up a menu, Len Dailey was reviewing his offer. "The more I think about it, the more sense it makes. You already know how the plan doesn't pass muster. Just tell us how it needs to be changed. It's not like we're cheating. We want to meet government rules. That's the objective. It's in both our interests."

"You make it sound very appealing. But to an outsider looking at it, it might not quite smell right." I didn't think Len would mind if I mixed my metaphors.

A waiter began to approach our table, but then a female voice came from behind me. "Tom, let me take this table. You take number six. Some women there. They'll give a stud like you a bigger tip." Then, addressing us, she stated, "I'll be your waitress today. My name is Jacqueline. Oh, Mr. Lendeman, I didn't know it was you."

"And I thought you worked elsewhere."

"I don't usually work here. But I have plenty of waitress experience, and I sometimes fill in for a friend." Jacqueline mentioned a special that wasn't on the menu, took our drink order, and departed, using her most seductive walk.

"You and Jacqueline good friends?" Len asked, showing

genuine interest.

"No, we both live in the same rooming house."

"Damn attractive young lady. Quite a body."

Len Dailey was probably around fifty, but that wouldn't prevent any red-blooded male from admiring Jacqueline, even if he were married.

We ordered lunch. Len went over his offer again and asked what sort of compensation I was interested in. I told him two hundred an hour, and I thought it would take about thirty hours of my time. He thought the amount was fair.

We enjoyed our lunch, talked about the hot weather and the need for rain. He also enjoyed watching Jacqueline whenever she was near our table. I could see that he left a particularly good tip when it was time to pay.

Later that day, I called Aaron and told him about Dailey's offer, and how I was reluctant to accept it. I also said that I thought the proposal could work if I would be excused from reviewing any revised plans. Aaron told me he'd have to double check with Joe before getting back to me. The next day Joe called back saying that they would let me do this work for Dailey if I'd assure them any revised plan met all government energy regulations. I thanked Joe.

"You see, James, that's the way we can do business in a smaller place like Savannah, away from all the bureaucracy in Washington."

"Yup, love being away from Washington."

X

Washington, 2053

A FEW DAYS BEFORE KATE returned from her countrywide trip, she sent instructions to assemble current data on oil and gas production, split by every major producing region in the world. Additionally, she wanted United States imports from each region and estimated reserves of each of those regions. This information was readily available from our databases, but Kate wanted it assembled onto a page or two, which she could keep at her fingertips.

Then came detailed questions regarding relations with each major producing country, an assessment of their political stability, their alliances, their form of government, their leaders, key political parties. The list kept on growing.

Of course, these requests came through Jane. "Call Kate back, and tell her I'm going to have to go to State in order to get the best answers to many of these questions."

"I don't think Kate would want you to do that. We try not to work through State."

"Isn't this what our State Department is for? Tell her I really think I need to. Would you want me to call Kate?"

"No, I'll do it." Jane did not want me violating her direct channel to our boss.

An hour later the answer came back—"Don't use the State Department."

"I'm going to call Kate and try to change her mind," I stated when Jane brought me the reply.

"Please don't. It won't help either one of us," Jane pleaded.

"I get hurt if she doesn't change her mind. So, I want you to call Kate back and tell her I'll try my best working on my own, but I'm not going to vouch for the quality of the final product."

"I can't tell her that."

"You want me to?"

"No," Jane replied hesitantly.

"Look, just quote me. You're only delivering a message."

"And the messenger *never* gets blamed." Jane smiled wryly and left.

I understood everything about the exchange that Jane and I had, except why Jane had come to my desk on this occasion. She had always asked me to visit her.

This was noted by others. A co-worker stuck his head in my office after Jane left. "I've never seen the aloof Ms. Sorel on this floor before. Surprised she could find her way here. You must really rate."

I only smiled in return. The less said, the better.

The next morning the old routine was reinstated. Jane asked me to stop by her desk. "I don't think Kate appreciated your comment."

"What did she say?"

"Not much really. She kind of made a sound—'hmmm.' Then she said, 'I'll talk to him when I return.' Didn't sound positive to me."

"Oh, well, you only die once." I tried to sound philosophical.

"Yes, but you have so much to look forward to. Like our third date."

"From the sound of things we should get that date in before Kate returns."

"We do have a weekend coming up," Jane said invitingly.

"Yes, we do. How about the Omniplex on Saturday?"

"Sounds good to me. But my roommate is going to be home

all weekend."

"Would I be too bold to suggest that I have an apartment and no roommate?"

"Boldness frequently wins out."

We covered the logistics of our date, which promised to stretch from Saturday afternoon into Sunday. As I returned to my own cubicle I needed to wipe the grin from my face. I had to stop thinking about my successful campaign to woo and screw the fair Ms. Sorel. Fortunately, I had plenty else to think about. I needed to complete this new voluminous assignment, and I would also have to find time to clean my apartment and get some food into the refrigerator.

I worked late into Friday night, completing Kate's assignment to the best of my ability. Saturday morning was spent cleaning the apartment. I tried to look at it through Jane's eyes and found it quite appalling. Taking out the garbage was easy. Cleaning mold from the bathroom tiles, grime off the kitchen appliances, and dust from every horizontal surface were all more challenging. I did some work, and then decided that I didn't even own the proper cleaning supplies to handle some of the jobs.

Fortunately, a supermarket was only a few blocks away. I came home with cleanser, sponges, paper towels, a few snacks, two bottles of wine, and orange juice, coffee, creamer, frozen waffles, and sausages for Sunday morning breakfast.

The work in my apartment was more difficult than Kate's assignment had been. By two in the afternoon things were as clean as they were going to get. I showered, shaved, and set off on the combination Metro and tram rides to get me to Jane's apartment.

I met Jane's roommate, Priscilla, who appeared to be several years older than Jane. She was pleasant, but not particularly attractive, except for her long auburn hair. Jane was ready to leave when I arrived, and we exchanged only enough pleasantries with her roommate to be polite. A small bag was packed with a change of clothes. We took the same Metro/tram path back to my apartment.

It was nearly five when we arrived.

Jane made a quick assessment of my quarters—a studio apartment. "Not bad for a bachelor's digs. Kitchen's kind of small, but at least you have a queen-sized bed."

"I don't do much cooking."

"But you do a lot of . . ."

"Sleeping."

We each had a glass of wine while sitting on the only two chairs in the apartment. They were wooden kitchen chairs and not too comfortable, but we weren't going to stay long. We soon headed via Metro to central Washington and the Omniplex, the large collection of theatres, restaurants, and shops near the Mall.

The restaurant I chose specialized in steaks. All the waitress asked was "how do you want it done and what do you want to drink?" I asked Jane if she wanted a rum and Coke. She answered that she'd let me guide her further into the world of wine. I ordered a bottle of cabernet. Salads were quickly brought, along with some bread. When we were done, the plates were whisked away, and the steak and *pommes frites* arrived. We lingered over the remainder of the wine and discussed whether we wanted to go to a movie.

We settled on Jane's suggestion of taking a short stroll around the shopping area to help digest the dinner. After looking in half a dozen stores, Jane said boldly, "Let's get back to your place. I'm in the mood for something, and it's not a movie."

"I think I get your drift."

Then Jane looked a bit worried. "Did I shock you?"

"No, not a bit. After all, this is our third date." But I did wonder how many third dates Jane had had. Oh, shit, did it really matter?

I began to wake Sunday morning, realizing that things were not normal, not necessarily bad but clearly not normal. I was sharing my bed and was lying on my right side. Another body was curled within mine, like two spoons in a drawer. She—and now I realized it was Jane—was using my arm as a pillow. I was awake, but my arm was asleep. I tried to extricate it from beneath her head. It would not move. I had to use my other arm to pull it free, and then it lay useless between us. Accompanied by the usual feeling of pins and needles, my arm began to function slowly.

"What you doing?" Jane awoke to my movement.

"Trying to get the feeling back in my arm."

"I'm glad something else didn't go to sleep last night. It was good—both times." Jane rolled over, facing me. She put her hand behind my head and planted a languorous kiss on my lips. Her breath was a mixture of stale wine and several hours' sleep. Yet the act was pleasurable. I kissed her back and was sure my breath was similarly scented. Neither of us complained. Our hands again explored the territory frequented the night before.

"I have to pee."

"Yes, so do I."

Jane hurried into the bathroom first and then after seeing me emerge, said, "I'm going back in to brush my teeth."

"I'll make coffee."

We did not return to our sexual post-play.

During breakfast, Jane asked, "What do you usually do on Sunday mornings?"

"I turn on my page palette and read the *Washington Post*. And what do you do?"

"I go to a café and read their *Washington Post*—at least the first section or two. And, on rare occasions, I go to church."

"Then you're a believer."

"I guess, but I go more from a sense of tradition or habit. Where else would you go on Easter?"

"What church do you grace with your presence?"

"I pick the closest one that's kind of mainstream—Presbyterian, Methodist—it really doesn't matter." We both fell silent for a minute. Jane was the first to resume. "Are you going to read the *Post* after I leave?"

"You're not going to leave. I'm going to take you home."

"That's very chivalrous."

"No. It's very appropriate."

"James, I figured you out. You're rather old-fashioned, very traditional."

The evaluation seemed almost a slur. "You say that just because I'm going to take you home?"

"No, there are other things."

"Name one."

Jane hesitated. "Well, you use an old-fashioned condom."

"You mean rather than the latex spray-on. I don't trust that type."

"Because you're old-fashioned. They're supposed to be ninety-nine percent effective, and they're more sensual."

"I wasn't sensual enough?"

"Now I've hurt your feelings. You were great. No, I mean more sensual for *you*."

"Did you hear me complain?"

"No. But I want you to feel maximum pleasure, so you'll want to do it again."

I looked at Jane quizzically. "What do you think I feel? 'I got Jane Sorel to go to bed with me—now I can move on to someone else'? No, I want to spend more time with you and have more sex with you."

Jane moved over to my side of the kitchen table, sat on my lap, and kissed me again—this time quite gently. "Maybe this Wednesday? A hump-day date."

"Kate's going to be back."

"Do we need her permission?" Jane smiled wickedly.

"No, you know what I mean. She's coming back from a three-week trip. She's going to dump a lot of work on me and maybe on you, too. We'll shoot for Wednesday, but I have the right to ask for a rain check."

Jane's forehead wrinkled. "What's a rain check?"

"You really don't know?"

"No, I don't."

"I guess it is an old-fashioned term. They used to play ballgames in outdoor stadiums. If the game was rained out, they gave you a 'rain check,' so you could attend the makeup game for free."

"Wow. Really? Isn't it much more efficient now? All baseballs games are played in six stadiums in Dallas. All football is in four stadiums in Chicago. And we can all watch on our entertainment centers."

"Very efficient, but I wish that the New York Yankees could actually play a game in New York."

"You *are* old-fashioned, James." I received a kiss on the forehead.

When Kate returned, the expected happened. A whirlwind hit the office. I was the second one to be called to her office. It was both an honor and a plague. She had a two-inch spiral notebook filled with observations from the trip.

"We're dying. It's not a quick death, but a slow death is even more painful."

"Excuse me for saying so," I tried to be respectful, "but didn't we know that?"

"You don't know the extent of it." I thought I had plenty of statistics at my fingertips, but I held my tongue. "It's worse than we think. The data we have are skewed."

"How so?"

"The regional offices are lying to us. They report energy supplies that are overstated. They understate usage. They fail to report shortages that emerge."

"Certainly the media would play up power downs, empty supply depots, etc."

"The media can't afford good regional coverage. So far, the rubber band hasn't broken. Sure there are depots that are dangerously low. There's a little outage here or there. The media are told we have a temporary disruption or a small misallocation.

They're not told how tight things are."

"And why do the regions do this?"

"Two reasons. They don't want to panic the locals or us here in Washington; and, second, they want to keep industry plodding ahead in their region. A publicized shortage would prevent any new projects or expansion of any existing facilities. Our regional office and the regional energy council would be blamed. The local economy would retrench. It's a delicate balance performed on a knife edge."

Again I thought a question was in order. "So what are we going to do about it?"

"I was just coming to that. We're going to play rough with our suppliers. That's why I wanted you to collect all that info on our energy trading partners."

"Isn't this a rather large policy change? We're talking about the president and State taking a different tack."

"We're going to have to take the lead. We've been the caboose. We need to be the engine and get up front and pull them along."

"Do you think we can exert the leverage?"

"We're going to have to try. We're going to have to starve some of our friends to get our share. From now on we have to think of ourselves as cannibals." My mouth must have fallen open. "Come on, James, we're going to work this out. I looked at what you gave me. It's pretty good but pretty tame. Now that you know where I'm coming from, I want you to go into greater depth. Let's start with Iran, Kuwait, Iraq, Canada, Mexico, Venezuela, Nigeria, and Australia as suppliers. Let's assume we can squeeze Western Europe. They can deal with the Russians. We'll leave Russia and Brazil alone for the time being. Get me the weak points on enemies and friends."

For the past several minutes, Kate had been pacing her office. She hit her desk to emphasize several points.

"And I still have to work on my own?"

"You can get help from a few trusted people in this

Department."

"But not State."

"Of course not. I think you can see why. Let's get back together on Thursday morning and see what we have. Questions, comments?"

"May I suggest that we leave out Nigeria and Venezuela? Their production is pretty well tapped out now."

"Okay. I'll buy that. Push everything else aside, including the work on revised regional fuel allocations. Allocations can stay as they are for the time being. This project gets top priority and top secrecy. Understand?"

"Yes," was my simple reply, but I only had a vague notion of how I was going to proceed.

Jane was in the outer office when I left. She arose from her desk and came over to me and stood dangerously close. "Everything okay?"

"I think so, but you won't guess what's happening, and I suppose I shouldn't tell you."

"Maybe Kate will tell me."

"I hope so. It will make things easier on us. Less need for subterfuge."

"Are we still on for Wednesday?"

"I don't know. Let's see how I progress today and tomorrow."

"Good luck."

I could tell Jane wanted to kiss me, but that was impossible.

Back in my office, I wanted to do my own pacing, but there was no room. I drummed my fingers on the desk. I needed more information, but where could I get it? I had tried the obvious databases. I would need to search in additional places, but where would they be? The Department of State was the perfect spot, but that was prohibited. Using expanded search criteria, I began to scan additional sources of information. From the first dozen, nothing promising emerged. I looked further.

I went deeper into each country's source information. These sites were bound to be self-serving. Yet they provided something additional, and I printed out items which I thought might be useful. If nothing else, they would add points of views and pad my earlier report.

However, I knew this additional input was not going to be nearly enough. It was going to give Kate nothing of interest. I searched further and came up with very little. In order to see how I might use the additional information, however slim, I put together reports on Mexico and Kuwait. The new reports didn't look much different than the old.

At this point there were two possibilities. First, I could go back to Kate, tell her that I was coming up with little else, and even show her the new reports to demonstrate that her restraints would not permit me to generate the information she wanted. Or, second, I could take some unorthodox approach.

The former direction was safe, unimaginative, and would hardly please Kate. The latter was dangerous. Success would put another feather in my cap, but failure or discovery of my method might spell ruin. I wanted to satisfy Kate, but more importantly, I needed to satisfy myself. I determined to produce no second-rate product.

I knew that my old roommate and buddy, Steve Durham, was back in Washington. He was in a position to help me, and I was fairly certain I could convince him to do so. Certainly he was in the State Department, but I reasoned that I was not approaching the Department in any official manner. Rather, I was approaching Steve, a friend.

My evening call to Steve's home number reached his voice mail. I asked him to call me back as soon as possible regarding an urgent matter, adding that he could call back at any hour and that I preferred a call at home.

I received no call that evening or night. On Wednesday I was back in the office, trying to figure out a way to accomplish my task without relying on Steve Durham. I was coming up blank.

At around ten, my phone rang. "Sorry I couldn't get to you last night. I'm in New York for the day. But since I reached you, I guess you survived the night."

"It's not a health issue—not exactly. But if I don't make some progress on an issue I'm working on, my head will be on the block."

"That's serious. Well, how can I help?"

"Look, I'd rather not talk on this line. Can I call you back in five or ten minutes?"

"Okay, but make it as quick as you can. I'm due in a meeting in fifteen minutes."

I ran from the office building with my personal phone in hand and headed to a bench in a small park squeezed between two nearby buildings. Steve answered promptly. "So, what's up?"

"I need your help and need to keep the matter highly confidential—no reporting this to your bosses."

"I better hear where you're going before I commit to that. I don't want to end up without a job or in jail. You might want to avoid those two outcomes as well."

"Okay, Steve, I agree. Here's what I need. I'm working on a top-level hush-hush project to reposition our energy policy, so we, meaning the U.S., get a better share of world energy output. Officially, I can't work with State."

"But I work for State. That's the rub."

"You're a friend. I'm talking to a friend."

"What do you need, *friend?*" I could sense wariness in Steve's question.

"I need deep intelligence assessments of petroleum production and usage in a number of countries. Even more I need assessments of their political weaknesses and strengths."

"What kind of countries—Middle East?"

"Some Middle East, but others like Canada, Australia, and Mexico."

"Is Kate contemplating some misadventures amongst our friends? We have not been at war with either Canada or Mexico for centuries, and I don't think we ever contemplated attacking the Aussies."

"Don't be funny."

"I don't think it's funny at all. Kate doesn't want you talking to State because she knows any steps in this area are going to be contrary to our international interests."

I tried to calm Steve down. "Look, I think you're getting the wrong perspective on this activity. We're just trying to assess how we can acquire a bit more petroleum."

"By strong-arming others."

"This probably won't come to anything. Just an intellectual exercise. But I have to feed her something. Wouldn't you rather have me involved in this project, so I can tip you off if something is really going to go haywire? Feed me some stuff, and I'll return the favor."

"I'm not permitted to give you classified information and I won't. But there's some pretty good stuff that gets extracted from classified information and is summarized in what are called 'State Department Briefs.' I'll give you the general file address and then you can search by country. I'm not even supposed to give you this info. It's treated as confidential even if it's not classified, so I'm not your source. *Comprendo?*"

I was not sure what language "comprendo" belonged to, but I understood. I wrote the computer address file designations Steve gave me on a small piece of note paper. I could swallow it at some point if necessary.

For the balance of the morning and well into the afternoon, I searched through my new source of information. Although much of it did not seem to be confidential, some of the analysis was insightful and altered some of my thinking about friends and foes. I made notes but avoided copying any of the material. By four o'clock, I was ready to put my own thoughts into writing. The phone rang. It was Jane. I had forgotten all about her.

"Hey, do you know who this is?"

"Sorry, Jane, I've been up to my neck. But I shouldn't make excuses. I could have taken a few minutes to call you."

"I guess you're telling me that our date for tonight is off."

"Yes, I'm afraid I'll be pulling an all-nighter."

"I was hoping the all-nighter would be with me . . . Yes, you can ship that by overnight to the following address." Jane gave the address of our office to the mythical caller and signed off. Obviously, Kate had come out of her office and approached Jane's desk.

I would have liked to call Jane back, but that was inadvisable for two reasons. First, Kate could still be at Jane's shoulder; and, second, I really needed to get back to work.

Ten minutes later the phone rang, and it was Kate. "Are you going to have something good for me in the morning?"

"I hope to."

"Is there anything I can take home tonight to read?"

"No, I'm not at that point. I just came up with some . . ." I tried to find the right words, "some new revelations."

"Sounds like a religious experience."

"Hardly, but I'm going to be working on it well into the night."

"Oh, poor boy. I'm making life difficult for you. Give me some good stuff tomorrow, and I'll make sure you have time to play." She rang off.

I worked late, assembling a document of sixteen pages. A little more than a third was thinly disguised summations from the State Department briefs. If anyone would have compared my report with the State Department material, the plagiarism would have been apparent. However, who would be inclined to do that? Another portion was lifted from my previous report. The remainder consisted of new observations and conclusions.

In the morning, I arrived early in order to double-check my work and then make copies for the meeting with Kate. With most other people I could have handed them a data file for their page palettes. I would have my copy and the discussion would commence. But I had learned that Kate wanted hard copy to look at. During a discussion, she liked to flip back and forth between the pages and found it too difficult to do that on the palette. Since copiers and printers were few and far between, I went to Kate's office, and Jane made the two copies for Kate and me. She mouthed, "Good luck," as I left for my cubicle to wait for a call bidding me to return.

I got a cup of coffee, picked up the report, and began to reread it. Immediately I began to detect flaws, or was I simply second-guessing myself? Too late to make any revisions now; *Go with what you got*, I told myself.

The call eventually came, and in five minutes I was sitting in a chair next to Kate.

"So, what do you have for me?"

"Here's a report which includes some new intelligence, and based upon that, I've developed some new thoughts." I then pointed out some of the most noteworthy new background material, leading to a different set of conclusions.

Kate flipped through the report, quickly dog-earing some of the pages. At first, she simply followed my explanations, saying little. Then the questions began. I thought I answered most competently. After half an hour, Kate observed, "This gives me something to chew on. There's worthwhile stuff here. You deserve the rest of the day off. Catch up on your sleep. But check in with me tomorrow morning. I might want you to expand this report in some directions. We'll have a lot of work to do over the next few weeks."

I had no idea what I was going to do with my newly acquired free time. Jane was at her desk. "I have the afternoon off," I told her.

"Good for you."

"Do you have the evening off?

Jane didn't answer. She merely opened her eyes really wide—a gesture which did not immediately register with me.

"Well, do you?" I repeated.

Kate's voice came from behind me. "If you want, I'll give Jane the rest of day off, and you two can really have a good time."

"I have a lot of work to do, Ms. Hastings," Jane said quickly.

"Do what you think is proper. But if you are sticking around, make another copy of James's report."

I left the two women quickly. I wondered what would transpire between Jane and Kate during the rest of the day. I also thought about what was going to happen with the additional copy of my report. How could I go home and sleep? On the other hand, I didn't want to stay around the office. I went to the Mall, entered a museum, and walked past scores of paintings without noting any of them. By mid-afternoon, I was hungry and getting tired.

I headed home, bought a large sandwich at the corner store, reached my apartment, flipped the TV on, and began to chomp on my meal. Mechanically but reluctantly I turned to the news. My mind raced in irrational directions. Would they report on two employees in the Federal Energy Department having an affair? Had my report been leaked to the press already? Of course, the news had nothing to do with Kate, Jane, or me. My nonsensical fear faded. I grew more tired. I flopped on my bed and fell asleep.

The phone awoke me. My room was dark, and I forgot where I had left it. It took a minute before I answered. Jane was on the other end. "What time is it?" I mumbled.

"Nine o'clock."

"Where are you?"

"On my way to your place, if you want me to come. Were you sleeping?"

"Yes, but come over. I'm awake now."

Twenty minutes later, Jane arrived. She kissed me firmly on the lips.

"Are we in trouble?" I asked.

"No, I don't think so. I think Kate finds it amusing that we're dating."

"I think Kate would have worded it more crassly."

"Oh, she did. She said, 'I thought you two might be screwing.'"

"How did you reply?"

"I just said, 'Yup.' And she laughed and said, 'Well, good for you two. Enjoy yourself.'"

Jane and I had every intention of enjoying our evening together. Overhanging our actions and thoughts, however, was the vague presence of Ms. Kate Hastings, now that we knew she was aware of our relationship. She didn't seem to object, but we recognized that she could make life difficult for us.

We opened a bottle of wine, and I found some crackers and cheese to accompany the cabernet. After half the bottle was consumed, we drew closer together on the couch. Our hands began to feel each other; our mouths began to explore territory beyond the lips. But there was some barrier restraining us. It was Kate.

"You're thinking about her," Jane said.

"I suppose I am."

"We better talk about it. Otherwise she's going to interfere, even though she's far away."

"Yet we both sense her presence."

"Her presence is only in our thoughts." Jane tried to minimize the issue.

"But we were both thinking about her."

"Yes. That I know. But, you are with me. Why are you thinking about her?"

"I could ask you the same question."

"You explain, first."

"I suppose because we were caught. I was wondering how we'd go on with Kate knowing about our relationship."

"You think she didn't suspect before today?"

"You're asking all the questions," I mildly protested.

"Okay, I think she suspected even before today."

"How could she? We were really careful."

"Kate has a sixth sense—like a witch."

"I thought all women were supposed to have a sixth sense."

"We do, but witches do better than others."

"And why were *you* thinking about Kate?"

"Because I could sense you were thinking about her. You were kissing me, but you had that blond witch in the forefront of your thoughts."

"You sensed that?"

"Yes, does that make me a witch?"

"I had another consonant in mind."

"You bastard." The banter had become more light-hearted.

"Screw Kate. Let's fuck," I exclaimed, using stronger language than intended.

"Sounds complicated."

I forced a scowl. For a while, we exorcised Kate from our thoughts.

The next morning, Jane and I headed to the office together. Kate had already discovered our secret, so we saw little point in taking a useless precaution. In the lobby of our building we took our separate paths. However, we did not feel secure enough to share a good-bye kiss.

Half an hour later, I called Kate's office. Jane answered.

"Ms. Sorel, is Ms. Hastings there?"

"Sorry, Mr. Lendeman, she hasn't arrived, yet. I'll give her a message when she does."

"I'd appreciate that."

"Kisses."

Since my cubicle was not sound-proof, I did not feel that I could respond in kind. I was sure Jane understood.

An hour later, I was passing Jane's desk and heading into Kate's office. She asked me to sit on the couch. She had her copy of my report, and I had mine. The session started with her asking some more questions, which I thought I answered fairly well. But she was always looking for additional information and ideas. Soon the requests came.

"Here are a few things I'd like you to do. Expand on how we can help the Canadians to exploit their oil sands more aggressively."

I interjected, "You know they're trying to conserve their reserves and—because of ecological concerns—they've agreed to limits on production."

Kate frowned. "Let's not be so sure they don't have more reserves than they claim. There are advances in technology to consider, too."

"Most governments have overestimated their reserves over the last fifty years."

"Please, let's continue." Kate was not appreciating my interruptions. "I'd like you to explore the possibility that additional finds in Mexico and the Mid-East can be uncovered. Additionally, give me some estimate of how much petroleum China is wasting through their inefficient use of resources."

I had no idea how the inefficiency of China's resource utilization could be turned into more energy for us, but I was not going to question Kate. I responded simply, "Yes, ma'am."

"Can you flesh out this information in two days?"

"That's Saturday."

"Yes, I'm quite capable of reading a calendar."

"I'll get it done by Saturday."

"Call me at home on Saturday morning. By the way, keep Saturday afternoon and evening open."

"Sure."

"Thanks," Kate said breezily as I got up to leave.

I stopped at Jane's desk. "I'll need Kate's home phone number, and I'm sorry to say I won't be available this weekend."

"Sounds like you got a weekend planned with Kate."
"I hope not, but I'm not sure."
Jane's brow furrowed.

XI

Savannah, 2061

I BROUGHT MY COMPUTER DOWNSTAIRS and got a cup of coffee from the kitchen. It seemed to be a nice morning, so I thought I'd work on Len Dailey's development application outside. Juggling the computer and coffee, I opened the back door, spotted Jacqueline sunning herself, and hesitated.

"Don't be afraid of me, Mr. Lendeman. I can put my top back on if you wish."

"No need to disturb yourself. I think I can handle the situation."

"Handle what?" Jacqueline pretended to misunderstand.

"Look, my friend, I have to do some work. You won't even notice I'm here, and I won't notice you."

"Are we friends now?"

"Haven't we been?"

"Then I have to make sure to call you 'James.' Is that what you prefer?"

"Yes. Now I'm going to start to work."

It required a bit of effort, but I began to review the development proposal and made some notes about the deficiencies I spotted. After about ten minutes, I was almost completely into my job and only noticed Jacqueline when she shifted position.

I could sense that Jacqueline wanted to talk to me, but I was in the process of jotting down a number of ideas about how Dailey's proposal could comply with energy usage restraints. Some energy saving devices came to mind quickly, but others would require more thought and, perhaps, engineering input. My own ideas would generate about fifteen percent energy savings. I estimated another ten percent would be needed to meet requirements.

For about fifteen minutes my concentration on the project obscured all of Jacqueline's antics. But eventually I sensed she was staring in my direction. I looked up from my papers to meet her gaze.

"Goodness, you're working hard."

"How can you tell?"

"You're working up a sweat."

"That's the heat and humidity. None of my work requires manual labor."

"I like a man to get sweaty," Jacqueline observed as she sat up on the chaise.

I was beginning to think Jacqueline would do something inappropriate in Mrs. Pinckney's garden. "Frankly, it doesn't sound very appealing to me."

"I guess that's because you're not gay, nor a woman."

"An accurate observation."

"On the other hand you're rather uptight and repressed."

"You can tell this just by the way I'm doing my work?"

"No, I can tell it by the way you're living your life." Jacqueline added a grin to the end of the sentence, and her eyes crinkled. Her statement was a challenge.

"What do you know of my life?"

"There's not much to know. You do some work, though not much. You read. You go downtown to do some research and walking. You stop in at the Georgia Historical Society."

"You must be spying on me."

"See, it's pretty accurate." She changed her tone. "I'm really sorry for you, James. You have no life."

"Let's not get judgmental."

"I'm just summing up what I know. It's not healthy for a man, who's still rather young, to be so limited. You're much younger, but

Mrs. Pinckney has a more active life."

"Well, maybe I like my relative inactivity. Maybe I don't feel so young."

"I know how to change your perspective."

"Please tell."

"I'm dancing at the club tonight. Come see me."

"That's over the border in South Carolina."

"Don't tell me you're on parole and can't go out of state."

"No, it's just the inconvenience."

"There you go, talking like a fifty-year-old. You can get there the way I do. You take the tram downtown. Then take the light rail toward Hilton Head. It runs every hour on the half-hour. Then you get off at the first stop in South Carolina. That's the one after Hutchinson Island. See? Simple enough."

"But time-consuming."

"With all due respect, all you have is time. I'll make it worth your while. I'll change your whole outlook and raise your spirits."

"You're pretty sure of yourself."

"I'm self-confident." Her chin jutted out.

"Unlike me, I suppose."

"You said it. I didn't. So you'll come?"

"I'll think about it. Maybe next week."

"Do it tonight or else you'll just keep on procrastinating."

Deep down, I wanted to go. My work, the book I was reading, my impersonal room held few attractions. "I tell you what. The energy council owes me the electrocar for one night. If I can get it for tonight, I'll come. I'll call them a little later."

"There's the phone. Do it now."

"You're like my mother, hounding me until I do my homework."

"Believe me, I'll show you I'm nothing like your mother."

I made the call. Joe told me I could have the electrocar for the night if I picked him up at his office and drove him home, first.

This I did and then returned downtown, parked the electrocar, and lingered over fish and chips and a beer at a mock English pub. Sometime around eight thirty I retrieved the vehicle, headed to Oglethorpe Avenue, and then over the Talmadge Bridge.

Electrocars were not designed for the steep slope of the bridge. Or, more properly, the pitch of the bridge was not designed for electrocars. With the accelerator jammed to the floor, I slowed to thirty kilometers per hour before reaching the apex of the span.

The Durango was a ramshackle building, covered in rough slabs of wood. Of course, there were no windows. It defied the shy to enter. However, there were several electrocar charging stations out front. I pulled up to one and put in enough money for a thirty-minute recharge.

Jacqueline spotted me shortly after I entered the club. She was wearing a long skirt and a tiny bikini top. She was mixing with the dozen or so customers who were already around the bar.

"I just finished my first show. You'll have to stay through three other girls before I come on again. You'll be able to compare, and you'll see I'm the best." She threw her head back and laughed. "Then after I finish onstage, we'll go in the back."

"And what do we do there?"

"You'll see. I have to leave you for a few minutes and spend some time with that guy who bought me a drink, or else he'll get rowdy. Get yourself a drink or two and relax."

I watched two girls do their topless dance. Both were bustier than Jacqueline, but flabbier. I was only slightly aroused, unlike most of the audience who vied to stuff money in their g-strings. The crowd grew to about twenty. Two were women. I wondered whether they were with some of the guys or satisfying their own tastes.

Another dancer came on stage. She was tall and quite skinny except for her breasts, which were probably enhanced. Quite a bit of money was tossed her way.

Finally, it was Jacqueline's turn. She began her routine while clothed in a slinky top and leotard-like pants. Soon those came off, and she was down to a gold g-string. Her perky breasts, which I had seen on a number of occasions, bounced rhythmically as she danced and swung around the center pole. Her moves were the most athletic of the night. Her flexibility was impressive as she employed the pole like a gymnast might. She showed no self-consciousness. In fact, she seemed to enjoy exhibiting her body and skills. Her routine was well rehearsed. By the time she was done, I would guess a hundred bucks was hung around the thin gold string circling her hips.

The impression was erotic but tinged with a bit of disgust. I should not have thought of Jacqueline as a friend. I felt she was demeaning herself. Yet she did not seem to mind; even when she had to slap a guy's hand because his gratuity was being placed too close to her crotch, she did it with a smile.

Certainly Jacqueline exuded sex appeal, and her performance aroused me. But the pure sexuality, for me, was muted by the feeling that the scene was sordid. Maybe Jacqueline was right. Perhaps I was old-fashioned.

It took Jacqueline more than five minutes to work her way to my seat. Every few feet she needed to exchange some pleasantries and hugs with the guys who had filled her g-string with fluttering currency.

By the time she reached me, she had added a low-cut top to the minuscule bottom. A pouch was hanging around her neck. Her tips had been stuffed in the pouch for safekeeping.

With Jacqueline sidling up to me, my sense of mild disgust was being replaced with sexual intrigue. I remembered my manners. "Can I buy you a drink?"

"Glad you asked." In the direction of the barkeep she yelled, "Gin and tonic."

The drink appeared instantaneously. "So, what did you think?"

"You know how to please the crowd."

"Meaning I'm sexy."

"Very. I think you enjoy this type of work."

"Sure, it's easy. I make a lot more money than waiting tables. I kind of like the guys looking at me. Gives me a bit of a high. And it's good for my ego. This joint is okay, too. They protect the girls. Nothing goes further than what I want."

"And how far do you want?"

She hesitated and did not reply directly. "Grab your drink. Come with me." She took me around the edge of the room, so we didn't mingle with the crowd that was now intent on ogling the buxom brunette on stage.

We entered a narrow corridor. Every four meters there was another door. She opened the fourth door on the left and pushed me into a dimly lit room. In one corner was a stand on which to hang clothing. A well-padded chair dominated the center.

"Finish your drink and sit in the chair." Jacqueline pushed a button. Some soft, rhythmic music emerged from speakers in two of the corners.

"You can take your shirt off. Then you can take my top off. Normally a customer is not allowed to touch. But you're not a customer. Right?"

"Anything you say." I was going on a journey and Jacqueline was going to be my guide. She sat on my lap, now only clothed in her g-string. Her body began to undulate in time with the music. I put my hands on her shoulders.

"You can go lower. I know you want to."

I put one hand on a breast. I wanted to let the other one jiggle as Jacqueline's body writhed sensuously. The sight fascinated me. After a minute I took the hand from her shoulder and reached between her legs. The moisture was immediately apparent.

"You know, that's against the rules."

"I thought you were suspending the rules," I replied boldly.

"What the hell." She undid my fly and reached inside.

No lengthy effort was required on her part. "Man, that was

quick. You really needed it," Jacqueline accurately observed.

"Yes, it's been a while. But it wasn't good for you."

"Not yet."

Jacqueline made me get out of the chair. She perched herself precariously on the back with her feet on the arms. "Now you put your knees on the seat."

"I see what you're getting at."

"You're pretty quick on the draw." She laughed at her own comment.

Jacqueline responded to my tongue. "I think you've done this before."

"Or just beginners luck."

"No way. But shut up and keep going." She bit her lip, perhaps to stifle a scream. At least I wanted to think so.

"Come on, let's clean up. Then you can take me home. Say, I don't know how to put this." Jacqueline hesitated. "I have to give Joe, the owner, a hundred bucks. He figures I get at least two hundred for a lap dance. Joe isn't in on our arrangement, and he'll want his share."

I reached into my pocket. I had eighty dollars. "This is all I have on me."

She reached into her pouch and added twenty. "Okay, this will satisfy Joe."

"I'll give you the other hundred and twenty tomorrow," I offered.

"Just the twenty. You're not a customer. Next time we'll do it in Mrs. Pinckney's garden. She doesn't expect anything, not like Joe." My face must have registered my fear. "Don't worry. I was just kidding. I don't want to be tossed out on the street. Now, let's go home, James."

XII

Washington, 2053

I RECEIVED A CALL FROM Jane Friday morning, shortly after I submitted the revised report to Kate. "James, today is your lucky day."

"I was hoping it would be my lucky night."

"That's right. We do have a date. Play your cards right and you may be lucky twice. But this call is about business—so to speak."

"It's business but not really business. You'll have to explain, my sweet."

Jane giggled. "Okay, here goes. Kate is your boss and, coincidentally, mine as well. This has to do with her; consequently it's business."

"But it's also *not* business?"

"You're invited to attend a soirée at her apartment a week from tonight—next Friday."

"Are you invited, too?"

"Don't be silly. This party is for important people."

"Well, I'm not an important person."

"To tell the truth, you're being invited because Hal Jeffers just canceled. You're a pinch hitter for an important person. But you're not supposed to know you're not on the 'A' list. Kate will kill me if she thinks I told you."

"Don't be naïve. Kate is assuming you'll tell me."

"Just don't test that theory."

"Okay, your transgression is safe with me. So, give me an idea of who the important people are."

"First of all, there's Thomas Santana."

"The writer?"

"Do you know any other Thomas Santanas? Also, Mark Leinster, the congressman, and Brody Stearns."

"Brody who?"

"Brody Stearns, the vice president's chief of staff. You need to know a person like that."

"Shame on me."

"Look, you'll be introduced to all these people at the soirée. Kate does not want the guest list released in advance. In total, there will be twenty of you."

"If I accept."

"You're not going to turn Kate down. I think Kate feels she's honoring you with the invitation."

"Then I won't refuse this distinction."

"Wise move."

During the first half of the week which was to be capped with Kate's soirée, I met with Kate only briefly on Monday and Wednesday. On neither occasion did she mention the Friday gathering. We reviewed progress on two projects, which, if the truth were told, were of rather low importance. I was working on revised rules for transportation fuel allocation. I rather enjoyed the subject. Kate did not. She did not want to concentrate on the division of an ever-diminishing pie. She wanted to go into the kitchen and cook another pie. More and more, she left me to my own devices in crafting rule modifications.

After meeting with Kate on Monday, it had occurred to me that I should read something by Thomas Santana. I recalled that a book of his had received much attention two or three years earlier. I quickly found a reference on line. The title was: *Cultural Cycles and the End of the Age of Materialism.*

Two sentences from a review stated: "In this rather readable mix of philosophy and history, Santana explores the economic decline of the West and how it forced an end to the materialistic three quarters of a century from 1950 to 2025. Although most people rue this decline, Santana contends that society benefited from a refocus on more realistic objectives."

I went to the media site AZAFNAC and found that I could download a copy for twenty dollars, fifteen dollars off the normal retail price. In ten seconds I had my copy. Late Monday I began to read it. I agreed with the reviewer who said that the book was readable in the sense that the discussion was not bogged down in pedantry and obscure terminology. Despite this, I found it soporific. I took my page palette to bed, started to read the second chapter, and then awoke in the morning, having read only a dozen pages.

At work the week progressed slowly. On a few occasions, I took the opportunity to open Santana's book and read some more. I mainly read the beginning and end of each chapter to get a sense of the key arguments and conclusions.

By five o'clock on Thursday, I was straightening my desk and verifying that confidential papers were locked away. The phone rang. Jane was on the other end, probably meaning that Kate was going to interfere with my planned early departure.

"Yes, *ma cherie*."

"Her highness requests your presence."

"Her wish is my command."

"I wish I could have the same influence on you."

"But you don't control my pay."

"You're very mercenary."

"I like to eat."

"So I've noticed."

"I don't think I'm going to extend this conversation. My sovereign awaits."

"And her handmaid knows she wants your ass over here pronto."

When I arrived at Kate's office a few minutes later, Jane barred my way. "Sorry, an important call came in."

"More important than me?"

"Much more. The vice president."

I took a seat, expecting my wait to be short. Presumably the vice president was not in the habit of chitchatting at length with an assistant secretary in the Federal Energy Department.

I waited. And I waited some more. I asked Jane, "Do you think this will take much longer?"

"Your guess is as good as mine."

"When do you get to leave?"

"When she tells me I can."

I returned to my seat. I wished that I had brought my page palette. My time could have been put to better use, even though the outer office was fairly dark. The general lighting had gone off at five thirty. Jane was using a task light. A few dim safety lights barely broke the gloom.

I turned back to Jane. "You still have work to do?"

"There's always work for me to do," Jane replied with a sigh. "I never seem to run out. Even when Kate is out of town, she can keep me well supplied."

"Well, she must go on vacation."

"Not very often, and her vacation is not totally a vacation. She'll frequently call in to . . . I think she just finished her call. I'll remind her that you're waiting."

"Good idea. Unless she has a very good long-term memory, she may have forgotten."

"I may have forgotten what?" Kate had emerged from her office.

"Forgotten that you were waiting to see me."

"I'm not yet senile. Come in and take a seat." Turning to Jane, "Have you finished the status report?"

"Yes, I printed a copy."

"Good. Let me have it. Then I see no reason for you to stay any later."

"Thanks, Ms. Hastings."

Then turning back to me, "Come in, James. No need to stand gawking."

"Sorry. Didn't mean to gawk."

I took my usual seat. Kate sat in her armchair. "I just want to go over a few ground rules for the soirée." I nodded, but said nothing. Kate continued, "There will be twenty people, including you and me. My apartment will be quite crowded. There will be a number of knots of conversation. Most of the people want to hear themselves talk and impress others. Half are from government and half from academia or the arts. I imagine you will do more listening than talking."

"I should be seen but not heard."

"You should be a good boy. Talk as you see fit. But, quite frankly, you'll probably find it difficult to squeeze in too many of your own thoughts. One warning: don't be tempted to impress anyone by using any of our confidential work, especially your latest project."

"Do you really think I'd do that?"

Kate paused. "No, and I'm sorry I felt obliged to warn you. At some point Brody Stearns, the vice president's chief of staff, may want to talk about your recent report. He's read it and feels it contains some useful points. You can discuss it with him, if he raises the subject. But it will be difficult to obtain adequate privacy in the midst of twenty people. Perhaps he, you, and I will have an opportunity to get together when the party winds down; perhaps not.

"Whether he discusses the report or not, he may take the opportunity to size you up."

"I'll try to look tall."

Kate frowned. "Try to act intelligent."

"And I should leave my flip comments at home."

"Let's leave it at intelligent and discreet. Needless to say, Brody is the best link to the vice president; and the vice president is our link to the president."

"I heard the vice president and president don't see eye to eye."

"They don't on some points, but they do on many. I'm counting on Chandler being able to convince the president that we need to be decisive about expanding our energy sources. We're hanging by our thumbs. The next step is to hang by our necks."

"Is Longworth inclined to show leadership on this issue? I've heard energy is low on his list of priorities."

"Then this will be a test for him."

I could not reply. The thought of Kate Hastings preparing a test for the president boggled my mind. *This woman has balls*, was my incongruous thought.

I arrived at Kate's soirée a few minutes early. She seemed glad to see me.

"The caterer arrived a little late because her normal supplier did not receive his roast beef delivery. She had to find another source. It's terrible when you can't rely on shipments getting to Washington. We're trying to get the last few things in place."

"Can I help?"

"Since you're here, sure."

I moved a small table and a few chairs, and then I helped the caterer unpack a few dozen glasses from their boxes. Kate continued to arrange some flowers. As I helped, I looked around the apartment. I could only see the living room, the kitchen, the dining alcove, and the entrance to the terrace. The living room was large by mid-twenty-first-century standards. It was well decorated, but it was impersonal. There were no photos, memorabilia or souvenirs. The furniture, except for a large couch which appeared comfortable, was angular. The paintings, lamps, tables, and side chairs were likely chosen by a decorator. The mixture of gray and peach tones produced a serene effect. I doubt if Kate chose the colors; she probably approved them.

Just as we were finishing our impromptu tasks, the first guest arrived. Kate greeted her politely but without warmth, almost as if she were a rival. Her name was Karen something-or-other. She was a lawyer in the Transportation Department.

Almost immediately two additional guests arrived. Both were from academia. Then some more people from government arrived, including Brody Stearns. Kate introduced us immediately and made certain that he connected me with the recent energy report. "James wrote the report that I forwarded to you recently."

"Ah, yes, some good concepts. The V.P. looked at it, as well. We'll talk more."

Stearns moved on. Kate attended to new arrivals. I was left by myself near the front door.

I heard a soft knock on the door, and a young woman hesitantly pushed her way in. "I assume this is Kate Hastings's party."

"You're in the right place. I'm James Lendeman. I work with Kate."

"I'm Pat Auriga. And I have to confess that I don't know Kate." I must have looked surprised. "You're probably wondering how I got an invitation. I know Brody Stearns. I've entertained at parties at the vice president's home."

"What type of entertainment?" I asked, while sizing up the petite brunette.

She looked up at me with fierce dark brown eyes. "As you can probably guess, I'm not a stripper."

"I'm not sure what a stripper should look like."

"Sure, you do. A sexier figure than I have."

"Of course, I wouldn't think a stripper would be performing at the vice president's place. So what do you do?"

"I teach music, in general, and voice, specifically."

"So you're a singer."

"Yes, but I teach more than I sing. This term I'm teaching voice, elocution, and music history."

"Sounds like a full schedule. Are you going to entertain us

tonight?"

"Doubt it. I don't have an accompanist."

A knock at the door interrupted us, and I fulfilled my newfound role as doorman.

"You are?" A tall, middle-aged man with a healthy shock of white hair addressed me in a preemptory tone.

"James Lendeman," I replied simply.

"That doesn't tell me much. I suppose Kate is somewhere to be found."

"Yes, either in the dining room or on the terrace."

"Very good. I'll keep my jacket." He moved on in search of the hostess.

I turned to Pat. "I must look like the hired help."

"So must I."

"Let's get away from the door."

Pat and I picked up drinks from a table set up as a bar. Then we grabbed some hors d'oeuvres. "I'm still curious. How did you get an invitation if you don't know Kate?"

"I don't exactly know. Brody called me and asked me if I wanted to go to a party where I'd meet some prominent people. I wasn't doing anything tonight, so I accepted. That was it."

"Why do you think Brody asked you?"

"If you notice, no wives are here. And the party is a little short on women."

I refrained from making a comment about short women. Instead, I asked, "What do you hope to get out of meeting some of these people?"

"Maybe some sponsorship of productions I supervise at school."

"What school?"

"Man, you can ask a bunch of questions. Will I get a chance?"

"If you want. But you didn't answer my last question."

"I'm based at American University, but I do some work at

other schools and some freelance, too. Now let me find out what you do."

"I work for Kate at the F.E.D."

"So you're a policy wonk."

"You might say so."

"And how did you wangle your invitation? Are you a very *special* assistant?"

"I'm not sure what you mean by that last comment. And I'm not quite sure why I'm here. Maybe I'm filling in for someone else who couldn't make it. At any event, I got an invitation, and found it difficult to say no to my boss."

We went on to discuss our tastes in music, which were hardly similar. Pat liked classical music, as I would have guessed, plus some rock from the last century. I told her I liked zoom and snake-bop. She grimaced. "But I do like the Beatles and the Eagles."

"Okay, you do have some redeeming qualities."

At that point, Kate came along. "Hey, you need to circulate." She was primarily talking to me. I introduced her to Pat. "Nice to meet you," she commented, but then turned back to me. "You see the bald guy in the camel-colored jacket. He's Lavery Buford from Georgetown. Go join that group. Lavery's interested in the work we're doing."

Kate left. I shrugged my shoulders, acknowledging to Pat that I had to obey my orders.

"I think I'll say hello to Brody," Pat told me.

Lavery Buford was a professor of economics, and the most talkative person in a group of five. One of the others was from the University of Maryland. A third was the lawyer from the Transportation Department. I never did identify the other two. I edged into the group. No one acknowledged me.

Buford and his coterie were debating the factors leading to the economic decline of the past fifty years.

"One might point to other major causes, but if I have to point to one, I'd choose the diminished availability of reasonably priced energy. Think of this. It has not only led to a decline in economic activity, it has led to out-and-out economic and societal disruption. The car industry is twenty percent of what it was, and what are we producing? Cheap electrocars. Vacations involving travel are down by more than seventy-five percent. Sure, train and light rail travel has increased significantly, but those industries have contributed very modestly to job growth."

"And the energy shortage led to the collapse of the outer suburbs," the UMD professor interjected.

"Exactly. Talk about a major disruption to both society and the economy."

"But consider the decline in the farm population in the early twentieth century. That might have affected farmers, but the U.S. economy prospered," another in the group countered.

Lavery smiled. "There was something called 'the Great Depression.' Maybe we should call it 'the First Depression.'"

"Certainly you're not suggesting that the depression was caused by a decline in farmers," Lavery's challenger persisted.

"No, but that was a part of the collateral damage. Look, the readjustment in farm population was a somewhat-overlooked phenomenon of the twentieth century. More workers were needed in the cities. Fewer were needed on the farm. Remember it was not only improved agricultural methods, which made food production and delivery so efficient, it was also the availability of cheap energy. In this century, expensive energy has reversed the situation. This has contributed to our long, painful decline. As people allocate more money to essentials—food, energy, housing, healthcare, etc.—less is available for discretionary spending."

"You included healthcare spending, but certainly that element has improved by the government assuming so much of the expense."

"My friend," Lavery continued with a touch of condescension, "we're paying for the differential with taxes. Perhaps I should have listed taxes and debt service as essentials. This spending on essentials has strangled the American consumer. At the turn of the century, American consumers were preeminent. A good deal of this was made possible by credit and, of course, by inexpensive essentials. Then the over-building of housing made possible by cheap credit led to a huge decline in housing values and the perceived wealth of many Americans. Banks next reined in credit card debt and tightened underwriting on auto loans. Tax receipts declined at both the national and state levels. Eventually, in the second decade, taxes were increased primarily through elimination of deductions and credits. Medicare and retirement benefit payments strapped the government when the 'baby boomers' retired in great numbers."

"That's when the term 'social security' was scrapped," someone piped up.

"Roughly," Lavery continued. "But I digressed. We were talking about energy and particularly petroleum energy as being the lynchpin of past success and current failure. I see that James has joined our little discussion group in the past few minutes. He's a government expert on energy economics."

I had no idea that Buford knew me or knew of my work. Perhaps Kate had pointed me out. Perhaps she had even briefed him on my recent report. Was this allegedly secret document now entering the public domain? My mind raced as Buford continued.

"We've made some significant and some, quite frankly, half-hearted efforts to close the gap between energy supply and needs. I'd rate conservation efforts as poor until the thirties and forties. It was at that point that homes, apartments, and offices were substantially redesigned and retrofitted. Transportation was shifting dramatically at that point, from private to public varieties.

"On the supply side, we had already begun to increase use of solar power and probably put too much weight there. We returned to building a few nuclear power plants. But we were too slow to employ wind power on a large scale, and lagged on exploiting natural gas for more uses. In the meantime, we tried to employ diplomacy and some bullying to acquire a larger percentage of other countries' petroleum output. In most instances, particularly in the case of Latin America, our efforts backfired."

The lawyer from Transportation interrupted. "I don't dispute your view of history, but here we are in 2053. Despite cutting energy use to the bone, we don't have enough. Our economy has been struggling. The country is still seriously in debt. What do we do?"

Lavery Buford directed a broad smile in the direction of the woman from the Transportation Department. "Ah, that's the trillion-dollar question. I could state my own opinions, but if our gracious hostess would favor us with her presence, she might enlighten us about the government's current efforts. Ultimately, it's the responsibility of the F.E.D. to pull the rabbit out of the hat. Since fair Kate is otherwise occupied, perhaps James, her right-hand man, can fill us in."

Eyes turned toward me. "Professor Buford, you well know that I can't discuss classified matters."

"Perhaps you can share some non-classified directions, so we know our government is active in this area."

"I can assure you, we're always working on something. We don't sit around simply collecting our pay. When we're ready to produce the rabbit, we will."

Lavery's brow furrowed. The lawyer from Transportation smiled at me. The little group began to break up to freshen drinks and revisit the hors d'oeuvres.

I encountered Kate. "Having a good time?" she asked brightly.

"Is that what I'm here for—to have fun? Isn't this party . . ."

"*Soirée.*"

"Sorry, *soirée*. Seems to me it's just an extension of work."

"Are you bucking for overtime pay? If so, sorry, you don't qualify. Sure, it's business. Do you think I'd choose to spend a Friday night with most of these people if I didn't think I could get something out of it? James, you have to learn how to derive pleasure from work. Anyway, continue to circulate. I have my own work to do."

Over the course of the next two hours, I listened in on groups that were discussing budget problems, the national debt, remedies for insomnia, the virtues of Bourbon versus Scotch whisky, the inefficiency of the judiciary (no representatives from that branch of government were present), and a number of inane subjects. Later in the evening, I edged into the group surrounding the writer Thomas Santana. Since I had managed to skim his latest book, I wanted to hear his informal comments. Perhaps the themes of his book had been discussed earlier. When I reached him, he was debating the value of attending a Washington soirée.

"I think it's solely an occasion for people to try to impress each other," someone stated.

Santana was short in stature with shiny black hair and mesmerizing blue eyes. A small smile was continually on his lips. "You may have a point, but obviously none of us declined Ms. Hastings's invitation and chose to stay home in order to contemplate more weighty matters. Do I want to impress? Certainly. Do I want to be impressed? Even more so. Earlier in the evening I made a mental note of someone's assertion that in the first decade of this century, no one stepped up to the plate and said '*après nous le deluge.*' Although the metaphor may be mixed, the observation is valid. Forty years ago, people knew that the seeds of decline were sown. However, there was no political will and courage to take the correct but difficult course. As a result, two generations have paid dearly for the self-gratification and complacency of the prior two."

Silence followed Santana's somewhat overwrought summation. Rather than let a new subject be introduced, I felt an urge to make a contribution. "It occurs to me that the last two subjects may be connected. We do have a desire to impress, in part because we want to add to our own stature. We are now an asset-strapped society. Few have the means to create ostentatious display. So we look for ways to boost what we have left, namely our egos."

"Interesting," Santana commented while fixing me with his hypnotic eyes. "I don't believe we've been introduced. I'm Thomas Santana."

"James Lendeman," I replied.

"I've made a mental note of your comment. It's worth pondering."

I moved away from Santana's clique, satisfied with my one and only contribution to the evening's discussions. Kate, I noticed, was absent from her own soirée at several points during the night.

Around ten thirty a few guests began to depart. No doubt they wanted to catch the Metro before service became more intermittent. Others noticed the movement and began to follow. A few people stayed on. Perhaps they had electrocars at their disposal.

Pat came over to me before saying good-bye to Kate. "I'm sorry we didn't have the opportunity to talk more."

"Maybe we'll have another opportunity," I replied casually.

"I'd like that. We'll work something out. Here's my card."

I glanced at the business card which Pat had pressed into my hand. It had her address and number at American University. I watched as she walked the few steps to where Kate was standing. They exchanged a few words, and Pat headed to the door, while Kate walked over to me.

"She's a cute gal," Kate commented. "A musician or something."

"So this is the first time you've met her?" I asked a question to which I knew the answer.

"Yes. Brody asked me to invite her."

"Why would he do that?"

"No concern of mine. When the V.P.'s chief of staff asks for a simple favor, I comply. Who knows? Maybe he's screwing her."

I was about to say, "No, I don't think so." But I really didn't know.

The last guests left. "Can I help you get things back in shape?"

"The caterer is doing most of it. I was going to leave the balance for tomorrow morning. But if you really want to help, we can probably get it done in a half hour."

Kate and I put furniture back in place and collapsed some folding chairs. She gave me a cleaning solution to treat some soiled spots on the carpets.

It was nearing midnight. The caterer had left.

"I guess I'll be going now."

"Will you be able to get a Metro train?"

"There should be one more right around midnight."

"If you have a problem, come back here. You can sleep on the couch."

"I'll try not to bother you."

"Don't be embarrassed to sleep here. I won't tell Jane. I won't even tell her that you were making a date with the little musician."

I sensed that Kate was only kidding, but I wanted to make my position clear. "Look, Kate, first of all I did not make a date with Pat . . ."

"But you will," Kate interjected.

I ignored the last comment. "Second, Jane and I are dating, but we're not even close to being engaged. If I want to date someone else, I can. So can she."

"Then if you're so independent, stay the night. Don't struggle with the train system at this hour. You'll stay in the living room. I'll use the bedroom. We don't even have to see each other." She grabbed my wrist. "I'd feel better if you do stay." She looked into my eyes, and I could tell she was sincere.

"If you insist," I relented.

"You can use the bathroom first, while I get a blanket and pillow."

Although the couch was fairly comfortable, I could not fall asleep. The pillow smelled slightly of Kate's perfume. I thought about her and how beautiful she had looked with her pale, blond hair piled regally atop her head, showing her arching neck. The image of a white swan came to mind—graceful and remote. But she wasn't remote; she was in the next room.

Then I thought about the evening. Missed opportunities to get involved and contribute came to mind. If I made an impression on anyone, it was likely negative. I never had a chance to talk to Brody Stearns. Perhaps Pat Auriga would recollect something positive about me. Hopefully her card was still in my pocket. Would I call her? Very doubtful. She was cute, and intelligent as well, but there was no reason to complicate my relationship with Jane.

I must have fallen asleep at some point, because I was awakened in the middle of the night. "Are you asleep, James?" Kate's voice was barely more than a whisper, but her hand was on my shoulder.

"I guess . . . I must have just dozed off," I replied incoherently.

"I'm sorry. I woke you up." Despite her apology, she did not retreat. I could see her silhouetted against moonlight streaming in the window. She was clothed, but not in anything substantial. "I can't sleep. Can we talk?"

I sat up, pulling the blanket over me because I wore only briefs. "Sure. Let's talk."

Kate plopped down on the couch, close to me. "It's chilly in here."

Her solution did not involve adjusting the thermostat. Instead she lifted the blanket and leaned against me. Instinctively I put my arm around her shoulder. She settled closer to me. I felt her slim frame curve into my body.

She wore some hip-hugging bottom and a thin bandeau top. A lot of her skin was touching me. This proximity was maddening. Kate seemed unfazed. "I keep on thinking about the conversation I had with Brody. You might have noticed that we broke away from the party for a while. Anyway, he told me about the vice president's initial reaction to our report.

"I should have let you know that I added some practical examples to your work. I tried to make some of the technical points more understandable and provide a path forward, as well."

Of course, Kate could do what she wished with my report, but I would have preferred to know where the report was going and in what form. This thought was transitory. I was primarily wondering if Kate noticed my unyielding erection.

She continued talking, with her head against my shoulder and her long hair draped over my chest. "Anyway, Brody liked the report. He thought it represented some bold thinking. He wouldn't have passed it on to the V.P. if he didn't like it or wasn't willing to back it."

"So what's the problem?" I asked, trying to show that I was following her train of thought.

"I'm getting to that. So the V.P. gets the report with a short briefing from Brody. He puts it aside and doesn't read it for a few days. But when he reads it, he likes it. At least, that's his initial reaction. He lets it sit for another few days. Then he looks at it again.

"He starts to think about how the president will react to it. Of course, he knows that the president will have to approve, and this will entail a reversal of current policy. The V.P. feels we need to acquire more energy resources even if we need to be devious or forceful. He knows that that would be alien to the president's thinking. At this point he has lost a lot of influence with the president. Evidently it was the V.P. who suggested we should push for a regime change in Indonesia. We know how that turned out.

"So the V.P. is thinking: 'I'd like to pursue this, but I don't have the clout to convince the president. Maybe,' he thinks, 'I can use someone else to champion the concept.' He eventually takes the report to Linskey."

"The deputy secretary of defense?"

"Exactly."

"Why not the secretary?"

"Well, he thinks the deputy secretary will view it more favorably, being more of a hawk. If Linskey agrees, the two of them can work on Reimer."

The moon was now visible, shining through the west-facing window. Would Kate now notice the bulge in the blanket? Would she care? For the time being, she just continued her narrative.

"So Linskey starts looking at the report. He skims most of it and focuses on only a few parts. Particularly, he notes my example of how to obtain more oil from Brazil."

"My report didn't touch on Brazil."

"No, but my addition did."

"How did you propose to get more oil from them?"

"Through a mixture of pressure and inducement."

"What sort of inducement?"

"Give them a few A-bombs."

"Why does Brazil need such a weapon?"

"Prestige. They'd join the nuclear club."

"So they'd become the twentieth or thirtieth country to have the bomb. Big deal."

"You're sounding like Linskey. He gave the report back to the V.P., and told him that he wouldn't recommend it to Reimer in the current form. The only positive thing is that he left the door open a bit. In principle, he'd like to put more pressure on a group of select petroleum producers. But he said we need a more subtle approach."

"We should work with the State Department."

"I will not work with those people." To emphasize the point, Kate punctuated each word with a tap on my chest. I could feel the long nail on her index finger perform the staccato beat. At the end of the sentence she left her hand on my stomach.

"I've heard your opinion about State before, but I don't know why you're so adamant about the subject." I realized I could incur Kate's ire in pursuing the subject, but I took the risk.

"Well, I don't like those haughty snobs from the top down.

But, more than that, they leak information that passes through their hands, particularly if it suits their purposes. Beyond the intentional leaks, they have a security problem. Their computer systems are administered by HALO."

"So?"

"HALO's just a shell organization. Pata and Pandit, the Indian conglomerate, bought it ten years ago. Almost all the work has been moved to Bombay. HALO only has a few hundred people remaining in this country—half in Bethesda and half in San Mateo. This is their front."

"Well, aren't most of our businesses owned by foreign countries and governments?"

"Most—but not those involving our security, except for the State Department."

"Aside from State, you can add airport security, most of our largest banks, rail traffic control, half of our refining capacity, sixty percent of our coal mines, eighty percent . . ."

"Okay, I get your point. But understand mine. I'm not going to deal with State on any substantive or confidential matters." No chest tapping was used to emphasize the last point. "Wow, James, look at the moon. Isn't it gorgeous? It's almost full."

"Waxing gibbous."

"What does that mean?"

"More than first quarter, but less than full."

"You have a lot of knowledge in that cerebral database." Kate moved her gaze from the moon to my face.

"Extensive, but not always useful."

"Don't sell yourself short. I appreciate your ability. You know, everyone I meet is opinionated, but so few are knowledgeable. You put knowledge first. That's one of the reasons I value you and like you. Do you like me? Or do you put up with me because I'm your boss."

"I enjoy working for you. I like the job—it's exciting. And I like you, personally."

"So you *like* me. And you find the job exciting. I thought you might swap the adjectives."

"Ma'am, I . . ."

"Where does 'ma'am' come from?"

"I did spend two years at the University of Georgia."

"And that's your means of putting some separation between us."

"Oh, I wouldn't want to do that. But aren't we getting into some dangerous territory?"

"You know me. I'm a dangerous woman." With that, she rolled on top of me and planted a kiss firmly on my lips. I nervously returned her kiss. Then she drew back. "I'm sorry, James. But that's going to be it. I told you when I invited you to stay that there would be no interaction of a sexual nature."

"And we must maintain the propriety of the boss-slash-subordinate relationship," I added.

"I don't give a damn about such old-fashioned restrictions. The important thing is that I keep my word. I said there would be nothing sexual, and I'm going to stick to that. But don't look so crestfallen. I think our collaboration is progressing quite well." She paused and then added, "I feel better now after talking." She quickly left the sofa and returned to her bedroom.

But I could not fall asleep. Kate's behavior totally confused me. It was billed as business, but it reeked of sexuality. Did she want to sleep with me? Would she even consider such a thing? Would I?

XIII

JANE AND I HAD A date on Saturday, the day after Kate's soirée. We met at a restaurant and then returned to my apartment.

"You didn't mention Kate's party," Jane commented, as soon as we closed my front door.

"Nothing much to say. A lot of people were doing a lot of talking, trying to impress each other. The food was good; the drinks were wet."

"Very funny." But Jane did not laugh.

"Well, I knew you made the arrangements for the caterer, so I thought you'd want a report on how they did."

"And Kate, did she treat you like hired help or an honored guest?"

"Some place in between. I helped her arrange a few things before the soirée started, and then I circulated. I listened a lot and barely said anything."

"Did Kate tell you to be a good little boy—be seen but not heard?" Jane's tone was clearly sarcastic.

"She gave me no such instructions. She was the ideal hostess. But let's not talk about Kate. This is our night. What do you want to do?"

"Let's choose a sexy movie, and then we'll see if we can do better than the actors."

I was glad that Jane dropped the conversation about Kate so quickly. "I might find it difficult to compete with a professional actor."

"Don't worry. You're a natural stud."

"Calling me a stud puts a great deal of pressure on me." Having spent the previous evening cuddling with a nearly nude blond goddess, I was incredibly horny. Despite my self-deprecation, I was sure I'd perform to Jane's satisfaction.

We began watching an X-rated film. We lasted through only the first ten minutes. Then reality trumped make-believe.

During the next week, Kate and I met three times. Our goal was to develop a more sophisticated and realistic set of steps to support the aggressive pursuit of petroleum resources we advocated.

We jotted down some ideas, but when we looked at them later, they looked no better than those in the original report. Toward the end of our last meeting on Friday, Kate stated, "I'm really frustrated." Our eyes met. "Get your mind back on business, James. For the benefit of your crude mind, let me restate. I'm disappointed that we can't present a good concept more effectively."

The deep-set blue-gray eyes stared at me again. Her mouth formed a thin line, signaling both determination and supplication.

I could provide no immediate help. "I guess I'm supposed to say something intelligent."

"That would be better than drooling."

"I'm not drooling."

"You're mentally drooling."

"A week ago an incredibly beautiful woman curled up with me on a couch, and the moonlight lit her hair."

"Very poetic. And on the next night you screwed her admin assistant. Twice."

"How would you know that?"

"Girls talk."

I was almost inclined to state: "bitches talk." I thought, too, of asking Kate what she had told Jane about what happened after everyone else left her party, but I thought it prudent to return to business. "Getting back to your earlier point, I think we're not succeeding because we lack the necessary expertise. We know energy. We're not experts in international relations."

"You're suggesting, again, that we get State involved."

"I know you won't do that."

"Then, pray tell, what do we do?"

"I have a friend in the State Department . . ."

"So do I, but I'm not going to get him involved. What's different about your friend?"

"He has a strong independent streak and is a bit anti-establishment. I think I can persuade him to avoid running to his bosses with our ideas."

Kate looked at me severely. Her eyes narrowed with skepticism. "You're saying this guy is a maverick. I can't imagine putting our most sensitive work in his hands."

"I won't pretend that there's no risk. What I'm trying to say is that my friend does not have an unduly high regard for the sanctity of the boss/subordinate relationship. I don't see him running to his boss to describe what we're doing or what we're asking him to do."

"You're stating it very diplomatically. In essence, you're saying he's a free spirit. Given that, I can't dismiss my concern about using him."

"I'm not sure . . ."

Kate cut my reply short. "Look, I'm not prepared to make a decision about getting your friend involved. I want to think about this over the weekend. But what you should consider is how we can acquire the expertise we need *without* using your friend in State."

With that, Kate dismissed me.

I didn't hear from Kate on Monday and, near the end of the day, called Jane to check that Kate was in the office.

"Oh, she's here alright. Been in meetings all day. Did she stand you up?"

"She was supposed to get back to me on something we discussed Friday."

"And she didn't."

"Right."

"Bad girl. She deserves a spanking."

"Okay, I don't need the sarcasm. Maybe she'll get back to me tomorrow."

"Should I give her a message?"

"No, thanks."

That night, I received a phone call from an unexpected source.

"Hello."

"James Lendeman?" a female voice asked.

"Yes."

"This is Pat Auriga. I don't know if you remember me . . ."

"I sure do. You're the cute brunette who acted as my assistant when I was playing doorman at Kate Hastings's apartment."

"Exactly." Pat accepted my description.

"So what's up?"

There was a slight pause. "This is a bit forward of me and a bit awkward. You see, I have an extra ticket for Wednesday night's concert at the National Theatre." Again, she hesitated. "I was wondering if you could join me."

"Thanks for the offer. What band is playing?"

"The National Symphony Orchestra."

"Oh, big band music."

"Yes, very big band." Pat played along with my joke.

"What songs are they doing?"

"I think you're trying to make this difficult. They're doing American composers—MacDowell, Gershwin, and King."

"I've heard of Gershwin."

"Good start. Well, the idea is that there's one composer from the nineteenth century, one from the twentieth and another from the twenty-first. So what do you think?"

I couldn't procrastinate any longer. I had to make a decision. Nothing was scheduled for Wednesday night, so I said: "Sounds good."

"Could you meet me there? The concert starts at seven."

"Can I take you to dinner?"

"I have a meeting at five, so I'll be kind of pressed for time."

"Maybe we can get a sandwich after the show."

"It's a *concert*," Pat was determined that I use the correct terminology. "A sandwich afterward would be good. So I'll meet you in the lobby a few minutes before seven."

"Great. Say, I've never been to a symphony orchestra concert. What do I wear?"

"Whatever you wear to the office will be fine."

On Wednesday, Kate passed me a message through Jane, saying that she was still pondering the wisdom of approaching my friend at State for help. After conducting this brief bit of business, Jane wanted to chat about other subjects, but I cut the conversation short, fearing I would end up divulging my plans for the evening. I could tell from the way Jane signed off that she was somewhat miffed. But I was certain that she would soon forget the brief telephone call.

I arrived at the concert hall at twenty to seven. There was no sign of Pat, but I was early. I found a spot that I thought was conspicuous and began to wait. By ten minutes of seven, the lobby crowd was thinning substantially as people began to head for their seats.

At one minute to seven, by my watch, Pat arrived in the empty lobby, slightly out of breath. "Sorry to keep you waiting. Got delayed at the meeting and then missed a Metro train. Here's your ticket. Let's go in."

I had no opportunity to say a word. We each took a program and then arrived at our seats a moment before the conductor came on stage. I saw that there were actually four pieces on the program: an overture by Samuel Barber, a piano concerto by Edward MacDowell, after intermission something called a 'brass rhapsody' by Tyrone King, and, finally, *An American in Paris* by George Gershwin.

At the intermission, Pat and I filed into the lobby. This was our first opportunity to talk. "So what do you think so far?"

"I liked the overture better than the piano concerto. It had a haunting melody that keeps going through my head." Pat hummed the tune I was thinking of. "Yes, that's it."

"Yes, it's memorable. MacDowell is largely forgotten now, but he was one of America's first serious composers. He was also a professor of music, so he's not forgotten among musicologists."

"Kind of the Pat Auriga of the nineteenth century."

"Hardly. I'm not a composer. Well, not really. I've written a few songs."

"I'd like to hear them. Do you play an instrument?"

"The piano. Even a little guitar."

"Maybe you should try a regular-sized guitar."

"Very cute. I never play the piano or guitar professionally. Just singing—that's my forte."

"Are you a soprano?"

"A mezzo. Hey, we're just talking about me. How about you? I know you work in the Energy Department. I suppose you have some specific education in that area."

"Yes, a master's degree. But quite a number of people in the department have accounting, math or even liberal arts degrees. My training helped me get the job . . ."

"Jamie," a voice came booming behind me. "I thought it was you, old buddy. How about introducing me to your pretty friend?"

"Pat Auriga, meet Steve Durham."

"It's a pleasure." Steve flashed his broadest smile.

"Likewise."

"I didn't realize, Jamie, that you liked this sort of music. Or have your tastes changed since college?"

"Now that I'm being exposed to it, I'm beginning to like it. But how about you? You never played this sort of stuff when we roomed together."

"Always been a great admirer of the three Bs. The Beatles, Bach and Beethoven."

"But not Brahms?" Pat asked.

"I like the *Double Concerto* a great deal; symphonies are pretty good, too." Steve always excelled at developing a rapport with women. "But, tell me, who are your favorite composers?"

"I don't think I have one favorite. I gravitate toward those who write for the voice."

"Pat's a voice coach," I interjected, trying to avoid elimination from the conversation.

"So you're a pro." Steve had turned back to Pat. "Therefore more than ever I want to know which composers you favor."

"Puccini, Handel, Lentz, Schumann—enough?"

"Where did you study?" Steve was unrelenting.

"I received my undergraduate training at Oberlin and then did advanced studies at the Curtis Institute." Then, changing tone, "Please don't think me rude, but I have to visit the restroom before the concert resumes." She walked away briskly.

Steve turned to me. "Your new girlfriend is fantastic."

"She's hardly my girlfriend. She had an extra ticket and invited me. We met two weeks ago." I was totally honest.

"So you and Jane didn't break up?"

"No, but we never said we were seeing each other exclusively."

"Gee, I thought you were." Then, changing direction slightly, Steve asked, "Do you think you're going to ask Pat out again?"

"I told you, *she* asked *me*. What's your point?"

Steve was never one to be shy. "If you're not going to date her, let me have her phone number."

My curiosity got the better of me. "Who are you with

tonight?"

"Oh, just someone from the office."

"Female?"

"Yeah."

"You're incorrigible."

"What do you mean?"

"You bring a date to the concert, but then at intermission you go out and hit on someone else."

"I was on my way to the john."

"But then you see me with a girl who's rather cute, and you have to hit on her."

Steve slumped his shoulders in mock humility. "I was being polite, just making conversation. Anyway, I'm checking with you to make sure you're not serious about her. See, I'm really a good guy."

"I thought you were going to the john. I don't want to see you piss in the lobby."

"I'll go as soon as you give me an answer."

"I'll think about it."

"Okay. But remember you owe me a favor and you might want some more favors in the future." Sometimes Steve seemed psychic.

"So you want me to act as a pimp?"

"You put things so crudely and over-dramatically. I'm just asking you to fix me up. You always think the worst of me."

"Sorry if I bruised your feelings. You're too sensitive, Steve."

"Now you're pulling my leg, Jamie. I am going to the john now, but don't forget my request."

After the concert, Pat agreed to join me for a snack. We settled for coffee and cake at a local café. We were both tired, and the conversation lagged. I could not properly evaluate a musical performance, and she was disinterested in the work of the F.E.D. At one point she asked a few questions about Steve Durham. Where did we meet? What did he do? Was he married? I answered the questions succinctly and honestly. But when she asked how he acquired his musical knowledge, I had to confess my ignorance.

On Thursday, I arrived at the office a little late. There was a message waiting for me saying that Kate wanted to see me.

I took a quick sip of coffee and headed to Kate's office. Jane intercepted me. "Kate's on the phone. She should be free in a minute."

"Okay."

"Say, I called you last night. Your phone was turned off."

"I didn't get a message from you." I tried to avoid Jane's inference.

"I didn't leave a message."

"Well, if you wanted to talk to me . . ."

"Kate's free. You better go in."

As I entered Kate's office, I was hoping I would hear of Kate's decision regarding the use of Steve Durham to aid our project. But, since she had delayed taking action so long, I knew not what to expect.

"Come in, James. It must have seemed like I was avoiding you this past week." I hadn't expected an apology, modest though it was. Kate continued. "Let's get the first issue out of the way. Regarding the use of your friend, I'm not prepared to share our report with him. But maybe there's a way to see what he can do without showing our hand."

My initial reaction was disappointment, but I sat quietly and listened.

"What I want to do is to name two countries, say Iraq and Brazil. Then let your friend come up with inducements that might be used to encourage those countries to direct a larger percentage of their crude oil to us. Don't scare him—or is it her?"

"It's 'him.'"

"Don't let him think we want to use aggression. Let him come up with the means. We'll see if he has imagination and daring.

Naturally we will expect him to suggest those courses of action having the greatest chances of success. I'd like him to justify his reasoning."

"You're asking for quite a bit of work to be done—all *pro bono* and in secret."

"Exactly. It's a test. I want to see what he can offer us, and what his sense of commitment is."

"Why should he be committed to our project, a project he hasn't even seen?"

"I don't know, maybe patriotism, adventurism. You figure out the inducement for him. That's *your* test."

"Thanks."

Kate could sense my sarcasm. "Come on, these challenges come with the turf. You know that working with me has its difficulties, but it also has its rewards. So get in touch with this guy and get him started. You're going to have to do that fast because we'll soon be going on a little trip. Do you have a valid passport?"

"I don't think so."

"Well, get a new one quickly. We're going to *Wien*."

"Where?"

"*Wien*. Vienna. *Wiener schnitzel*."

"I get it."

"Have you been there?"

"No."

"Neither have I. Of course, we're not going as tourists. We have a situation to pursue. It could lead to something worthwhile, or it could be a complete waste of time. We're going to meet with some Russians to see if we can join together to get something out of the Chinese. Of course, we want a share of some of the oil allocations they've been amassing. At this point we have no clue what the Russians want.

"Of course, we need to be accompanied by some nursemaids. There will be one, maybe two people from State and someone from Defense. I hope it's no more than that.

"This is mainly an exploratory meeting. We want to see if we can get the Russians to put their cards on the table, and if so, is the *quid pro quo* worthwhile? We expect we'll only get a hint of what they want, and we don't want to divulge too much at first. So there would likely be meetings later on at a higher level. It's just investigatory at this stage. Questions?"

"When do we leave?"

"Probably a week from Sunday. There's a trade meeting going on in Vienna. That's our cover. Officially, we're delegates. But we won't go to the trade meeting. We'll meet with the Russians."

"How long will we be gone?"

"Plan on a week. It might be less or a little more. When I get more information about our departure, I'll let you know. But get that passport this week."

"I imagine you'll be telling Jane you're going to be away."

Kate smiled. "I will let her know we're both going to be traveling. She'll know we'll be in Vienna. But I'm not going to tell her anything more."

"Understood."

When I left Kate's office, Jane asked me if I had a good meeting.

"It was interesting. We'll talk later."

In truth I didn't want to talk to Jane, not right away. I was too excited about my upcoming trip, and I feared that I would reveal too much information. I needed to deal with my own emotions before talking to Jane.

The next few days went by quickly. I had an open-ended ticket to Vienna with a return date left open. A passport was produced on a haste basis.

By the weekend, Kate had informed Jane about the trip. Jane came to my apartment and helped me wash the clothes I'd need for Vienna. I guess Kate had warned Jane about the confidential nature of the trip, because she didn't pump me for further information. We went to a local restaurant for dinner and then watched a movie.

Jane spent the night. Sex was almost obligatory, given our upcoming separation. Obligation did not lead to passion. The sex was workman-like. We dispensed with it and then began to talk. But we couldn't talk about what we wanted to discuss—at least not the mission. Jane knew that we were going to Vienna, that we did not know the date of our return, and that we were staying at the Imperial Hotel.

"I hear the hotel is very nice," Jane offered, not being able to discuss anything else.

"That's good."

"Very old-world."

"I'd expect nothing less."

The desultory exchange continued for a few minutes before we fell asleep on opposite sides of the bed.

In the morning, we had breakfast and built a conversation around things we could discuss—the change to colder weather, whether Jane would visit her family during the holidays, whether I should visit my mother. Around eleven, Jane sensed it was time to leave. I usually accompanied Jane home after she stayed at my apartment. This time, Jane discouraged me. "You have a lot of things to do. I'll go home by myself."

"I should really go with you."

"Please don't. You'll waste the rest of the day."

I relented quickly. When we kissed, there were tears in her eyes. "Why the tears?"

"Nothing. Just a woman thing. Stay safe on your trip."

"You'll see me all this week."

"But it will be at the office. I can't act the same there, and you'll be so busy. I really must go. You take care of yourself."

When Jane left, I tried to reach Steve Durham. Unfortunately, I only reached his voicemail. I did not want to leave a message. I tried again in the evening with the same result. Although it was not my preference, I would have to reach Steve at his office. But a call to his office on Monday brought no better result.

It was not until Wednesday that I reached Steve on his cell phone.

"Jamie, my boy, good to hear from you." His greeting was excessively jovial.

"I was trying to reach you."

"Funny, I don't have any messages from you."

"I didn't leave any."

"Then I'd find it difficult to return your call."

"I chose not to leave a message."

"Oh, something hush-hush."

I didn't answer Steve's question directly. "I need your help."

"Don't you always? Something to do with your upcoming *pas de deux* with the Russkis?"

"What do you mean?"

"You and your comely boss are going on a little junket down the Danube."

"Where did you get that from?"

"Hey, man, I work at State. We're involved, too."

I was dumbfounded that Steve knew about the Vienna initiative. Perhaps he knew more about it than I did, although it was more likely that he had heard only a vague outline, but was naturally intrigued since Kate and I were involved. I sensed that if I now presented Kate's request, he would think it was somehow connected to the Vienna trip. So I needed to proceed cautiously.

"Jamie, are you still there?"

"Yes, I am."

"I thought the phone went dead. What do you want?"

"First of all, I want to give you something you asked for."

"What's that?" How quickly he forgot.

"You still want Pat Auriga's number, don't you?"

"Oh, absolutely."

I gave him the number. "Now, there's something else I'd like to get to."

"Shoot."

"This will probably be fun for you."

"Bet it won't be," Steve shot back.

"Anyway, let's say we want Brazil to funnel ten percent more of its petroleum output to us, what inducements, trade or otherwise, could we use to get them to cooperate?"

"Didn't we go through this before?"

"No, we're not talking about strong-arm tactics or anything like that. What does Brazil need or want? How can we have more effective trade arrangements?"

"You got to be kidding. Doesn't Brazil use two-thirds of her production to satisfy domestic needs?"

"Actually about sixty percent."

"Okay. So that leaves forty percent. We probably get about twenty percent of her output right now."

"Fifteen percent."

"So if we take another ten percent, that leaves fifteen percent for all her other neighbors and trading partners."

"So how do we do it?"

"I don't think you do."

"Surely there must be something Brazil needs from us. Security? Armaments?"

"I can't believe that's coming from a pacifist like you. Has your boss gotten to you? Or maybe vice-versa?"

"I resent the implication."

"Look, it's a compliment. If you could score with Kate, you'd be the envy of almost every guy in Washington. Anyway, you want me to work on this nonsense?"

"Yes, I do. And it has to be kept strictly confidential—more confidential than this upcoming trip to Vienna."

"Okay. I'll do a little thinking about it. But don't expect me to be able to solve your problem."

"It's the country's problem," I interjected.

"Sure, *the country's* problem. Look, if it was so easy, we would have solved it already."

"Maybe we haven't been bold or creative enough."

"Yes, I know—*l'audace, l'audace, toujours l'audace*. Okay, I'll try to give it some thought. I'll see what I can come up with by the time you get back from your Austrian vacation."

"You're a real pal." I hoped my tone was both appreciative and sarcastic.

"Sure. I'm always ready to help out my buddy. But at this point I figure you owe me about ten favors."

"I just gave you Pat's number."

"That took you one minute. I'll spend a week thinking about your issue."

"Bullshit."

"If that's what you're looking for, I can certainly comply."

"Enough. I have other things to do."

"Give your boss a hug for me."

XIV

Vienna, 2053

KATE AND I MET AT the Dulles Airport gate for a flight to Paris. Of course, Kate was in first class, and I was in steerage. We arrived at Charles de Gaulle airport and joined up again on the tram heading to the gate for the Vienna flight.

"Get any sleep on the flight?" Kate asked.

"Maybe an hour or two. I bet you did better up front?"

"Yes, somewhat. But I'm still tired. At least we won't have any business until tomorrow."

The flight to Vienna had no segregation by class. Kate and I sat next to each other. We had not had a chance to meet in the office for several days. Our Friday phone call had covered the reference materials I was bringing.

"Will there be any papers for me to look at?" Kate had asked.

"If you want something special, I'll print it out here. Otherwise, it's all in my computer." I sensed Kate's grimace over the phone.

"You're bringing your computer?"

"Of course."

"I don't understand why people can't be separated from their computers."

"No, not until death do us part."

"There's seems to be more fidelity in that relationship than in a marriage," Kate observed.

"You never leave your purse behind when you go out, let alone travel."

"Of course not. It holds all sorts of essentials—my wallet, my passport, and, most important, my makeup."

"Leaving aside the makeup, a computer contains much more valuable information and is smaller than your purse."

"But it can't make you look good."

"If it helps me answer your questions, it makes me look good. I'm sure you'd prefer that I have answers at my fingertips as opposed to my wearing makeup."

"Okay, you bring your computer, and I'll bring my makeup case." I thought of a number of retorts, but I thought they might lead in risqué directions. So I said nothing and Kate continued. "You're supposed to say that my mind is my greatest asset, not my looks."

"I'd never denigrate your looks."

"Impertinent fellow," Kate exclaimed, but she added a chuckle.

At the Vienna airport, a representative from the embassy met us and helped us through customs. He had an electrocar waiting and whisked us through the light traffic that was dominated by street trams. Although it was only mid-afternoon, the day was gloomy; the city looked gray and grim. Our driver pointed out some of the sights we passed. Neither Kate nor I reacted with enthusiasm. We entered a portion of the *Ringstrasse.* There was a sense of style and grandeur despite the all-encompassing impression of dark gray stone.

The lobby of the hotel lightened our mood. Old-world opulence and competent service was immediately apparent. Our reservations were quickly found. Kate noted my room number and I memorized hers.

As we were about to separate to be led to our respective rooms, Kate asked, "What are you going to do now?"

"Sleep."

"Don't get more than two hours now or else you won't be able to sleep tonight. I'll call your room around seven and make sure you're up. Then we'll go to dinner."

"Yes, ma'am."

I unpacked some of my clothes, then climbed between the sheets, and promptly fell asleep. All too soon the ringing phone jarred me awake. Still groggy, I searched to find the source of the noise. I eventually reached for the phone and knocked it to the floor. Picking it up, I said "Hello."

A female voice returned, "*Guten abend.*"

"I'm sorry, I don't speak German, *deutsch.*"

"James, you're still half asleep."

"Oh, Kate, I didn't recognize . . . I didn't know you spoke German."

"I know maybe a hundred words. Anyway, this is your wake-up call. Do you think you can be ready in about half an hour and meet me in the lobby?" She did not wait for an answer. "Bring along a coat. We have a short walk to the restaurant."

"Okay," I replied simply.

I needed a shower. I needed a shave. As I looked around, I saw that the room was in disarray. It took some time to find my shaving kit, a toothbrush, and the clothes I needed to wear.

As I showered and shaved, my level of consciousness rose, although I was still tired and a bit disoriented. I knew I was running behind schedule. I nicked myself shaving, and that required a little more time to stop the bleeding. I tried to move faster but couldn't. Eventually I left my room, but then reentered because I had forgotten my coat. I turned the wrong way, and then had to retrace my steps to the elevator.

While descending to the ground floor, I looked at my watch. Seven-forty. Was Kate expecting me at seven thirty? I didn't know, because I never checked my watch when Kate awakened me.

I looked around the lobby. No Kate. Had she left without me? She would have called my room again. Wouldn't she? I tried to remember her room number. Was it four-oh-five or five-oh-four? I found the hotel phone and tried four, zero, five. The phone rang six times, but there was no answer.

A voice from behind said, "Trying to get a *fraulein* for the night?"

"I was just trying your room."

"I hope you don't think I'm going to be your *fraulein*."

"Please, Kate, I'm still half asleep. I won't even try to match your repartee."

"You usually can't anyway. Sorry to keep you waiting, but I had to take care of some business. Ready to go?" I nodded. "I gather you got some sleep," Kate commented as we exited the hotel and stepped onto the Ringstrasse.

"I slept soundly until the phone rang. Wish I could have gotten more."

"When you try to sleep tonight, you'll be happy it wasn't more."

"Where are we going?"

"A restaurant off the *Kaertnerstrasse*. The concierge said it's only a five-minute walk and authentically Viennese. I think it's better to get some fresh air, rather than stay in the hotel."

"Agreed." The cold November night was bringing me out of my stupor.

"Look. The sky is clearing."

There was a sprinkling of stars. Hints of constellations appeared here and there. With the clouds that remained, and the city lights—though relatively subdued—I could not get my bearings. My father had taught me most of the major constellations. *Let's see—November—I should be able to see the great square in Pegasus.* But I couldn't make it out.

"You can put your head down now. I don't want you to trip and break your neck."

"Yes, Mom."

"Do I remind you of your mother?"

"Except for your motherly advice from time to time, not at all.

You're entirely different."

Kate didn't react to my comment. She changed the subject. "I understand the Kaertnerstrasse is one of the most fashionable streets in Vienna. Nice shops, *n'est-ce pas?*"

"That's French, not German."

"You're so perceptive and *schmartlich.*"

"Is that a real German word?"

"Probably not."

"*Peut-être nous pouvons parler anglais?*"

"*Très bien, Jacques.* Yes, I think we better speak English. But don't you think it's wonderful to visit an old European city like this?" I had no chance to answer. "The Hapsburgs; Johann Strauss; schnitzel; strudel. And remember OPEC used to be headquartered here."

"Now there's something I can relate to."

We walked several blocks, occasionally pausing to look in a café or store window, all the while checking the names of streets we crossed. The concierge had told Kate that the street we should look for was the *Vibergstrasse*, or something like that. It was five or six blocks on the right. The restaurant had an impossibly long German name, but Kate remembered that it contained the word "*weiss.*"

So far, none of the street names looked anything like "Viberg." The next street name attracted my attention. "Look, the next street is called *Weihburggasse.* Could it be *gasse* rather than *strasse?*"

"I guess so." Kate admitted, "I didn't pay attention as to whether it was a *gasse* or a *strasse.* Let's look down the street and see if we can spot the restaurant."

As we turned the corner, the establishment with the impossibly long and unpronounceable Germanic name came into view. Our reservation was in order. The *maitre d'hôtel* took us through a front room and into a second. The interior had a rustic ambience with wood paneling and an occasional antler on display. The maitre d' suggested one table, but Kate indicated she preferred another in a quieter nook.

We began to study our menus which were in German with English translations. Kate requested the waiter bring us a good Austrian white wine when he asked if we wished to have a drink. Our dinner selections were made after some discussion. We decided to order different main courses, so we could try some of each.

After we ordered, I began to feel, somewhat dangerously, that I was out on a date rather than with my boss. I looked at Kate's silvery blond hair falling over her shoulders and navy blue blouse. She saw me looking and vaguely smiled. Then her eyes scanned the room. We were nearly alone.

"I guess we can talk a little business, so long as we're discreet."

So much for my date. Although no other diners were within four meters of us, I wondered if a listening device could have been planted, anticipating that two representatives from the F.E.D. would be discussing their deepest secrets. Such paranoia, I concluded, was not warranted. Yet avoiding critical topics would be prudent.

Kate began. "Tomorrow's agenda will be light. We have a ten o'clock meeting with State to discuss procedures for our encounter. They'll no doubt insist on taking the lead in ferreting out our . . ." Kate hesitated, trying to find the right terminology, ". . . counterparts' interests. Actually, I don't mind them doing the initial probing. They know we have to get our oar in the water at some point when it comes to any energy deal. I think we should hold back and let our friends do the heavy lifting."

"I understand. Obviously, I don't have any experience dealing with our counterparts."

"I certainly don't, either," Kate acknowledged. "But I've done a lot of negotiating. And all negotiations take a certain course. You have to properly assess the strengths and weaknesses of your own position and then try to do the same for your opponent's. Then you see who has the best leverage. Ultimately you either make a deal or walk away." Kate continued in this vein for another minute or two, and then she realized she was repeating herself. She came to an abrupt halt. "I'm talking as if I'm senile."

"Senile? That's a term that applies to old people."

"And you don't consider me old?"

I didn't know if Kate was serious or just fishing for my reaction. "You're a young woman."

"If I told you that I'm nearly ten years older than you, would you still consider me young?"

"Well, first of all, I wouldn't believe it. Of course, you're the one who has access to personnel records. But I would think you could pass for my age. Certainly no one would think you're ten years older."

"I said '*nearly* ten years older.'"

"Sorry. Anyway, if I saw you on the street I would guess you were no more than thirty." I lied slightly.

"Women who walk the street must appear a bit younger."

"Kate, you know what I meant."

"Yes, I know. You're sweet." She reached across the table and squeezed my hand.

Her touch felt electric. I would have liked to respond as a close friend and confidant, but I didn't know if Kate was playing a game with me or being honest. For some reason, Kate seemed to need my reassurance and compliments. Was her need a weakness or a normal human emotion? But her behavior, human or otherwise, in my estimation brought her down more to my level. Yet this was an evaluation that was dangerous to make.

We finished our schnitzel and Viennese-style chicken, shared a dessert, and then passed on having coffee. Kate, being of higher rank, paid the bill. A moment later, we were back out in the bracing air, and Kate began to comment on the wind which had picked up. As we walked, she turned right on the Kaerntnerstrasse. I thought we were heading in the wrong direction but said nothing. Shortly we entered a huge open square. The sign said: "*Graben.*" A large cathedral loomed to the right.

"I think we made a wrong turn," Kate declared.

"Yes, I think we should have made a left turn on the Kaerntnerstrasse."

"You should have told me."

"Well, you took the lead."

"From now on, you lead the way on excursions. I don't have a very good sense of direction. Now you know my weakness."

In reality, I thought I had discovered two of Kate's weaknesses that night.

After having breakfast together, Kate and I waited in the lobby for the driver who would take us to the embassy. The drive took only a few minutes. At the desk we showed identification and then were escorted to a conference room. A man, probably of Kate's age, stood up to greet us.

"I'm Doug Stein. We'll be working together on this project." He flashed a broad smile, displaying his large, even teeth. Despite the season, he appeared to be sporting a bit of a tan. His dark hair was perfectly combed. "I trust you were comfortable at the Imperial."

"Quite luxurious," Kate answered for both of us.

"We're waiting for our colleague from Defense. His name is Ken Bader. I haven't met him. I don't suppose you have?"

"I don't think so." Again Kate made the response.

"Kate, can I call you 'Kate'?" Kate nodded her assent. "Kate, you're the highest-ranking person on our team. But in this encounter with a foreign power, State should assume the lead in discovering what the Russians are after. Since what we're looking for in return is primarily energy supply, I would hope you would speak to that issue when the time comes."

Kate nodded again. Our team member from Defense arrived. Introductions were made. Despite being a civilian employee of the department, Ken Bader had a decidedly military bearing. His back was ramrod straight. His handshake was firm. I noticed that Kate winced as she tried to extricate her hand quickly.

Doug took the lead again. He spelled out how he thought the discussion might go. We discussed roles: Doug assuming the lead; Kate, when the circumstance warranted, speaking to energy demands; Ken giving us perspective on any military concerns that could arise. The overall purpose of the encounter was to lay out positions. No conclusions would be reached, no agreements made.

From the original contact which led to this meeting, we knew that the Russians were seeking some concessions from China. We wanted to obtain a share of Chinese oil contracts which they had negotiated with producing countries over many years. The Russians were still energy sufficient. Which meant they wanted something else. Perhaps food, perhaps land, perhaps manufactured products—we'd soon find out. The Russians evidently had some ideas as to how to put pressure on China. For some reason, they thought we could help. At a minimum, they didn't want us to interfere.

The meeting was adjourned at noon. Lunch was served in the embassy dining room. We had soup and sandwiches, and—for those who wanted dessert—ice cream with chocolate sauce.

As we left, Doug reminded us that in the evening we would receive instructions at our hotel regarding meeting arrangements with the Russians. A preliminary discussion over lunch was expected. We knew not where. The Russians would supply the details.

Kate and I were driven back to the hotel. In the lobby, Kate asked, "Want to explore a bit? It looks like we have the afternoon free."

"Sure."

Kate wanted to look in some of the shops which had been closed the night before. We walked down the Kaerntnerstrasse again. At about every other store Kate paused to look in the window. "I guess I should get a souvenir from Vienna."

"Why?"

Kate assumed my mono-syllabic question reflected disapproval. "You're right. Such trinkets only gather dust. The memories are the important thing."

"I suppose so."

"You're being very cynical today."

"Sorry, I'll try to be better company. How about walking down to that big square we spotted last night? Then maybe we could visit the Hapsburg palace," I suggested.

"Sounds like a good plan."

We spent an hour looking in windows and stalls in Graben and some surrounding streets. Kate saw a small porcelain of a Lipizzaner stallion. "I wonder how much it is?"

"Only one way to find out."

"Yes, let's ask. If it's under a hundred euros, I think it would make a great souvenir." So much for the game plan.

When we arrived in the vicinity of the Hofburg, I was carrying two of Kate's purchases and she was toting another. We spent a few minutes looking around a small church adjacent to the palace.

Kate confessed she was getting tired and wanted to take a nap before dinner. She asked to skip the Hofburg itself. I led the way past the opera house and back to our hotel. I carried my share of Kate's acquisitions to her room, which proved to be a suite with a well-furnished living room and a large bedroom behind sliding doors.

"Let's discuss what we'll do for dinner," Kate suggested.

But I had something else more urgent to do. "Can I use your toilet?"

Kate pointed to a door near the entrance to the suite. When I returned, Kate was in the bedroom taking her street clothes off. "Don't be shy. You've seen me wearing less."

"I remember *touching* you when you had less clothing on."

"Really. Funny, I don't recall. But I'm sure you were a

gentleman."

I spread out my hands as if to say, "What else would you have permitted?" But no words came to mind to accompany the gesture.

"You know, James," Kate returned to the earlier topic, "you needn't feel obliged to have dinner with me, if you have something else you'd rather do."

"What else could I possibly do that would be more enjoyable than joining you for dinner?"

"Hmm." Kate reacted mysteriously, then adding, "So gallant and politically—or should I say administratively—correct. Anyway, how about just eating in the hotel's dining room?"

"Fine with me."

"Meet you at seven?"

"Fine."

"Would you make the reservation?"

"Gladly."

"You're so agreeable."

"I aim to please."

"Hmm."

I made what I hoped was a graceful exit.

Again I arrived first in the lobby, and chose to wait outside the restaurant. Five minutes later, I spotted Kate.

"You could have gone in and gotten a drink. I wouldn't have minded if you had a head start."

"I'm too much a gentleman for that."

"I suppose so. Let's go in."

Much of dinner was consumed by small talk. We came to one conclusion: if we were going to stay in Vienna a few more days, we would take in a concert.

"What's your idea of a concert?" Kate asked.

"I don't know. What sort of bands do they have here?"

"How about the Vienna Philharmonic? An operetta? Or some

Strauss?"

"Is Strauss a guitarist?"

"You're joking, of course. He's been dead for two hundred years."

"Then he can't be very good."

"James, he's an institution in Vienna. He was a composer. He . . ."

"He was the 'Waltz King.' I was just pulling your leg."

"So you're not a total illiterate when it comes to music."

"To be honest, I know very little about classical music. I've not been exposed to it much. But I'm always willing to learn." I thought about Pat Auriga. Was it only a few weeks earlier that we had attended the concert? I wondered if Steve had called her.

During dessert, Kate admitted that she was a little nervous about the next day's meeting. "If you don't mind, I'd like to go over some stuff after dinner and do some role playing."

"Perfectly fine with me."

"I'll get a bottle of champagne sent up. The real stuff."

I glanced at the bottle of Austrian wine which was only half finished. It was a bit tart for my taste. I had had only one glass. "Great," I concurred.

After dinner, we headed up to Kate's suite. Had anyone noticed, they would have likely misconstrued the purpose of our liaison.

Kate immediately called room service and ordered a bottle of Roederer and then added, "I'm going to put on something more comfortable."

"And I'll take my jacket off."

"Quite audacious. I'll just be a minute."

The champagne arrived while Kate was changing. I signed for Kate and found a two-euro coin for the tip. The bottle was still closed in the wine bucket. I began to twirl it slowly in the icy slurry.

"You do nice work." Kate had come out of the bedroom. She

wore gray hip-hugging sweat pants and a blue tee shirt—possibly these served as her pajamas. Kate looked at me. "You don't look very comfortable."

"My wardrobe is not handy."

"You could get something from your room."

"I'll survive. I'll roll up my sleeves, if that would help."

"It's a start."

I began to wonder where the evening would lead. But Kate quickly turned to business. "Let's open the bubbly and discuss what tomorrow might bring."

I looked around the room. A number of pieces of faux-Louis XV furniture were artfully arranged. There was a TV (*not* Louis XV), shelves, bric-a-brac, lamps—all sorts of places to hide a bug.

Kate read my thoughts. "We'll be discreet. No deep, dark secrets. But I need to talk through a few things. And, please, let's start attacking that champagne.

"I've always fought battles in the domestic arena. I've dealt with opponents in business and later in government. I know them. I generally can pretty well size them up and figure out what makes them tick. But here we're dealing with the Rus . . . with foreigners. I'm not schooled in that sort of thing. I don't have that experience. I need to know what to do."

Kate looked at me, staring intently with her piercing gray eyes. I did not answer immediately. I wanted to think. I took a slow sip of champagne, while Kate drained her glass and sought a refill.

"I think you're putting too much pressure on yourself," I began. "You're used to being in charge and calling all the shots. In this case, Doug Stein will be running the meeting for our side. I'm pretty sure you'll be able to observe and see where the discussion leads. You'll only have to jump in when you find the right spot."

Kate had been bending toward me, her hands clamped under her chin. Now she leaned back. Her tee shirt was fairly short. Her bare midriff was now exposed. I remembered her creamy skin from that moonlit night in her apartment. I remembered the intensely erotic feeling it produced then, which was now being repeated. I forced my mind back to the discussion. I knew I had to continue to talk business, even if Kate had spotted me looking at the area around her navel. "We can be listeners. We're not supposed to make any commitments. If some potentially damaging proposal is made regarding our areas of interest, you simply say that we need to evaluate the idea, the numbers, whatever."

"But we may be asked to put our ideas on the table. I should avoid that, but you know me. I'll be inclined to push our agenda."

"I'll nudge you under the table."

"Give me a good kick. And sit close to me." An inviting suggestion on Kate's part.

"I will. But if Doug's right, our friends are going to put forward their proposals."

"They might be totally unacceptable."

"Sure. But we don't have to tell them that in the meeting. We can talk about the need to evaluate." I was warming to my role of coach.

"Deferring the talks might kill any possibility of a deal."

"We're not obliged to make a deal, especially a bad one."

"Very true. But if there's something we can build on, I'm going to speak up, even though I won't commit."

Kate was still reclining on the couch, looking a bit more relaxed. I sat in an armchair, which I had pulled to a meter away.

She glanced around the room. "We didn't say anything inappropriate."

"I don't think so."

"I feel better now. I guess I knew a lot of what you suggested, but you helped to coalesce my thoughts. You simplified things. I was right to bring you along."

"Glad I can help."

An awkward silence followed. "I guess I should go," I suggested, in order to solicit a response.

"Do you want to go?"

"Not if you want me to stay."

"Do you want to watch a movie? It's still early." Kate looked at her wrist, but she had already removed her watch.

"It's only nine thirty," I confirmed.

"We have some champagne left. I tried to get a movie on the TV earlier, but it wouldn't work. You know me with electronic gadgets."

"I'll take a look at it." I got up and took two steps toward the TV.

"No, it's the one in the bedroom."

I turned into the bedroom, surprised by Kate's ill-disguised gambit. I took the TV control and sat on the front edge of the bed. She followed me and sat next to me, placing her arm around my shoulder and pretending to look at what I was doing with the remote.

"Well, the remote seems to be turning the TV on." Kate's head was now against my upper arm, allegedly to get a look at the buttons on the remote. "Let's try the menu button. Here we go. See, one of the choices is 'movies.' We just use this arrow to scroll down to the movie button and press 'select.' *Voilà*. Here comes a list of movies. Spot any you want to watch?"

Kate said nothing. I turned my head. Her face was only a few inches from mine. "Should we quit the pretending?"

I tried to think of a clever reply, but I could only say, "Good idea."

"It would make me feel better if you could spend the night. And I don't mean sleeping on the couch. I'm going into the bathroom. Don't go away."

"I'd really like to go to my room and get a toothbrush." Actually I wanted to check my toilet kit for a condom.

"No need to go. I'm sure the hotel left a travel toothbrush amongst all the amenities. There are a bunch in the bathroom near the front door."

"Okay, fine with me."

Kate held my arm and planted a kiss on my cheek. "Do that, but take that shirt off and leave it here. You look so formal."

Odd, I thought. Was my shirt being held hostage pending my return? I went to the john and then found the cellophane package, which contained the diminutive toothbrush and tube of paste.

When I returned, Kate was still in her bathroom. She heard me. "You can come in. I'm just finishing up."

Kate was wearing the terry cloth robe that the hotel supplied. I was quite sure there was no clothing underneath. She was finishing washing her face and then applied the washcloth to her crotch. Unabashedly, she explained, "I just got over my period two days ago." She grabbed a bottle of cologne and applied a few drops behind her ears and also to the area that had just been rinsed.

Again, Kate had surprised me with her frankness. Responding to her attitude, I began to take off my slacks.

"Now you're getting into the spirit of things." She closed the distance between us. Her robe was covering her breasts but was open from the waist down. Instinctively my eyes shifted lower. Her pubic hair was mostly shaved, except for a tuft, perhaps left to prove that she was a genuine blonde, albeit less platinum than her coif would have one believe.

She pressed against me. "You are responding to the moment." Her hand was now on my penis. "Let's not stand here between bathroom and bed." While still in an embrace, we edged toward the bed. The phone rang. Kate rushed back to the bathroom to take the call on that extension. I listened to Kate's side of the conversation.

"Pick up at ten. Got it . . . We'll wait in the lobby . . . No need to call James. I'll get the message to him." Kate grinned in my direction as she ended the call. "Did you get the message? Ten o'clock in the lobby."

"Got it."

"I guess it was better getting the call when we did, rather than ten minutes later. I believe we were heading to the bed."

Kate let her robe drop as she took the remaining four or five steps. I took off my briefs. I began to put my arms around her invitingly slinky body.

"I have to warn you about one thing. We're not going to have sex." The astonishment must have registered on my face. "Oh, don't worry. We're going to enjoy each other. I promise we'll both be satisfied. But I'm deathly afraid of getting pregnant."

I could have mentioned that she probably was not fertile this close to her period. I started to suggest, "Well, there are ways of . . ."

Kate didn't want to hear about prophylactics. "No, we won't argue about this. We have to do it my way. It's not just my fear of having a baby. We will also be able to say honestly that we never had sex. That's appropriate given our . . ." Kate searched for the right term. ". . . relative employment situation."

I had begun losing my erection. Kate noticed. "Oh, my poor dear, I'm turning you off. Don't worry. We'll enjoy each other."

She pushed me, so I fell on the bed. She knelt near the bottom and grabbed my flaccid member which needed to be revived. It soon was in her mouth, and then she began to lick its head like a kid would attack an ice cream cone. After a minute or two she stopped. "Okay, now that I've got your attention, kiss me. Kiss me all over."

I didn't need to say anything. I rolled Kate onto her back and started at her mouth. I moved on to her neck and nibbled on her ears, for the first time sampling the cologne which she had applied a few minutes earlier. I worked my way lower. Her nipples were hard. I licked one and then the other. Kate's eyes were closed. She was evidently pleased with my exploration of her anatomy.

I slid lower on the bed and kissed her stomach and then went below the navel. That part was slightly soft but with an underlying firmness. Kate began to moan in an aroused but contented fashion. I lingered there for a minute, but I couldn't stop. I caressed and kissed her thighs. Her thin legs were perhaps not her best feature, although when clothed they gave Kate a statuesque appearance. I went back higher and gave a gentle tug to the tuft of pubic hair, which had attracted my interest and smelled more of Kate's cologne. From there it was a short distance to the ultimate target, which I found juicy and sweet. "That's so good," Kate murmured.

I continued for a few minutes to explore the cavity with my tongue. More and more I focused on a specific target.

"James, do you know what you're doing to me?"

I wanted to reply, *Sure, your little pea is now BB hard*, but I recognized a rhetorical question when I heard one, and anyway my mouth was otherwise occupied.

I heard stronger moans. Her arms began to flail. "Stop," she directed. Had I gone beyond some unknowable barrier? "I'm very close and you're not. I want to be on top of you and get you in my mouth."

Such consideration. If this doesn't deserve a boss-of-the-year award, what does? I mused whimsically.

We both shifted positions. She began working me aggressively while I kept my tongue jabbing and licking at a furious pace. I grabbed her calves with my hands. My face was totally buried in a moist, cologne-scented wonderland. Kate's pelvis was now heaving furiously. I probably had no way to breathe, but death would come exquisitely. My tongue responded with even greater fervor. She began to gasp, and I could tell she was stifling a scream. My cock fell out of her mouth. "Oh, my god. Hold on, my sweet James. Give me a moment . . ."

But she did not realize that I was only a few seconds behind her. I ejaculated. It was on her face and, worst of all, in her hair. Her emotion changed from ecstasy to mild horror. "Oh dear, I need to clean up. You can use the bathroom by the front door."

We went in opposite directions. When I returned three minutes later, Kate was still in the shower. I didn't know whether to get dressed and leave or wait around. I compromised. I partially dressed and sat on the bed to await her return. Soon she emerged with a towel wrapped around her wet tresses.

"Well, we had a slight faux pas. But I truly enjoyed what we did. Did you mind doing it my way?" she asked softly.

"Quite enjoyable."

"Just 'enjoyable'! You fucking bastard." She grabbed a pillow and hit me. Then she kissed me hard on the mouth. "You were kidding, weren't you?"

"You shouldn't have called me a fucking bastard."

"Well, that's what you were trying to be."

"But we never fucked. Isn't that the line?"

"Okay, you're just a bastard. Give me a good hug and then you can go."

I obeyed my boss. I suppose the faux pas led to my early exit. She had forgotten that, earlier, I had been invited to stay the night.

The same cast we had previously met with was assembling at the embassy the next morning. Again, Ken Bader was not present when Kate and I arrived. Doug Stein tried to fill the gap with small talk. "Did you both have a good evening?"

"Nothing very exciting," Kate answered. "As a matter of fact, James and I were thinking that if we stay here another night or two, we should experience something typically Viennese. Would you be able to suggest anything? Perhaps a concert."

Stein only needed to ponder the question for a second. "The *Volksoper* is probably putting on an operetta. Would you want me to see if we can get two tickets?"

"That would be great."

"For tonight?"

"I guess so. Don't you think we'll likely be leaving tomorrow or the next day?"

"Who knows? We'll know better after our meeting. Let me see what the embassy can do." He stepped out of the office. After a minute he returned. "We'll check for tickets. Evidently there's a good program at the Volksoper. Some Strauss, some Lehar. Just the type of thing you're looking for."

At that moment, Bader arrived. Again, Doug Stein tried to be the gracious host. "I'm checking on tickets for tonight's performance of Strauss and Lehar. Would you like to be included?"

Bader furrowed his brow. "That's old time music?"

"Yes, waltzes, operetta."

"Thanks for the offer. I'll pass."

The meeting turned to logistics and protocol. The Russians had arranged for lunch in an out-of-the-way restaurant. After lunch we would get into the business part of the meeting. The Russians were going to put forward a proposal and would seek our reaction. We could respond if we were certain of our position. Otherwise, we could demur and say we would give the suggestions serious consideration.

Doug laid out a number of do's and don'ts, some of which were repeated from the day before. After about a half hour, there was a knock on the door; two people entered. We were introduced to our translator, Katerina Larman, and to an electronics technician, Paul. Only his first name was given.

Katerina was a fairly attractive brunette, with flowing hair and white skin. Paul was prematurely balding and a bit pudgy.

Doug explained that the Russian translator would perform the primary service, but Katerina would verify that the job was being done accurately. Paul would perform a sweep for listening devices before we got into any serious discussions. The Russians would likely do the same, since we were entering a public facility. Even though we would have a private room.

As soon as this information was communicated, Doug announced that we would be leaving in ten minutes, which meant it was a good time to use the "facilities."

While returning from the john, I tried to strike up a conversation with Ken Bader from the Defense Department. "Aside from Defense, I bet you've had military service."

"You would have won that bet."

"Marines?"

"Army."

"Are you based in Washington?"

"We should be heading back."

But we were heading back.

Two cars were needed to take the six of us to the restaurant. Doug put Kate and me with the translator, while he rode with Bader and the technician. The route took us along a few wide boulevards and then through a number of smaller streets. The trip took about fifteen minutes.

A man emerged from the restaurant to greet us. It turned out he was a member of the restaurant staff. With a combination of gestures and halting English, he led us to a room up one flight and down a corridor. I could see why the Russians had chosen this secluded location. Two people were present in the room—a man and a woman. They explained that several more of their delegation were on the way. It turned out that the woman was the second-ranking person on the Russian team. The man was the translator. She told us that three others would be coming, including Anatoly Ryshkov, their chief.

Our electronics expert began to conduct a room scan. I wondered whether he would redo the process once the other Russians arrived. On the other hand, both the Russians and we were more concerned about a third party eavesdropping. We would know what each other were saying.

All of a sudden, a stocky man with bushy, graying hair burst into the room and announced loudly, "I am Anatoly Ryshkov. Excuse my lateness." Two acolytes followed at his heels. Ryshkov shook hands with each of us. His grip was firm, and when he encountered Ken Bader a clash of wills took place. Ryshkov said good-naturedly, "You're a strong man. Military, no?"

"Former," was Bader's Spartan reply.

Ryshkov turned back to all of us. "Let us have a glass of wine.

Lunch will be brought in. The restaurant specializes in Hungarian food. I hope you won't find it too spicy. But they'll bring in platters of several types, so you can choose or try some of each." Ryshkov explained all this in English.

As we began to take our seats, Kate asked, "Mr. Ryshkov, where did you learn your excellent English?"

"A few years of schooling in England, madame."

"And what did you study?"

"Economics and history. Frankly, I prefer the history. I think it is very important to know what different countries experienced over the ages. It helps explain the national character. Although quite often we have experienced the same types of things, only at different times."

"How do you mean?" Kate prompted again, as waiters with platters began to enter the room.

"For example, both of our countries, and Britain, too, fought civil wars. They occurred in different centuries. And many people would say they were fought for different reasons; although, of course, there are always underlying economic reasons."

"Certainly the English Civil War was fought for other reasons," Kate asserted.

"Don't be so sure, madame. Power and the purse are never far apart. But the conversation has become serious too soon. Let's enjoy the food."

I dug into a piece of chicken *paprikash* and thought, *There's still a strong streak of economic determinism in Russian thinking. Or could it have been the English schooling?*

No serious topics were raised as we ate. I noticed that almost everyone limited himself to one glass of wine and then turned to mineral water. After a half hour or so, the platters and dishes were cleared. Coffee and little pastries were brought in, along with a bottle of sweet wine and a decanter of brandy. No one touched the brandy. A few took a small glass of the sweet wine. Kate eschewed both, and I followed her lead. The waiter withdrew.

Anatoly cleared his throat to get attention. "I think it's time to get down to business. My government, I believe, initiated the proposal that we get together to discuss where we have common interests vis-à-vis China. So here we are to put our cards on the table, and we'll see if we have some similar views."

Since Ryshkov was speaking in English, we needed no translation. One of the Russians could not follow, so a simultaneous translation was given to him *sotto voce*.

"As we all know, China has been an enormously successful economic power since the beginning of the century. They have accumulated wealth for the state, although not as much for their citizens. They hold great interests in your companies and your debt. Similarly, their economic tentacles have reached into our country, although probably not as much as into yours. Not rich in natural resources themselves, they have cornered markets in important commodities.

"You've probably considered ways in which to alleviate this economic pressure. Perhaps you have not taken the steps because they conflict with principles you hold dear, or perhaps you fear reactions from China or others. We have considered some steps to take, too. If our principles are not quite as deep-seated in our constitution as yours, we still would not want to unduly upset countries with which we have no quarrels. Yet we do not want the Chinese noose to be pulled tighter. Perhaps you can see what I mean?"

Ryshkov's speech was attracting Kate's full attention. She began to nod involuntarily in agreement, which was no doubt a faux pas. I could also see that her eyes had widened. When Anatoly paused, she urged, "I can appreciate what you're saying, please continue, Mr. Ryshkov." Judging by the look on Stein's face, he was not pleased with Kate's affirmation of Ryshkov's position.

"Thank you, madame. We Russians have seen the United States—a country we admire greatly and against whom we've never fought a war—we have seen your own power and influence wane. Don't misunderstand me. We still have the utmost respect for your economic, technological and military prowess."

I thought Ryshkov was laying it on a bit too thick. Kate was still following closely.

"At any event, between the two of us we should possess the means to encourage China to, as the expression goes, level the field."

"The *playing* field," Kate interjected.

"Thank you again, madame. So some pressure, discreetly but firmly applied, could benefit us both."

"You have some specific thoughts in this regard?" Stein inquired.

Ryshkov stroked his chin. "It is really not very difficult to envision. In the military sphere, both of us could conduct simultaneous exercises. You might employ your navy near your former outpost of Taiwan. We could have army maneuvers along our mutual border. Economically, we could threaten to nationalize some of their economic interests. I don't know if politically you could threaten the same, but it would be a powerful message."

"And what do you want from China?" Doug again asked the question.

"I can't be terribly precise, you understand. But let us just say that we wish to purchase back some assets that were previously granted to the Chinese under excessively favorable terms."

"And, of course, you don't want to pay full price," Kate commented. Anatoly only smiled. "So tell us, what do you envision for us? What do we get out of the deal?" I could see Doug squirm. He would have approached the subject more deftly, but Kate was getting to the key point, and anyway, there was no way he could keep her quiet.

"Well, let's see. What do the Chinese have that you could use? As we both know, China has acquired an incredible amount of petroleum rights over the past fifty years. They were wise to do this. The reserves they hold in foreign lands can satisfy their needs for another twenty years or more. And they have only slightly cut back on consumption, not nearly as much as you have. I say to myself, if I were in your position, I would not like this situation. Of course, you might say, not to like it is one thing, but to do something about it is something else.

"But let's say, through our combined pressure, we can get the Chinese to negotiate a few things. For us, the reacquisition of assets. For you, the reassignment of some oil contracts."

"How much oil would you be thinking about, Mr. Ryshkov?" Kate could not restrain herself.

"I don't know precisely. Unlike you, I'm not an expert in this area, and fortunately my country has an adequate supply at present. Would a hundred thousand barrels a day sound appropriate to you?"

I could see that Doug Stein did not want Kate to respond, but Kate would not be deterred. "That's a ridiculously small amount."

"Well, then tell me, what would you consider appropriate?"

At this point Doug broke in. "We'll have to consult more on that point. But tell us more about what Russia is seeking?"

Anatoly paused. "This, of course, is a delicate matter, and I can't go into details. Some of the natural resources we possess and provide to the Chinese are worth much more than when we drew up the original agreements. We've talked about reasonable negotiations. They want us to adhere to the contracts in all their specifics. They have become the most ferocious capitalists. We think they need more encouragement to alter their point of view. That is about as much as can be said."

"I see," said Doug. "I'm not sure we can accomplish much more at this meeting. As for us, we need to consult our government. Will you be able to stay in Vienna for another few days, if we are able to advance the discussions?"

"We are closer to home than you are. I plan to be here through tomorrow. Of course, we can return quickly should the situation look promising."

Except for handshakes and a few pleasantries, the meeting was at an end. We returned to the embassy for a post-mortem review.

Doug opened the meeting with a one-word question: "Reactions?"

Kate, never shy, led off. "We certainly need more oil. A hundred thousand barrels per day is not worth bargaining over. I'd consider five hundred thousand to be a minimum we should consider. Of course, if we're bargaining, we'll have to propose a million or two to start."

"I suppose you will want to consult with your Secretary," Doug suggested. "The secure line will be available this afternoon."

"I will tell him what I think, and I'm sure he'll agree." Kate was miffed that Doug did not appreciate her standing within the F.E.D.

"I'm going to forward this up the line within State. But I think the Secretary is wary of proceeding too far with this *démarche*. We will need further evaluation." There was a pause. "And, Ken, any opinion from Defense?"

"Can't give one. Looks like we'd be expected to have a role. Needs extensive planning. No final judgment now. We'll be cautious pending further information and review."

"Okay. Let's see if we can get any quick reactions from our departments. We'll meet here again at eleven tomorrow morning. I expect we'll not be able to pursue this initiative immediately, if at all. But we'll see where we stand tomorrow."

Bader and Doug left quickly. Kate and I were collecting our things. Doug came back into the room. "Good news. You have tickets to the Volksoper tonight."

"Thank you very much," Kate said, accepting the envelope.

Kate availed herself of the secured line to call her boss's office. She did not reach him, but she probably didn't want to. She left a confidential voice message. "Told State that less than five hundred thousand barrels per day is not worth pursuing. Doubt if the negotiations will proceed satisfactorily. Leave a message at the embassy if you disagree. Kate."

She turned to me. "Let's go. We'll try to enjoy our last night in Vienna. I'd like to get the late flight out of here tomorrow. State and Defense have no interest in seriously pursuing this. They don't share our perspective."

I was surprised that she so quickly sized up the situation in this fashion.

We started the evening at the Volksoper. We listened to Johann Strauss and Franz Lehar selections in the first half of the program. At intermission, Kate asked, "You enjoying this stuff?"

"It's alright. Plenty of waltzes."

"There are more waltzes to come. *Rosenkavalier*. A different Strauss. Would you mind if we skip the balance? We could get some strudel and then head back to the hotel."

"Sounds like a better plan," I replied quickly, hoping that the point about returning to the hotel contained a subtle message.

At the café, I ended up with the strudel. Kate, being an ardent lover of chocolate, had the *Sacher torte*. We did not linger over our coffee.

In the elevator, Kate asked, "Can I invite you up for some champagne?"

"I'm not sure I'm in the mood for champagne."

"You're invited anyway."

That gave me the answer I wanted. "I'll just stop in my room and then be along in a few minutes. Okay?"

"Permission granted."

When I arrived at Kate's room, she greeted me in her robe, which was opened almost to the waist. "Love your outfit."

"Enjoy it now. It won't be on for long. What do you have there?"

"A bottle of cognac."

"A good idea. Exactly what I need."

"And I brought this." I showed Kate the condom.

"You're spoiling the whole mood. Put that thing away. I told you the rules."

"I just thought . . ."

"Don't think. Just play along and enjoy. It has to be my way or no way."

"I'm sorry."

"Open that cognac, and we'll try to loosen the atmosphere."

From that point on I kept my mouth shut—except to drink some brandy and perform the necessary services for Kate, which, I must admit, she seemed to enjoy once again. I was more careful in my approach, lessening the fervor and perhaps a bit of my pleasure, but this time committing no faux pas.

Later, as she lay in my arms, I thought, *This is wonderful, but also sad. I'll probably never enjoy another night like this. We'll get back to Washington and return to a boss/subordinate relationship. Kate won't even invite me to her apartment. She'll have all her Washington friends at her disposal. Who knows how many important men get invited over?* Then I told myself, *You're crazy and sick. Just enjoy the moment.*

XV

Savannah, 2061

DOWNTOWN SAVANNAH WAS DRESSING ITSELF for Christmas. Decorative lights had been banned for years, but Santas, reflective Christmas trees, and all sorts of spangles and balls dangled from homes and storefronts. The weather was changing, too. Days with highs in the brisk teens and lows in the single digits were replacing those which reached the balmy twenties. One night the temperature fell below zero, and early that morning frost was still on the grass.

Mrs. Pinckney was introducing some heartier dishes to the menu. On the windows, the second overpane had replaced the screens. The fountain was drained. Jacqueline no longer sunned herself. And if I worked in the garden, I needed a sweater.

One somewhat warmer morning in early December, I was lounging in the garden, making leisurely progress on a proposal for the regional energy council. Mrs. Pinckney's head poked out the back door. "James, do you have your phone with you?"

"No. I think I left it in my room."

"I believe it's rung several times."

"Okay. Thanks for letting me know."

The message was from Aaron Smith. I returned the call and reached him directly. "Hey, James. This call has nothing to do with energy council business." I was a bit surprised, but just waited for Aaron to continue. "You're an economist, right?"

"Not exactly. I've done my studies in energy utilization. Some people consider it a branch of economics."

"And energy is at the center of all economics in this century."

"Well, it's been an important element," I conceded. "So what's this all about?"

"There's a vacancy at SCAD, really a joint course with Armstrong. You know some courses are offered to students from both schools." I didn't know that, but I let Aaron continue uninterrupted. "The class is billed as 'Economics of the Twenty-First Century. How energy supplies have affected our society.' You have an advanced degree, right?"

"A master's degree."

"That should be good enough for an adjunct lecturer. Look, if you're interested in pursuing the job, you can call the assistant dean. Her name is Joan Gwinnett." Aaron put the emphasis on the last syllable. He gave me her phone number.

A few days later, I found myself heading to Dean Gwinnett's office in a brick building on Bull Street. I had decided to find out more about the job, exactly what I would be expected to teach, how much it would pay, the schedule, etc.

Certainly I could use the income. Like many Americans I was cobbling together several part-time jobs in order to make ends meet. My consulting pay along with the trickle of continuing income from the F.E.D. covered my ongoing bills with no margin for safety. None of the work was reliable. On average I probably worked only twenty hours a week. I was neither fully occupied nor financially secure. Another job could fill out my schedule nicely. On the other hand, I had never done any formal teaching, just some coaching of subordinates. I was not sure I would be good at it.

Joan Gwinnett turned out to be a plump woman, likely in her mid-forties. Her dark hair was beginning to be streaked with gray. It was pulled back and tied with a brown ribbon. Her pants were black, her top pink; both were a bit wrinkled. She made few attempts to make herself look attractive. Perhaps she had concluded that the task was not worth the effort.

She shook my hand warmly. "I'm glad you're here and seriously considering taking on this job. Your résumé was quite impressive and certainly more than adequate for teaching a mid-level economics course."

I thought I was going to be interviewed for the position. Instead, it seemed that Dean Gwinnett viewed her task as convincing me to take the job. However, I did not want to take the job under false pretenses. "You can see that neither of my degrees was in economics."

"Yes, but in all other respects you reek of economics."

"Sorry. I had no idea."

"I'm glad you have a sense of humor. The students will like that. Really the course is not that difficult. It's a survey course of the economic history of this century. You can slant the material toward your strengths—history, economics, fuel consumption, probably some of each.

"Gordon Frazier taught the course for the past two years. Unfortunately, he's recovering from some heart surgery."

"So you're going to be stuck with me."

"There's your sense of humor again. But, seriously, you're closer to the age of the students than Gordon is. I think you'll relate. And, if you're willing, I'd be pleased to have you take the job."

"May I ask you a few questions regarding things like pay, class size, schedule, etc.?"

"That was inconsiderate of me. Of course." She spent the next fifteen minutes responding to the half dozen questions I posed. Her answers were good enough for me to take the position. She handed me a six-page outline Gordon Frazier had used to give the course. It wasn't much, but it was a start.

For most of Savannah, the focus was now on Christmas and New Year's preparations. With nothing much to do for the holidays, I worked on my own ideas for the course. In total, I was required to deliver thirty lectures, each to last one hour. My first sketches showed that I could fill ten lectures with ease. Where would I go from there? Perhaps there should be some repetition in preparation for the mid-term and then for the final exam. Each student would need to write a paper. One class, possibly two, could be devoted to choosing and developing topics. In another class, the best papers could be read. The term was beginning to take on flesh.

Mrs. Pinckney told her lodgers that she would like us all to join her on the Sunday afternoon before Christmas for some finger sandwiches, punch, and cookies. The punch proved to be punchless. Perhaps the alcohol was omitted in deference to Jacqueline's tender age. Mrs. Pinckney thought of Jacqueline as a teen-ager, underestimating her age by a good five years.

Despite the blandness of the fare, Mrs. Humphreys, Jacqueline, and I thanked Mrs. P. profusely for thinking of us at the holidays. In order to make conversation, Mrs. Pinckney asked us what we were doing for Christmas. Mrs. Humphreys was going to spend Christmas with her daughter. Jacqueline said that she was going to stay around and work. She could earn some extra money doing yet another part-time waitress job. She pointed out that there was a great demand for wait staff during the holidays. Mrs. Pinckney admitted that she had no idea that such was the case.

Then it was my turn. I told the little gathering that I, too, was staying in Savannah to work on notes for a course I was going to teach. Mrs. P. and Mrs. Humphreys posed a number of questions. What was I going to teach? Where was the course being given? How many students would I have? I answered the first two questions, but I admitted that I had no idea how many students would sign up.

"Well, I intend to take your course," Jacqueline piped up. "So long as you promise me an A," she added. Mrs. Pinckney frowned in Jacqueline's direction.

"Jacqueline, you know I can't do that," I replied sanctimoniously.

"Oh, of course, I do. I was just kidding. But I bet I can earn the A."

Mrs. Pinckney smiled approvingly. I, however, sensed that Jacqueline's meaning was less pure.

Two days after Christmas, I encountered Jacqueline in the parlor. She was reading from her page palette. "I'm getting a head start on my reading for your course."

"You're quick. I just posted the reading list yesterday."

"And I just registered today."

"I hope you'll enjoy the course. Economic history can be a little dry."

"I'm sure you'll manage to spice it up. But I have one little problem."

"What's that?" My suspicions were aroused.

"I don't want to miss your first two lectures. Unfortunately, my boss is forcing me to work those two nights. Maybe you could give me some private tutoring?" She smiled sweetly and imploringly.

"If you have to work, you have to work. Is it waitressing or dancing?"

I received a petulant look in response to my question. "I think you're being judgmental."

"Okay, forget it."

"So you're not going to help me make up the classes?"

"No, I will. And you can dance your little butt off."

"You're cute." Jacqueline smiled seductively.

"Is that the way you talk to your professor?"

Jacqueline said nothing. She came over to my chair, put her hands on my knees, leaned over, and planted a gentle kiss on my lips. "*That's* what I think of my professor."

XVI

Washington, 2053-54

KATE AND I RETURNED FROM Vienna to a chilly Washington. For a number of years, Washington winters had been unusually mild, with only a few dozen nights dipping below zero. Even in January, a number of days had reached ten degrees. This winter was beginning differently.

After a few attempts at restarting discussions, both the Russians and we thought it best to suspend further talks. Kate told me that she had always considered the mission to be a wild goose chase. However, she felt obliged to pursue any chance to acquire more petroleum supplies for the country. Unfortunately, we now feared that the Russians would pursue concessions from the Chinese without including us in the process.

At the beginning of 2054, the State Department initiated contact with the Russians to restart the earlier discussions. The Russians proved to be evasive.

Kate's interest turned to politics and the congressional elections that would be held later in the year. Perversely, she hoped that President Longworth's party would lose seats, so that he would feel obliged to take a more aggressive stance on energy policy. But early polling indicated that the opposition was viewed with less favor than the incumbent's party. She looked at the key Senate races, and concluded that none of the candidates was worthy of consideration.

Kate's interest in her job seemed to wane. She found fault with almost everything in government. In part, this was due to her not having the influence she craved. She was distrustful of each proposal made by any other department that touched on energy supply or usage. Quietly she dropped the pursuit of trying to extract more petroleum supplies from countries such as Brazil and Mexico.

In a one-on-one meeting in late January, she further denounced the Vienna mission. "Mark my words, those Russians are up to no good. They wanted to get us involved as a cover for some nefarious scheme. But they were going to slice the pie very much in their favor. They wanted the big piece and wanted to leave us the crumbs. Those people are devious. We'll see something come out of the Vienna junket, and it won't be any good for us. You just wait and see."

After a typically mundane meeting in February, Kate stated, "I'm getting awfully tired of the Washington scene. If I stay here, I'm going to have a boring time for the next few years. Longworth doesn't want this department to do anything creative. All we can do is chronicle the continuing strangulation of the American economy and our standard of living. I'm not going to be a statistician."

"What else would you do?" I asked.

"Return to the private sector. I'd do much better there. At least I could make three times as much."

"Money's always good."

"It can get me some of the things I want. Do you know what I've wanted for twenty years or more?"

Although I had been close to Kate for the past year, I didn't really know what made her tick. I thought it might be power, not anything material. "I can't even guess."

"Sure you can."

"To be your own boss."

"Not a bad guess. Maybe I'll achieve that at some point. This may sound strange, but I've always wanted a hot, red convertible."

"You mean with a gasoline engine?"

"Exactly. Something with acceleration. A car that can push

you back in your seat when you take off. Not a dinky electrocar."

"The use tax alone on that will be over fifty thousand a year."

"Closer to a hundred thou'. How else should I spend my money?" Kate stared at me, watching my expression as she outlined her fantasy. "I have no offspring to care for. I like some nice clothes, but I don't acquire much jewelry—just a few pairs of decent earrings. Why not ride around in a head-turning car?"

"You don't need a car to turn heads."

"You're an incorrigible flatterer. You embarrass me." But a broad grin attested to her appreciation. "And what do you want, James? A better job? A family?"

"Certainly not a family."

"Why not? You know, Jane would love to marry you." Kate watched my face as she let this information slip.

Kate's comment stunned me. Of course, I didn't expect a sexual (or whatever Kate would call it) relationship to resume after Vienna. But on the other hand, I didn't expect her to act as a matchmaker for me. "Have you two been talking about me?"

"You know we girls gossip on occasion." She smiled wickedly.

I hardly thought of Kate as a gossipy girl. "Have you been comparing notes?"

"What do you mean by that?" she asked suspiciously.

I knew in Kate's mind we hadn't had sex, but Jane and I certainly did, and it had resumed after my return from Vienna. "Do the two of you discuss my qualities and deficiencies?" I thought I made a respectable recovery.

But Kate still looked at me through narrow-slitted eyes. "Jane talks about you. I don't. But I did confirm that you are an honorable and upstanding person."

Upstanding? In Vienna she saw me horizontal more than vertical. Before I could get in another comment, Kate changed direction. "Professionally, what do you want to do?"

The stock answer came to mind. "I'd like a job with more responsibility."

"And more pay?"

"Hopefully, that would come with more responsibility."

"Do you think you're ready to head a regional office?"

"I think so. Of course, I haven't had the supervisory experience."

"But you have more technical expertise than just about anyone in our regions. I think you'd handle the supervisory aspect just fine. Heck, there are only fifteen to twenty people in most regions, and the bigger ones have good seconds in command. And because of your technical background, you'd be able to handle the energy councils. I think you're ready."

"I appreciate the vote of confidence."

"There's an opening or two coming up. If you had a choice, would you pick Dallas or San Francisco?"

Kate's thought process was moving more quickly than mine. "I've never been to Dallas."

"But you went to Stanford, so you feel comfortable in San Francisco."

"Yes, somewhat . . ."

"So it's San Francisco," Kate drew the conclusion.

"Am I being shipped out?"

"Isn't that what you want?"

"All this has come on so suddenly. It would be a big change." Another thought came to mind. "Do you need my spot for someone else?"

"My goodness. Do you think I'm so Machiavellian? Remember, I'm not counting on being here. You could even take my administrative assistant with you."

"She can't work for me. That would be improper."

"I'll find her a job in another department in San Francisco. See what I'm willing to do for the two of you?" Kate flashed a benevolent smile.

"You have it all figured out."

"Talk to Jane. You have to do that part."

"I guess I should thank you."

"I think you should. And don't worry, someday we'll be back here in Washington together. Then we'll be in a stronger position to influence the course of . . . We'll be able to get things done."

"I'm glad you can see so well into the future."

"I know you're being sarcastic. But I can see it clearly. Trust me."

I left the office earlier than normal that day. My head was swimming. I couldn't think about the everyday tasks in front of me. I wanted to think in private about what I wanted to do with my life—and what Kate wanted me to do. I didn't want to discuss my thoughts with Kate. I didn't want to discuss them with Jane.

At home, I poured myself a drink. It was Scotch, the only hard liquor I owned. I looked for something to eat, although I was not sure I was hungry. I made a scrambled egg and a piece of toast and mechanically ate them. I didn't try to evaluate how well the Scotch accompanied the food.

I tried to assess objectively what Kate had proposed. The transfer to San Francisco would include a promotion. It was a good career move and a logical next step, but I had visualized myself moving up the ranks at Kate's side. If she left the department, I would lose my mentor and essentially be off on my own. Perhaps it would be better to be five thousand kilometers away in San Francisco, rather than serving as a lackey to a new crew in Washington. In San Francisco, to a certain extent, I would be my own boss.

Strangely enough, I would miss the energy usage rules that I was working on. Kate felt their development tedious. But I thought they represented a challenge, and she gave me a lot of latitude in approaching the drafts as I saw fit. I might miss that aspect of the job. But who knew what I'd be doing under a new boss if Kate left. At least a regional director had clear-cut responsibilities.

And then there was the issue of Jane. I liked Jane; I liked her a great deal. I enjoyed sex with her, the real stuff, not Kate's ersatz version. But sex with Jane, though varied and pleasurable, was never as exciting as non-sex with Kate. Nonetheless, I had to forget about Kate. She was unattainable, and—even if obtained—would be toxic. Living with Jane would be more comfortable than serving Kate. But was comfort the objective?

I tossed these themes over in my mind for several hours and reached a decision about the job in San Francisco, but not about Jane. I wondered if Jane would even be willing to come with me to the West Coast without being married. But if I took her, that would be tantamount to marriage, because I couldn't abandon her after taking her across the country. This was a complicated issue. It involved both feelings and ethics.

I didn't know if Kate was right—that Jane wanted to marry me. We had never explored the subject of marriage. How long had we been dating? Six, seven months? Others dated for years without marrying.

I was searching for ways to make a decision. I really needed to answer only one question: Did I want to spend the rest of my life with Jane? And that was a question I chose not to answer too quickly.

In the morning, I was back at work. For a while I handled only insignificant tasks. Just around noon I sent an email to Kate, saying I wanted to accept the assignment in San Francisco. My hope was that Jane would be at lunch and would not intercept the message. I remained in my office through lunch, having only some crackers and a cola. Around one, I decided that I was being a coward and left a voicemail for Jane, saying that I would like to speak with her that afternoon and, if possible, in person.

For several hours I heard nothing from Kate or Jane. Then a bit after four Jane stopped by. She closed the door, although that did not assure privacy since the office partitions were not ceiling high.

Jane kept her voice low. "Kate got your message. She asked me to tell you that she foresaw no problem in getting you approved for the San Francisco job. Formal approval should come in about a week, but you can start making plans for departure. I guess that's it." Jane hesitated. She had delivered an exit line, but she clearly didn't want to go.

"Don't leave yet," I said unnecessarily. "I want to talk to you."

"Okay." Jane's two-syllable reply seemed to encompass both agreement and anxiety.

"You know it was a difficult decision for me to make—taking the job in San Francisco."

"It's a logical move for you and a good opportunity. You're not obliged . . ." Her voice trailed off.

"Do you feel I'm abandoning you?"

"I have no claim on you. We've had our good times. But you need to make your own decisions and follow your own path." Jane's words were brave, but her face betrayed her deep disappointment. Her ill-concealed emotion produced a deep sense of sorrow, perhaps even guilt, in me.

Contemplating marriage out of a sense of guilt, I knew, was ridiculous. But my mind was drifting in that direction whether I intended to or not. "You didn't answer my question."

"What was the question?"

"Am I abandoning you?"

"We never signed any contract. I think I better leave."

Clearly the conversation was not going well. "No, don't go like this."

"Like how?"

"Angry, maybe disappointed."

"I'm not angry. And if I'm disappointed, it's in myself, not you."

"Why be disappointed in yourself?"

"I don't know. I don't wish to explain it."

"Which one is it?"

"Leave me alone. That's what you're planning anyway."

I was messing everything up. "Look, I haven't expressed myself properly. Would you be willing to come with me to California?"

"You can find a new girlfriend there."

"Is that what you want me to do?"

"You can do what you want. I'm not even sure what I want myself."

"What I want is for you to come with me." Jane said nothing. She just stared at me. Almost involuntarily I added, "We can get married."

Jane's face barely brightened. "If that's a marriage proposal, it's the most unromantic offer I can imagine."

"Then let me try this."

"Don't get down on your knee. Your door has a glass window."

"Okay, how about this?" I took Jane's hands in mine. "Will you marry me?"

A small smile appeared on Jane's lips. "Okay, that's better."

"Is that supposed to be a 'yes'?"

"Not exactly. Let me think about it overnight."

"Talk about being unromantic. You make my marriage proposal sound like a business deal."

"You made it sound that way. I'll have to relocate. I have to leave my job with Kate. At least you know San Francisco. I've never been west of Chicago."

Jane's negativity surprised me. "I guess you need to assess the pros and cons for yourself. But I think you're dwelling on the negatives."

"What do you mean 'negatives'?"

"For example, you mention leaving your job with Kate. But what if Kate leaves her job here? Where does that leave you?"

"Do you know something I don't?"

I realized that Kate had not confided in Jane. "No, not really.

But Kate's not the type of person to stay put too long. Kate's a candidate for all sorts of jobs—in government or outside."

"Maybe you're right. My head's swimming at the moment. All of this is so sudden. Sure, I'd like to go to California with you. That's my gut reaction. But let me think about it until tomorrow."

"Go ahead. But I bet I could seal the deal right now if I gave you a kiss."

"I don't know. And I don't think you should try. There are probably several pairs of eyes watching us."

"The hell with them." I put my arms around Jane and kissed her with almost theatrical passion.

After fifteen or twenty seconds, Jane freed herself from my grasp. "Damn you, yes."

"What does that mean?"

"Yes. I'll marry you." She ran out the door. Five minutes later, Richard from a few offices away stuck his head through my door. "What's going on between you and Kate's admin?"

"Sexual harassment."

Richard retreated.

XVII

Savannah, 2062

JACQUELINE MADE AN APPOINTMENT TO hear my first lecture on January 2, 2062, which was a holiday for most people. It was an opportunity for me to practice the delivery of my material from the rough notes I had made. I hoped that I could even receive some constructive feedback.

We went into the parlor at two in the afternoon. I stood with my back to the window. Jacqueline took a seat in an armchair a few meters in front of me. She leaned back as if she were going to watch a movie.

"Are you prepared to take notes?"

"I have a recorder."

I looked Jacqueline up and down but couldn't guess where the recorder was concealed. "It's a micro recorder," she offered, responding to my apparent but unstated question. "Do you want to try to find it?"

"Jacqueline. This is a class, not play time. Let's get down to business." I paused to collect my thoughts and establish an atmosphere of decorum. "This course is going to cover economic history from the beginning of the century to the present."

Jacqueline raised her hand. "Shouldn't you introduce yourself to the class?"

"I'll be sure to do so when the full class is present. Now, if I may continue . . ."

"Am I permitted to ask questions during your lecture?"

"If you have a legitimate question about the material I'm

presenting, then go ahead and ask the question. If you want to critique my delivery or the lecture content, why don't you save that for the end? Okay?"

"Understood, sir." Jacqueline settled back and seemed prepared to listen.

"Before we explore the economy of the twenty-first century, we should recognize that the last decade of the twentieth century was a period of relative calm and prosperity. The Cold War had ended. Eastern Europe was beginning to establish a more diverse and prosperous economy, with turbulence in the Balkans being an exception. The decade served as a preamble to the dynamic emergence of China, India, and Brazil at the beginning of the new century.

"America basked in its economic success through leadership in computerization and the use of the internet, which became pervasive at that time. Stock markets soared to dizzying and, in fact, unhealthy heights in the case of some technology companies. At the end of the decade, the United States even managed to have a balanced budget.

"The following decade, the first decade of the new century, saw a reversal of this fortune through some circumstances outside of the control of the United States and through some bad decisions on the part of government and the business community. After the terrorist attack on the World Trade Center in New York City, the United States—through some tortuous reasoning—became embroiled in a lengthy war in Iraq. A lack of attention to a reemerging fundamentalist threat in Afghanistan led to a protracted military effort in which NATO allies shouldered a modest portion of the burden there.

"Financial misjudgment in the home loan industry, including the packaging of these loans as third-party investments, led to a housing collapse which nearly brought down the banking and insurance structure of the United States and affected a good part of the rest of the world. I should add that other economies made some of the same kind of mistakes as the United States did.

"At about the same time, oil prices reached then-record heights. People attributed the spike in the price of crude oil to three factors: political instability in some oil-producing countries, the rapid growth of new economies—for example China and India—and sheer speculation. After the world entered a lengthy period of recession, the pressure on oil prices eased, but they never returned to levels seen at the very beginning of the twenty-first century.

"The general consensus, based on a half-century of hindsight, is that gradually the demand for oil outstripped new supplies coming to market. This situation still affects the price of petroleum to this day. It was not recognized at the time, but world oil production peaked around the middle of the second decade of the century. I don't want to imply that there were no new petroleum discoveries after twenty-fifteen. However, the new amount found could not replace the quantity being lost through exhaustion of old, formerly highly productive oil fields. Furthermore, the newer finds almost always required deep water and/or innovative drilling techniques. Oil that could be extracted at twenty dollars a barrel was being replaced by that which cost two hundred dollars or more to produce.

"Contributing to the country's difficulties was uncontrolled government spending. We were fighting two wars, trying to stimulate a moribund economy, and attempting to extend health benefits to all citizens. The debt of the United States tripled in one decade. The trade deficit with other nations grew rapidly, especially when the price of crude oil was high.

"At any event, the recovery from the world recession of two thousand eight to two thousand ten was slow and improvement gradual. In fact, job creation in this country never fully recovered because many jobs—which were shipped overseas to low-cost labor markets—never returned. The American standard of living has never again attained the level we experienced in the year two thousand."

Jacqueline raised her hand.

"Yes, Ms. Bellan?"

"You're going at a very quick pace. It will be difficult for students to keep up."

"That sounds more like an observation than a question. And I thought you promised to keep observations for the end of the class."

"Okay. Sorry."

"But to address your point, my intention is to provide the class with an overview of the entire period during the first two class sessions. In later lectures I will drill down into the details."

"Then perhaps you should let the students know that up front," Jacqueline boldly added.

"Point well taken, Ms. Bellan. Now back to the lecture.

"Not only was the government greatly in debt, but so was the typical American citizen. It was said that the generation reaching maturity in the late twentieth century sought immediate gratification of their desires: large automobiles, larger houses, second homes, electronic gadgetry, expensive vacations, etc. Credit was too readily available, and too many Americans took full advantage of it. The economic reversal at the end of the first decade of this century changed all that. Whereas, previously, credit was lavished on the American population, it now became restricted. The American consumer was no longer the powerful growth engine that he or she once was.

"There were two positive segments of the American economy that continued into the second decade of the century; namely, agriculture and exports. The weaker U.S. dollar, as well as the strength of emerging economies, provided the market impetus. The developing world developed an appetite for American food, so to speak."

"You don't have to say, 'so to speak.' Everyone will know you're making a joke, so to speak."

I bypassed Jacqueline's impertinence. "Thank you, Ms. Bellan.

With your permission, I'll continue.

"The second decade of the century provided a transition from the economic excesses of the first decade to the severe economic challenges of the third, while providing a foretaste of these dislocations. Some trends continued into the second decade: high oil and gasoline prices, a gradual increase in inflation, and excessive government and personal debt. In this decade we saw more municipalities default on their debts. This was due to the deterioration in the tax base, centered on housing problems—foreclosures, abandonment of properties and significant declines in the value of home and commercial properties."

Jacqueline raised her hand and asked a question of sorts. "I'm not sure I understand how a fall in home prices would affect the taxes a city receives."

"Good question, especially since you and most students would not have been property owners. Most municipal tax receipts, particularly before twenty thirty-five, came from tax assessed on properties. The value of the property determined, along with the tax rate, the amount of taxes paid."

"Thank you, sir." I hoped all my students were equally polite.

"One thing should be recognized. Although I spoke of higher oil and gas prices, greater inflation and higher interest rates, the increases did not come in a straight line. Rarely do such metrics move consistently on a month-to-month or even a year-to-year basis. However, when you look at the data over a decade or two, the direction is incredibly clear. By twenty thirty, crude oil passed eight hundred dollars a barrel. Even though this reflected the continuing decline in the value of the dollar, the price of oil—in inflation-adjusted terms—tripled in a decade. Gasoline became prohibitively expensive for the average consumer. If a person needed to use a car, gasoline became one of the largest elements in an individual's budget. Gasoline consumption declined greatly, but not enough to reverse the general price trend.

"Because vehicle usage was such a financial burden, the exurbs and outer suburbs became less viable as bedroom communities. In the outlying areas, property values declined even more than in the more interior suburbs. Homes were abandoned. Some were reconverted to farmland; some new construction in outer suburbs was never purchased. This hastened the re-concentration of population to urban and inner-suburban areas.

"Where rail service from suburban areas could be easily enhanced, the trend was less pronounced. In several respects, America was returning to modes of living akin to the nineteen fifties—fewer cars, more commuter rail travel, business centralized in urban or inner suburban areas, etc.

"Europe, being more centralized and possessing better public transportation, needed adjustments on a much lesser scale and, therefore, possessed a certain economic advantage. However, Europe did not escape the economic turmoil of the twenties. Some of the less-productive countries could not meet the qualifications to remain in the Euro zone. In fact, the strong euro hurt their economies. Several needed to exit the Euro zone. Although a few—such as Italy—after restoring their finances, returned to the euro. Countries whose economies grew greatly at the beginning of the century were also better prepared for the change because they adapted to the new economic circumstances as they grew.

"The United States government, through the first three decades of the century, took small, but not truly dramatic, steps toward energy conservation. Much was discussed in terms of shifting larger vehicles to the use of natural gas, increased usage of electricity or hybrid sources for passenger vehicle purposes, etc. Also contemplated was greater emphasis on the use of wind, solar, and nuclear sources for home and commercial power. Much change became bogged down in the political process. No overall plan was developed.

"Conservation was mainly prompted by economic necessity. Americans gave up the second and third family car. The ones they chose were increasingly more fuel-efficient. In general, car companies responded well to consumer needs. They had to; otherwise, the competition would beat them to the punch. They consistently bettered the government-mandated fuel efficiency requirements. Where feasible, families switched to electrocars. Natural gas was used for business fleets, trucks, and buses. But natural gas for passenger vehicles was limited by the slow expansion in the refilling station infrastructure.

"At home, insulation was improved. Houses were kept warmer in summer and cooler in winter. Some people installed solar panels, especially where and when energy tax credits were available.

"In the area of energy production, a few nuclear plants were completed between twenty fifteen and twenty twenty-five. The second decade of the century saw the birth of many windmill power fields in suitable locales. However, the greater use of wind power was hampered by a failure to invest significantly in the modernization of the country's electric grid. Coal-fired plants remained at a fairly constant level, albeit with some adaptations to control pollution emissions.

"Strangely, environmental concerns were somewhat abated by the leveling off of fossil fuel usage in the established economies due to general economic stagnation. However, periodic accidents in deep-water drilling, pipeline and oil transport mishaps, and nuclear power plant crises temporarily refocused the country on environmental issues and slowed the adaptation process. Fossil fuel usage in emerging economies never quite reached anticipated levels, but of course their level of use was much greater than at the end of the twentieth century.

"All the production and conservation steps occurring in the teens and early twenties did not forestall the more drastic dislocations emerging in the late twenties and early thirties. Gasoline did not just become more expensive, it became scarce. Priority was given to commercial needs, and private citizens were deprived. Gasoline theft became all too common, and a black market developed. Home heating oil supplies were inadequate. The Northeast was particularly hard hit. Winter illnesses, such as influenza, became more prevalent.

"Some light rail lines were built where traffic projections warranted, but America had not yet concentrated industry and population sufficiently to make many such ventures viable. Another decade or two would be needed.

"Certainly the country could have benefitted from significant improvements in infrastructure, particularly in the areas of mass transportation and energy distribution. However, the U.S. had one big problem: it was financially strapped.

"It should be pointed out that after World War Two ended, the country experienced an unprecedented increase in the birth rate. This was called the 'Baby Boom.' It started right after the end of the war and reached its peak in nineteen fifty-seven. These 'Baby Boomers,' as they were known, reached prime retirement age in the teens and twenties of this century. They were owed Social Security benefits and Medicare, the old age health benefit then in effect. Both of these programs, especially Medicare, were grossly underfunded. A few rather futile attempts at reform were attempted. But, by and large, politicians were not prepared to tackle a controversial issue and waited for the avalanche of retirees to come. They came, and the government went further into debt to fund these benefits. By twenty thirty, eighty-five percent of Federal expenditures went to pay debt service and entitlement programs. That left very little for the military, education, and all the other services people expected.

"The rate of inflation increased throughout the decade of the twenties, topping at twenty-five percent, in twenty twenty-eight. That was a presidential election year. Americans were shell-shocked and apathetic. Neither political party seemed to be able to tackle their problems. A number of congressional candidates ran under a new political banner: the National Unity Party. Both old parties played down their nominating conventions, and neither candidate ran on his party's record. Americans, with some good reason, sensed that the system was broken, and a certain significant percentage felt it was beyond repair. Americans' perennial optimism was at a low point. For two decades, the vast majority of Americans were just getting by. Unemployment remained stubbornly high, and fewer well-paid middle class jobs existed. The standard of living had declined over the second and third decades of the century.

"The next four years did not bring improvement. By the election of twenty thirty-two, only forty percent of American families owned a car. Only three percent owned two. Gas was frequently unavailable at any price, and the price reached a hundred dollars a liter. Of course, a loaf of bread cost fifty dollars—just to give you an idea of the inflation that had occurred.

"Americans had had enough with halfway measures. In twenty thirty-two, over sixty percent voted for John David Koster, the candidate of the National Unity Party who promised drastic changes. He was honest enough to warn the electorate that the medicine required to cure the nation's ills would not be very palatable. But the majority of Americans were willing to try it.

"Koster and a pliable Congress quickly got to work. He did not advocate protective tariffs. Instead, the U.S. required letters of import to document all products entering the country. These, Koster explained, were instituted so we could track shipments in case of defects, safety problems, etc. Of course, these letters of import came with hefty fees to cover government administrative costs and then some. But, Koster insisted, they did not represent a tariff.

"Koster did not raise taxes on most Americans. However, he was concerned that Americans were not saving enough for their own security and retirement. So Americans soon found that five percent of their income was going into a government-run savings account. If one withdrew money in the first three years, negative interest was paid—or subtracted, depending on your point of view. For the next three years, no interest was paid, but, thereafter, five percent per annum accrued. Thus long-term savings was encouraged, and coincidentally billions in interest-free loans were given to the government in the guise of savings accounts.

"The term 'Social Security' was officially replaced by 'Social Assistance' to highlight the fact that distributions to the elderly would only provide a small portion of what they would need to live on.

"Healthcare in many ways helped to bankrupt the United States. Medicare had never operated on sound economic principles. With the addition of millions of Baby Boomers to the Medicare rolls, it required huge subsidies to stay afloat. Koster took the dramatic step of consolidating health plans for the young and old. A standard base plan of care was established and offered through a number of insurance organizations or, as a last resort, through the federal government. There was a lifetime cap on the amount the base plan would pay on behalf of any individual. Supplemental plans could be offered by sanctioned insurance companies. Large physician networks allied with regional hospital systems were encouraged. A single set of rules for medical reimbursements was established. Within two years, the system was up and running. Within four years it was operating on a break-even basis with incoming premiums equaling medical payments and administrative expenses.

"The medical system solved one economic problem, but it engendered complaints from physicians (who deemed themselves underpaid), and from claimants (who might have been restricted from certain costly and unproven medical treatments). Certain procedures, such as joint replacements, experienced waiting periods.

Jacqueline, after a quarter-hour of silence, piped up. "Isn't this really the medical system we have today?"

"With some modifications, yes, it's essentially the same system."

"It can be okay, but sometimes it sucks. I had a . . . well, I had a problem. It was difficult to find a doctor to treat me quickly, and time was important."

I wondered whether Jacqueline's problem was with the medical system or whether the procedure was one that many physicians in the socially conservative South chose not to perform. But I would not pry. "Yes, the system is hardly perfect. But it's what the country can afford. Let's move on."

"Anything you say, professor." Jacqueline smiled sweetly.

"The last major economic change in Koster's first term involved a revaluation of the currency. On January 1, 2035, seventy-three old dollars became one new dollar. It would have been easier to divide by one hundred, but Koster didn't want people to continue to calculate wages, prices, etc. in terms of the old dollar. A factor of seventy-three made such a task more inconvenient. And, sure enough, in a few months people were comfortable with the new dollar.

"At the beginning of Koster's second term, under the guise of simplifying the tax code, he eliminated the charitable deduction, capped the amount of mortgage interest that could be claimed in any year, and canceled a dozen other tax credits and exemptions. The clergy denounced Koster as an atheist. The construction industry said he was destroying the American dream of home ownership. However, private home ownership had already been greatly in decline.

"In return for the elimination of these tax preferences, the two lowest tax brackets had their rates reduced by two percentage points. Overall the changes brought in more revenue rather than less.

"I should mention that the biggest changes in Koster's second term were not economic but, rather, governmental. People had been unhappy with the cost and inefficiency of government. They were sick of the endless political campaigns, particularly when they despised a fair percentage of the candidates running for national office. A major change was made, and it required a constitutional amendment.

"In response to the common complaint that the major objective of any politician was to get reelected, term limits were established. Both congressmen and senators were limited to two consecutive terms. In addition, a congressman's term was lengthened to four years, so the election season was not continuous.

I noticed that Jacqueline's eyelids were beginning to close. "I think, class, we'll stop here, and save the rest of the overview for next week. Any questions?"

Jacqueline perked up. "Aren't you going to tell us what sort of tests will be given? Are there any papers to do?"

"Yes, I guess I should cover that, but I haven't made a decision."

"You probably have to give a final," Jacqueline suggested the minimal requirement.

"Plus a mid-term exam and a paper, I should think."

"Please remember that many of us have jobs and don't have an endless amount of time to spend on studies." Jacqueline made one last pitch for a modest workload.

"And I hope you'll remember that I want to provide a legitimate college-level course. Any other comments?"

"Just one. There was something I thought you'd include, but didn't."

"And what was that?"

"The chaos and lawlessness of the twenties. Weren't there all sorts of protests and gangs of thieves roaming the streets of many American cities?"

"Yes, that's true. And the suburbs weren't immune, either. Of course, the course is about economics. I'm sure I'll include something about the violence when we drill down into that period later in the course."

Jacqueline looked puzzled and was determined to make one last point. "Are you saying that this thievery and the protests weren't related to economic conditions?"

"Hmm. You have a point." I looked appraisingly at Jacqueline. I always figured she possessed a lot of street smarts, but there was real intelligence behind the pretty, albeit rough, exterior. "They were stealing to get money. Gas delivery trucks had to operate in convoys for protection. If I recall correctly, since the twenties, eighty percent of the wealth in this country has been in the hands of the wealthiest five percent of the population. Many of the protests centered on wealth imbalance. I will have to talk about the violence in this context."

"That would be good. It would add to the level of interest."

"You found the information dull?"

"No. Not at all. But a lot of students' minds wander. Violence always makes people sit up and take note."

"I'll keep that in mind and look for more examples to spice up my lectures. If there's nothing else, class dismissed."

Jacqueline approached me, put her hand on my shoulder, and planted a kiss on my cheek. "Thank you for giving me a personal lesson."

"It was my pleasure, Ms. Bellan."

"You said the class was dismissed. You can call me Jacqueline again, James."

XVIII

San Francisco, 2054-56

BEFORE LEAVING FOR SAN FRANCISCO, Jane and I were married in New Jersey, a location convenient for both of our families. We invited a modest number of friends, including Kate Hastings and Steve Durham. Neither ended up coming. In total, only eight friends and a dozen relatives attended.

Jane wore a tailored cream-colored dress with no veil. A justice of the peace conducted the ceremony. Jane's mother felt obliged to observe that neither the ceremony nor the brief party that followed was traditional enough for her tastes. However, Jane and I felt that a modest affair was in line with current practices and economic circumstances.

After spending our wedding night in a hotel near Newark Airport, we flew directly to San Francisco. We had rented, via the multinet, a furnished studio apartment for a month. Under my moving plan provisions, the government paid the first two weeks' rent. In addition to my airfare, the moving plan provided a lump sum of eight thousand dollars to defray other expenses. Since we were moving few belongings, we figured we could pocket most of the amount.

Before starting work, we took a few days to tour San Francisco. During my college days, I had spent a few days in the city, but, to Jane, it was all new and even a bit exotic. Her initial impressions were favorable.

Through Kate's efforts, Jane had been assigned to an admin assistant position at the customs office. Her rank was reduced and her pay cut a bit, but with my increase we felt we could get along quite well.

What we hadn't counted on was the higher cost of living in San Francisco. We first looked at apartments in the city, and quickly found that any acceptable ones were out of our price range. The furnished studio we rented for our first month was in a convenient location within the city, and consequently we could not afford to stay there without the initial aid we got from the government. So there was some pressure to find something affordable. We finally did. It was outside the city limits near a BART line that headed to the airport. The apartment was dark and uninviting. The area was rundown. But it was what we could afford.

Our first several months in San Francisco were exciting. Jane and I worked about a kilometer apart. Occasionally we met for lunch. More often, we stayed in the city for dinner. Over the course of three months we must have tried nearly twenty different Chinese restaurants, plus a sizeable number of others—Italian, continental, seafood—all representative of San Francisco's bounty.

We also took two long weekend trips. One was to Sonoma County, north of San Francisco. Half the wineries had closed since its heyday near the beginning of the century. With the reduction in tourism, many of the bed and breakfasts had shut their doors, as well. We did find one in Healdsburg. I borrowed the electro-hybrid that was assigned to my office, and Jane and I made the two-hour trip one Friday afternoon. We toured three of the wineries that still accepted visitors, and later had a good meal at a restaurant on the town square in Healdsburg. On Sunday we headed home with a half case of wine serving as our souvenir.

A month later we scheduled a bus tour down the coast to Carmel and then on to the Hearst Castle at San Simeon. The trip was delayed by a week because the tour company did not receive its full natural gas allocation on time. The bus was comfortable, and made more so by its being only half full. We spent the first night in Carmel before heading farther south. The Hearst mansion was open to tourists only on weekends. It was obvious that the property could have used better maintenance, but I suspected the reduced tourist traffic through the relatively remote area didn't generate enough revenue to keep the facility up to standard. On the way home, we spent the second night in Monterey. When we returned home, Jane and I wondered if the sojourn had been worth the two thousand dollars spent. We vowed to start economizing. We could not continue to dip so deeply into the cornucopia that was San Francisco as to jeopardize our finances.

Suddenly we found saving was more important than ever. Jane was pregnant. She worked through continual nausea in the first trimester, and then growing discomfort in the next. By the end of the seventh month, she had had enough of contending with mass transit and work and began a maternity leave—from which she would never return.

After a lengthy labor, she gave birth to a healthy, good-sized boy, whom we named Mark. Two days later, I brought Jane and Mark back to our one-bedroom apartment. Suddenly, I had to learn to get a decent night's sleep with a baby crying in the same room. Jane was breast-feeding Mark. So I had no obligation to get up for any feedings. Still, once awake, I found it difficult to get back to sleep.

This led to my being less congenial when in the office. Fortunately there was a good second in command, Keith Wheatley, who, at least temporarily, became a buffer between the staff and me.

My boss did not look over my shoulder. He was back in Washington. Leo Frase was the Director of Administration and a veteran of the department. I knew him well when I worked for Kate. Of course, Jane knew him, too. He wore old-fashioned black-rimmed glasses and had an unruly mane of salt-and-pepper hair. He provided advice to me as if I was one of his offspring—or at least an offspring of the Federal Energy Department. I thought of him as an old salt, although he was probably no more than fifty.

It was Leo's goal to visit each of the regional offices at least once per year. He always took an extra day in San Francisco. If possible, he even made two trips to the West Coast per year: one in summer to escape Washington's heat, and one in winter to escape the cold. But he always seemed to have a good business reason for the visit.

During Leo's third or fourth visit to San Francisco, we dined at a French bistro-style restaurant. We talked for an hour about regional issues. Then Leo asked, "What do you want to be doing in five years?"

An employee or applicant for employment should always be prepared for this question, but I was not. "I don't know. It's not something I think about frequently."

"But you do on some occasions." Leo pressed the issue.

"I suppose I do. I guess there's one thing I'm sure of. I don't want to be running a regional office." I saw Leo's jaw stiffen. "Not that there's anything wrong with administration. I just don't think that's my strong suit. I'm a policy guy."

"Perhaps you shouldn't limit yourself," Leo suggested.

"I think my training and preferences lead me in that direction."

"You know, if you return to the policy area, Kate won't be there."

"I'm not looking to return to Kate; I'm looking to return to what I like the most."

"Okay. I'll accept your reasoning. I have another issue. Your office has two vacancies on the books. With the economy lagging, the president wants the government to do its part in helping the employment situation."

"With the slow economy, we have more than enough staff to handle our responsibilities. Our workload, as you know, fluctuates with economic activity."

"I understand your point, but I want you to be creative. Increase cross-training. Attend to lower priority items. You'll figure it out."

Leo winked.

I had enough of a political sense to avoid suggesting that he was asking me to devise "make work" projects. Instead, I merely said, "I get your point."

Leo looked at the dessert menu that had just arrived. "Now, how about some profiteroles?"

Early the next morning, Keith Wheatley popped into my office, curious about how my dinner with Frase went. I assured him it had gone well. "As a matter of fact, there's a little job for you to do coming out of our discussion."

"What's that?"

"Leo wants us to fill the two vacancies we have on our books."

"Really? Activity is low right now."

"That's what I told him. But larger issues are involved. I imagine we have a bunch of resumes we can go through."

"Hundreds. I was about to toss the ones which came in more than three months ago."

"Why don't you select the promising ones? In fact, you and Tanya can go ahead and hire the admin assistant. I don't have to be involved in that decision. I trust your judgment. I would like to interview the two or three top candidates for the entry-level technical position."

"Got it," Keith responded and quickly left my office, no doubt intent on immediately starting on the new task.

When Mark was ten months old and beginning to crawl around the apartment, Jane and I came to the conclusion that we needed more space, even if it required moving farther from downtown San Francisco. After looking for a month, we found a two-bedroom apartment we could afford, which was past the airport. It had not been maintained well and required some sprucing up. Jane and I decided to paint the two bedrooms ourselves, intending to do the living room when we had the time.

A few weeks after moving in, I received a call at the office. "James, you son-of-a-bitch, you must have moved and didn't let me know."

"Nice way to say hello, Steve."

"You deserved it."

"I haven't heard from you for months. What's on your mind now?"

"I called to find out how you're doing. How's your lovely wife? How's the bambino?"

"We're all fine. How about you?" I asked, knowing that Steve would get to the intent of his call in his own good time.

"Couldn't be better. I wanted to let you know that I'm taking an assignment in China. I'll be in Beijing for at least six months, but it will probably last longer. What do think of that?"

"Sounds fascinating."

"I'll be passing through San Francisco. Can I invite myself to dinner? I guess I already did."

"Then all you have to do is tell me if you're accepting your invitation."

"Gladly."

"And do you mind telling me when you're arriving?"

"Friday night."

"The day after tomorrow?"

"Glad to see you can still read a calendar. Is there any problem?"

"No. Jane will be happy to see you. Do you need a place to sleep?"

"No, the U.S. government will pick up the tab for a hotel at the airport."

"Well, we live close to the airport. That will be convenient."

"Say, I'll have a friend with me. Actually, she's a friend of yours, too. You remember Pat."

"Pat Auriga? I sure do. I didn't realize that you and Pat were still seeing each other."

"Well, it's a long story. We split up before you got married. Somehow or other we got back together about three months ago. She's going to spend some time with me in China."

"That's nice."

"You said that like you don't approve."

"Don't be silly. You two do what you want."

"The government's not paying for Pat." For some reason, Steve was feeling a bit guilty—a strange emotion for him—about the arrangement.

"You don't need to explain to me."

"I thought I should let you know, so you don't think you can be a whistle-blower and turn me in." Steve forced a laugh.

"Steve, you're acting weirder than normal."

"You think so? Thanks. I wouldn't want to start appearing normal. Anyway, I'll call you when we get into town."

When I told Jane about Steve's visit, she reacted coolly. "We'll have to figure out something to feed him."

"Them. He's bringing his girlfriend."

"Great," Jane reacted sarcastically. "Women are fussier than men. We could have given Steve a hamburger, and it would have been okay."

"You wouldn't have done that."

"No. I suppose not. We'll get some steaks, and you can grill them."

I had expected Jane to ask some questions about Steve's girlfriend, but she didn't. Evidently her curiosity was not aroused.

Jane welcomed Pat warmly when she met her. Perhaps she had expected Steve to bring a flashier date. Pat was a bit shorter than Jane. She was still an attractive brunette, but certainly not beautiful, and she was obviously not some young chippy.

Pat picked up Mark, when he crawled over to greet her. She told Jane that she thought he was handsome and strong for his age. I doubted that Pat had been around many babies, but I said nothing.

Steve gave Mark a cursory look. "Yup, he's a baby." At dinner, Steve faced away from Mark, so he couldn't see the mashed peas being shoveled into the baby's mouth. He seemed pleased when Mark was about to be put to bed. Whereas Pat gave Mark a goodnight kiss on the cheek, Steve gave him a wave of his hand, as if to dismiss the baby from his presence.

When Jane returned from Mark's bedroom, Steve declared, "I have some stuff that I don't want to carry into China. We should use it tonight. Better than bringing wine. Right?"

"What sort of stuff?" Jane asked innocently.

"Oh, it has many names—Mary Jane, pot, grass, weed. It's legal here in California, isn't it?"

"It's legal for medicinal purposes." I added, "But no one gets busted for indulging at home."

"Then let's do it. Wine and weed—great combination."

"Let's do it," Jane assented with surprising enthusiasm.

While Steve rolled a fat joint, I put on some rock music from the last century. Steve struck a match as "Light My Fire" began. Jane took a healthy draw. Pat barely participated. "It's rather harsh. I'm afraid for my voice," she explained, by way of an excuse.

The marijuana along with another bottle of Sonoma pinot noir soon produced a mellow effect, lowering inhibitions. The bottle of wine, like the joint, was passed around communally while we all sat on the floor. Jane tried to match Steve in terms of gulps of wine and inhalation of the mild narcotic. She was seated between Steve and me and across from Pat. As she drank more, she leaned against me and then against Steve. "I wanna find the most comfable . . . comfortable lap. Maybe it's James, maybe it's Steve. Maybe I'll even try Pat's."

Pat shrugged at Jane's behavior. Steve, on the other hand, reacted suggestively: "Put your head on my tummy. Any lower and you'll find it too hard for your liking."

Jane may not have understood Steve's insinuation. "I always like a hard pillow."

"This ain't no pillow."

Steve and Jane laughed uncontrollably. Pat and I didn't even smile.

Steve soon added. "I have an idea. Why don't we all strip to our underwear and get in a pile. We'll see who ends up with who."

"Great idea," Jane quickly responded and began to fumble with her blouse buttons. "But why stop with the underwear?"

"Janie, you're a girl after my own heart." Then Steve turned to me. "Jamie, did I ever tell you what a great wife you have?"

The question was rhetorical, and I did not respond. Steve quickly added, "And I bet she has great tits, too."

"You'll see in a minute. These damn buttons must be glued." Steve laughed heartily at Jane's comment, but only Jane joined in the laughter.

Jane continued to fumble. "With your permission, Jamie, I'll give Jane a little helping hand."

"You *don't* have my permission."

"Steve, I think we should leave," Pat added.

"Oh, you're both prudes. But we're not, are we, Janie?"

"Are what?" Jane had stopped fumbling with buttons, and had, in fact, stopped doing anything, including comprehending the conversation.

"I don't want to go. I'm having fun," Steve declared loudly.

"Steve, let's leave. You're going to wake the baby."

"Babies wake up. Then they go back to sleep. Let's have an orgy."

"No one else wants an orgy." I tried to set Steve straight. "Not me. Not Pat."

"But Janie does. Don't you?"

By this point, Jane was falling asleep and did not respond.

"Janie, I'm talking to you," Steve raised his voice again.

Pat said, "I'm going to make some coffee. I think Steve and I need some. Then we'll go."

"I need nothing of the sort. I need another joint, more vino, and some sex."

Without replying, Pat went into the kitchen, and I followed to help with the coffee. "I apologize for Steve's behavior."

"He tends to get carried away when he's high. I've been his friend for a long time. I've seen him like this more than you have."

"I'm going to give you the rest of the grass. I don't want him to be tempted to take it into China. All we need is some diplomatic incident." Pat gave me a little smile.

"I'll take it, but I'll probably flush it down the toilet."

"Do with it as you wish." There was a pause. Then Pat asked, "Do you think it's a mistake for me to go with Steve to China?"

"I'm in no position to judge."

"I'm supposed to be there for three months. I doubt if I'll stay that long."

"Then why are you going?"

"Steve can be charming and very persuasive. Plus, it's a grand adventure. I'm going to study traditional Chinese music."

"So you're on a professional assignment."

"I try to think of it that way. The coffee's ready. Let's get some into Steve, and we'll be on our way."

Fifteen minutes later, Steve and Pat were ready to leave. Steve was in a bad mood as he came down from his high. "I'm not coming back here soon. Treated like a complete shit."

"You *were* a complete shit." The words came from Pat, not me.

"I was delightful, and if you had had some grass, you would have thought so, too."

Pat pushed Steve out the door and kissed me on the cheek. "I hope we meet again under better circumstances." She thrust a small cellophane bag into my fist.

XIX

BY EARLY MARCH, SAVANNAH WAS well into its spring weather. Publicity for the St. Patrick's Day celebrations was omnipresent. The parade—which a half-century earlier was the second largest in the country—now was limited to local families of Irish descent walking the three-kilometer route, joined by a few marching bands and three or four local fire trucks. Gone were the firefighter fife and drum corps from faraway cities and a host of elaborately decorated floats. The spectators were primarily from Savannah and some surrounding towns, and River Street—although still the center for bar hopping—no longer was filled elbow to elbow.

The economic history course that I was teaching was at the middle of the term. I felt that I was doing a pretty good job. Few students had dropped the course. Generally twenty-five to thirty students attended each lecture. Jacqueline missed about a third of the classes. I tried to give her summaries.

I graded her mid-term first. She did reasonably well, showing that she retained most of the material from class and did a good deal of the assigned reading. I gave her an "A," although perhaps an "A minus" was more appropriate.

In general, I tended to be generous with grades. As a new lecturer, I did not want negative comments to circulate among the students. Although I didn't expect to teach beyond the current semester, I didn't want to burn my bridges.

As I was finishing grading the last exams, my phone rang. An unfamiliar incoming number was displayed. "Hello, James?"

"Yes."

"This is Pat, Pat Auriga."

"Hi. I thought I recognized your voice." I probably would have done so after a few more words were spoken.

"How are you doing?"

"Okay. Keeping out of trouble, which for me is an accomplishment. And how are you doing? Still the nightingale of Washington?"

"Well, I suppose you don't know I left American University six months ago."

"I don't think we've spoken."

"I'm not sure that was a great decision. The university provided a steady income. Freelancing is hit or miss."

"I'm sorry things are not going better for you." My sympathy was genuine, and I certainly could relate to her situation.

"It's not all gloom and doom." Pat probably reacted to the pity implied in my tone. "I'm in a group called 'Chanterelle.' We're going to start on a tour shortly. One of our first stops is in Savannah. That kind of led me to call you. Maybe we could get together when I'm in town?" There was a tinge of doubt in Pat's voice. Perhaps she thought I would reject her invitation.

With extra enthusiasm, I replied, "That would be absolutely great. I'll take you out to dinner."

"I'll get you a ticket to the show."

"Don't you mean 'concert'?"

"Well, yes. But I thought I'd make it sound more enticing."

"Believe me, I'm looking forward to it already."

Between this call and a follow-up conversation, Pat and I completed our arrangements. Pat's group was performing as part of the annual music festival, which lasted one week. Fifty years earlier, the festival was three times the size, but as with all such events, it had been periodically scaled back to keep it in line with travel restraints and demand.

Chanterelle's concert took place on a Sunday afternoon. The group was composed of eight female singers. Their skill was apparent, even to a dilettante like me. They were not accompanied by any musical instruments. The program ranged from renaissance to contemporary music, no doubt designed to show off the full extent of the group's abilities.

The concert was held in the Lucas Theatre, a hall with an ornate interior, dating from the early twentieth century. I guessed that the capacity was about twelve hundred; however, the audience may have numbered six hundred. Having never been to a concert at the Lucas before, I did not know whether the turnout represented a success. I felt bad for Pat, singing to a half-empty auditorium.

Employing the regional energy council's electrocar that was on loan to me for the evening, I took Pat to a restaurant in the City Market area. I selected the restaurant for two reasons. First, I was quite sure that Jacqueline did not work there. Second, it was quite dark but spacious, providing a location where Pat and I could dine slowly and talk. The décor was sparse, with a few old photos enlarged to poster size hung on old brick walls.

We ordered glasses of wine and did not even open the menus. I told Pat that I enjoyed the concert a great deal. Unfortunately, I could not come up with appropriate musical terms to describe my appreciation. I told her that I was impressed with the group's coordination despite not having a conductor, and that I was amazed at the various harmonies eight singers could produce.

Pat smiled and thanked me for the compliments. But she did not want to talk about the concert. "Tell me, James, how are you doing? I sense you're living the life of a hermit."

"No. I'm doing okay. I'm teaching a course, and I enjoy that. It's a challenge. I've never taught before. I do some consulting when it comes my way and provide advice to the regional energy council. All that keeps me rather busy." I tried to put a good light on my somewhat grim existence.

"And how about you? You didn't seem thrilled with your life when we spoke on the phone." I tossed the ball back in Pat's court.

Pat shrugged. "I guess I'm doing fine. I'm doing the concert tour, and that will be interesting while it lasts—traveling to different cities, performing before different audiences. But I feel that I'm stuck in a rut. I have a few private voice students. I don't know where my life is heading. I'm approaching forty . . ."

"You're not really. You don't look it."

"Well, I'm certainly over thirty-five. Forty is just around the corner. To be forty and doing the same things that you were when you were twenty-five—that sucks. Shouldn't life progress?"

I might have told Pat that remaining at a given plateau was preferable to going downhill, but I chose to concentrate on Pat and deflect the conversation from me. "So what would you want to be doing?"

"I've thought about that a lot. And the trouble is, I just don't know. Don't get me wrong. I'm a musician. I like being a musician. I'm doing the work I'm trained to do, work I like. It just seems that there should be more."

I wondered whether the problem lay more in Pat's personal life than in her professional life. "Did Steve hurt you?"

"Let's not talk about Steve Durham. That's a closed chapter," Pat replied emphatically. "In fact, let's not talk about the past. You don't want to do that either, do you?"

"No, not at all. So talk about your future."

"I'm not Nostradamus."

Our waiter came over to the table. This was his third approach. We quickly referred to the menu and ordered salad and seafood main courses. With the waiter gone, we returned to our conversation.

"Where were we? Oh, talking about you not being Nostradamus."

"That's right," Pat concurred.

"What would make your life exciting?"

Pat thought for a moment. "A trip to the moon."

"Seriously."

"I just don't know."

I tried to be helpful by sparking a thought. "A new boyfriend?"

"Please. That's just what I *don't* need. Unless you're volunteering."

"You're being kind. Okay, how about a new job?"

"I've been changing jobs. It's akin to going from the frying pan into the fire."

I continued. "Change of scene? Move away from Washington?"

"Where would I go? Did moving to Savannah improve your life?"

"Perhaps it did a bit. Less pressure than in Washington."

"Are you referring to the locale or your job?" Pat questioned.

"Hey. We're trying to focus on your problem, not mine."

"Maybe they're not very different."

"Then if we can solve your problem, I'll have a head start on mine. So let's get back to you."

"You're tricky, James."

"I'm probably one of the most transparent people you know."

"That's what I love about you." Pat blushed. She probably hadn't meant to use the word "love," but having let it out, she couldn't take it back. She could only ignore it. "So what am I going to do?"

I sensed I was hitting a brick wall. I thought quickly. "Where is your tour taking you?"

"After Savannah, we go to Orlando, Sarasota, Charlotte, and Raleigh."

"Maybe you'll find something exciting in one of those towns."

"James, you're reaching. We're trying to set up a tour in

Europe this summer. That's more likely to provide excitement. But I'm not sure it will pan out."

"It would be extraordinary." Perhaps my enthusiasm was overstated. "Where would you be going?"

"No large cities, like Paris, London, Rome. We're pursuing some medium-sized places with festivals of some kind or another. Like Avignon, Florence, Verona, Edinburgh."

"Marvelous. How about taking me along? I could carry the cello."

"We're singers. We don't have a cello."

"If I can't carry the cello, I'll carry you."

Pat was smiling now. She was prettier when she smiled. "You're crazy."

"I'm looking for a way to get on this tour."

"Well, we have no cello. I can walk quite well on my own. I can even wheel my own suitcase."

"Okay. I know when I'm being rejected."

Pat knew I was joking, but she probably thought some truthfulness lurked beneath the surface. She put her hand on top of mine. "You know if I could take anyone along I'd take you. But how would you get along with eight high-strung women?"

"I could try."

"You're being funny."

During our meal, the subject changed. Pat wanted to know more about Savannah. It was a safer subject. In fifteen minutes I hit the highlights: the founding under James Oglethorpe; the siege during the Revolutionary War, including the death of Casimir Pulaski; the invention of the cotton gin; prosperity as a cotton port; the focal point of Sherman's march to the sea; the restoration of the historic district.

When we finished the main course, we passed on dessert. There was still some daylight. I drove down Bull Street and then back on Abercorn to show off a few of the historic squares. The nineteenth-century beauty of the town impressed Pat. We parked on Bay Street and walked down a ramp-like lane to River Street. A few tourists were going from shop to shop. I offered to buy Pat a souvenir. She insisted that I save my money.

We returned to Pat's hotel. She needed to get to bed early because she was leaving at seven for the bus trip to Orlando. "I'm sharing a room. Otherwise, I'd invite you up."

"Then we'll just say good-bye."

"I truly enjoyed this evening."

"And I loved the concert."

"I hope it won't take us another two years to get together."

"I agree," I replied sincerely. "Then let's make a pact to meet before two thousand sixty-four ends."

"That sounds too long. We must keep in touch." Pat kissed me on the lips. It was slightly more than just a friendly kiss. There was a hint of emotion in it. "That seals the deal," she added.

XX

San Francisco, 2056

ON THE MORNING AFTER STEVE and Pat's departure, I had to change Mark's morning diaper and give him breakfast. Jane slept until nine when she stumbled into the kitchen, "I have a bit of a headache. Was I very bad last night?"

"You didn't have much of a chance. Pat and Steve left before things progressed too far."

"What things?"

"You and Steve were thinking about having an orgy."

"But not you and Pat?"

"No. But, of course, you had more grass than us."

"Did I?"

There was no need to answer.

"I'm sorry if I got carried away. I've felt so constrained over the past year with the baby and all. You, at least, have your work."

"You think that's my outlet to blow off steam. How often did you ever see me blow off steam in the office?"

"Well, that was Washington. Here you're the boss."

"And all bosses get out of control."

"You just don't understand my point. Forget it."

We were arguing over a few unfortunate comments and over a night, which I remembered all too well—and Jane could not recollect at all. Admittedly, she had been high, but in my opinion she behaved like a slut. I was ashamed of her more than I was bothered by Steve's actions. Steve was Steve. But Jane revealed a side of her that I didn't know existed and that I certainly didn't like.

"The coffee's ready," I told her.

"You forgive me?"

"Of course."

Jane put her arms around my neck. It would have been better had she not. She smelled of stale wine and too much partying. But I couldn't push her away.

On more and more occasions Jane and I found reasons to argue. Jane would complain about my staying late at work or about my failure to help her around the apartment. I would point out that she had little to do to maintain a two-bedroom apartment and that, at a minimum, she could seek a part-time job to help with the expenses. She, in turn, would declare that a part-time job wouldn't even pay for daycare for Mark.

My real desire for her to get a job stemmed from my feeling that she was becoming lazy. A job would break the cycle of returning to bed after breakfast, doting on daytime TV, and then not even planning a dinner. These thoughts I was reluctant to express.

I knew a communication gap was forming between Jane and me. I chose not to confront it, and so did Jane.

After the disastrous reunion with Steve and the balance of the weekend with Jane, I was pleased to return to the office. I looked at email, including department circulars. Keith knocked on my office door, fifteen minutes before the staff meeting scheduled for nine. Obviously there was something he felt he needed to cover in advance.

"I think we need to tell people that we're adding to staff. They've seen strangers coming in for interviews. If they don't know what's happening, they'll expect the worst."

"And what would that be?"

"That we're replacing some of them with newcomers."

"That's pretty far-fetched."

"Aren't most rumors?"

"Yes, but some rumors are true. How far are you along in the hiring process?"

"I'm about to make an offer for the admin assistant position. The woman has over ten years' experience. Her company went out of business two months ago. She has excellent references. She's very professional."

"And not good looking."

"How did you know?"

"The 'very professional' phrase. But I bet she has a nice personality."

"Okay. But we can't hire for looks," Keith added didactically.

"Just pulling your leg. How's the other position coming along?"

"I'm down to two candidates. I think you should interview them to confirm my opinion. One's a guy. The other's a rather tall, lanky young woman. Her looks might appeal to you."

"I'll have to see if your description is accurate. At any event, let's get them in for interviews, and I can assure you, looks will not influence my opinion.

"The difficult part," I continued, "will involve coming up with meaningful work. I hate to take work away from productive people and divide it up. It makes good people lazy and insecure." I was talking about the office but briefly Jane came to mind.

"For a few months the new person—he or she—can tag along with some of the experienced staff and learn the ropes."

"True," I agreed. "But the newbie has to be heading in some direction toward a legitimate position. I hope activity picks up."

"Don't we all?"

Two weeks after my discussion with Keith, Lisa Ann Karns became an administrative assistant in the office, and two weeks after that Allison McLean joined us as a technician, grade seven. She had less relevant experience than the man we had interviewed, however, she showed a genuine enthusiasm for the job, while the man gave the impression that he would simply deign to accept this entry position for which he was too well qualified. Allison had a bachelor's degree in chemistry from Michigan, and two years' experience working in a laboratory and another year doing temporary work while helping her husband get a master's degree in Texas. They had now separated, and she decided that she needed a change of scene. She always thought she'd like San Francisco and moved there on impulse.

Keith had accurately described Allison. She was tall, only a few centimeters shorter than I, and quite attractive—with long dark hair and large brown eyes. She gesticulated quite a bit when talking, and her long fingers flowed rhythmically like a conductor leading a chorus.

Her training plan was divided into two areas: reading essential departmental policy documents and sitting with experienced staff to see how they performed various tasks.

In order to keep the staff relatively busy during those slack times, Keith and I instituted follow up visits to projects, which had been approved and implemented over the past three years. This was unusual. Normally we would complete the approval process, and then as the project was in the construction phase, we would do one review to determine that implementation was occurring according to plan. Now we were going to review projects that were in operation to make sure that no modifications had been made which would negatively impact energy efficiency.

Keith and I jointly did the first review. Based upon that experience, we made a few changes to the steps and questionnaire that would be employed. Then we each took an experienced staff member on the next two reviews. We found some minor issues to comment on in most visits. The staff knew that this work was not critical, but they were pleased that some work was being added, rather than eliminated.

After conducting these reviews for two months in the San Francisco, Oakland, and San Jose area, I decided that we should range farther afield. Keith took a pair of reviews near Salinas, and I chose two in the Napa area. Allison had not yet been on one of these reviews, and I decided to take her with me.

"Planning to combine business with pleasure?" Keith teased me.

"I hope you're not going to spread such a comment around the office."

"I won't have to."

I gave Keith a sharp look of non-approval. He simply smiled in return.

Three days before Allison and I left for Napa, an unusual report came across the news channels. Russia and China were accusing each other of aggression, invading each other's territory, and causing a significant number of civilian injuries and deaths. Various analysts were trying to sort out the truth from the vague and conflicting statements.

The first reports came in early in the morning. Jane was up taking care of Mark. She asked me, "What do you make of this conflict in China?"

"I don't know. We don't even know if it's occurring in Chinese or Russian territory."

"Some report said it was in northwest China."

"Well, then you know more than I do."

"You don't think this has anything to do with the trip you and Kate took to Vienna?"

"How do you figure that?"

"You were meeting with the Russians. They wanted some cooperation from us with respect to China."

"You're not supposed to know that."

"Oh, come on. You're not answering my question."

"I don't know. It could be connected, but the Russians never really spelled out what they wanted in China."

"Well, as far as I'm concerned, they can kick the shit out of each other. So long as we don't get roped in, we can't get hurt. We might even profit from their conflict," Jane concluded.

When I reached the office, I put a call through to Leo Frase on the secured line to Washington, which I rarely used. He was in conference and couldn't be disturbed. I asked for a call back.

Eventually, around three o'clock West Coast time, Leo returned my call. "James, I need to get out of here for a dinner meeting, but I wanted to reach you before leaving. What's up?"

"That's what I want to find out from you. What's happening in China?"

"You probably know as much as I do."

"That's not an answer." I used Jane's tactic.

"Look, as far as we know it has nothing to do with energy. Ergo, the F.E.D. is not in the loop. State and Defense are on the point."

"In other words you can't tell me what's going on."

"Just stay cool. I'll let you know more when I can. But I really don't know much. And as far as I can tell, regional offices are not impacted at all. Okay?"

"Not really. I'll expect to hear something from you soon."

"We'll see what happens. Just don't hold your breath."

Despite the approach of the dinner hour on the East Coast, I called Kate.

"Hello, James. I bet I know what you're calling about." There was almost a lilt of merriment in Kate's voice.

"What do you know about this situation involving Russia and China?" I got right to the point.

"My friend, I've been out of government for almost two years."

"You didn't answer my question. And I know you still have your sources."

"James, James," she said petulantly. "I really can't talk. But you know that the Russians have had a bee in their bonnet for some time about squeezing China for the resources they've cornered."

"So there's clearly a connection between what's happening

now and what we were doing in Vienna."

"I didn't say that."

"No. You didn't."

"James, just settle down. Don't get in trouble over this. I'm sure people will be filled in on a need-to-know basis."

"And I won't need to know," was my sour reply.

"Let's change the subject. When are you coming to the New York area?"

"There's a regional director meeting in New York in another six weeks."

"Let's get together."

"I'd like that."

"There's something I want to show you."

"What's that?"

"It's a surprise." Kate paused. "And forget about that thing you were talking about. You can't do anything about it anyway. You'll just be frustrated."

"I'll try to put it out of my mind," I told Kate, but I suspected it wouldn't be possible.

On Wednesday morning, Allison McLean and I left the office a little before ten o'clock. A few pairs of eyes followed our exit. It was not that men and women did not go on business calls together, but Allison was the most attractive, youngest, and least senior technician. Why was she going out with the regional director on an overnight trip?

We had an appointment in the afternoon in Petaluma and another the next morning in Napa. We crossed the Golden Gate Bridge, which had one side devoted to cars, trucks and buses and the other side to a light rail line. Traffic leaving the city at ten was negligible. Once over the bridge, the electro-hybrid hummed along at eighty kilometers per hour.

During the ride north, Allison and I talked about work. She took the opportunity to ask a number of questions. One involved the history of the review we were about to perform. I told her that the review was recently created, but had been based on the reviews we did when a project was nearing completion. I explained that we had decided to initiate these reviews because we were concerned that organizations may have deviated from requirements after our final inspections. Such was my convenient lie. I did not want to tell Allison that her position was not needed and that we had to devise work to keep the staff occupied.

We arrived in the Petaluma area around eleven thirty and decided to go on toward Santa Rosa to find a place to eat. At lunch, Allison asked me what I thought about the confrontation between Russia and China. I told her that I was not sure what to think. I had no inside information. Probably the people in the State Department knew more, but not us. I thought briefly about Steve Durham, still in China, and wondered whether he was caught up in the affair in some way or another. Strangely, I was not worried about him—Steve would always manage to wheedle his way out of any tight corner; plus he had the State Department behind him— but I was concerned about Pat Auriga. I hoped that she had left China before everything happened. She had visited us four months earlier. Perhaps she had wrapped up her work in Beijing.

My mind had drifted, and Allison noticed that I was not paying attention. "You look like you're far away."

"A few thousand kilometers away. I have friends who are probably in Beijing right now."

"I hope they're safe," Allison said, appropriately but blandly.

"Yes, I hope so."

Our meeting at the warehouse operation went smoothly, once we overcame some suspicion of the local manager that we were on a faultfinding expedition. We told him that we only wanted to advise him of procedures which might be short of commitments made when the operation was expanded five years earlier. If we found deficiencies, the facility would have ample time to make adjustments. No penalties would be incurred.

I was not sure that my words or tone really represented assurances, but the manager relaxed both in body language and conversation. We asked a series of questions, and then took a tour of the operation. We reviewed some data on energy usage.

The portion of the facility which had been converted to agricultural storage attracted most of our attention, since more energy was required to assure proper humidity and temperature control. Although we found no serious areas of concern, we did point out some small issues that warranted change. The manager realized that these items could be rectified rather easily. We concluded the wrap up meeting, promised a written summary, and shook hands.

Around five o'clock, Allison and I left Petaluma and headed toward Napa where our hotel was located. I drove slowly along the back roads in order to enjoy the rolling scenery. The hotel contained only about fifteen rooms, but was mostly empty despite the grape harvest being in progress.

We freshened up and then went to a local restaurant that the hotel manager had recommended. The décor was rustic, but a corner booth provided some privacy and a degree of comfort.

I asked Allison about her initial impressions of the F.E.D. and the job she had taken. She told me that she was still bewildered by the scope and structure of the department, overall, although she felt comfortable in the local office. As for the job, she appreciated getting the opportunity and was finding the work interesting.

Then she turned to her personal situation. "I really didn't think I'd get the job. I thought you'd have candidates with more relevant experience. My last job was part-time and clerical in nature."

"I think your enthusiasm tipped the scale in your favor," I suggested.

"Thanks. I really needed the job badly. I came out to California on a lark—or maybe it was an escape. Ted, my former husband . . . no, I guess he's still my husband. Our divorce is not finalized. Anyway, he got a job in Atlanta. I wanted to head in the opposite direction.

"After helping him get his master's degree, I found he really liked a certain petite blonde more than his tall, brunette wife. Karen was another student in his master's program. I think they planned to get together after graduation. They let me help Ted financially until he finished the degree, and then I got dumped. They both ended up in Atlanta. I was used and deceived. That hurts more than the breakup of the marriage itself."

"You got a raw deal."

"True, but I can also say that I was fortunate to find out what a bastard Ted was before we spent many years together and had kids and all that."

"It's good that you can see the positive side," I commented mechanically.

"What else can I do? I'm still young. I have a lot of my life ahead of me. Can't cry over spilt milk." Allison had said all that she wanted to say about her marriage. "I guess I've talked about myself enough. Tell me about yourself, if you don't mind. I hear you have a little boy."

"Yes, his name is Mark. He's one and a half and gets into everything. I guess all toddlers do." I veered away from further talk of my family. "I grew up in New Jersey. Then I went to college at Stanford."

"So you knew the area before you took the job in San Francisco."

"I spent practically all my time in Palo Alto. Even a decade ago, it was expensive to get around. And San Francisco is not a cheap place to visit."

"Or to live in."

"True. And then I got a master's degree at the University of Georgia."

"In Atlanta?"

"No, the bulk of the university is in Athens, about a hundred kilometers east of Atlanta. Then I went to work for the F.E.D.

Spent some time in New York, then Washington, and now I'm here in San Francisco."

I realized that I had breezed through a lot of personal history very quickly. But I didn't want to go into many details. I didn't want to talk about Jane or Kate, or cover my frustrations or even successes at the F.E.D.

I steered the conversation back to Allison. I asked her about her time in Ann Arbor and then found out that she grew up in a Chicago suburb. Chicago was a city I had only visited once. That part of the conversation petered out.

Being in the Napa Valley, we talked about food and wine. Allison told me that she hoped to learn about California wine, since she now was visiting prime wine country. I started to share some knowledge, not mentioning that much of it came from Kate. Wine was a safe subject, conjuring up no unpleasant memories for either of us.

The next morning we had breakfast together, put our minimal luggage in the electro-hybrid, and traveled the ten kilometers to the wine storage facility we were going to audit. The introductions were made, and we followed Kyle Brant, the manager, to his office, so we could explain our task.

He listened politely for a few minutes. Then he asked, "How long will this take? You know we have to close the office at noon to let employees get home by two."

I was stupefied. "Why are you closing? What's happening?"

"You heard the warning this morning. It's all over the news."

"We didn't listen to the news."

"There's some fear that nuclear fallout is coming over the West Coast at some time between late afternoon and tomorrow morning."

"Is it a power plant problem?" Allison asked.

"No. It's probably something the Chinese or the Russians did. Set off a dirty bomb when the border fighting started."

I suggested that Kyle take Allison on a brief tour of the facility.

I wanted to call my office, and based on the information I received, the balance of the review could be postponed.

I reached Keith instantaneously. He spoke before I could. "Where have you been? I've been trying to reach you."

"I guess I turned the phone off last night and forgot to turn it back on this morning. What's happening?"

"I told the office staff that they must all go home at noon. That's what businesses and government offices have been instructed to do."

"But what's happening? Why the emergency?"

"I haven't gotten any details from Washington, but Leo wants to talk to you. Maybe he'll be able to tell you more."

"I'll call him, and if there's more to tell, I'll call you back."

I expected Keith to sign off; instead he asked, "And what are you going to do? You and Allison shouldn't be caught on the road this afternoon."

"Your point is well taken. We'll figure something out."

After ending the call with Keith, I immediately phoned Leo Frase. He spoke before I could. "Where the hell are you?"

"North of San Francisco, doing a facilities audit."

"A what?"

"The work you want done. Nevermind. Can I get some real info about what's going on this time?" I put the onus back on Leo.

"The world's going to hell. That's what's happening. Evidently the Chinese exploded a dirty bomb to deter the Russians. Some of the material, through some sort of error, got into the atmosphere. Winds are bringing it across the Pacific. Using satellite data, a number of scientists think that northern California might get some of it."

"What are we expected to do?"

"Well, it won't be a Chernobyl, but there's some Cesium-137, Strontium-90, and Plutonium in the jet stream. Orders have been issued for people to stay indoors from this afternoon through noon tomorrow. If we detect fallout, we'll try to identify the hot spots and cordon them off until they can be cleaned up."

"But those elements have pretty long half-lifes. If we get fallout, it doesn't dissipate in a day or two. It takes years."

"That's true, Einstein. That's the point in finding the hotspots and cleaning them up. We can't keep people bottled up for days. We have to get a handle on the situation. Maybe we'll all be okay. We don't know more at this point. If you're religious, you can pray." I said nothing. Leo continued. "Is Jane with you?"

"No, she's at home."

"She probably has gotten the word, but you better talk to her."

"Yes, Dad, as soon as I finish with you."

"Now you know everything I know. Maybe you even know more. You were with Kate in Vienna."

"You think it has a connection to that trip? Nothing ever came of our talks."

"Nothing for us. But the Russians had something in mind."

"I bet the two aren't connected," I said with more conviction than I possessed.

Immediately after ending the call with Leo, I tried to reach Jane. There was no answer. This made me uneasy. I wondered why her phone was off.

Kyle, the manager, was now returning with Allison from their tour. He looked nervous and confessed to me that Allison had spotted a problem. Their only problem, he added quickly. Non-insulated doors led to the loading dock. Originally, proper doors had been installed, but they warped and malfunctioned. Plywood doors were put up. New doors had been ordered a number of months ago. They had not arrived yet. Someone had forgotten to follow up. Kyle berated himself for not doing so himself. He hoped no fine would be imposed.

I pointed out that we were not there to punish. We simply wanted any deficiencies to be rectified.

Kyle thanked me for my understanding. I told him that, in view of the pending emergency closing, it was probably best for Allison and me to leave. We might return in another few months to complete the audit. Of course, by then we would expect the door problem to be fixed.

Kyle swore it would be.

At that moment, Jane returned my call. I asked for some privacy, so both Allison and Kyle waited in the corridor.

Jane had been speaking to her mother before I tried to reach her. Her mother was frantic after hearing the news reports. She was sure San Francisco would be ground zero for some disaster which was only vaguely defined in her mind. Jane stayed on the call for nearly an hour, trying to calm her mother. Then Jane noticed that her phone battery was low, and she turned it off, so it would recharge faster. That's why she missed my call.

"I understand. I just wanted to make sure that you and Mark are safe and know what precautions to take." Jane told me that she did. She needed to run out to get some more food in the apartment. Then she and Mark, she assured me, would barricade themselves inside. She asked if I would get home by two.

"I'm not sure. I might have to stay up here for the night. Will you be okay without me?

"I wish you could make it back."

"I'm not sure I can in time."

"Then, of course, you'll have to stay. Mark and I will be okay for the night. It's not going to be the apocalypse. We won't have high winds and thunder."

"No, all that might happen is some radioactive material may fall. But trained crews will promptly clean that up. When the all-clear is given, everything will be fine." I tried to state all this with an air of assurance, which in truth I did not possess. "Jane, I'll call you back in a little while and let you know if I'm staying or will be home this afternoon."

I exited the office and joined Allison and Kyle. I looked at my watch. It was now ten thirty. "I guess if we leave right now, we can make it back to San Francisco by about one."

"Unless the emergency causes delays," Kyle suggested.

"Then, of course, we have to get home from the city." I turned to Allison. "Where do you live?"

"Near Walnut Creek. It takes me about forty-five minutes to get to my stop on the BART from downtown."

"And then how long from the station to your home?"

"It's a ten-minute walk."

"There's no margin for error. Everyone might be taking the trains at the same time. It seems like we're cutting it too close. Maybe we can get our hotel rooms for another night."

"The hotel was practically empty." Allison seemed inclined to stay. "Of course, I don't have another change of clothes."

"Neither do I."

"We'll be grubby together."

I called the hotel. They told me that the rooms were available. The assistant manager was going to sleep at the hotel to attend to guests' needs. However, they advised us to bring sandwiches, drinks, and something for breakfast. There would be no food available, only ice, a few soft drinks, and coffee.

We stopped at a grocery store, which was busy with people getting last-minute supplies. We bought four sandwiches, snacks, donuts, and plenty of soda and bottled water.

At the hotel, a freckle-faced young man, about twenty-five years of age, greeted us. "I'm Sean. I'm the assistant manager. I'll be staying here tonight to share the adventure. We only have six guests tonight. Feel free to use the lounge to eat in. There's an ice machine just through those doors." He pointed past the lounge. "I'm going to shut off the water supply to the ice maker at two, so we don't get radioactive ice." Sean chuckled. "But we won't turn the water to the rooms off. Shower at your own risk.

"Frankly, I think the government is trying to scare us. They always do. That's politics."

I couldn't comprehend what political advantage could be gained from radioactive fallout. Nor did Sean suspect that he was talking to federal government employees.

Sean continued, "So just make yourselves at home. If there's anything I can do for you, let me know, although I don't know what I can actually do, since I'm trapped here, too.

"Let's see. You have rooms eight and nine. You both stayed here last night. So welcome back. Don't worry about the scare. I'm sure it won't amount to anything. It never does."

"I'll bow to your expertise," I squeezed in the comment to end Sean's monologue. We snatched our keys and went upstairs.

Outside our doors, I asked Allison if she wanted to go to the lounge to eat our lunch sandwiches.

"No, thanks. Let's leave Sean to his own devices. I think he enjoys having a captive audience. Why don't you stop into my room when you're ready to partake of our magnificent feast."

"I'm going to unpack and call Jane again. So give me about a half hour."

Jane had assumed that I was staying in Napa. She had not yet left the apartment to get the extra provisions because Mark took an unusual late-morning nap. He was waking now, and she assured me she would leave as soon as possible. I urged her not to delay.

With sandwich and cola in hand, I went next door to Allison's room. The TV was on, and she was focusing on the latest news about the radiation threat. Monitoring devices indicated that normal levels were being detected at high altitudes two hundred kilometers west of the coast.

The hope was that no precipitation would fall. Rain would bring down radiation from the higher altitudes. Currently the chance of precipitation was ten percent. The frequent San Francisco fog, being near the surface, was not expected to be a factor in determining fallout.

After spending an hour with Allison, digesting both the news and the food, I went back to my room. I checked to see if there was more precise information about the emergency coming from Washington. There was none. I switched the page palette to a book I had started to read before leaving home. In the background, the TV was on, so I could read and follow news updates at the same time.

At four o'clock a report stated that a few readings in the San Francisco area showed a slight elevation in background radiation levels. No precise locations were given for these results. It was pointed out that the readings obtained were not dangerous, but people were reminded to stay inside for the night and especially cautioned not to get involved with clean-up crews which could begin work as early as six in the evening.

I called Jane again. She answered immediately. "Is everything okay?" I asked.

Jane hesitated for just a second. "Yes, of course."

"Everything fine with Mark?"

"Sure. He's taking another nap. We'll be fine. We're just waiting, trapped like everyone else. What are you doing?"

"I've been reading."

"Will you be able to get something to eat?" Jane suddenly realized that my situation might be less cushy than hers.

"I bought a few sandwiches earlier. I'll be fine."

"Good."

There was nothing else to say except good-bye. Gone were the days when we closed a conversation by saying that we loved each other.

A little later, I rejoined Allison. We ate our dinner sandwiches and watched more news. Outdoor shots were restricted, but there were no reports of emergencies. The elevated radiation levels had now crossed the central valley and were heading toward the mountains. Higher readings were obtained above three thousand meters. Ground level readings were declared to be "acceptable," whatever that meant. Allison asked me questions about interpreting the information being received. I could provide few insights.

We turned the TV to a music channel and began to converse. She told me more about her failed marriage, and the abuse, verbal rather than physical, that she had endured. Her husband criticized her for only having a part-time job. He wanted her to earn more money, even while he was earning none. He didn't like scrimping while he obtained his degree. He found fault with Allison's height, with her nose (which seemed fine to me), with her hair (which he said was too long and straight), with her cooking.

Allison pointed out that he knew all these things before they were married. Why did he find fault with everything about her once they were wed? He didn't have a good reply. Of course, the answer was that he had found someone else who appealed to him more.

She stopped her monologue. "I shouldn't be going on like this." She touched my arm lightly. "I apologize."

"No need to apologize. I can see how difficult it was for you. Everyone needs to talk on occasion." I didn't know exactly what to say. I sensed I was pouring one platitude on top of another. "I suppose no marriage is perfect. Only half survive. It's not worth saving a failed marriage." I was not sure whether I was talking about Allison or myself. But no, my marriage had not failed—yet. I needed to work better at it. I vowed to discuss the difficulties rationally with Jane.

Allison and I returned to the news. Nothing of substance was added to what had been reported previously. Even so, normally scheduled programming was preempted. News was continuous. But it didn't change. I thought about how difficult it was for a reporter to spend hours on the air when there was nothing to say. San Franciscans were told to stay indoors until noon on the following day.

I told Allison that I was going back to my room to read a little before going to sleep. "See you around eight for our magnificent breakfast."

"No problem ordering—it's donuts and the hotel's coffee.

Wonder if it will be instant?"

"Hardly a feast."

"It's no picnic."

The next morning, Allison and I made breakfast out of the mini-donuts bought the day before and the weak coffee in the hotel lobby. We needed to wait for noon before leaving. All restaurants in Napa were still shuttered as we left. On the outskirts of Vallejo we spotted a fast food joint that had just opened. We voraciously gobbled down hamburgers and fries.

There was no point in going back to the office. All non-essential business and government facilities were closed for the day. I dropped Allison at her apartment and then headed across the Bay Bridge to home. Jane seemed genuinely happy to see me. We talked about the radioactivity, which was being found in small amounts. She never asked about my business trip.

Within two weeks, the radioactivity scare was fading into the background. A few dangerous sites in the Sierra Nevada Mountains were closed to civilians while clean-up activities progressed. The San Francisco area was declared safe.

If the radioactivity cloud had passed, office discussion about my trip with Allison had not. Keith came into my office late one afternoon when almost everyone else had departed. "I feel, James, there's something I should tell you, even though it's a bit awkward."

"Go ahead."

"There are comments . . . insinuations going around the office about you and Allison and your trip."

"Yes, we did take a business trip. What's the issue?"

"The gossip centers on you staying an extra night."

"This is laughable. We had to stay. Doesn't anyone remember the radiation lockdown?" I was showing my irritation.

"Of course. You *had* to stay." There was a hint of doubt in Keith's tone.

"Well, the whole notion is absurd. Allison and I were strictly on a business trip. That's the way we behaved. There's nothing going on between us. Ask her. Who's spreading this crap around?"

"How can you tell where rumors start?" Keith responded.

"I want it to stop. These are lies. It's slanderous."

"If we overreact, it will create the impression that something in the story is true."

"There's nothing in it that's true. It's a malicious falsehood. Allison and I both know that. Check with her."

"I don't need to. You told me the story is a lie. I believe you."

"So what do we do?" I needed someone else's advice.

"Nothing. Let it die. If nothing else revives the story, it will eventually pass. But it might take some time."

"What do you mean by 'reviving the story'?"

"Things like Allison getting favored treatment; you two going on another overnight trip. Those sorts of things."

"I get the picture."

XXI

I ENJOYED SEEING PAT, BUT a week after she left, my mood was turning negative again. Perhaps I was suffering from her malaise: not finding anything exciting in life. Perhaps I had my own type of malaise. Just as I couldn't help Pat with her problem, I couldn't solve my own.

As another month ended, I prepared the final examination for the course I was teaching. I had thought I would look forward to the end of the term and being relieved of a duty that was alien to me. In reality, I found the prospect of the course concluding depressing. I would have less work to do and more time on my hands.

The day came when I delivered my final lecture. A few students came up to me and told me they enjoyed the course and learned a lot. If I were a cynic, I would have thought that they were angling for better grades. I chose to think that they were being honest. Most students, however, simply pushed on to their next courses or went home.

I noted that Jacqueline had exited this final class early. The next day she saw me at Mrs. Pinckney's house. "Sorry I had to duck out of your class early. Did I miss anything important?"

"I was probably just summing up at that point."

"Well, I guess I better start studying for the final. You're not going to make it too tough?"

"I think I've been fair up to this point. I don't intend to change now."

"Yes, you've been very fair. I appreciate the extra help, especially when I had to miss a class. And I did like the course. I never thought I'd be saying that about an econ course."

"Glad you enjoyed it," I replied simply.

"Well, thanks again." Jacqueline gave me a peck on the cheek and rushed out the front door. Through the window, my gaze followed her. A young man, at least a decade my junior, was waiting for her. They kissed and then walked briskly toward Abercorn Street.

For a few days I was busy grading final examinations. Jacqueline's effort was reasonably good. It deserved a B-plus. I gave her an A-minus.

I saw her a few days later. "I guess an A-minus was fair, but I was hoping for an A."

And I was hoping for a blow job, I thought of replying, but I kept the conversation on a professional level. "I tried to be fair to all students."

"I'm sure you were, Mr. Lendeman," came the cold rejoinder.

After the term ended, I felt isolated. Jacqueline chose not to lay out on the chaise lounge in the garden. My consulting assignments dried up. The regional energy council had no work for me. The weather was too sultry for long walks around the squares and through the parks. I remained in my room for long periods, playing mindless games on my computer.

Even Mrs. Pinckney seemed to be absent. In fact, she was gone for three days to visit relatives in Augusta. But even when she returned I rarely saw her. This was just as well. I wanted to be alone. At least that's what I told myself.

I began a list. I called it my "tally." In actuality it consisted of two lists: what was positive in my life and, conversely, what was negative. The latter list soon became much longer than the former. The positive list tended to contain more trivial points, such as: I like fried chicken; I like strong coffee. The latter list was composed of more meaty fare: consulting is tedious; I'll never find employment I like; I have no friends.

Both lists were written on one piece of twelve by six notepaper. Each list was assigned one side. I had to write small to permit all of the "negative" items to fit.

I began to carry the tally around, so that I could add thoughts as they came to mind. I realized that the tally was becoming an unhealthy obsession. But, in a perverse way, that thought pleased me.

On a hot day, much too hot and humid to work outside, I was reading in the front parlor. Mrs. Pinckney approached me. "I think this might be yours." She was holding my tally, which must have fallen out of my pocket.

I snatched it from her hand. "I hope you didn't read it," I blurted out, injudiciously.

Mrs. Pinckney was not one to shrivel in the face of an accusation. "I had to look at it to find the owner. I hope you don't mind my saying this, but it's one of the saddest things I ever saw. I think you need some help."

"As strange as it might seem, that piece of paper is good therapy."

"You know what I think?" Perhaps Mrs. P. expected a comment from me, encouraging her to continue. I said nothing. She continued, anyway. "I think you should come to church with me, meet my minister. He's a very caring man. I think you need support and fellowship."

"Thank you for your concern. But I think I can take care of myself."

"Are you so sure?"

"Quite sure. And a church would hardly be the answer."

She looked appraisingly at me, no doubt wondering what sort of antipathy I held for religion. I, of course, was not going to explain. "Think it over, James. I've known you for almost two years. You need more in your life than what's found within these walls." With this admonition, Mrs. Pinckney turned and left the room.

I stuffed the tally in my pocket, making a mental note to be more careful with it in the future.

September is still a hot month in Savannah. A change in season is not apparent until October. Mrs. Pinckney spotted me in the parlor one afternoon.

"I'm leaving a salad in the refrigerator because I'm going to be spending some time at Mickve Israel this evening."

"Thanks. By the way, you told me once that you'd explain why you occasionally help out at the synagogue. You never did."

"Oh, did I promise that?"

"Yes, you did."

"Well, it's really quite simple. You know my full name is Charlene Minis Bulloch Pinckney. I must have told you about the Bullochs."

"That you did."

"Then it's time to cover Minis. The Minis family was a family of early Jewish settlers in Savannah. I've tried to trace back the origins of the name in my family, but I was never totally successful. It was used from time to time as a middle name for some in the family extending back into the nineteenth century. I'm not sure there ever was a true Minis in my background or whether it was picked up as an old Savannah name. At any event, even if I don't have a drop of Jewish blood in me, I wanted to maintain contact with the Jewish community here. I have a number of Jewish friends, and I help out at the synagogue particularly around the high holy days."

"Interesting story."

"Yes, I think so. As I recollect, I offered to bring you to the Presbyterian Church and you refused. Would you be more interested in Mickve Israel?"

"If you want to know if I'm Jewish, I'm not, although I think one of my great-grandfathers might have been."

"I still think you need some religion in your life."

"And I respectfully disagree. Some people find comfort in religion and some people are hurt."

"Hurt by religion? I can't imagine how."

"There was something called the inquisition."

"That was centuries ago. You were never subjected to the inquisition."

"Of course not." I did not want to explain why my feelings were so strong. That would have required talking about a painful period in my life. No, Mrs. Pinckney didn't need to know. Not now, not ever.

Near the end of September, my phone rang around nine o'clock in the evening. As I went for the phone, I sensed—I don't know why—that a woman was calling. I hoped it was Pat Auriga. But when I reached the phone I saw from the display that it was a woman, but not Pat. "And to what do I owe this honor, Madame Secretary?"

"Just thought I'd give you a call to see how you're doing," Kate replied.

I was suspicious. Kate never made a casual call; she always had a purpose in mind. "I'm doing okay. How about you?"

"Just okay." Kate ignored my question. "I was hoping to hear that you were doing very well."

"I receive some disability pay from the government. A *very small* amount, I might add. What else can I say?"

"Disability pay, my ass." An image of Kate's tight buns came to mind while she continued. "Seriously, are you enjoying Savannah? I can't imagine why you're down there. Did you really need to escape so desperately?"

"I'd rather not relive that period. It's past. I try to put it aside, but it can't be undone."

"And you hold me responsible?"

"Kate, it's too complicated." I wanted to switch the subject. "Let's talk about you. I like to talk about success rather than failure."

"Damn it, you *are* feeling low. You know, you're not the only one with problems. Let me tell you about one of my problems. That's one of the reasons I called. And I'm going to ask you to help me."

Now I was completely mystified. I merely said, "Me?"

"Yes, you, my good, old friend." I was surprised by the categorization. "I'm going to need you to come to Washington." Now I was even more surprised.

"You have to be kidding."

"I wish I were kidding. This is not a joking matter. I need some medical treatment. I'll explain more when you get here. I need you to watch over a few things for a few weeks, maybe even a month or so. Can you get here tomorrow?"

"No way. I have to do a few things here." I lied.

"But you will be able to help me out?"

I hesitated. "Yes, I guess so. I assume I'll get paid."

"You'll get full consultant's pay and use of an apartment, *gratis*."

"In addition to the pittance I already get from the government?"

"Sure. Do we have a deal?"

"I guess so. I'll try to get there on Friday."

"Make sure it's Friday. Take a morning flight."

"I'm not sure there's a morning flight from Savannah."

"Then go through Atlanta. I need you here. Confirm your arrangements with my admin assistant."

"What's her name?"

"Sam."

"Samantha?"

"No, Samuel, you sexist pig."

After the call ended, I asked myself, *Why do you jump when*

Kate asks for something? That was the nature of our relationship. Whether she was my boss or not, I sensed it would never change.

XXII

San Francisco, etc., 2056-57

IN NOVEMBER 2056, THE REGIONAL directors met in New York. The two-day session, which was generally held once a year in Washington, was moved to New York for no particular reason that I could discern. The meeting was an opportunity to share information about what was going on in our regions, plus to get word from our bosses about what they anticipated for the coming year. A new president, Hector Villeros, had just been elected. He came from the same party as his predecessor, but a new president would no doubt put his own stamp on policy. So the get-together provided an opportunity, strictly on an informal basis, to try to predict what initiatives might be forthcoming from the administration.

At one point in the conference, Leo Frase took me aside. "A month or so ago, I got an anonymous call from someone who claimed to be from your office. The person implied that you were having an affair with someone in the office. I never put any stock in anonymous calls and detest the people who make them, but I thought I'd mention it to you. I don't imagine there's any truth in this." Leo paused, making the statement into a question.

"Absolutely not. I was on a business trip to Napa when the radiation emergency arose. A woman from the office was with me. We could not get back to San Francisco before the curfew was imposed. We spent a night at a hotel and had separate rooms. Nothing happened, but I heard that some malicious gossip was circulating."

"I was sure there would be nothing to it. It sounded from the get-go like a crank call. That's why I didn't mention it until we were together. By the way, how are Jane and your little one?"

"Just fine." I knew Leo was trying to remind me that I had a family, just in case there was a germ of truth in the allegation he supposedly dismissed.

The second day of the meeting ended at three, giving some of the attendees an opportunity to get home that same evening. I stayed over an extra night in order to have dinner with Kate Hastings.

She was now a high-ranking officer with the Wainright Corporation, headquartered in Newark. She told me to take a train to the Short Hills station, and she would meet me there. She would drive me to dinner and then back to my hotel.

Kate was easy to spot among the small group of those waiting to meet commuters at the station. She looked like none of the housewives. Since I had seen her last, her beauty had not diminished. She kissed me on the cheek and then led me to a parking lot where a few rows of electro-cars filled scarcely a quarter of the spots. Her car was a sleek red sports car.

"You got the flashy car you always wanted."

"Yup, unfortunately it has to be a hybrid. Even so, I have to pay a fortune in use tax."

"I bet."

"You want to try it out?" she offered.

"No. I wouldn't do it justice."

Kate took a few back streets to a highway leading west from Essex into Morris County. She accelerated on the highway. I was pressed back into my seat, a feeling I hadn't experienced for years. "I want to get into the hills, so I can show you what this baby can do. We have a reservation at a restaurant in a town called Mendham."

"I know it. I grew up in this area. Remember?"

"Should we drive by your old house?"

"No," I replied a little too brusquely. "It will be dark anyway."

The restaurant was one I had gone to when I was young, particularly on special occasions such as Mother's Day. It was composed of an old inn in the center of town, plus an annex. This night, only two small rooms were open for service. Three tables were occupied in one room, and we were given a table by ourselves in the second.

Kate filled me in on her job, which combined public relations with government affairs. She was paid well, she had no reluctance to tell me. I estimated that she was probably earning more than twice what she had been paid in Washington.

It wasn't until during the main course that she confessed that she missed Washington, primarily because it was at the center of power. She was sure she would return one day, but it wouldn't be to the position that she had left.

Kate asked about Jane and the baby. She probably didn't remember Mark's name. I told her everything was fine, not willing to get into a discussion of the marital difficulties that come and go. She asked me about my job in San Francisco. I told her it was fine. (I wished I had come up with a different term.) She heard from contacts she still had that I was well regarded in the department. She thought that some regional directors would soon be rotated, and if possible, I should attempt to get the New York job. That would be a logical stop on the way back to Washington. "You do want to get back to Washington, don't you?"

"Of course." I replied promptly, giving the expected reply automatically.

"Being out of government, I can't help you now. Although I do still have my information sources," she included unnecessarily. "My influence is very indirect. But I'll be back some day. I'm as sure of that as I live and breathe."

"You have the reputation, the contacts, and the desire. That will make it happen," I observed.

"Yes. You know me well."

As we left the restaurant, Kate noticed that her gas was low. The onboard computer indicated that one gas station in Morristown was open until ten. The trip was downhill and the road was empty. The gas held out, and we arrived in time. Kate put thirty-six liters in the tank.

"How much does it hold?"

"Thirty-eight liters, if I remember correctly."

I offered to pay part of the hundred-and-fifty-dollar gas bill. "Don't be silly." Kate dismissed my offer brusquely.

We drove back east to a hotel near Newark Airport where I had booked a room. I thanked Kate for dinner and for the opportunity to get together. She brushed my cheek with hers and murmured, "Until the next time, my friend."

Thanksgiving, Christmas, and New Year's were spent quietly. Jane and I were encumbered by lack of cash and a toddler. We bought Mark a few presents, and—like most kids his age—he was most fascinated with the ones that made noise. To compensate for the noisy toys, Jane and I treated ourselves to a new TV with a better sound system, spending more money than we should have. We spent New Year's Eve at home, indulging by getting a take-out dinner and a bottle of sparkling wine from Mendocino County.

Then we settled in for the winter, which was much tamer in San Francisco than in most areas of the country. Winter temperatures seemed to average only six or seven degrees less than in summer, unless you ventured inland. But winter could be gloomy, and Jane's mood took on a hue to match.

Sometime in February, she commented, "I think Mark has something wrong with him."

"A cold, probably. All kids get colds in winter. You had one in January."

"No, this is something else. He's pale and listless. I think he has a bit of a fever."

"If you think there's a problem, take him to the doctor."

"Haven't you noticed a difference in him?"

"Not really. But you're around him much more than I am."

"Maybe I'm imagining it," Jane was second-guessing herself.

"Maybe, but maybe not. If you have any doubts, take him to the doctor. That's what doctors and medical insurance are for."

"I guess I'll make an appointment, if he's acting the same way tomorrow."

However, she did not make the appointment the next day because she perceived that Mark's symptoms had abated. "You can see; he seems somewhat better. Do you agree?"

"I'm not sure. I think mothers are more sensitive to these things than fathers are."

"Well, I think I've seen an improvement," Jane stated, a bit more emphatically.

"That's good enough for me."

A few days later, she had a different opinion. "Mark does not seem right to me."

"Did you call the doctor?"

"I will tomorrow."

This time, Jane made an appointment. Mark's visit to the pediatrician resulted in some tests being done. When the results came back, the doctor told Jane that the tests were inconclusive, and he referred her to a clinic in San Francisco for more tests. Jane learned that the clinic specialized in blood disorders.

Since the clinic was only about a kilometer from my office, I joined Jane and Mark for the appointment. About an hour after the blood was drawn, we were escorted into the office of Doctor Ann Milram. She was a pleasant looking brunette who, strangely, bore some resemblance to Pat Auriga.

"I don't want to draw any definite conclusions at this point. But there is a definite imbalance in Mark's blood. The red blood cell count is a bit low. We really need to do some additional tests.

We'd like to put Mark in the children's hospital overnight. Mrs. Lendeman, you can stay with him at the facility. Would you be able to do this tomorrow?"

"I guess so," Jane replied, automatically.

I could tell Jane was a bit bewildered and not prepared for what the doctor was saying.

The tests in the hospital led to more tests. Then the diagnosis came. Mark had something that the doctor called a "leukemic type condition." It had started to appear in children between one and five years of age, and was more common in Northern California than elsewhere. Most children affected were responding to a mild form of chemotherapy. Naturally the term "chemotherapy" scared both Jane and me. The doctor tried to allay our fears by telling us that there were only mild side effects. I don't think her strategy worked. We left the office, and Jane burst into tears. "Why does this have to happen? What did we do wrong?"

"Nobody did anything wrong. Shit just happens. It's pure chance."

"It was that radiation from China," Jane declared.

"We have no reason to think that." But I had thought exactly the same thing.

Mark's treatments began. Most were done on an outpatient basis. On occasion, he stayed in the hospital overnight. We were told he was making progress, that the "readings" were improving. Jane would say that she sensed he was improving—and then a day or two later she would say the opposite.

I tried to concentrate on work, but also to be supportive of Jane and Mark. The truth was that I could escape to the office. Jane could not. She wallowed in the details of Mark's treatments. She followed his ups and downs, some imagined and some not.

For me, there were out of town meetings to attend. One in May took me to Washington, and it lasted three days. I came home, and all seemed the same with Mark. Jane, however, seemed withdrawn. As the weeks went by, she tended to neglect cleaning—except for Mark's room. She had never been an enthusiastic cook. Now she limited the menu to one of three things—hamburgers, spaghetti and meatballs, or broiled chicken. She never wanted to go out to dinner—she wouldn't trust a babysitter with Mark, given his health. Many nights she slept on an inflatable mattress in Mark's room. Sex was limited to about once per month. I knew Jane no longer enjoyed it, and in turn, I, too, found it obligatory, mechanical and unsatisfying.

People in the office were sympathetic to my situation. Keith and others worked a bit harder so I could join Mark for his doctor appointments and treatments. Of course, no one was under great stress because economic activity was still slow, leading to moderate workloads in the office. Leo Frase told me to take whatever time off I needed.

In July, the doctors told us that Mark would get a hiatus from treatments. They wanted to see how he would react to a withdrawal of medication, and felt his young body needed a break.

For a few weeks, Mark's energy seemed to improve. Then it began to fade again. The doctors evaluated the latest tests and recommended that Mark go back on treatments, albeit with a slight adjustment in medication. Jane was frantic. She sensed that Mark was going to slip away from us, and she was losing faith in the doctors. She thought she needed an alternate way to save him.

She began to go to church. At first, she went to the local Methodist church. Mark was put on a prayer list. This was not enough for Jane. She found a less traditional denomination where the preacher laid hands on Mark and personally prayed to Jesus to save Mark. These more-active attempts at intervention satisfied Jane—at least for a while. She donated quite a bit of money to the church, more than we could afford.

Jane thought that Mark's condition was improving through these efforts. She even occasionally skipped a medical treatment. I received a threatening call from the clinic, saying that they felt Jane was endangering the welfare of the child. I confronted Jane with this information.

"Yes, they called me, too. But the fact is: their treatments aren't doing much good. Mark needs stronger healing powers than they possess."

"You mean at the church?"

"That's one possible place."

"What does that mean?"

"None of your business," she replied brutally.

"What do mean 'none of my business'? He's my son, too."

"I'm the one who looks after him. You go off to work."

"I pay for his care, and I shell out the money for your god-damn church."

"Don't you ever say that. You're going to kill the child."

"No, *you* are," I countered.

We had long since passed the point of rational discussion. I'm sure that—at that moment—Jane and I detested each other.

A few days after that encounter I had to go to Washington for a two-day meeting. I was one of the regional directors added to a committee to develop a three-year plan for department initiatives. The planning effort would take about three months. Much work could be done through conference calls and document exchange, but three face-to-face meetings were planned. It was decided that I would host the second in San Francisco. It would be held in October, with the last meeting being held in Washington a week before Thanksgiving.

When I came back from the first meeting, I tried to talk to Jane about how Mark was faring. She answered with brief responses or evasions.

"Did Mark see the doctor?"

"He's being cared for."

"How's he doing?"

"Okay."

"How are you doing?"

"Do you really care?"

During the meeting in San Francisco, I spent one night at the hotel with the other attendees. Jane was not empathetic. By this point we were barely talking—and certainly not conversing. Frankly, I was happy to spend a night away from home and share some drinks with other department associates.

Leo Frase was in attendance. He asked about Mark and Jane. I answered in the abbreviated form that Jane used with me.

"There's more of a problem than Mark's illness, isn't there?" Leo asked perceptively.

"The illness is producing tensions between Jane and me."

"Not at all unusual. I'm sure you two can work it out if you will each meet the other half way."

"I'm not sure that will work."

"Then you two can get counseling."

"Maybe." I left it at that.

By the time I traveled to the final committee meeting in Washington, Jane and I rarely spoke to each other. We tended to leave notes. I was not sure if she read mine. My flight was the red-eye, which left San Francisco around eleven at night. I thought I might have dinner with Jane before I left. She took her plate and sat in front of the TV, ignoring me. I sat at the kitchen table and did not follow her.

At eight o'clock, I took my bag and headed to the front door. "I'm leaving now," I declared.

"Good-bye," Jane replied, without taking her gaze from the TV.

There was no question of a good-bye kiss. Two years earlier, we would have made love the night before I left on a business trip. There was no expectation of that, either. And I knew when I returned I should not expect an embrace, let alone any greater form of intimacy.

In fact, when I did return, there was not only no embrace, there was no Jane. It was late afternoon and the weather was blustery. Could she have taken Mark for a walk and some fresh air? Perhaps she was doing shopping?

As I looked around the apartment, I sensed that it had been vacant for a while. There were no lingering food smells. There were no toys scattered around. No trash was in the kitchen container.

I explored further and noted that items were missing: a small picture of Jane's mother that had sat on a table in the living room; some of Mark's favorite toys were not in the toy box; the teddy bear he slept with was gone; Jane's cosmetics and toothbrush were missing. Jane was evidently prepared to spend a night, perhaps several, elsewhere.

Where could she have gone? She had few friends. In a few days it would be Thanksgiving. On impulse, could she have gone to her mother's for the holiday? A cross-country trip, given our finances, would have been highly impractical. But Jane's thinking was no longer logical.

Despite my misgivings, I put a call in to Jane's mother. My voice obviously surprised her, but I quickly got to the point. "By any chance is Jane with you? When I returned from a trip, she was gone."

"No, she's certainly not here."

"She's not on her way there?"

"No, I wouldn't think so. We haven't spoken for a week. When did you last see her?"

"Three days ago, when I left for Washington."

"So you just got back."

"An hour ago."

"Maybe she's just . . ." Her voice trailed off. Then slowly she continued. "I guess I should mention this. We last spoke about a week ago. She called me to say that I shouldn't be worried if she couldn't be reached for a while. She said she needed to go away, and she was taking Mark."

"Did she say how long she planned to be away?"

"No, just what I told you. She said 'a while.' Did she leave you a note?"

"I haven't found one."

"Well, I guess there's nothing more to do. Just wait for her. Would you call me when she returns?"

"Of course." Even though Jane's mother was told she was going to be away, I was still concerned, particularly about Mark.

A bit later I found a note in a drawer in our bedroom. It wasn't signed, nor was it addressed to me, but it was in Jane's handwriting.

I left with Mark. We'll be okay. I'm doing the right thing for him.

I sat on the bed, looking at the note, and tried to figure out what Jane was up to. After several minutes, I decided to call the police to see if they would handle her disappearance as a missing person's case. They told me an officer would stop by in the morning to get my statement and look at the information I had.

The officer arrived as promised in the morning. She asked me to describe my return from Washington, my call to Jane's mother, the items missing, and the legitimacy of the note I found. "Is there any indication of foul play?" the officer asked. I had thought she would determine that.

"Not that I found."

"What's your relationship with your wife?"

I paused to think before answering. "It's been somewhat strained." I told her about Mark's illness, his treatments, Jane's doubts about their effectiveness and her search for alternative cures. I explained that we didn't see eye to eye about these things.

"I see what you're getting at," said the officer, but with some restraint. Being a woman, she might have harbored some gender bias. I didn't know if I was getting a fair hearing. "Do you have another sample of your wife's handwriting?"

"I'm sure I do." I searched quickly. She had left a binder with some recipes. A few were written by Jane.

"So you have no reason to think she might be in danger?"

"Not particularly. Except she has no friends in the area. Who would she turn to? And she can't have much money with her. I'm even more concerned about my son."

The officer noted the name of the clinic where Mark received his treatments. She seemed to be running out of questions. "We'll make inquiries and let you know if anything turns up. You tell us if you hear anything." She gave me her card.

A few days later, Jane's mother called to ask if I had heard from her daughter. "No," I replied.

"Aren't you concerned?" she asked with a strong dose of exasperation in her voice.

"I am concerned—about Mark more than your daughter. That's why I've gotten the police involved."

"And what do they say?"

"They're looking into it."

When I ended the call with Jane's mother, I called the officer who had taken the case. She was not available. The next day she called back and told me there was nothing to report.

"What does that mean?"

"We have no leads."

I didn't have the audacity to ask if she was pursuing any leads. Instead, I asked, "Would you suggest I hire a private detective?"

"That's up to you."

I thought it best to inform Leo Frase and Keith Wheatley, my second in command, about what had happened. During my narration, Leo repeated at several points, "Very strange behavior, very strange indeed." Of course, he had not spoken to Jane in over two years, and had no idea of how she had changed from the efficient admin assistant he had known.

Keith's reaction was more direct. "I'd get a lawyer if I were you. She's abandoned you. That's grounds for divorce."

"I'm not sure I want a divorce."

"I'd still get a lawyer involved. He can give you good advice about the whole situation. I know one who's pretty savvy, and he doesn't charge an arm and a leg." He went to his desk and, in two minutes, returned with the lawyer's name and number.

It took another week for me to make up my mind to make an appointment with the lawyer. I wanted to meet face to face with him, and I was pleased to note that his office was located in a lower-rent area south of Market Street.

Grant Sherwood was a stocky man in his early fifties. He had a large head topped with tousled brown hair, flecked with gray. His bushy eyebrows shared the same color scheme. His open-ended direction to me was: "Describe the situation with your wife and child." As I did so, he leaned back in his reclining desk chair, closed his eyes, and put his feet up on the well-worn desk. His shoes could have used some polish.

It took about ten minutes for me to relate the history of the past six months. Sherwood was more interested in Jane's behavior than in Mark's illness. He asked for a copy of the note that Jane had left for me but, since, had been given to the police. In response to his request, I gave him the police officer's name and phone number. He told me that he'd find out what the police had done and were prepared to do. But, he warned me, "We're probably going to have to hire a private investigator to find out where your wife went."

"How much will that cost?"

"I can't say exactly. I know one who's good at tracking down people. He charges a thousand a day plus expenses, last I checked. That's pretty reasonable. It might take him a few days, maybe a week to find her."

"I see." I could see myself going into debt. I also got an estimate of the lawyer's fee, and then I told him I'd get back to him in a day or two to give him the go ahead. He urged me not to delay. The trail might get cold, and it could take the investigator longer to track Jane down.

Over the next two days, I wrestled with the decision to hire an investigator. Jane's mother called to find out what I had learned from the police. I told her that they did not seem to be pursuing Jane's disappearance aggressively, and that I was thinking of hiring a private investigator. She thought it was a good idea but did not offer to share in the expense. Of course, I did not ask.

I sought Leo's opinion. He thought it was a good idea to hire the investigator and pointed out that I could get a loan from my retirement savings account if I was short on cash. This I knew, but I thanked him for his advice.

After I spoke to Leo, I called the lawyer and told him to proceed. He assured me that I was doing the right thing and asked for a three thousand dollar retainer for himself and the investigator.

Although within the office I had told only Keith of Jane's departure, it became apparent that others knew. I could see it in their faces. They looked like they wanted to express some sympathy or understanding or pity, but they didn't know how to approach the subject. Instead, many avoided looking directly into my eyes.

This office knowledge was finally confirmed when Allison entered my office very late one afternoon. We had been avoiding any one-on-one contact since rumors of an affair had circulated.

She began directly, "I've heard rumors that Jane left you and took Mark."

"You heard correctly," was my straightforward reply, and I did not ask her to disclose the source of her information.

"I'm sorry to hear that. I just wanted to let you know that if you could use a home-cooked meal, we can set something up." I did not react immediately. "I guess I'm inviting you to come over if you want. If you think that's inappropriate, I understand."

It probably was inappropriate for us to get together, but I didn't care. "At some point, I'd like that meal."

"Should we set a date?" Allison persevered.

"What would you suggest?"

"Saturday evening?"

"Sounds fine to me."

"Around six thirty, then. Do you remember where I live?"

"I'm sure I do."

It took nearly an hour and a half to get from my apartment to Allison's. I handed her a bottle of Napa cabernet. "A remembrance?" she asked.

"Not the best occasion to commemorate, but hopefully the wine is good," I replied.

Allison led me into the living room section of her studio apartment, which probably totaled around forty square meters. We nibbled on hors d'oeuvres and sipped some wine while a chicken and noodle casserole gradually cooked in the oven. I did most of the talking, occasionally prompted by Allison's questions. It was not difficult to tell her about Mark's health problem and the deteriorating relations with Jane. She provided a sympathetic ear, having had her own marital problems.

When it came time to leave, I looked deeply into Allison's eyes. I could sense that she wondered, as I did, how far we should proceed on what some would consider a date. I thanked her for the dinner, the company, and the conversation. She thanked me for the wine. Our faces were close. I kissed her gently on the lips. She kissed back and let her lips linger for a few seconds on mine. I think she would have liked me to stay a while longer to see where this initial embrace might lead. However, my inconsiderate mind reminded me that I was her boss, and I hesitated. I'm sure Allison read my thoughts. We reluctantly pulled away from each other.

"Next time, can I take you out to dinner?"

"Yes, I'd like that," she answered quickly.

XXIII

SAMUEL, KATE'S ADMIN ASSISTANT, ARRANGED for a car to meet me at Dulles airport, so I wouldn't have to drag my luggage on a shuttle bus to Washington. I knew I was staying several weeks, and I had packed accordingly. Kate was giving me preferential treatment. I would even have the use of an F.E.D. apartment in northwest Washington.

The car, however, did not bring my luggage and me to the apartment. We went directly to F.E.D. headquarters. Sam met me at the front door, gave me an identification badge, and ushered me to Kate's office.

Kate was on the phone, but I was waved in. I sat in front of Kate's desk while she concluded the call.

"James, thank you for coming on short notice. You look just the same. How long has it been—two years?"

"Yes, just about. You look great, Kate. The job must agree with you." I had lied. Her face was drawn. There was dark, puffy flesh under her eyes.

"I look like shit. You're a lousy liar."

"No, seriously."

"James, we've known each other too long for that. Let's get down to business."

I nodded in acknowledgment.

"I'm designating you a special assistant for the next five or six weeks. I want you to be my eyes and ears. I need someone I can trust."

"You have a staff of hundreds right here in this building."

"Obviously I do, but I don't know them as well as I know you. They have their own agendas. You're not involved with the office politics. Plus, we go back a long way. We've been . . ." Kate hesitated to get the right words. "We've been through a lot of things together and have maintained our mutual respect."

Kate looked at me, perhaps expecting my concurrence. I sat and listened.

"The reason I need you here is that I have to go into the hospital. I have a tumor in my breast. It's malignant. It has to be removed."

I was shocked. I had thought of Kate as indestructibly eternal. Suddenly I understood why her appearance had changed. "I'm so sorry to hear that. I find it difficult to believe."

"I wish I were joking." She paused and then continued. "The tumor alone will be removed. Then I'll have a few radiation treatments. It's a short sequence. They say it's supposed to be ninety-five percent as effective as the longer series, which really knocks the shit out of you. Anyway, five or six weeks is as much time as I can afford."

"You should really put your health first," I offered the obvious advice.

"I'm a big girl. I made my decision, and I'll live with it."

My brain added, *Or die with it*, but I couldn't articulate the phrase, and I was even ashamed to think of it.

"So here's the game plan. I'll be out for two or three days because of the surgery. Then I'll need to be off a day or two for each of the weekly radiation treatments. Of course, the doctors need to check the result of each treatment and confirm I can move on to the next. But I'm determined to keep to the schedule and get this over with."

I wished Kate had more concern for her course of treatment, rather than viewing it as something to dispense with as quickly as possible. But I knew that any suggestion of this sort would do no good and furthermore would not be appreciated.

Kate moved on to cover what was more important to her than her illness; namely, the things she wanted me to keep my eye on during her absences. It seemed that she didn't totally trust her two deputy secretaries, particularly Wayne Sickles, who was thought of, in some circles, as a rising star. She knew he had strong opinions, which were not necessarily aligned with hers. In her absence, she feared he would push his own ideas.

Sickles had been an executive in the solar energy industry. His interests, Kate felt, were still focused in this area. He tended to think of Kate's pursuit of additional sources of crude oil as quixotic. He realized that crude was needed for certain purposes, such as aviation and the military, but even here he thought more effort was needed in the area of alternative fuels.

Kate appreciated Sickles's intelligence, and even his willingness to state a novel opinion. However, she thought he pursued his contrary notions even after she rejected them and they were excluded from department priorities.

Kate and I met for an hour, taking us to noon. Kate informed me that we would have lunch with Wayne Sickles and her other deputy secretary, Hazel Dumas. Unlike Sickles, Hazel Dumas was a long-time employee of the Federal Energy Department. I had met her on a number of occasions, but had never worked closely with her. However, I was not in Washington to monitor Hazel. Wayne was my primary target.

Our lunch was cordial. Kate explained that I was going to act as a special assistant for the month and a half during which she was to undergo surgery and treatments. Obviously, Wayne and Hazel had received some earlier briefing on Kate's health. Wayne, responding in a politic fashion, assured Kate that he would be delighted to work with me. Hazel merely smiled. Her smile, however, disappeared when Kate stated that Wayne would be attending any cabinet meetings taking place when she was absent. Kate went on to state that Wayne and Hazel should keep me informed of any staff meetings they were holding, so that I would have the opportunity of sitting in.

After lunch, which had been brought into Kate's conference room, she asked me to stay. "I'm going to give you some information on the major projects we're working on."

"Good. I'll review them this weekend."

"There's one other thing I'd like you to do over the weekend, if you're willing."

"Just tell me."

"I'm going to have the surgery Monday morning. I don't want to be alone Sunday evening. Could we go out to dinner or go to a movie or both?"

"Of course."

Kate smiled weakly. "You're sweet. Somehow I can always count on you."

Samuel, Kate's admin assistant, gave me the reading material that Kate had promised. Then the department's car drove me to the apartment, which was just off Dupont Circle.

The early October day was warm. The apartment, when I arrived, was stuffy. I checked the thermostat. The governor would not allow it to go below twenty-six degrees. The F.E.D. had to adhere to its own rules. Perhaps it was one I worked on—I really didn't remember. I stripped to my undershirt and slacks.

I sized up my new quarters. It was a one-bedroom apartment, which included a combined living room and dining area, a small kitchen, and a bathroom that featured both a tub and a stall shower. The refrigerator contained a six-pack of domestic beer, six colas— three diet and three regular—six bottles of spring water, a small tub of margarine, a quart of milk, some cheese spread, and a loaf of raisin bread. The freezer was empty except for a package of French toast. In the cupboard I found instant coffee, tea bags, and crackers. Obviously the apartment was equipped for snacking, but not much more.

I unpacked my two suitcases. October could bring both warm

and cool weather to Washington, so I had packed accordingly. The armoire was more than ample to hold my socks, underwear, and a dozen shirts. The closet had more than enough hangers for my needs.

Once unpacked, I decided to scout out the neighborhood. A block away I found a Chinese restaurant, which featured a hefty takeout menu. A grocery store, small but adequate, was around the corner. Some fancy restaurants were located within a few blocks, but I doubted that these would be needed.

Kate asked me to come to her apartment around four on Sunday afternoon. In the interim, I had two days to kill. Of course, reading would fill a number of hours, but that still left plenty of time.

An idea came to me as I was walking back to the apartment. I reached for my phone and found the number I wanted. A woman's soft voice answered.

"Pat?"

"Yes."

"It's James, James Lendeman."

"James, delightful to hear from you. To what do I owe this good fortune?"

"I'm in Washington for a few weeks, so I wanted to give you a call."

"I'm glad you did. We'll have to get together."

"That's exactly what I was thinking. Are you doing anything tomorrow night?"

"I'm sorry. I have something planned. But I have plenty of other time available over the next few weeks."

We agreed to reserve the following Saturday night. Pat offered to cook dinner, if I'd take her to the movies. I readily agreed.

I walked to the grocery store again and bought an initial stock of food. After putting some frozen and refrigerated items away, I decided to get a start on my homework assignment. The warm apartment, along with the dull, analytical material and my earlier travel made me doze off. I slept until after seven. The Chinese restaurant that I had located earlier supplied my dinner that night, as it would on a number of subsequent occasions.

One seat at the dining area table faced the TV. I put my takeout, a plate, a glass of beer, and utensils in front of me. I sought some sporting event to watch. I was not optimistic. College football in my youth was primarily played on Saturdays, pro football on Sundays. Basketball had not yet started. Baseball, which was now reduced to an eighty game season, was over. Of course, all games were played at the national centers, leading to a waning of hometown interest. I found a rerun of a bicycle race—at least that was an energy-efficient sport, albeit boring.

As I began my second beer, the phone rang. Kate was at the other end. "How are you adapting to your return to Washington?"

"I'm doing fine. Eating some Chinese takeout."

"I'm envious. I'm having some canned soup."

"Can't a cabinet member do better than that?"

"It came right out of my own cabinet." I forced a chuckle in response to her lame joke. "I hope I'm not interrupting anything important."

"No. I'm here, all alone. I don't have many contacts left in the city. How are you doing?"

"I'm going crazy. I can't concentrate on work, and I don't want to dwell on my surgery."

"What can I do?" I suspected Kate already had something in mind.

"I don't want to drag you out of your comfortable apartment tonight. It is comfortable, isn't it?"

"It's fine."

"That's good. But I can't go through this weekend by myself. Could you come over tomorrow? You haven't planned anything else?"

"Just the reading you gave me. I'll gladly interrupt that."

"Not that fascinating?"

"Not as fascinating as you." As the words slipped out, I wondered if I had gone too far.

But Kate's reaction was bland. "I'm not sure how fascinating I can be, given the circumstances. I want you to get my mind off myself. Maybe we could do something in the afternoon, then have dinner together. Then we'll spend Sunday doing something. We'll figure it out. I just hope I won't bore or depress you."

I hated to hear this powerful and important woman plead for attention. "Kate, I'll be happy to do whatever you want. And I'm sure I'll enjoy being with you. I always do."

"Look, I don't have a car assigned to me on the weekend. Can you get over to Arlington? It's only a few blocks from my old apartment." Kate gave me the address, and I agreed to arrive around noon. She told me to bring a change of clothes in case I wanted to spend the night.

"Is your couch comfortable?"

"I have a better job now. I can afford a guest room."

The Metro took me to a stop only a block from Kate's apartment. I arrived in her neighborhood at a quarter to twelve, toting a suitcase that was embarrassingly large for an overnight stay. I wheeled it around the block to kill ten minutes before entering her lobby. A guard, who looked like he might be a government employee, questioned me and asked for identification before buzzing Kate's apartment.

The inner lobby and elevator were filled with security cameras. I suspected that the building was home to a number of high-ranking government officials. To get to Kate's apartment on the tenth floor, I was told to take the elevator to eleven and then go down one flight. On the eleventh floor I encountered another security guard, who checked my identification again, asked me to open the suitcase, and then directed me to a small elevator that served the ninth through twelfth floors.

Kate's apartment was at the end of the hall, and I correctly surmised that it occupied a corner of the building. Kate answered the door and planted a kiss on my cheek. "Looks like you're planning to stay a while." Kate was eyeing my big suitcase.

"Remember, you asked me to stay in Washington for a month. I had to bring two large suitcases, not an overnight bag. Are you afraid your neighbors will notice?"

Kate took my comment seriously. "No. Everyone minds his or her own business around here. Come in. I'll show you around."

I immediately noticed that much of the furniture had come from her old apartment. Obviously, it had followed her around over the past few years. The apartment had a balcony that faced Washington.

Indeed, Kate now had two bedrooms. Her own had a canopied bed hung with pink and gray fabric. Opposite the bed, a long, low Chinese-inspired dresser was topped by a mirror which extended about two-thirds of its length. The guest bedroom contained a queen-sized bed with no headboard. A plain chest of drawers was stuck in a corner; a small, undistinguished print hung on an otherwise bare wall. Obviously, Kate had invested little in the guest bedroom, perhaps reflecting its usefulness to her.

We walked back into the living room, past the small galley kitchen. "I had some sandwiches delivered. There's a very good deli a block away. Are you hungry now?"

"I'll eat when you feel like eating."

"Strangely enough, I'm starving." Kate went to the refrigerator, which, I noticed, was largely empty, except for the platter that contained six half-sandwiches. "There's tuna, corned beef, and turkey. Do you want a beer?"

"I'll have soda if you have any."

"Of course."

We sat at the dining room table, which had a view of Washington beyond the balcony. "Pretty, isn't it?" Kate commented, looking at the city. "It hides the ugliness within."

"That's a rather negative point of view."

"Probably more jaded than negative. Excuse me. I'm afraid my disposition has taken a turn for the worse. I'll probably be lousy company."

"Well, let's do the best we can."

The day was sunny and pleasantly warm, a few degrees cooler than on Friday. We went to the Mall and wandered through several exhibits. A few people obviously recognized Kate, but none became intrusive. After looking at Kate, some looked at me. They were probably thinking, "Who the hell is the guy with the Energy Secretary?"

In mid-afternoon we stopped at an outdoor café for drinks. Kate sat facing the sun. I could see the signs of aging: the crow's feet at the corners of her eyes, some slack skin under her chin. She was still a beautiful woman, but she was clearly a woman in her forties, possibly approaching fifty. It occurred to me that I didn't know her true age.

We watched the families enjoying their day off. Some youngsters were happy; some were arguing with their parents.

"I think I'm happy I never had a child. I would have been a lousy mother."

"People can learn to be good parents."

"But Jane wasn't."

"No," I agreed. "But she tried to be in her own misguided way."

The conversation stopped for a few minutes. We watched the human parade, each consumed by our own analysis of these passing figures. I liked to people watch. I suspected that Kate rarely engaged in such an activity. She was a doer, not an observer.

Our drinks were long finished. "Can I get you another?" I asked.

"No. If you don't mind, I'd like to go home now."

We arrived at Kate's Metro stop. There was a street leading away from her building. It appeared to contain a number of shops and restaurants. "That looks like an interesting street," I observed.

"I never go that way. My driver pulls into the garage. Occasionally I have to take the Metro, but I don't explore."

"Do you want to?"

"I'm a bit tired. But you go ahead if you want to."

"No, we'll do it some other time. I'll go upstairs with you."

Kate told me she was going to lie down for a half hour and suggested that I think about what I'd like for dinner. I turned the TV on, but couldn't find anything interesting. I logged onto my computer and looked for restaurants in Kate's neighborhood. As I suspected there were several in the street that I had pointed out. One was Chinese—but I had had Chinese food the night before. Two were Italian. One was essentially a pizzeria. The other looked higher class with northern Italian specialties. Another was a sushi bar, but with the diminished transportation schedules I was wary of eating raw fish.

An hour went by and I could hear no stirring in Kate's bedroom. The door was closed. I turned the handle slightly. It was not locked. I could hear Kate's regular breathing. I decided to wake her. I gently touched her arm.

Kate awoke with a start. "Oh, James, it's you." She did not seem angry. "I'm not used to having anyone else in the apartment."

"You said you were only going to rest for a half hour. You slept for over an hour."

"I was tired. What time is it?"

"Around seven."

"In the evening?"

"Yes."

"Then it's getting close to dinner time. Are you getting hungry?" For some reason Kate now put her hand on my arm.

"I'm sure I'll be hungry by the time we're ready to eat. I noticed that there are two Italian restaurants nearby. One has pizza; the other seems to be fancier."

"I've ordered pizza from a restaurant called Pazzi."

"That's the one."

"The pizza was pretty good. Do you mind if we don't go out?"

"Fine with me," I replied, although I would have preferred to dine at a restaurant.

The pizza, which had to go through an interesting clearance process, turned out to be quite good, if a little cool. The wine that Kate supplied was much better. Kate's larder was rather bare, but she possessed a temperature-controlled wine cabinet in the corner of the kitchen. It was stocked with Bordeaux and pinot noir, plus a sprinkling of champagne and chardonnay. In total, there were about fifty bottles.

Kate picked an Oregon pinot noir. "I'm not sure if this will go well with pizza, but I'm sure we'll enjoy it anyway." And so we did.

Kate ate only one slice of pizza. I ate three. We both lingered over the wine. Kate's conversation jumped from work to politics to health concerns and, ultimately—and surprisingly—to family. "Did I ever mention I have a sister?"

"I don't believe so."

"She's an older sister, eight years older than me. She lives in Connecticut. I haven't seen her in five, maybe six years. She doesn't know of my health problem."

"Maybe you should tell her."

"I think not. She has two daughters. They're at least in their twenties, maybe even thirties. Time goes by so quickly. I send them Christmas presents each year. One writes me a long thank you note; the other just a few words. That's my family. Your mother's still alive?" Kate asked.

"Yes, she is. But I don't get to see her often."

"Does she still live in New Jersey?"

"Yes."

"Maybe while you're here in D.C., you should go up there. Spend a day or two."

"I'll give it serious consideration. But you're my priority

right now."

"You're sweet. Or is it because being my companion is a paying job?"

"Kate! You don't do me justice."

A little later we watched a movie, which we both pretended to enjoy. After the movie was over, Kate said she was going to get in bed and read. I asked if I could continue to watch TV if I lowered the sound. To which Kate replied that I should treat the apartment as my own.

I searched the TV offerings first for movies and then, not finding any to my liking, I entered "history" in the search field. The first ten offerings included a special, which had been prepared for the two hundredth anniversary of the battle of Antietam. The anniversary, I was reminded in the early minutes, had just passed, since the battle was fought on September 17, 1862.

My interest grew as the docudrama made me recollect the key events of the period: Union soldiers finding a copy of Lee's orders wrapped around several cigars; McClellan's initially energetic response; and later his hesitation as the battle progressed from the Union right to left. With my renewed connection to Georgia, I paid particular attention to Robert Toombs's brigade's stand against Burnside in the final stage of the battle. During the time I spent in Athens, I had noted a sign recognizing Toombs as a prominent graduate of UGA. And I had finally learned of one of his accomplishments.

Kate entered the living room as the program was coming to an end. "What are you watching?"

"A history of the battle of Antietam."

"That was a Civil War battle." Her statement was half a question.

"That's right. It took place two hundred years ago, just up the Potomac in Maryland."

"How far is it from here?"

"I'm not quite sure. Maybe a hundred kilometers." The credits were rolling across the screen.

Kate's interest in the subject had been sated. "I'm having trouble sleeping. Would you come into my room and lie next to me? It would comfort me."

My thoughts returned to her former apartment and to our junket in Vienna. I wondered whether I was about to experience exhilaration or frustration. "Sure, if you really want me to."

"I asked, didn't I?"

Kate was wearing a robe. She took it off. With only a night-light coming through the open bathroom door, I could not see what she was wearing underneath. She quickly slid beneath the covers and urged me to do the same. I stripped to my undershorts and took the opposite side of the bed.

I dared not touch Kate until she took the initiative. She made no immediate move to do so. As my eyesight became adjusted to the darkened room, I could see that she was on her back, looking up at the ceiling.

"I'm scared, James. I'm scared of being sick. I'm scared of getting old. I'm scared of being alone."

"You have me here. And I'll be here while you get your treatments and when you're cured."

"But then you'll be gone. You have your own life."

"It's really not that much of a life, especially compared with yours."

"Do you have a girlfriend in Savannah?"

"Not really."

"What does that mean?"

"That means 'no.'"

"You're a young man and good looking, James. You shouldn't act like a hermit. I suppose I shouldn't, either. You know, I haven't had a man in this bed since I became secretary. I must be intimidating. Or just old. Or ugly."

A compliment was called for. "Kate, you're still a beautiful woman. You're the most interesting and exciting woman I ever knew or could imagine knowing." Had I delivered the compliment before? It didn't matter. Kate appreciated it.

She rolled over and was now on her side, leaning against me. "I've missed you, James. You make me feel so good, and I trust you." She kissed me lightly on the lips. I returned her kiss. She opened her mouth a bit. In rapid steps the kissing became passionate.

I put my hand on her thin thigh. She was wearing an extremely lightweight nightgown. It reached only to her hips, and was now riding up higher.

A few moments later she moved my hand between her legs. It was quite clear what she wanted, and I was only too pleased to accommodate. No strenuous or lengthy effort was required on my part to satisfy her.

I started to withdraw my arm. "No, James, hold me. Hold me close to you."

Her back was now against my stomach. My nose was in her hair. A sweet, fruity smell made me bury my face beneath her long tresses. I nibbled on her neck. She purred and gyrated her hips against my groin. Her action bore some resemblance to Jacqueline's specialty, but it soon faded away.

"I'm afraid I can't do for you what you did for me." Kate was going to disappoint me, but given the status of her health, I could understand.

"I'll go back to my bedroom."

"No, you won't. We can work something out. Come with me into the bathroom."

She led me by the hand.

It was not clear what Kate had in mind. She made me face the sink. Then she put some oily substance in my right palm. Now it was clear what she expected me to do.

"I don't think I want . . ."

"Yes, you do," she interrupted. She removed her nightgown and came up behind me. She pressed her body against mine and wrapped her arms around me with one hand on my chest and the other on my abdomen. I did what was expected of me.

I spent the night in Kate's bed; the next night, too. In between, we killed Sunday over brunch and a long walk around Georgetown. Later we had a light dinner at the Chinese restaurant near Kate's apartment, but she was supposed to eat very little.

She was concerned about the operation. We tried to watch TV but couldn't. Through the evening she stretched out on the couch with my arms around her. We put on some soft music and talked. She did not want any form of sex that night, but she wanted to be held. I enveloped her thin form in my arms, and she fell asleep that way.

XXIV

IN FEBRUARY 2058, THREE THINGS occurred in rapid succession. I received a report from my lawyer and private investigator; Leo Frase made me an offer that I decided to accept; and my relationship with Allison McLean reached a bittersweet climax.

On Monday, February 11, I received a call from my lawyer. He had not called me in a few weeks, and I feared he was trying to avoid me. "James, we have some news for you."

"About Jane?"

"Sure, what else would it be? Rather than talk on the phone, can you come over around four. The investigator will be here."

I looked at my calendar. A staff meeting was scheduled to begin at three. Normally it would last until five. But hearing from the investigator took top priority. Keith could take over running the meeting. "Yes, I'll be there."

I left the office at three forty-five and practically jogged to the lawyer's office, arriving five minutes early. When I was ushered into Grant Sherwood's office, I was introduced to Baylor Bixby, who didn't look much like a private investigator. He looked about forty-five years of age, quite bald, and rather short and paunchy. He extended a flabby hand, which gripped mine weakly.

Sherwood got down to business promptly. "Tell Mr. Lendeman what you found."

The detective was not about to be too concise. Since his investigation amounted to seventy billable hours, he wanted to make sure that I knew I was getting my money's worth.

"First, I had to find out when and how your wife and son got out of San Francisco. I went under the assumption that they didn't have the resources to take a private car and probably not even a commercial flight. I concentrated on train and bus stations. I knew within a few days when they left. But I had to talk to many ticket agents. Finally I found one who recognized your wife and son from the picture I showed them.

"Even then, she wasn't sure where they went. I had to go through a bunch of records to find the ones where an adult and a child under the age of five were ticketed, making payment by cash, since you never received a credit card charge.

"I checked about ten leads. The most promising one led to Mendocino. Now Mendocino could have been the end of the line. Or they could have gone on from there.

"One possibility led farther north to Eureka. Finally I found a person in Eureka who thought she saw your wife and son get in an old panel truck and head south of town. Now such trucks are unusual and may not even be hybrids. I asked about such a truck around town. I thought a few people knew about it but were afraid to say.

"Finally, I found one old mechanic who had the guts to tell me. The truck belonged to a cult called 'The Great Diviners.' They claim to be intensely religious. But people think they engage in group sex. They grow pot; even sell some of it under government seal, but quite a bit more that's illegal. They also possess a hefty arsenal—rifles, automatic weapons, maybe even hand grenades. There are about thirty men, sixty women, and a hundred children. Neither the local police nor the state troopers want to mess with them. They're happy to leave them alone so long as they don't cause problems outside of their own commune.

"I took a car as close as I could get to the area. I saw the truck come and go. I couldn't get close enough to identify your wife. But I'm sure she's there."

At this point the investigator concluded his narrative. The lawyer added, "So now the investigation phase is concluded, and we have to decide what else we want to do."

"What else?" I asked, not understanding.

"Well, for one, you probably want to pursue a divorce. Then there's the custody of your son to consider. Although everything will be complicated, not being able to serve papers."

"I see. I guess I'll have to think about what I want to do."

"Sure. Take some time. But I suggest you don't put it off for too long."

I didn't ask what "too long" meant.

The night after finding out about Jane and Mark, I barely slept. My mind was churning. I tried to figure out what made Jane take such a desperate and ridiculous step. Had Mark's illness totally destroyed her sense of logic? I had forgotten to call Jane's mother and tell her what I had learned. I made a mental note to call her the following day. I looked at the clock. It was already the following day.

I arrived a little late at the office, and immediately called Keith into the office. I thought he deserved to hear what I had learned, especially since he was covering for me more and more.

The tale I told surprised him. "Wow. Where do you go from here?"

"I'm not sure. I guess I could get a divorce. But, frankly, that's not very important to me. I'm more concerned about Mark. But even the investigator wouldn't go near the compound."

"It's confusing and complicated." Keith's summation echoed my own thoughts.

"I've decided not to make any decision right away." I realized the statement sounded stupid, but I let it stand. "Maybe I'll find some inspiration or revelation."

"Good luck."

I struggled through the day. I sat in on a meeting Keith chaired.

I yawned all too frequently and lost the gist of the discussion. After
the meeting, I asked my admin assistant to screen calls and told her
I had not slept because I had a stomachache. I'm sure she knew I
was prevaricating.

By three in the afternoon, I was trying to figure out how to
struggle through another hour or so. Then a phone call came in
which my admin assistant indicated I needed to take.

"How you doing?" Leo Frase asked.

"You probably don't want to know. I'm bummed out. I found
out that Jane took Mark to some kind of cult compound in an
inaccessible part of California."

"Nonsense. All of California is accessible. It's all urban or
farmland."

"Leo, in this case you don't know what you're talking about.
The police don't even mess with these people."

"Really?"

"Absolutely."

"Shit. I'm sorry to hear this. What are you going to do?"

"I'm not sure. I'll think about it for a while. There might be
nothing to do until she chooses to come out."

"I wish I could give you some sage advice, but I'm drawing a
blank. And here I was calling to make you an exciting offer."

"What's that?"

"I want to move you to the position in New York. We're
thinking of doing a three-way rotation. We think Boykin would
be a better match for Dallas. Biondi would take your job in San
Francisco. But now with what you just told me . . ." Leo's voice
trailed off.

"So you're withdrawing the offer?"

"Well, considering the problem with Jane . . ." Again a
sentence was left incomplete.

"Do I need a wife to do the job in New York?"

"Of course not."

"Unless I'm going to storm the compound and rescue my

wife, who, I'm sure, wants no rescuing, I might as well go to New York. There's nothing to keep me here."

"You're making a decision just like that?"

"Why not?" And then the thought of Allison crossed my mind. Not Jane, but Allison.

"James, I'm about to have dinner. Let me call you in the morning. Sleep on it for one night. You've evidently absorbed a lot of information recently."

Sleep I did, despite the importance of the decision facing me. I was sure that it was best to move on—escape, some might say.

The next morning, I passed Allison's desk. She looked carefully at me. She knew something was happening. There were no people close by, so I said quickly, "I'll call you tonight." She handed me some papers, as if she was delivering a report she owed me. I took the papers into my office. They were blank.

Leo's call came in a few minutes later. "Have you reconsidered your decision?"

"I've reconfirmed it," was my simple reply.

"Can you get to New York by March fourth?"

"I think so."

Leo continued to talk about the assignment and what he hoped I could accomplish in New York. In turn, I told him that I was excited about the prospect of returning to the East Coast and assuming responsibility for the New York office. He went on to speculate on the wonderful opportunities that could open up to me by being in New York. He continued to sell me on a proposition that had already been sold. I listened politely. He concluded by warning me not to communicate anything in the office before one o'clock West Coast time on Friday. A few loose ends still needed to be tied up.

After ending the call with Leo, I remembered that I had once again forgotten to call Jane's mother. I reached her immediately and explained what I had learned from the private investigator.

"This is preposterous. I know my daughter. She couldn't do

anything like that."

I thought, *She knew her daughter but that was a few years ago.* I had thought that I knew Jane, too. I did not try to refute her. Instead I replied simply, "Well, that's the information I received."

"Maybe you should get another detective."

"I really couldn't afford the first one. You can get one if you wish."

She had no retort.

Now that I was leaving the San Francisco office, each additional meeting and task seemed irrelevant. I glided through the day, delegating even more work to Keith. Allison and I made an appointment to meet for dinner on Thursday after work. We left the office late—and separately—and then met at an out-of-the-way Chinese restaurant a block off of Grant Avenue. Near the end of the meal I mentioned that an announcement would be made the next afternoon that I would be transferred to New York.

Allison absorbed the information. I could not tell what she was thinking. "I hope this will be a good opportunity for you."

"I was told it should be. It will be a matter of what I make of it." Without hesitating, I added, "I'll miss you."

We both realized that we didn't know each other well enough to say more. I walked Allison to the BART station. We kissed like a husband and wife parting at a train station.

Friday night, after the announcement about my transfer was made, I called Allison. "I'd like to take you out to dinner. Since I'm leaving, maybe you won't want to bother."

"Bother is hardly an appropriate term. I'd love to."

We made a date for the next night. She told me there was a nice Italian restaurant near her apartment, and she would make a reservation for seven. Allison made another suggestion: "Instead of going back to your place, why don't you plan on staying over? My couch converts to a bed."

On Saturday, I arrived at Allison's apartment at six. She kissed me warmly. "I guess you're not my boss anymore." She kissed me again, with more fervor. A bottle of wine was already opened. We drank half before heading for dinner.

The restaurant menu was enticing from appetizers through dessert, but we each ordered only a main course. We knew dinner was not going to be the highlight of the evening.

At one point, Allison declared, "I'm glad you're not my boss anymore."

"I suppose I am for another few weeks."

"Not as far as I'm concerned. It's been announced. We're free to do what we want."

"And what do you want?" I asked, feigning innocence.

"The same thing you do."

We returned to Allison's apartment and grabbed the remains of the wine. As we sat on the couch, I gave Allison one last chance to depart from the path we were heading down. "It seems like this will make a very comfortable bed."

"For whom? You know you're not sleeping here."

"Not if I get a better invitation."

"Consider yourself invited."

We went to bed incredibly early.

That weekend I learned something from Allison that I hadn't learned from Jane or Kate or anyone else. When you're with someone appealing, it's touch—skin to skin, lips to lips, fingers to flesh—that's erotic. Proportions and contours matter much less.

Allison's body was thin, but not thin like Kate's. It was firm and angular. Her breasts were small. When she lay on her back, they nearly disappeared. Perhaps this is what her husband found unattractive, but I did not. I found her athleticism and flexibility exciting. When she was on top of me and let her long brunette hair cover both our heads, her sensuality was at its peak.

Our sex might even have been enhanced by the knowledge that we had so little time left together and had to make the most of it.

When I left for New York I took a picture of Allison with me. It showed her face, hair and shoulders. In the photo it was not apparent that she was nude, but I knew that she had been when it was taken, and that fact would help me when we separated.

XXV

Washington, 2062

KATE'S OPERATION TOOK PLACE ON Monday morning. A car picked her up from the apartment at six and drove her to the hospital for the pre-op work. At the same time, I departed for my apartment where I changed for work, had some orange juice and toast, and then departed for the F.E.D. building.

Kate had arranged for me to take over a small conference room just down the hall from her own office. She had entrusted Sam to bring me incoming communications of various types. Hazel Dumas left me a voicemail message, saying that she was having a staff meeting at two o'clock and inviting me to attend, if I wished.

Two hours passed slowly. I read reports and tried to become acquainted with the current issues facing the F.E.D. Frequently my thoughts turned to Kate. Sam stuck his head through the door around ten thirty. He was smiling. He said there was good news from the hospital. Kate's operation had gone well. She was in the recovery room. She would be kept in the hospital for one night and would likely be released the following morning. He gave me a number where Kate could be reached after three o'clock.

Before leaving to pass the same information on to Hazel and Wayne, Sam invited me to join him for lunch if I didn't have other plans. I immediately accepted.

As it turned out, Hazel Dumas joined Sam and me. We mainly talked about what was facing Kate. They assumed that I would stay with Kate for a few days, while she recuperated. Kate had

never made such an arrangement with me, even though it made
some sense. Nothing was said about Kate being a single female
and me being a male.

At an early opportunity, Sam made sure he told me how
much he was in awe of Kate and how grateful he was that she
gave him the opportunity to be her admin assistant. Hazel smiled,
a bit condescendingly, and asked, "Don't you think you earned the
position?"

"It could have easily been given to someone else. There were
dozens of qualified people to pick from."

I thought I detected a frown on Hazel's face, which would
have been odd, given her own success under Kate's tutelage.

During the meal, Hazel's conversation seemed guarded.
Perhaps it was Sam's presence; perhaps it was mine. I figured I
would have many opportunities to get to know her better.

I attended her staff meeting. Her part of the department was
responsible for data collection and reporting, not the part that
particularly interested me. As Hazel's subordinates, a few of whom
I knew, discussed glitches in assembling statistics and their need for
systems improvements, I was glad that I had forewarned Hazel
that I needed to duck out at three.

When I returned to my office, I called the hospital room
number Sam had given me. No one answered. I waited a half hour
and called again. This time, a groggy Kate responded.

"How are you feeling?" I asked the obligatory question.

"I don't know. Sleepy."

"No pain?"

"I think they gave me a lot of medication."

"I heard the operation went well."

"I'm sure that's what they always say. They're not going to tell
you they fucked up."

"No, what they'd tell you is that they encountered some
complications. But they didn't say that."

"Marvelous. But they cut me up pretty good. I'll probably

need the painkillers for a few days. I'll be going home tomorrow, they say. Will you come to the apartment to keep me company?"

"Of course." That was part of my job.

Kate's operation had been on Monday. Late Tuesday morning she was released from the hospital and driven back to her apartment. I was there to meet her. I stayed the night, sleeping in my own room. Kate was told to remain home on Wednesday, and she complied with the instructions. I stayed with her.

On Thursday, she went to the office. I rode with her in the electrocar that was sent for her. I did not meet with her until after lunch. By that point, I could see that she was fading.

"Can't you go home now?"

"No. I have two more meetings. I'll try to keep them brief. Maybe we can leave about four."

Kate and I had dinner together. I asked her if she would mind if I went back to my apartment that night. She was scheduled to have a follow-up appointment with her surgeon on Friday morning. A car would take her there and, subsequently, bring her to the office.

Kate teased me about having a date that night. I told her that I needed to wash some clothes. Her comment, however, reminded me that I did have a date, but it was on Saturday night.

I thought I better get the news out of the way. "Kate, I have a confession to make. I have an appointment on Saturday night. Do you mind if I keep it?"

"One doesn't have an appointment on Saturday night; one has a date. But that's beside the point. Of course keep it. I don't control your personal life. Tell me, is she attractive?"

"I guess so. We're only friends. I'm not sure I've ever kissed her, and if I did, it was only on the cheek."

"Hmm." Kate was suspicious of what I told her.

"I think I met her for the first time at a soirée at your apartment."

"What's her name?"

"Pat Auriga."

Kate shrugged, not recognizing the name.

"She used to go out with a friend of mine," I said, by way of further explanation.

"I told you, your having a date is fine with me. I give you my blessings." Kate forced a smile.

Although I felt a bit guilty leaving Kate alone that Saturday night, I was looking forward to spending some time with Pat. I called her on Friday to confirm that we still had a date for the following night. She replied that we certainly did, and she was looking forward to seeing me. After the brief call ended, I realized that I had used the word "date" rather than "appointment." So what, I concluded.

A half hour later, Kate stuck her head into my office, having returned from the follow-up session with her surgeon. "My doctor says she's pleased with the way my operation went and my post-op recuperation. Of course, that's what I expected. Anyway, I have the go ahead to proceed with my first radiation treatment on Tuesday."

"That's good news."

"I guess so."

"Do you want some company tonight or Sunday?"

"Actually I have an *appointment* tonight." I thought Kate put some emphasis on the word "appointment." "But give me a call on Sunday. Maybe I'll let you take me out to dinner."

"It would be my honor."

"So gallant, Sir James."

Somewhat before six on Saturday I arrived at the Metro stop a few blocks away from Pat's apartment in northwest Washington. It was one stop away from where I used to live. And, yet, it produced no sense of nostalgia.

Pat's apartment was on the second floor of a high-rise building.

She had a courtyard view. The combination living room/dining area was small. The dining table, placed against a wall, could seat only two comfortably. A love seat, easy chair, entertainment center, and low table comprised the living room furnishings. The kitchen, hardly in keeping with the balance of the apartment, was fairly large and well equipped.

After Pat greeted me with a hug and took the bottle of wine I had brought, she retreated to the kitchen to finish the meal's preparation.

"Do you mind if I watch?"

"I might even put you to work."

"Fine with me. But I have to warn you, my cooking skills are nil."

"You can open the wine. I'll do the cooking."

As I entered the kitchen, a raft of wonderful smells reached my nostrils. "Smells great."

"Just some chicken with mushrooms, spices, and red sauce. It's my own concoction."

"*Chicken Auriga.*"

"There's also a risotto with asparagus, and, to start, just a small caprese salad. I'm not much on desserts, but I could open some store-bought biscotti, if you wish."

"Sounds like a big feast, even without dessert. I should have brought a magnum of wine."

"And then we'd fall asleep at the movies. I'm going to hold you to your promise to take me out. There's a two-screen theater a few blocks from here."

"What's playing?"

"One's an animated picture which would probably be more appropriate for children."

"And the other is X-rated?"

Pat formed her lips into a pout. "Do you think I'd suggest something like that?"

"No. Sorry, ma'am." Perhaps Kate would have made the

suggestion.

"The other is a French language film about a family living in a poor neighborhood on the outskirts of Paris. My description doesn't sound great, but it got very good reviews."

"How's your French?"

"Don't be silly. It has subtitles."

"Then let's try it."

Dinner was excellent. I thought the risotto was particularly good, and I complimented Pat effusively. If she could cook like that, I wanted another invitation. She reacted shyly, suggesting it was not her cooking skill, only her Italian heritage, that was coming through.

During dinner, I told Pat what brought me to Washington. She expressed sympathy for Kate and told me that she had an aunt who successfully fought breast cancer. The implication was clear: it was a disease that could be whipped.

Then the talk turned to Pat's career. She was back at American University, teaching two courses, but still doing some freelance work with a singing group. However, she was pursuing something quite different involving work in Europe. When I pressed her for details, she demurred. "I don't want to jinx it," she explained.

"Is the job in France?" I probed further.

"I'm not going to tell you until it's all settled."

"Is it . . ."

"James, we're not playing twenty questions. I'll tell you if something materializes."

No doubt, Pat enjoyed the film more than I did. I tried to understand some of the dialogue, but could only pick up some phrases here and there. The French that I took in high school and college was fading from lack of practice. I consoled myself with the thought that a lot of slang, which I never knew, was employed.

I walked Pat back to her apartment. She offered me a cup of coffee or espresso if I wanted. I refused, saying either type would prevent my sleeping. Pat said that she had enjoyed the evening, and I agreed. She said we should get together again during my remaining time in Washington. Again I agreed, but we did not set a date. We gave each other hugs, and Pat kissed me on the cheek.

XXVI

New York, 2058

ON A TEMPORARY BASIS, I had rented a furnished studio apartment in the area south of Houston Street. I figured that during my first month in the city I could look for a more permanent address. I brought very few things from San Francisco. Most of the furniture that Jane and I had bought was sold. Only a chest of drawers, a TV, and kitchen utensils were shipped. There were no memories from the California apartment that I wanted to preserve.

I sent a message to about a dozen people, including Kate and Allison, giving my new address. Only one person immediately reacted—Jane's mother. "Why in the name of God did you leave California?"

"I was transferred," I responded blandly.

"But you have a wife and son somewhere in California."

"How do you know that?"

"You told me."

"But you doubted the report."

"Let's not play games."

"Remember, your daughter ran out on me. I didn't leave her. She could even have moved on elsewhere. I have to get on with my life. And that's that. If I hear anything about your daughter, I'll let you know." There was nothing more for either of us to say.

The New York office had not changed a great deal since my brief tour of duty there eight years earlier. About two-thirds of the staff was the same. Such is the way of a government bureaucracy.

The office was responsible for a region covering most of New York State, all of New Jersey, and the western half of Connecticut. To fulfill these responsibilities, my staff was fifty percent larger than the one I had had in San Francisco, and I had two assistant managers. One was a man about my age who had moved up in the organization only one notch since I was last in New York. The more capable person was a fifty-year-old woman, Carla Pettone, who had been on disability during my first tour. Within the first two months, I found that I could rely on Carla to manage both her projects and her staff effectively. I wondered why she hadn't been put in charge of a small region, since she had over twenty years of service in the department. At some point, I heard the rumor that she was an alcoholic. I, however, saw no evidence of this.

Kate called me a week after I assumed my new duties. She congratulated me on my new job and said we needed to get together. I asked Kate to name a date, but she begged off, declaring that she was way too busy to schedule anything. A month later, we made an appointment, but she ended up cancelling.

During my first month, I found an affordable one-bedroom apartment in Hoboken, New Jersey, and moved in in April. Directly across the Hudson River from Manhattan, Hoboken had a mass transit link directly into the city. It took me only twenty minutes to get to the office. I bought a cheap, second-hand bed, and a folding table and chair for eating. After a few weeks, I added an easy chair, again second-hand, and a small side table.

Allison and I spoke every few days when I first arrived in New York. After a while, this contact dwindled to once in a while. It was difficult to maintain a relationship across a continent and with no ability to meet face to face. I knew my feelings for her were waning when I found myself hoping she had found a man whom she could love. I knew I would not be that person. I figured she was probably doing better than I. I went to some bars where I should have been able to find a companionable woman. Somehow it didn't happen.

During the spring and summer, I found myself taking a trip—

naturally by railroad—to Washington every few weeks. I was put on two committees. One was the Regional Director Advisory Committee—the New York office was generally represented. The other was an ad hoc group to develop approaches to assure steady energy supplies over the next five years. That was as far ahead as Washington wanted to look.

As I was walking through the halls of the F.E.D. building during one of my trips, I thought I saw Kate in the distance. I tried to catch up with the statuesque blonde, but she evidently turned into an office because I couldn't find her.

That night I tried to reach Kate by phone, thinking we could meet if we were both in Washington. She did not answer, and I didn't leave a message.

At about the same time the economy perked up. Construction projects in the New York area were receiving funding. This meant more work for the office in reviewing the energy impact plans. I was happy to be busy with more activity in New York, plus the Washington committee work. The workplace kept my mind off the fact that my life outside of the office was empty and unrewarding.

Sometimes I wondered whether Mark was still alive. Perhaps he had made a miraculous recovery in the wilds of California's Humboldt County. I tried not to think of Jane. Her mother didn't call anymore, and that was fine with me.

I considered myself a bachelor, even though that was not my legal status. Sometimes I had trouble filling out forms, such as those in doctors' offices. Marital status? Who should be contacted in an emergency? I tried getting away with leaving these areas blank. If forced to choose, I answered "single." For the other question, I'd make up some fictional name and phone number.

I had opportunities to visit my mother and sister, and I did on one or two occasions. After I'd gotten settled in, Carla invited me to dinner after work. She had been married and then divorced three years later, but that was a long time earlier. She was nearly twenty years older than me. It would be a friendly evening with casual conversation occasionally touching on our mutual work. She made a salad, rigatoni with a *ragù* sauce and added some store-bought cannoli for dessert. It was a simple Italian meal, except the meat sauce was homemade, and preparation probably took several hours.

"You're married, James, aren't you?"

"Yes and no."

"I'm confused. Didn't you marry Jane Sorel who worked for Kate Hastings?"

"Yes, but we're . . . I'd guess you'd say . . . separated." For some reason I felt comfortable talking to Carla. It took me ten minutes or more to give her a summary of how my marriage deteriorated and then, in effect, ended with Jane's flight with Mark.

Carla listened carefully. "That's terrible. I feel so bad for you. I guess getting away from California was a good move."

"I think so."

"You like the office?" She meant the New York staff.

"They're fine."

"You know most of us are very happy to have you. Maybe I'm talking out of turn, but your predecessor was out of his depth. You have the education and background that's needed."

I was embarrassed by the praise, and tried to redirect the conversation. "And how do you like your job?"

"In general, I like it a lot. And I'm grateful to have it. I kind of went astray at one point. You might have heard something about it. So I'm happy to have an occupation which is meaningful and interesting and provides a decent living."

I did not know the facts, only the rumors. But I was not about to pry while her guest. I ate a cannoli, and Carla tried to get me to eat a second, which I resolutely refused. I left before any more food was foisted upon me.

At the beginning of December, I received a call from Kate. "How would you like to have dinner with me?"

"I'd love to. I thought you were trying to avoid me."

"In a sense I was, my neurotic friend. But I want to talk with you now."

As Kate was talking, I looked at my calendar. "Would Friday be good?"

"I was thinking about tonight. I'm in the city. Let's meet at six."

Of course, I had nothing planned for the evening, and Kate was being her insistent self. "Sure. We can do it tonight."

Kate gave me the name and address of a small restaurant in Greenwich Village. "We shouldn't encounter anyone we know there."

I had a little trouble finding the restaurant, which was designated by only a tiny plaque next to the front door. Kate sat in a back corner, looking at her watch. She already had a half-empty glass of wine in front of her, even though I was only five minutes late.

"Let's get you a glass of wine, so you can catch up," was how Kate began. She seemed wound-up and tense. "How are you doing?" she asked out of politeness.

"Fine, and you?"

"Couldn't be better."

"That's great."

"You ever find out what happened to Jane?"

"No, I haven't. I don't really think of her anymore. But I wish I knew what happened to Mark."

"Sure." Kate barely paused before moving on to a subject more to her liking. "Say, I hear you've gotten off to a good start in New York."

"You probably know better than I. I haven't gotten much feedback."

"You know you can do that job blindfolded and with one hand tied behind your back."

"Maybe so. I'd just have problems getting from my apartment

to the office."

"You were always somewhat of a wise ass. After we order, I have to tell you something important but highly confidential."

"Why wait?"

"Have some patience. We'll put our order in, so I can get out of here at a reasonable hour." Kate beckoned the waiter over to our table. "I'll order for both of us. I know what's good here."

"Sure. You're the boss."

"Not yet." Then, turning to the waiter, "We'll both have the salad with your house dressing, and then the *côte de veau* for two, medium rare. And let's have a bottle of that Volnay that I like."

"Very good, madame." He left quickly, somehow sensing that Kate did not want him to tarry.

"The waiter seems to think you're married."

Kate at first didn't understand my point. Then she educated me. "Women of a certain age are called 'madame,' whether they're married or not. I'm afraid I'm well past that point. No, I'm quite sure he realizes that I'm not married, considering the various companions who accompany me here. The way I spend money, he probably thinks I am either very rich or run a high class whore house."

"I could picture you in either role."

"Let's not get too frisky. Here's what I want to tell you. I'm returning to the F.E.D. I'm getting a deputy secretary position, but I'm told that Lantier wants to leave in the next six months. I think they'll be happy to have him go. Then, unless I really screw up in the interim, I'll get the top job."

"I'm impressed. Congratulations."

"That's premature. I wouldn't come back for the deputy position. You can say congratulations when I get the secretary spot. The news about my appointment should be announced on Monday. Don't say a damn word until it's out."

"I won't. Whom would I talk to anyway?"

"And don't get too settled in New York. I'll get you to

Washington when I can."

    "Sure. I'll put my fate in your hands."

    "Aren't you excited by the prospect?"

    I knew what I was expected to say: "Of course."

XXVII

Washington, 2062

FOR SEVERAL WEEKS AFTER KATE began her radiation treatments, she spent more time out of the office than I would have expected. Naturally, she took each day of a treatment off, and, in addition, almost always the following day. I was glad to see that she was putting her health first. But, beyond that, I sensed she was not fully engaged when in the office. She appeared distracted. Her ability to focus, always very strong, was now intermittent. Issues that would have been of great importance to her were now quickly delegated to a subordinate.

Hazel Dumas continued to include me in her staff meetings and occasionally forwarded a copy of communications she thought would be of interest to me. Most of these seemed to be innocuous in nature, and I wondered if more meaty items were withheld.

Never did I hear from Wayne Sickles unless I initiated the contact. He always expressed his desire to cooperate, but his actions belied his words. His area of the department focused on policy, my old specialty. Within his organization were a number of people whom I knew well. I would have welcomed contact with any of them, but they seemed to be avoiding me.

John Blount, one of Sickles's direct reports, was an old acquaintance. After being stonewalled by his boss for several weeks, I put in a call to him. "J.B., this is James Lendeman."

"I was wondering how long it would take to hear from you."

"So you were expecting my call?"

"What do you think?"

"Maybe we should get together for lunch and chat," I suggested.

"Think not, old friend."

I thought his response was positively rude. "You were told to avoid me or just not to cooperate?"

"You be the judge. Look, I'm not going to have lunch with you, and I don't want to talk on my office phone. But you are an old friend, and I wouldn't object if you wanted to buy me a beer."

"Okay. You name the time and place."

"You're staying near Dupont Circle. I know a nice bar near there. You going to be in your apartment around five thirty?"

"I'll be there."

"I'll call you."

Around the designated time, I received J.B.'s call and soon was heading down P Street, looking for The Duke's Pub. Blount was waiting just inside the door. "Buy me a pint of the Chandler's, and I'll get us a table back in the corner."

The pub was less than half full, so we were able to find a reasonably isolated table with adequate separation from any neighbors. "I suppose we're safe here," I commented.

"Is one ever totally safe? But we can talk." J.B. took a healthy swig of his beer, downing a third in one gulp. I hoped this would lubricate his tongue. "So here you are back again, working for your girlfriend."

"She's hardly my girlfriend."

"That's not the scuttlebutt around the office."

"I guess I can't stop tongues from wagging."

"Not if you spend the weekend at her apartment."

I was not in a position to refute the last point. I changed the subject. "You enjoy working for Sickles?"

"No better, no worse than anyone else." J.B. took another healthy drink from his glass.

Drink up, J.B., I thought. *We can't keep this pointless dance going much longer.* "Can I get you another pint?"

He looked down at his nearly empty glass. "Thanks, James. I guess the damn thing evaporated."

I went back to the bar and returned with a pint for him. My first was hardly touched.

"Thanks, James. You're a real sport. So what do you want to tell me?"

"I don't have anything to tell you. I just want to have a discussion."

"What do you want to discuss?"

"To start with, why doesn't your boss cooperate with me? Kate wants me to keep in touch with him, but he doesn't want to deal with me."

"James, you're going to be around maybe another month. He wants to be around for several years."

"So I represent a threat to him."

"Only in the sense that you're Kate's spy. You know, Wayne and Kate don't see eye-to-eye on some subjects. Plus, Wayne sees his star rising. Kate, even leaving aside her medical problem, is losing the ear of some top people." J.B. looked at my face for a reaction. "She probably wouldn't tell you this."

"No."

"I appreciate your honesty, James."

"So, tell me, what's the point of contention between Wayne and Kate?"

J.B. took a swig of his beer, a bit smaller than his earlier ones. At twelve dollars a pint, I hoped I would not have to buy another. "My boss thinks that Kate is still fighting the last war. And we lost that one."

"Meaning?"

"Meaning, Kate is still trying to get the U.S. a larger share of petroleum output. Wayne wants to have us cut our reliance on oil even more."

"We've cut so much already. We use so little now compared

with what we did fifty years ago. What do we use petroleum for now? Mainly aviation and military transportation."

"Wayne would say, 'Why stop at aviation?'"

"You want planes to fly on wind power?"

"How about a hybrid plane? Use aviation fuel to get off the ground and then let the plane fly on solar power. The sun always shines above the clouds."

"Not at night."

"Eliminate or severely restrict night flights. Also, get rid of relatively short-distance flights, like between Washington and Boston. They're very energy inefficient. Put in some more high-speed trains."

"These are huge changes you're suggesting."

"The collapse of the suburbs wasn't huge? The near elimination of private car ownership wasn't monumental? We've gone through a lot of big changes. Why not one or two more?"

"You made your point. But you expect a solar plane to fly?"

"First of all, it's a hybrid. And yes, it not only will fly, it has already."

"A full-size passenger plane?"

"A scale model. But that's not the point. The technology is there now. We can do it. We just need to concentrate on science and not foreign adventures."

"So you and Wayne think that Kate's leading the F.E.D.—and the country—in the wrong direction?"

J.B. put his hands up in a defensive position. "Hey, I'm just pointing out what might be done in this country. We're a technologically advanced country, and we can put that advantage to greater use."

I took a swig of my own beer, which was still only half drained. "I can't disagree with that," I confessed.

"Then do me a favor."

"What's that?"

"Talk to Kate. For some strange reason, she trusts you more

than anyone in the department. Open her eyes to other possibilities. You know, she was always strong willed, even in her first tour with the F.E.D. But her mind used to be more open to other points of view. She seems to be fixed now on a few narrow objectives."

It hurt me to hear these comments about Kate coming from a respected veteran of the department. Even if I dismissed some of J.B.'s argument as the normal sniping, which occurs in any organization, I had to admit that it contained an element of truth.

J.B. turned away from F.E.D. matters and asked me about how I was doing in Savannah. I asked about his family. But, essentially, our conversation had finished. He downed the last of his second beer and said he needed to head home. He thanked me for the beers, put his jacket on, and headed for the exit. I waited behind to finish my last sips of beer and ponder what I would do with the information I received.

During her treatments, I spent less time with Kate than I would have expected. She told me she wanted more time alone, that it was nothing to do with me, but solely was due to her own mood. I did not totally understand her point. I certainly could have helped her around the apartment.

Usually there was one day of the weekend when she would ask me to join her. We would find some place to walk. But these strolls would be short because the weather had turned fairly cold and blustery. I'd join her for dinner, and then generally return to my own apartment.

Only once did she ask me to spend the night. She must have felt particularly lonely or, perhaps, fatigued on that occasion. Kate asked me to lie next to her until she fell asleep. Then I returned to the bedroom reserved for me.

During this period, she did not complain of pain. But I sensed she was enduring quite a bit of discomfort in silence. She would remain silent for lengthy periods of time, and apologize for being such poor company.

One cold evening in early November, Kate asked me to join her for dinner. I arrived at six thirty. She was wearing jeans and a wool sweater over a cotton top. On her feet were faux fur slipper boots. The apartment was chilly. No doubt the thermostat was set at, or below, the requisite nineteen degrees.

"I don't want to go out tonight," Kate stated as her unusual form of greeting. "But I'm sick of pizza and Chinese food. Do you have any suggestions?" Kate shifted the burden to me.

I thought for a second. "There's a place on the next street with barbecued chicken and ribs. It looks like they do take-out. Does that appeal to you?"

Without enthusiasm, Kate replied, "It's different. I'll settle for that."

"What do you want—ribs or chicken?"

She thought briefly. "I don't really care. Surprise me." She handed me a hundred dollar bill. "Do you think that will be enough?"

"I would hope so." I headed back out, never having taken my coat off.

The place was called the "Barbecue Pit" but was more of a store than a restaurant. There were half a dozen tables for those who wanted to dine in, but all business was done at a counter with a display case. The food was already prepared. So the line, which consisted of only three customers when I entered, moved quickly. I ordered some chicken, ribs, French fries, and coleslaw. The total came to about seventy dollars, a bargain considering prevailing prices and the upscale neighborhood.

I returned to Kate's apartment in fifteen minutes. "That was quick. Did they even bother to cook the food?" She commented.

"They do a big take-out business. It's prepared in advance." I put her change on the kitchen countertop. "Are you hungry?"

"A little bit. I'll manage to eat something." After the food was unwrapped, Kate took a chicken leg, a few French fries, and a spoonful of coleslaw. She poured a Diet Coke for herself, since she was supposed to avoid alcohol for the time being.

"Not bad," Kate observed after her first bite. For a minute we were silent as I ate, and Kate snacked. After she finished most, but not all, of the meager amount she had on her plate, Kate wiped her hands and lips with her napkin, a sign that she had finished. I was sorry to see this, because she had obviously lost weight over the past six weeks. Weight loss was something Kate could ill afford.

When her hands were clean, she patted my forearm. "I want you to know, James, that I appreciate what you're doing both here at home and in the office. You keep me company, even when I'm not good company. I've been in business and in government, and I guess I've been too busy to make many friends. I count you as one of the most important."

I was touched by Kate's little speech. It was difficult for me to reply. "It's an honor to be your friend. I've always admired you so much for your abilities, your intelligence, your determination. Frankly, I never could understand why you've shown an interest in me. I'm so ordinary when compared with you."

Kate shook her head. "You sell yourself short. At first I noted your academic and technical knowledge, something I really don't have. Then I grew to appreciate your counsel and level-headedness. I always felt I could count on you. You never had your own agenda. You were loyal, almost to a fault. You probably shouldn't have been so devoted to me. Your loyalty may have helped your career initially. Later, it may have held you back."

I listened to Kate and wondered if she was talking about the falling out we had had two years earlier. It had been a painful time for me, a time when I needed to escape from Kate. But even back then she helped me break away, and we generally forgot those differences and difficulties.

"You know, I have something else to confess. I always enjoyed having a handsome man around." Kate smiled, perhaps at herself.

"Me? I don't consider myself good looking."

"You're so humble. I think I know something about looks. Just accept the compliment."

"It's more than a compliment coming from an unquestionably beautiful woman."

"You see me as I was when we first met. I guess you haven't looked at me lately."

"Kate, you haven't lost your looks. You have a health problem right now. After you're finished with this, you'll again be the reigning beauty of Washington."

Kate laughed. "You're such an unabashed flatterer. I'm a faded beauty now. And I doubt if I'll be in Washington a year from now."

Kate's comment shocked me, because I misinterpreted it. "Please don't say that."

"Oh, I don't expect to be dead in a year. I'm talking about leaving government. This illness made me think about how I'm enjoying my job less and less. There's too much backbiting and sniping.

"Also, I could be earning twice as much in private industry. I have to think about saving more money. This illness made me realize I'm getting older, and I need more money in the bank. I have to think about taking care of myself." Kate looked at me, seeking some reaction. "Aren't you going to say something?"

"I'm not the person to advise you in these matters. I live from month to month. I can understand your wanting to earn more money. I also realize that there are conflicting views within the department."

"You've heard people publicly expressing doubts about what we're doing within my department?" Kate eyes flashed a touch of anger.

"Yes, a bit. Isn't that what you were referring to when you mentioned back-biting and sniping?"

"I was talking about government in general. What goes on between the executive and the legislative branches. What you find between one department and another. What did you pick up in the F.E.D.?"

I knew I was going to attract Kate's ire, but now was my opportunity to share the information I received from John Blount. "There are some people who feel that more emphasis should be placed on conservation and new technology, while moving further away from petroleum dependence."

"Move further away from petroleum dependence! God, we only use it for aviation, agriculture, chemical production, and the military. We've cut to the bone."

"I heard the suggestion that we could develop hybrid passenger planes."

"I see where this is coming from—Wayne Sickles. He'd like my job, but he's not ready for it. If I leave in two years, he might be. But if I leave in six months, he'll be passed over.

"But here's my real point. There are two things you should think about. First, I've heard this proposal for a hybrid plane. Look up the data about how much fuel is used to take off as opposed to cruising at altitude. You're not going to get a plane in the air using solar power.

"Second, you've got to realize that there's a Department of Transportation, a Commerce Department, a Defense Department. The F.E.D. has more to do with controlling the fuel supply than determining its use. We can't step on the toes of all those other departments. We can advise, but we're expected to collaborate. Transportation has looked at the hybrid plane and does not want to pursue it. Even if I wanted to exercise more control over everything connected with energy, the president would not permit it."

Kate had stated her points firmly and probably didn't expect a rejoinder, but I still wanted to explore some middle ground. "I realize you can't control the work of other departments, but when it comes to energy usage and technological innovation, we have generally been able to exert some influence."

Kate did not react immediately. She took a drink of cola. "Yes,

I suppose we still should exert some influence, but the hybrid plane is a loser." Almost without hesitating, she went on to say, "That chicken was really good. You got it just down the street?"

"Yes."

"I'll have to get their menu."

"I'm sure I brought one back."

Kate did not return to a work topic. Her energy level seemed to flag after our somewhat heated discussion. Her mind turned elsewhere. She talked about having a vacation once she was fully recovered from her surgery and treatments. Paris was at the top of her list. She told me that she had spent a week there fifteen years earlier and vowed to return.

I mentioned that I had spent three nights in Paris as part of a brief European tour I took after graduation. We talked about why we liked the city—its incredible beauty, the food, the ability to stroll the streets. I commented that I liked to linger in a café and watch the people passing by.

Kate rejected that idea. "Why would I want to look at other people? Maybe they want to look at me. No, I don't want to sit and watch the world go by. You know me. I want the world to revolve around me. Egotistical, I suppose. Don't you think?"

What could I say in return? If I agreed with her, she would find it offensive. If I objected, I would be lying. "No, not really." It was only a white lie.

I could see Kate's eyes were closing and suggested that I leave. She did not object. I put my jacket on. She planted a good-bye kiss on my cheek as I departed.

XXVIII

New York, Washington, 2059

AS SHE HAD FORETOLD DURING our dinner in Greenwich Village, Kate was nominated by the president to be deputy secretary for energy policy. The press release included some biographical information, highlighting her experience in government as well as private industry. Her nomination was quickly approved by the Senate, and she moved back to Washington in January 2059.

Once Kate was settled in her job, I expected to receive a prompt call to report to Washington. I was mistaken. For four months I waited in New York.

In the spring, Kate toured the regional offices, including a one-day visit to New York. She made a speech to the staff in which she promised that they would be involved in new and exciting work, without giving any specifics. She met individually with several people of different ranks. Kate and I took six staff members to lunch. She was gracious but not informative.

At three in the afternoon Kate met privately with me before leaving. She told me that she enjoyed her visit. I asked if she wanted to impart any words of wisdom based on what she heard and saw. No, she told me, it appeared that the office was running well. After delivering some additional platitudes, she seemed ready to leave.

"If you have another few minutes, Kate, would you mind giving me an update about my potential transfer to Washington?"

"James, have a little more patience. We're trying to work out some moves, one of which would involve you." She didn't excuse what I considered to be a delay and evasion on her part. She clearly didn't want to say more. We shook hands, and she departed.

Carla was one of my staff who had had a one-on-one meeting with Kate. I asked her to join me and give me her impressions of the meeting.

"Kate said she was enjoying her visit and that she wanted to get updated on activities, since she had been out of the department for two years."

"Did she ask any difficult questions?"

"No, not at all. In fact, for someone who was seeking information, she talked a surprising amount and didn't ask too many questions. I guess she did listen to the answers I gave her."

Probably I shouldn't have given Carla my opinion. "Yes, that's Kate's major weakness—she should be a better listener."

"Maybe I shouldn't tell you this," Carla continued without my prompting. "But Kate spoke about you. She said the office was fortunate to have you in charge."

"I hope you agreed with her."

I'm not sure if Carla realized that I was kidding. "I didn't have a chance. She continued with several more compliments. If I didn't know better, I would think she had some fondness for you."

How did Carla "know better," I wondered, picking on her turn of phrase.

Kate kept me waiting for the call to come to Washington. Then, as usual, she wanted me to respond immediately to her summons. One steamy day in late June, the first day that announced we were truly entering summer, Kate called a few minutes before noon. "Say, James, I hope you're not planning any vacation in early July."

"I'm planning to take July fourth off."

Kate sidestepped my attempt at humor. "I'm talking about a real vacation—a week or two."

"I have no vacation plans." Why would I? Where would I get the money? Where would I go?

"Good, because I'll need you to come down here for a day or two. We're going to announce that you're taking Leo's job when he moves to Treasury." Kate had communicated a lot in one sentence. I also noted that I was offered no choice in the matter. Additionally, Leo's job would not have been my first choice. I was digesting all this. "Are you still there, James?"

"Yes, sorry. I heard you. I'm trying to take it all in."

"Let me be clear. On paper you're taking Leo's job, which is mainly administrative in nature, as you know. But I want you to spend a lot of time on policy issues."

"That's good."

"After we make the announcement, I'd like you to wrap things up in New York and get down here by August first at the latest."

"Okay. And who's getting the New York job?"

"Hasn't been fully worked out yet. And, of course, keep all this hush-hush until we're prepared to make the announcement."

"I assume Leo knows of the change at this point."

"Assume nothing. *Entendu*?"

I had no idea what caused Kate to lapse into French. But I responded, "*Bien sûr.*"

Monday, July 7, was the day of the big announcement in the Federal Energy Department. Leo Frase was going to an equivalent position in the Treasury Department. I was taking Leo's job. No information was given about my assuming some policy responsibilities. An assistant, Joan Leach, was being brought in from Denver to be my second in command. Perhaps some people wondered why I needed an assistant, when Leo did without. Tea Montfort was moving from Chicago to New York to take my former spot. Her second in command in Chicago was to be promoted into Tea's position.

The staff in New York congratulated me. They knew that the move meant a promotion for me. In a sense, they would not be removed from my supervision because Tea, as well as the other regional directors, now reported to me.

After the announcement was made and I went back into my office, Carla followed me. "I'm happy for you. Remember your friends in New York after you leave the Big Apple and return to the big circus."

"Don't worry, you'll get to see me from time to time."

"I hope so. Say, what do you know about Tea Montfort?"

"Not a great deal. I've been in a few meetings with her. She seems bright and knowledgeable."

"How is she to work for?"

I saw where Carla was heading. "I really don't know."

"You may not realize this, but I haven't had a woman boss for years. And that was not a pleasant experience. I hope this time will be better."

"Well, I'm going to have a female boss, too."

"The same one you had a few years ago. I'm sure you know her real well. And obviously she had a say in picking you for the new job. It takes no genius to see that she likes you."

"We got along." I tried to minimize our closeness.

"But this Tea hasn't ever met me."

"You'll be a big help to her, just as you've been to me."

What surprised me—in our day and age—was that Carla was concerned about having a female boss. Our discussion was the type that might have occurred in the prior century.

I saw no point in lingering in New York. Tea Montfort spent a day with me in mid-July. She was introduced to the staff, and we discussed ongoing projects and some issues unique to the New York region.

By July twenty-fourth I was in Washington looking for a short-term lease on an apartment. On Monday, July twenty-eighth, I reported to Kate and was immediately surprised.

"James, meet T.T. Basso."

I stared at a good-looking man of medium height with wavy

black hair and piercing blue eyes. The name that Kate had offered sounded like "tittie," which could not have been correct.

As I shook the man's hand, I needed to rectify my ignorance. "Sorry, I didn't quite catch the name."

"Basso, T.T. Basso."

"James Lendeman."

"Kate was just telling me about you. I gather we'll be working a lot together."

"Great," but somehow I suspected that it would not be the case.

At this point Kate broke in. "I hired T.T. to help us with some policy initiatives. He's spent a number of years in business. I met him while in my last job. He worked for a competitor."

Later, I found out that the title T.T. assumed was "Director of Policy Issues." It was a title I would have liked. My fear of getting bogged down in routine administration was magnified. I barely knew Joan Leach, the assistant director Kate had chosen for me. I hoped she would be able to handle most of the day-to-day issues and command enough respect to serve as the primary point of contact for the regional directors. In that way, my time would be freed up to work in the policy arena, assuming that Kate would fulfill her promise.

My first task was to get accustomed to my new duties. Having dealt with Leo Frase for several years, I had the perspective of a regional director as to what should be done in Washington. Two keys responsibilities were coordinating and supervising the activities of the regions. Aiding regions which might be deficient in staff or talent was another. After two weeks on the job, with Kate having given me no special projects on which to work, I made an appointment to visit the Boston office. I had never had occasion to visit Boston and knew the regional director only from us both being present at the same meetings. The visit was a get acquainted opportunity.

When visiting Boston, I tried not to make Kate's mistake. I

asked plenty of questions and listened to the answers. Tim London, the regional director, had just about made a career in his position. He had been promoted to his current job eight years earlier, after having spent ten years as the prior director's assistant. He made my visit pleasant. His assistant, Emily Verlingham, was quite young. With her youth came enthusiasm. Before I left, London told me to keep my eye on his assistant. He thought that she should get an assignment in Washington within a few years, so she wouldn't get lost in the organization. I wondered whether he was also alluding to his own experience.

Since I considered my visit to Boston a success, I decided to schedule another regional visit. This time to Pittsburgh. I planned to acquire some experience doing these visitations in nearby offices before venturing across country.

As I began to leave Joan Leach on her own to handle routine office activity, I became impressed with her intelligence and proactive approach to problem solving. She also helped me gather some information about the newest addition to the F.E.D.—Mr. T.T. Basso.

He had been trained as a lawyer, and I suppose in some sense he worked in the broad area of corporate law. At several points he worked for a few large manufacturing and technology firms. At times he had had his own consulting business. His specialty involved helping his own company or clients dissolve or break contracts that might prove to be financially disadvantageous, in other words, "money losers."

People variously described him as very clever, wily, and even "smarmy." He was just a tad over forty, twice-divorced, and not known to have any current romantic attachments. He had lived in the northeast, Chicago, Los Angeles, and Houston at various times. His law degree had been obtained at Tulane. One additional fact emerged: his given name was Thurston.

More difficult to determine was why Kate thought she needed Basso's talents. It briefly crossed my mind that she found him sexually attractive. But I dismissed that notion, because Kate almost always put business before pleasure.

In October, Kate asked me to do something, which she characterized as a favor. "Please take T.T. to a few regional offices, so he can get a feel for what goes on there."

"Sure," I replied, but I was not all that happy about the request.

The following day, I told Kate that I would take T.T. to New York, Chicago, and Atlanta.

Kate's reaction came quickly, "Oh, he's been to those places all too often. How about throwing in Dallas and San Francisco instead of New York and Chicago?"

I was about to ask whether these trips were designed to tour offices or cities. I held my tongue. "I'll include Dallas, but I don't want to take him to San Francisco."

Kate gave me a sharp glance. "Does this have something to do with Jane? You're going to have to deal with your phobia."

"I will when business requires."

"I see. You think these trips with T.T. are just junkets?"

I chose to think the question was rhetorical, and therefore, I didn't respond.

With T.T.'s concurrence, I scheduled Atlanta and Dallas for one trip, going first to Atlanta for what amounted to a short day's visit. We flew into Atlanta on a Tuesday morning in November. Hartsfield Airport was a monument to overcapacity. Two terminal buildings continued in use. The others were boarded up.

We took a taxi, electric-powered of course, to the regional office, which was at the northern edge of the city center. The interstate winding north to, and then through, the city was also a testament to an era that no longer existed. At places the road was five lanes wide in each direction. Now two lanes sufficed. The balance had either been closed, so no maintenance was required, or was employed for a light rail system.

We arrived at the office around noon and immediately went into a conference room, where Max Montgomery, the regional director, had arranged for us to have sandwiches and soft drinks with a few members of the staff. T.T. looked somewhat disappointed with the set-up. Probably he had hoped to go to a restaurant for lunch. With reluctance, he opted for a roast beef sandwich on white bread and an iced tea.

After lunch, several members of the staff delivered presentations on current office activities. I had arranged such events for visitors to San Francisco and New York. We called them "dog and pony shows." T.T. demonstrated only slight interest. He asked a few questions when a fairly attractive redhead delivered her segment. After the presentations, we walked around the office, during which Max described what was done in each section.

At some point—probably around four—T.T. looked at his watch and said that he needed to make some calls. Max offered his office, so T.T. could have some privacy.

Max and I walked away, well out of earshot. "What do you make of him?" Max asked.

"T.T.? I don't know. I'm not sure what he's supposed to contribute. But Kate is shrewd. She must have something up her sleeve."

"He doesn't seem very interested in our work. Why did he want to take this tour, anyway?"

"I'm not sure he wanted to do the tour at all. I think it was Kate's idea."

In due course, T.T. rejoined us. We had a short, meaningless discussion with Max. T.T. looked at his watch several times. Finally, he asked, "Do you think there's anything else for me to learn here?"

Max didn't want to answer the question. I responded, "It depends how much depth you want to go into."

"I'm a big picture guy," T.T. asserted.

"Then I think we've concluded our visit," I said succinctly.

T.T. and I went back to the hotel. He said he had more calls to make. Then at six thirty we went to dinner. Although we clearly didn't relish each other's company, dining together was preferable to dining alone. We both ordered steaks, perhaps our first point of agreement during the trip. The steaks were only passable. T.T. doused his with ketchup.

The conversation started slowly. "You've known Kate for quite a while," T.T. stated, but clearly he expected a response.

"I guess it's approaching ten years."

"I met her about a year ago. She's quite a woman."

I preferred to express no opinion on the subject. T.T. continued, "Has she ever been married?"

"Not to my knowledge."

"She's not a lesbo."

"I'm pretty sure she's not."

"Good. I wouldn't want to think of her wasted on a woman."

Again I didn't interject my thoughts. T.T. didn't seem to care. "She's bright and tough. She wouldn't take shit from anyone."

"She can take care of herself," I responded mildly.

"Yeah, self-sufficient." T.T. made an abrupt shift in the subject. "You like this energy stuff, don't you?"

"This is my training and background."

"I suppose you know I'm a lawyer." T.T. was trying harder than I was to keep the conversation going.

"So I heard. But to tell the truth, I don't quite see where your skills fit into the organization."

"Yeah. I suppose I'm kind of the mystery man. I'll give you a little clue, because it seems that we're bound to work together. But keep this info to yourself. I understand, and you would know better than I, that certain parties have locked up more than their share of world oil resources. We have to see if we can break more loose."

I might have said, *Been there, tried that,* but I kept that thought to myself. I wanted to hear more from T.T.

"We've got to change the momentum. It's our patriotic duty.

I have some talents to contribute to the process. My consulting business focused on, what should I say, such things." Suddenly, T.T. stopped. "I think I've said as much as I should. Kate will have to fill you in."

We continued eating somewhat in silence, except when T.T. took some calls. He had left his phone on. Each time a call came in, he'd go to a quiet corner and talk for a few minutes before returning. I thought it a bit rude, but frankly I didn't mind his absence.

The next day, in Dallas, we went through much the same routine that we had followed in Atlanta. During a break in the middle of the afternoon, T.T. asked me, "Are they going to cover anything different?"

"They're reviewing the type of work they do. With small variations, all the regional offices perform similar functions."

T.T. looked perturbed. "Then why the hell are we visiting three offices?"

"That's what Kate wanted." I saw the scowl on T.T.'s face.

"Is there anything different about Chicago?"

"Michigan Avenue and deep-dish pizza."

"You know I lived in Chicago for a year."

"Then you know all about deep-dish pizza. You won't learn anything new. I'll talk to Kate. We'll cancel next week's trip and save the taxpayers some money."

Upon my return to Washington, I managed to spend a few minutes with Kate. I told her that T.T. and I thought that additional visits to regional offices would not add much to T.T.'s knowledge. Kate exhibited a brief flash of displeasure, because the visits had been her idea. But then she dropped the subject quickly, saying, "Whatever you think is best. Did you get the invitation to my holiday party?"

"I didn't see it, but I haven't gotten through my inbox yet."

"I'm sure it's there." With that, Kate looked down at some papers on her desk, indicating that my time was up.

"I hope you don't mind my asking, but when . . ."

Kate cut me off. "I know you're looking for the big project I had talked about. Nothing's going to happen until after the holidays. Then, hopefully, we'll get started."

Two days before Kate's party, it was announced that Gregory Lantier was resigning as head of the F.E.D. He was scheduled to leave at the beginning of January. Kate would be acting secretary until her nomination for the position of secretary was confirmed by the Senate. Since Kate had recently been approved for the deputy secretary job and had not done anything egregious in the interim, all expected quick confirmation.

About one hundred people attended Kate's party, which was held in the rotunda of the F.E.D. building. The holiday aspect seemed to take a backseat to the celebration of Kate's nomination. An impromptu receiving line formed. Kate filled the role of fairy princess admirably. I barely had a chance to utter my few words of congratulations before having to move on, pushed to the side by other well-wishers. I spent time chatting with department colleagues and a few members of Congress. The party was supposed to end at nine, but it lasted well past ten.

The F.E.D. party proved to be my office party, Christmas party and New Year's Eve party all rolled into one. In the middle of December, with no prospect of meeting family or friends for the holidays, I was feeling particularly lonely. The F.E.D. staff qualified as acquaintances, not friends. There was only one person in Washington whom I cared to talk to, and I hadn't seen her for over three years.

It took me two days to gather my courage to call Pat Auriga. I didn't reach her directly but had to leave a message. Surprisingly, she called back within an hour. "James, this is Pat."

"Thanks for calling back. I've returned to Washington and wanted to say hello."

"I'm glad you called. How long has it been since we've talked?

Two years?"

"I think more like three. You and Steve were passing through San Francisco on your way to China."

"I guess you know it didn't work out between Steve and me."

"I suspected it didn't. But I haven't kept in touch with Steve."

"That makes two of us. How are Jane and your son?"

The question made me realize how much had changed over three years. "It's a long story. We're no longer together. Mark got sick, and she took him away. I haven't seen either in about two years."

"Oh, my. I'm so sorry. Are you working in Washington now or just passing through?"

"I'm living here and still working for the F.E.D."

"Didn't I hear that your old boss is going to be secretary?"

"She's my old and current boss. And yes, she's nominated for the job. You're still teaching at American University?"

"Yes, among other things."

"Do you think it would be possible to get together and catch up on news?"

"Sure. I'd like that. We could get together for coffee sometime."

"Do you want to name a date?"

"I'm taking a little year-end vacation with my boyfriend. Can we get in touch after I return?"

"Sure. You have my number." I hoped my voice had not betrayed my disappointment. But why shouldn't Pat have a boyfriend? She could have been married by now. She was attractive, intelligent, and personable. A woman like that doesn't stay single forever.

Between Christmas and New Year's I continued feeling low. My conversation with Pat had not improved my spirits, and, in fact, may have produced the opposite effect. I decided to contact Allison. I remembered having sent her notice of my new address in Washington. But neither of us had called the other.

When I called, Allison recognized my voice instantaneously. "James, how good of you to call. Merry Christmas, Happy New Year."

"Yes, same to you."

"I imagine by now you're all settled in Washington. When did you get there? September?"

"Actually, July."

"How are you doing?"

"I'm doing okay. Are you enjoying the job?"

"Yes, it's fine. It's the personal relationships that tend to be the challenge."

"I hope you're not referring to you and me?" I asked.

"No, I was thinking of my husband. But things are looking up now. I've met a man who I'm really attracted to, and I think the feeling is mutual. He's nothing like my former husband. He's Australian."

"What does he do?"

"He's trying to get established as a swimming coach. He's very good at it."

I thought, *I hope he is; otherwise, you'll end supporting him just as you did your husband.* Instead, I said, "That's fascinating. I hope it works out. I didn't realize San Francisco's a swimming center."

"It's not. He mainly works in Los Angeles, but we get together as much as possible." Allison realized that her description of the relationship made it seem tenuous. "I guess the situation doesn't sound ideal. But we seem to be able to make it work."

"That's good. I wish you all the best."

We spoke for another few minutes about work. She hoped I could visit the San Francisco office, and we could get together for dinner or a drink. I thought it was possible, and didn't point out that, in a sense, I was again her boss.

We ended the conversation by wishing each other a prosperous and happy new year. Did I feel better after talking to Allison? Probably not.

XXIX

Washington, 2062

KATE'S TREATMENTS CONTINUED FROM OCTOBER into November. I was still going to the F.E.D. daily. This activity, however, amounted to attendance rather than work. At home Kate needed me less and less. She kept me on and kept paying me.

I began reading a series of mystery novels. I felt that I was getting lazy and falling into old, bad habits.

Around the middle of November, Pat Auriga called me. "How come I haven't heard from you?"

"Didn't we talk last week?"

"No, more like three weeks ago. Are you still in Washington?"

"Yes, still baby-sitting Kate."

"So that keeps you busy morning and night?"

"No, of course not." I realized that Pat wanted some attention from me. "Gee, I'm sorry. I've been preoccupied, running all sorts of errands for Kate." I lied.

"Okay, I'll accept your apology. Anyway, I have some news to share with you."

"What is it?"

"Why don't we get together? I'd rather tell you in person."

"Sure, that would be great."

"You can come over for dinner."

"Can I take you out to a restaurant this time?"

"You don't like my cooking."

"It's not that. You're cooking is excellent, but I'll feel guilty if you keep on cooking for me. It's my treat this time."

Pat relented and we set a date for the upcoming Wednesday. I wanted to avoid the weekend, in case Kate might need me. Pat and I ended up at a non-descript neighborhood restaurant, which provided an eclectic menu. The food proved to be no better than adequate, but the leatherette booth gave us a moderate amount of seclusion and quiet.

After we ordered, I quickly urged Pat to divulge her news. She took a sip of her chardonnay before beginning. "I don't know where to start. Well, you know I've been thinking of doing something different to add some excitement to my life."

I nodded in assent.

"So, I thought that I'd pursue a job in Europe. Living in a foreign country, learning a language, acquiring a new set of friends—all this should keep me challenged."

"I bet it will. I wouldn't even know how to go about getting a job overseas."

"I did it the same way I'd go about it here—networking. Fortunately the music community tends to be international in character. I spoke to acquaintances in France, Italy, Germany, and the Czech Republic. I got a number of leads and eventually two panned out."

"So where are you going and what will you be doing?"

"Give me a chance." Obviously Pat wanted to add to the drama. "I pursued two jobs, one in Germany and one in Italy."

"You're going to Italy," I guessed.

"Okay, you got it, but your chances were fifty-fifty."

"It wasn't pure luck. You can speak some Italian and you're of Italian heritage. The old country attracted you."

"I'm not sure those were the reasons. I speak some German, too. We singers need to have familiarity with a number of languages."

"*Sehr gut.*" I inserted my few words of German, and briefly my thoughts turned to a stroll along the Kaerntnerstrasse with Kate, almost exactly nine years earlier.

"I chose the job in Italy because I think it will be more interesting."

"Will you be roaming around Italy or based in one city?"

"Oh, I guess I didn't say. I'll be in *Firenze*, Florence."

"Florence is a great city for art. But how about music?"

"It's not quite like Rome or Milan. There's a nice concert hall and some other venues for chamber music. There's a modest music festival, which mainly features younger musicians. I'll be doing work for the festival. But also I'll be giving some voice lessons. The music part will be interesting, but imagine living amid all that art and history. I always wanted to learn more about Renaissance art, and I'll be in the place where the Renaissance started."

"I'm envious."

Pat looked into my eyes and could see I was being honest. "Couldn't you find something in your field in Europe? No one's forcing you to live in Savannah."

"No, Savannah was my choice for a getaway. But I couldn't work in Europe. My expertise is not a good fit there. They have their own energy specialists."

"And they have their own musicians."

"*Touché*. It's a little different when national interests are involved. Plus you have more familiarity with the languages. I took some French in college, but I haven't used it in years. I think I'll just stay put in the U.S. where I can stick with English."

"You could learn a foreign language," Pat persisted. "There are all sorts of computerized language programs."

"I suppose so," I replied without enthusiasm.

Pat told me that she would be leaving for Florence after the first of the year. She asked about my schedule, and I projected that I would be in Washington for another two or three weeks. Kate was coming to the end of her treatments. Unless there was some setback, she would have no further need for my services. In fact, I confessed to Pat, I felt I was helping Kate little at the F.E.D. I was serving more as a companion than an aide. During my weeks in Washington I found it difficult to get involved in the work of the department and make a contribution. Despite my background, I felt like an outsider, and to a large extent I was treated as such.

Pat listened to my modest complaint. She was not very sympathetic. "So you had to put up with a less than meaningful job for a month or so. Millions of people are doing that every day. And you'll be back in Savannah before too long, maybe doing an even less meaningful job."

"You're cruel."

"Sorry, didn't mean to be. But I've been stuck in lousy assignments. It happens to practically everyone. You can live with it, grouse about it, or try to do something to change it."

"But that's frequently easier to say than to do."

Pat shrugged and then changed the subject. "You'll be around Washington until early December?"

"Or at least until the end of November."

"Do you have any plans for Thanksgiving?"

"I haven't even thought about it. I'll either cook myself a frozen dinner or try to find a neighborhood restaurant that's open."

"No, you won't. Practically every restaurant is closed for Thanksgiving. And just to fill you in, it comes on the twenty-third. Here's what I propose. I'm invited to a friend's home for Thanksgiving dinner. I'm sure she'll let me bring a friend."

"I'm the friend you have in mind?"

"Who else?"

"I'm flattered." It suddenly crossed my mind that Kate might want my companionship on Thanksgiving. "Can I get back to you tomorrow? I really want to join you. But I need to check on something."

"You need to see if you can get a better offer," Pat teased. But perhaps there was some honesty lurking beneath the surface.

"To be truthful, I need to check to make sure Kate doesn't need me. You know I'm a hired hand. But be assured I'd rather spend the holiday with you."

"Now it's my turn to be flattered. I hope Kate gives you the day off."

Our dinner had ended. I paid the bill, and we walked back to Pat's apartment. As we parted, Pat planted a kiss on my cheek. I wondered whether we would ever find it appropriate to kiss on the lips.

XXX

Washington, 2060

IN MID-JANUARY, KATE CONVENED a small meeting. Attending were T.T., Paul Reiner from the policy section, me, and—of course—Kate. She announced that we were going to take a look at how the United States could acquire a larger share of world petroleum production. *Here we go again*, I thought. Kate acknowledged that we had taken a look at this problem before and were not successful. This time, she had convinced the president that a small commission should be established to attack the issue. "Attack" was Kate's term.

She asked us to generate ideas on how the group should be structured. There was a flip chart in the corner of the conference room. Kate asked Paul Reiner to man the flip chart and capture all ideas. At first we all were reluctant to speak. Then Paul, who evidently had some experience at this sort of thing, told us to just throw out ideas and not prejudge if they were good or bad. After we generated a good number, we'd start to group them, evaluate them, and select the ones we liked the best.

Kate started, and tossed out three or four ideas in succession. I remember one of hers was making sure we had a balance between men and women. That led me to propose that all major stakeholders needed to be represented. Someone asked me to elaborate. I told them that, unless we included people from the various governmental departments that would be affected, as well as from industry, from consumer groups, etc. our eventual proposals would be attacked by the parties who did not have a chair at the table. With the ice broken, everyone started throwing out ideas, including Paul, who had to ask us to slow down a few times in order for him to capture our thoughts.

After forty-five minutes, the action slowed down. We took a break. Then we got down to lumping similar ideas together, and finally prioritizing the items into those that we had to do, those that would be nice to do, those that could be done if convenient, and those that could be dropped. I sensed some pride of authorship. T.T. particularly lobbied for a few of his proposals that the rest of us thought had little merit. However, we worked through these issues and ended up with a list of ten principles to guide us. One of mine, which made the cut, was about including all stakeholders. Kate insisted on making one modification: "I don't want any environmentalists on the commission. We use so few polluting fuels, they need not be concerned by a slight increase."

The commission was put together amazingly quickly. In part this was due to Kate's insistence on keeping the membership small. Presumably this would enable us to avoid getting bogged down, but the narrowness of representation could lead to criticism by those omitted from the process.

In addition to the original four people from the F.E.D., and one person from each of three government departments—State, Defense, and Transportation—two people from private industry, two scientists, and an economist were included. Before the full commission met, Kate scheduled a planning meeting, which included the four of us from the F.E.D., plus the representative from the Defense Department, Darren Lee. Since Kate tended to distrust State and Transportation, their representatives were excluded from the preliminary meeting. Kate wanted to work on having some ideas ready to put before the full commission at the first meeting.

The five of us met in Kate's conference room a week before the first meeting of the full commission was scheduled. Despite

Kate's desire for balanced representation on the commission, Kate was the only woman at the meeting, but she was the person in charge.

Paul was again assigned to act as facilitator and stood by the flip chart. "Paul, you realize you're going to have to destroy the charts after you capture your notes." And then, turning to all of us, Kate warned, "What we discuss has to remain top secret. If anything is leaked, I will personally assure that the life of the offending party will be made miserable."

I thought T.T. was probably the most likely to violate a confidence, and I was the least likely. After all, I was living as a veritable hermit.

Kate posed the objective of the meeting. "I want to end up with a half dozen great ideas about how this country can get a bigger slice of the petroleum energy pie. So just throw out your thoughts. I don't care how outrageous they might be. We'll refine the best ones later. In fact, that's what the commission can do."

We talked quickly. Paul wrote quickly. In an hour, he had jotted down thirty or more concepts. We began to pick the ones we wanted to explore further. T.T. was one of the first to speak. "Why can't we get Canada to speed up production from their tar sands? There's a shit-load of oil still up there ready for the taking."

I could have responded, but Paul spoke first. "About thirty years ago, Canada signed an accord which limited its annual production from the tar sands. The accord was part of a broad-based treaty to reduce carbon emissions. As you probably know, quite a bit of energy is required to get the petroleum products out of tar sands. Actually, Canada was not reluctant to approve the agreement. They took the long view, figuring that by the end of the twenty-first century they'd be one of the last big producers standing. The Middle East, Venezuela, Russia are all running low on reserves. Even Brazil's production has peaked. But Canada can continue producing at current levels for another fifty years or more."

T.T. spread his arms in a gesture that combined exasperation with disbelief. "Let's get them to break the agreement. They're supposed to be our friends."

I looked at Paul, who was rolling his eyes toward the ceiling. Kate saw the interaction between the two of us. "Hold on a second. Let's hear T.T. out."

"Look, I've seen thousands of contracts over the years. There's almost always some way to break them. And if you do it cleverly, you don't get your ass in trouble. A treaty, an accord, call it what you will, is no different than a contract. Let's get our hands on a copy of that treaty. I'll figure a way out."

"But . . ." I hated to start a sentence that way in Kate's presence. She looked at me sharply. "But, it's not up to us to break it; it's up to the Canadians."

There was a moment of silence before Kate spoke again. "Okay, hold on. It's tricky, but it will just require a three-step approach. We need to give Canada a carrot; maybe it's no more than a premium price for its production. Second, we need to show them how they can break the agreement so that it looks reasonable to the rest of the world. And then, third, we need to corner that excess production."

Kate looked around the table. No one responded immediately until T.T. declared, "Well, boss, this sounds like one idea we definitely need to pursue with the commission."

Kate turned to Paul. "Put a check mark by this idea. Let's move on."

We continued our discussion for another half hour, took a break, and then got back to work. Even some crazy ideas were eliminated only after heated discussion. One idea, certainly not a scientifically practical one, proposed a giant pipe—something like a giant straw—to suck petroleum from a foreign field. At times, I felt like Alice after having gone through the looking glass. But we continued to whittle down the list and ended up with a half dozen that we—or at least Kate—thought had some potential.

Two were put at the top of list. One was about Canada's

more rapid exploitation of its tar sands. The other involved getting Brazil to alter its agreements with China, so that the U.S. could get a larger share of Brazil's output. We figured a combination of efforts would be needed. Brazil would have to be induced, either through cajoling or intimidation, to renegotiate its arrangements. Then they would have to strike an agreement with us for the share which was freed up. To produce the results we wanted, we even speculated on Machiavellian steps, such as inciting Argentina and Venezuela—Brazil's two covetous neighbors—to threaten some sort of belligerency. This, in turn, would encourage Brazil to look to us for support and weaponry. As a *quid pro quo*, we would get the additional oil.

This all sounded pretty preposterous to me, especially since we had gone over similar ground a few years before. I suggested, "Perhaps we shouldn't work this issue too much. We will have a commission that can add their opinions and expertise. Certainly State will want to provide input."

Darren Lee, who had been doing relatively little talking, spoke up. "That's a good point. I couldn't give a final opinion on any action such as the one proposed."

Kate remained silent for a moment, then said, "Okay, I think we've taken these issues about as far as we can without putting them before the Commission. Since Defense, State, and Transportation will be involved, I want to plant some seeds among my peers."

After the meeting I went home with conflicting feelings. On one hand, I was happy to be working again on a major project. On the other, I was concerned about the objective. It was to be another attempt to extract petroleum reserves by questionable means. We would have to convince not only skeptical—and even hostile— nations to bow to our desires, but also our own government would need to agree to undertake these aggressive steps. I wondered whether I wanted to go through this effort, and whether I even believed in the legitimacy of such actions. My initial excitement over beginning a new assignment was being replaced by a feeling of lethargy and pessimism.

We were bound to encounter significant obstacles within our own government. I couldn't see the State Department providing quick consent. Kate would have to convince the cabinet that even studying these ideas was worthwhile. Then, someone in the White House, at least the chief of staff if not the president, would have to approve us looking into such sensitive issues. Even the exploration of these notions could present dangers, if our efforts were exposed to public scrutiny.

A few days after the meeting, with my spirits sagging, I considered calling Pat Auriga. We had talked about getting together. But did I really want to hear about what a wonderful vacation she had had with her great boyfriend? She'd tell me about her extraordinary holiday, and I'd tell her that I ate a frozen dinner for Christmas.

After considering all these points and realizing that a promise was a promise, I chose her number on my phone and put the call through. Pat seemed pleased that I was on the opposite end of the line. "James, I'm happy to hear from you. I was getting to be concerned that you wouldn't call back."

Briefly the thought crossed my mind: if she cared to talk to me, she had my number and could have called. But I put my petty reaction aside and asked if we could meet for lunch at some point. "Of course," Pat replied promptly.

That Friday, we met at a small restaurant near the American University campus. It was not a place students were likely to frequent for lunch. Most would want to spend less on a midday meal. Yet more than half the tables were occupied. The tables were faux butcher block, plastic rather than wood. And there was too much neon signage. However, Pat promised that the food was better than the décor.

"Do you want a drink?" I offered.

"I better not. I have a two o'clock class. Some of my students might sleep, but I can't afford to." She ordered a mineral water. I matched her temperance with a Coke.

Pat started the conversation by telling me that she was surprised that Jane and I had split up. She asked what had happened. For some reason, I found that it was easier to talk to Pat than I would have expected. Maybe I simply needed to talk to someone. I spent fifteen minutes or so, describing Mark's illness, Jane's increasingly bizarre behavior, and her sudden flight to a cult compound in northern California. My outline reminded me of the ones I had given earlier to Allison and Carla.

"So you haven't talked to her in quite a while."

"I could never contact her after she left. It's been about two years. I don't know where she is—or even if she's alive. And I don't know if Mark's alive. That means more to me."

"I feel so sorry for you." There was compassion in her voice and in the expression on her face.

By this point, we were well into downing our sandwiches, and I had done the majority of the talking. "So how was your vacation?"

"It was okay."

"Just okay?"

"Bud and I had a few disagreements. I guess we patched things up." The last sentence was delivered with little conviction. Secretly, I gained a bit of pleasure—call it *schadenfreude*—from Pat's less-than-perfect vacation. Why this was so, I couldn't fathom. I had never had a real date with Pat. She was simply a friend, I told myself— someone who was enjoyable to be around, but just a friend.

In February, we had the first full meeting of what Kate called "her commission." To be honest, I never thought the group was truly a commission. The president didn't call it a commission, and it had no publicity, which was probably for the best. There were to be no hearings or public input.

Those of us based in Washington—Kate, Paul, T.T., Darren Lee from Defense, Beckley Stubler from Transportation, Franco Pelletieri (a scientist residing in northern Virginia), Jerry Kennedy (an economist), and I—met in the video conference room in the F.E.D. building. The representative from the State Department, Elaine Masarek, normally would have been present, but she was out of town and phoned in. Kate asked her if anyone else was in earshot. The answer came back, "Of course not." I might have asked if the line was secure, but Kate didn't bother. The others—C. Lane Vaught, from the petroleum industry, Robert Smith, from an electric utility, and Clyde Timkin, another scientist—were projected in from their remote locations via videoconference facilities.

After introductions, Kate took some time to set forth her goals for the project. Rather than set a specific number, she talked in general terms about maintaining—but preferably increasing—petroleum supplies over the next ten years. She told the group that some ideas had been generated by her and a few of her associates. These would be forwarded to all members so opinions could be aired at the next meeting. However, she stressed that they should not hesitate to put forward any of their own ideas, which could be sent to her directly.

Kate described how we would be organized. She wanted the commission divided into several working sub-committees. T.T. would work with Stubler from Transportation and Jerry Kennedy, the economist, to assess the practicality of proposals from a legal and economic perspective. I would work with Elaine Masarek from State and with Darren Lee from Defense to assess international implications. Kate would work with the balance of the commission to prioritize ideas, as well as to fold in any new suggestions, assess the ramification for various industries other than transportation, and in general be a focal point for commission actions.

I personally thought that the structure was awkward and, in some instances, misaligned. For example, I thought T.T. should work with State. If we were going to attempt to have any countries break agreements, State would need to provide input. I felt the economist should work with me.

Robert Smith, who was president of a fairly large Midwestern utility, asked if he was limited in the number of staff he could assign from his own company. Kate hesitated. She might have been thinking that each member would work on his or her own. Having had experience in business, Kate should not have been caught off-guard by the request. "I guess you could have one or two assigned, but I want to have each cleared. You know we prefer to keep the number of participants small to preserve confidentiality and to be able to move expeditiously."

Smith shot back, "Then I'll send you the names of two people tomorrow."

Lane Vaught, who was a vice president in his company, asked to assign only one additional person.

Once these requests were dealt with, Kate began to summarize the meeting and move toward adjournment. Kate and I exited the conference room side by side. "You look concerned," she commented.

"Just preoccupied."

"Well, we have work to do," which was Kate's way of saying "get control of your emotions and attack the project."

During the remainder of the day, my thoughts returned to a few related themes. T.T. was given the job of looking for loopholes in Canada's oil production limitations, and in Brazil's contracts with China. Obviously these tasks suited his background and talents. It was impossible for me not to believe that Kate had anticipated such an assignment when she hired him. I felt that Kate was acting as a puppeteer who had already concocted the script by which the remainder of us would perform. I never minded playing my part, but I didn't like being manipulated.

I set up separate meetings with Darren Lee and Elaine Masarek to discuss our path forward. Darren's was first. I figured it would proceed quickly because he had been in on our initial meeting. We sat down over coffee in my office, and I had a chance to size him up. His age was difficult to judge, because he was in very good shape. I figured he had been a Marine who retired young. The "Lee" no doubt came from China rather than Virginia. But there was evidently some Western blood in his veins. In the course of our conversation he told me that he was one quarter Chinese, one quarter Irish, one quarter Czech, and one quarter too many other things to mention. But he was obviously one hundred percent American.

"Me too," I said.

"Funny, you don't look Chinese."

"I mean, I'm American, but ethnically too diverse to try to analyze."

I covered some operational procedures I figured we would be following. Darren assumed that when we wanted some policies to be approved for pursuit, he would need to consult several ranks up the chain of command. In turn, I told him we would want to know which people were involved. I gave Darren a binder with several pages of information that Kate had provided regarding principles to be followed while working on the commission. He looked at them quickly and then put them in a briefcase. Many points concerned security. Darren assured me that security would be respected in the Defense Department.

Two days later, I met with Elaine. She did not want to come to the F.E.D., and I didn't want to go to her office. So I was pleased when she suggested we get together on neutral ground, namely a bar in her neighborhood. She assured me it was near a Metro stop. And when she gave me the address, I recognized it as being close to Kate's former place in Arlington.

"How will I recognize you?" I asked.

"Just look for a rather non-descript broad, sitting alone in a booth."

At six thirty on the appointed evening I entered the dimly

lit bar and let my eyes adjust to the light level. There were about a dozen booths. Half were occupied, and in one I spotted a sole female and walked toward her. Her short brown hair, parted a bit to one side, seemed to be under the control of contrary forces—the wind that had been blowing outside only a bit offset by the effect of gravity—rather than a brush and comb. Her eyes were mostly hidden behind black-framed glasses. She had not removed her coat, but her figure seemed to be more than ample.

"Sit down, James Lendeman. You've found the object of your quest." Elaine was drinking some sort of cocktail. A waitress arrived at the table, and I ordered a beer. Now that I was sitting across from Elaine, I could see even more clearly that she was not an attractive woman. Her nose was fleshy, her mouth too large, her jowls sagged. I guessed she was in her late thirties.

I felt a bit uncomfortable discussing a confidential project in a bar, but my initial comments were devoted to administrative matters. Suddenly, a younger woman approached our table. Her shoulder-length hair was jet black, her eyes hazel, her nose and mouth were small and well-formed. She carried her coat over her arm, and I could see that her slim figure was enticing.

"Laine, I'm frantic. I can't find my set of keys. Could you have walked off with both sets?"

Elaine began to rummage through her purse. I was staring, somewhat impudently, at Elaine's roommate. She noticed my attention and smiled.

"Haven't I seen you before?" I asked.

She laughed. "Don't you have a better pick up line than that?"

"No, I'm serious."

"Do you watch the ten o'clock news on channel four?"

"Of course, you're . . ." but I couldn't come up with a name.

"Laetie Varenne," she supplied.

"James Lendeman. Pleased to meet you."

"Nice meeting you, too." We shook hands.

Elaine held up two sets of keys. "Sorry. Guilty as charged."

Laetie grabbed one of the sets. "Look, I'm running late. I could only close the door behind me. It's not properly double-locked. Maybe you could break away from your date and see to the apartment."

"I'll do that when we finish our drinks."

Laetie turned and left without uttering another word.

Elaine turned to me. "Maybe it's best if we conduct the rest of the meeting in my apartment. You'll probably be happier than doing it here in public, although I hear it's been weeks since any Chinese spies visited this establishment."

"Let's do that." I finished the rest of my beer in a single gulp and paid for both of our drinks. We went out into the night, which was blustery but quite warm for February. Elaine's hair was tossed this way and that, but I sensed that it would end up in much the same state as I first observed in the bar.

Elaine began to talk as we walked. "Laetie's a pretty thing, isn't she?" I nodded my agreement. "We've been together for over a year. I think I'll lose her soon. She's going through a crisis."

"Problem with her job?"

"Nothing that simple. Trying to decide if she prefers women or men. I bet she'd like you."

I was glad it was dark, so Elaine couldn't see me blush. "What makes you think I'm available?"

"Just my perception. I'd bet you're divorced."

"Separated."

"Same thing. Here's the apartment. I hope I didn't misplace the key."

She hadn't. Elaine had no beer. She offered a mixed drink or wine. I asked for a soft drink, which she managed to produce. I opened the folder I had brought and gave Elaine a copy of the same papers I had given Darren Lee. She looked quickly at the material and concluded they were administrative in nature and could be reviewed later.

"You should have received some of our initial ideas directly from Kate Hastings. We will need your, that is, *State's* evaluation of the feasibility and means by which the top items can be pursued." I spoke a bit more about how we saw the commission functioning. Then I asked what sort of approvals she would need from her department.

"Those things from Kate are the type of proposals we're going to work on?" Elaine asked her own question.

"Yes. You have concerns?"

"They go beyond my modest powers to judge. But I think I'm safe in saying State isn't going to look with favor on these types of adventures."

I retorted with a line that Kate might have employed. "It's not a matter of what State or any other department wants, it's a matter of what the country needs."

"The country doesn't need to create turmoil among our friends and allies."

"If they're friends, they'll cooperate."

"Some of these proposals involve coercion. No person or country likes that." I did not reply, so Elaine added, "I don't know you, but I know something about your boss's ideas. This is what she wants to pursue. I bet you're supporting your boss rather than the proposals."

"You're not expecting me to respond to that."

"Your failure to reply says it all."

I changed the subject. "You never answered my question."

"What question?"

"What sort of approval level will be required within State?"

"Some of this stuff will need to go all the way to the top. Don't you think these are Cabinet-level issues? But let me take a closer look. I don't want you to think that State is going to be an automatic veto."

"Good. Let's see how the project progresses."

I finished my cola and headed home. Two thoughts occupied

my mind during the Metro ride. First, I wondered how I would fare while working on a project that I didn't believe in. And second, I thought about the odd pair—Elaine and Laetie Varenne. I could understand why Elaine would live with Laetie, but I couldn't see Laetie living with Elaine. Could someone appear to be so feminine and yet not be? I probably would never see Laetie again—except on the ten o'clock news—let alone get an answer to my question.

XXXI

Washington, 2062

ON NOVEMBER TWENTY-THIRD, I found myself with Pat and six additional people at Thanksgiving dinner. Pat's friend, who hosted the party, was a colleague from the music department at American University. I had cleared my attendance with Kate, who told me she had an invitation to a friend's house. I suspected that Kate fabricated her response, but I acted upon it and accepted Pat's invitation.

Except for me, all the others at the dinner were employed in artistic professions—music, dance, or graphic arts. I spent some time talking to an attractive woman named Linda, who was a dance teacher. Unlike most of the others, she professed interest in what the F.E.D. was doing.

Pat later noted that I had spent a fair amount of time with Linda. "Did you find Linda interesting?"

"She seemed to be somewhat interested in what I was doing at the F.E.D."

"While all the rest of us were talking about music and art. But you must have noticed how striking Linda is with those green eyes and auburn hair."

I could have acted innocent and claimed not to have noticed, but there was no point in lying to Pat. "Aside from that, she's kept her dancer's figure."

"You like skinny women?" Then Pat quickly answered her own question. "Of course you do. Just look at Kate."

"I can't believe we're standing here, talking about Kate."

"We were talking about your likes and dislikes."

"Well, I like you and you look nothing like Linda or Kate."

"You like me as a friend."

"Of course. I enjoy being with you, hearing about what you're doing, discussing your plans."

"But you don't consider me attractive."

"Of course I do." I tried to turn the tables. "Why are we talking about looks? Don't tell me you offered to take me to your friend's Thanksgiving dinner because you think I'm good looking."

"Of course not." Pat waved the idea away with her hand.

"So you think I'm ugly." I continued to fence.

Pat forced a laugh. "James, stop pulling my leg. How did we get into this stupid argument? I guess we're destined to be friends."

"Do you think we should alter that relationship?"

Pat looked deeply into my eyes. "We'd mutually have to agree to that. As of right now, I think we should rejoin the others."

We had been standing on the balcony. Suddenly I realized how cold I was.

The apartment where we had dinner was not that far from Pat's apartment. I walked her home. She asked if I wanted to come up for a drink, and I accepted.

We talked about her upcoming trip to Italy. She was obviously looking forward to the challenge and adventure. There was a sparkle in her eye when she spoke about Florence and the work she'd be doing there.

I told her that I would miss her, despite the fact that we only managed to get together on infrequent occasions. She assured me that she would miss me, too, but I could not tell whether she said so because she was being polite or because she truly felt that way. She suggested that I could go to Florence and visit her. We'd have a great time together.

I thought any such visit would be impossible, but of course I didn't say so.

After finishing the glass of brandy, I said I needed to leave.

"Really?" Pat seemed reluctantly to have me go.

"Yes, really."

"Then let me give you a hug. We may not see each other for quite a while."

We put our arms around each other. Our faces came closer together. We kissed, quite warmly, but somewhere deep down there was a hint of restraint.

XXXII

Washington, 2060

MARCH BECAME APRIL. CHERRY BLOSSOMS appeared, but I barely caught a glimpse of them. The commission had been functioning for two months. Generally people were working by themselves or in small groups. Kate had met with the entire commission only twice. My sub-committee, since the three of us were based in Washington, managed to meet every week or two.

Defense was contributing its reports on time. In the meetings, Darren Lee was a constructive contributor, effectively playing a good soldier on the project. State was another matter. Elaine always brought concerns to the table. State's assessment was that neither Canada nor Brazil would cooperate with us. Furthermore, exerting pressure on either was bound to backfire. Elaine presented State's analyses of the character of the governments in question.

Of course, I had to inform Kate of State's opinions. She felt that the State Department's perennial objective was to thwart her initiatives and serve as her nemesis. "The perfidious bastards," she exclaimed. "You have to convince this Elaine what's-her-name . . ."

"Masarek."

"Whatever. Anyway, this situation needs to be remedied. You need to work on this. It should be your top priority."

I pushed back. "I thought you had State in line. You were dealing directly with Weaver."

"Yes. But Weaver will say anything in a cabinet meeting to

avoid confrontation. Then his staff will take the line that they want. I don't think Weaver runs the department. Rather, the department runs him."

"Rather different than here."

Kate gave me a look that was difficult to interpret. Hostility? Anger? Amusement? "You better believe it."

I agonized over finding a way to open Elaine's mind to our— rather Kate's—point of view. Clearly my masculine wiles, if indeed they existed, would be useless on Ms. Masarek. I tossed the issue around in my mind, realizing that Elaine would be a tough nut to crack. She was interested in only two things: her job and Laetie Varenne.

I wondered, could I find a way to get at Elaine through her girlfriend? The idea was too repugnant and outlandish to consider seriously.

Yet, over the next week or so I spent an unreasonable amount of time trying to figure out what to do about Elaine. Either I would have to change her mind, or Kate would have to exert influence through Sam Weaver.

A few additional weeks passed, and the problem was no nearer resolution than when Kate told me that it was my top priority. She followed up and asked what progress I was making. I had to confess that the situation had not changed. I told Kate that Elaine was impervious to pressure and reasoning from me.

"Figure out something, or else this whole . . ." Kate paused, seeking the proper expletive and then chose not to use it. "This whole damned initiative might as well be chucked. You can get this Elaine to play ball; I know you can." This last comment was meant to be encouraging, but it came across as a threat.

I half expected to wake up one morning, having dreamt of a marvelous solution to my dilemma, but no such epiphany occurred. I stayed away from my office one day, telling my assistant that I had a touch of food poisoning. The following day I went to work, but pretty much closeted myself in my office pondering my problem and wasting time. By this point, Joan Leach had taken over the duties of keeping in regular contact with the regional offices. No routine matters needed to cross my desk, and I found that preferable.

Another two weeks went by. I held a perfunctory project meeting. Nothing moved forward. The sub-committee members' interests were waning. Elaine Masarek visibly yawned during the hour-long meeting. Any initial enthusiasm we once possessed was gone.

Kate kept badgering me about making progress. I had nothing substantive to report and could not disguise that fact. My platitudes and evasive answers did not work. She told me that I needed to get things moving in the next two weeks. T.T., who was already completing his part of the project, was held up as an example. I could have countered that his work required no cooperation from the State Department, but I chose to keep quiet and take my medicine.

It was obvious that I had to take some bold action, however irrational and desperate it might be. Only one ill-formed idea had come to mind. I called Laetie Varenne at the TV station. I did not reach her and could only leave a message. I expected no return call.

Surprisingly, she called back within an hour. "I knew you were going to call me," she asserted with a bit of a giggle.

"Why?"

"You're intrigued by me. You can't quite figure me out. So you want to learn more about me. And, of course, you admire me."

"You're damned sure of yourself."

"I can't afford to be shy and retiring. Not in my business. Even if I'm dead wrong, I have to sound like I know what I'm talking about."

"Okay. Since you have all the answers, what's going to happen next?"

Laetie hesitated not one second. "You're going to ask me out. And I'm not going to refuse."

"Shall we go to dinner?"

"Not for a first date. Just a rendezvous for drinks."

"This coming Saturday?"

"No, Saturdays are not for drink dates. Make it Sunday. Sunday at six."

"What spot have you picked?" I kept asking the questions.

"The same bar where you met Elaine."

Two days still remained in the workweek, but I didn't work. I put in an appearance at the office. I answered the phone when it rang, which was infrequently. I checked for emails but tried to avoid replying to any. On both days I took a late lunch and left the building. On Friday, I didn't return. I walked around the city for an hour and then went home.

I was thirty-five years old. My health had never been a problem. Now I found it difficult to sleep. Disturbing dreams about work woke me after only two or three hours of sleep, and then I would lie awake, thinking about the dream or about work, which was becoming a nightmare in itself. I was not succeeding in my work. My assigned task was unfair, and so was my boss. Kate was burdening me with an objective she could not accomplish herself. Yet she showed no inclination to let me off the hook. Incredible as it seemed, she was prepared to use me as a scapegoat.

After going through such thoughts for an hour or two, I realized that I would not get back to sleep that way. I took my page palette and went to a Dickens novel that I had loaded earlier. Even Dickens, an author who rarely sparked my interest, could not put me back to sleep.

I listened to Mozart. I liked Mozart about as much as I liked Dickens. *Eine Kleine Nacht Musik* proved as soporific as the *1812 Overture*.

By the time my date with Laetie arrived, this sleep pattern, or rather lack of sleep pattern was well established. Without knowing exactly how it would come to pass, Laetie, I thought, would somehow be the source of my salvation and relieve me of my torment. In some way, she would provide the means to soften Elaine's opposition. I had begun to think of Elaine as a personal enemy, the individual who was determined to thwart my plan— really Kate's plan—no matter what. I convinced myself that Elaine determined State Department policy with respect to the commission. Her opinions, even her whims, would seal the fate of both the project and me.

On occasion, when I did manage to catch a bit of sleep, Elaine entered my dreams, usually distorted into some sort of grotesque form. I was always trying to accomplish something, maybe a task as simple as taking a trip on the Metro or giving a presentation. There Elaine was, interrupting, intimidating, obstructing my efforts. I never managed to reach my destination or conclude my speech. Such is the nature of dreams, but my dreams were becoming reality.

I made sure to arrive on time for my date with Laetie, but she was already in the bar. Instead of sitting in a booth, she had picked a small round table, such as found in a Parisian café, near the front door. The empty chair was placed near hers. Laetie seemed even prettier than I remembered. Even more, she was stylish. Her gray slacks and burgundy top showed off her figure and raven tresses. She offered me the seat next to hers. "Hi. You're right on time."

"And you're early."

"I'm used to being early. If I'm on camera at ten, I'm at the station before nine."

"But you have preparations at work. You didn't need to prepare for me."

"Didn't I?" she responded enigmatically. "Anyway, what do you want to talk about? Probably not work."

"Definitely not work. You probably hear enough from Elaine."

"Elaine never talks about her work. So sometimes we talk about my work. Or maintaining the apartment. Or we fight."

A waitress arrived, and we each ordered white wine.

"How did you two meet?" I ventured.

"I'd rather not discuss that," she cut me off quickly. "Let's talk about you."

Quickly, I covered my childhood in New Jersey, education at Stanford and Georgia, and tours of duty with the F.E.D. in New York, California, and Washington. Laetie then shared some equivalent information. She had grown up in Connecticut and gotten a degree from Penn State. Then she worked for a station in Harrisburg and moved twice to larger markets before getting the job in Washington. From the timeframe she described, I calculated that she was no younger than thirty and probably not older than thirty-three.

She asked me what I liked to do in my spare time. I told her I liked to read and occasionally watch old movies on TV. She did not pursue my specific tastes. She told me she liked to jog and listen to popular music. Naturally she had to keep up with the news, but she didn't view this as a chore.

As we spoke I felt her leg rub against mine. At first, I thought the action was inadvertent, but it recurred. I wondered what she had in mind. We had simply been chitchatting, and it seemed a rather aggressive tactic.

We had just ordered a second round of drinks, when Elaine came through the door. "Well, look who's here," she exclaimed, obviously surprised at seeing Laetie and me together.

"James and I are on a date," Laetie responded promptly.

"Are you? How pleasant."

"Yes, we're having a lovely time. It's amazing how much we have in common." Laetie was providing all the responses, whether accurate or embellished.

"Well, I don't want to interrupt, but I thought your note . . ."

"I was just letting you know I was in the bar in case you needed me," Laetie replied, all too quickly.

"I see," Elaine replied coldly. "I'll leave you two to your *date*."

Suddenly I realized that Laetie had turned the tables on me. I was hoping to use her to get at Elaine. Instead, she was using me.

The conversation lagged after Elaine's departure. Laetie seemed distracted. Neither one of us wanted a third round of drinks. We vaguely spoke about getting together again, but I knew it would never happen.

The morning after my unsuccessful "date," I went into the office, albeit somewhat late. My admin assistant caught me as I arrived. "Ms. Hastings called about a half hour ago. She wants to see you. She said as soon as possible."

I went into my office, finished the coffee that I had brought, and then decided to amble over to Kate's office. "Kate wanted to see me," I told her admin assistant.

"I know, but she's busy at the moment. Why don't you have a seat? I'm sure she won't be very long."

"I'll wait in my office. You can call when she's ready."

The admin looked at me wide-eyed, as if to say, "Are you trying to commit suicide?"

Ten minutes later, I was sitting in Kate's office. She looked at me for nearly a half minute before saying anything. Then she posed an open-ended question, "What's happening?"

"What's happening with what?"

"What's happening with you?"

"What do you mean?"

"Stop answering my questions with other questions." She was trying to control herself.

"Okay."

"So?"

I really wanted to say, "So what?" but Kate would have hit the ceiling. "I don't think anything's happening with me. I'm trying to do an impossible job. It's frustrating. It's depressing."

"Are you ill?"

"No. I'm just a mid-level person in this department. I can't convince the State Department that they're wrong and you're right."

Kate looked somewhat hurt by my comment. "Is that what you think I'm asking you to do?"

"Yes, pretty much so. You want me to convince Elaine that we need leeway to use leverage against some friendly nations, and then you want her to get approval from her bosses to do something they don't want to do. She doesn't support our position and neither do her superiors."

Kate looked at me through narrowed eyes, and I thought I could detect confusion in her expression. "That can't be the case. Weaver told me he supports us. He said so in a Cabinet meeting just the other day."

"Maybe he's telling you one thing and then telling his staff something else."

"People don't play games with me," Kate replied angrily.

I could say nothing in return. After a minute, Kate went on. "I think you need a rest. I think it might be best if you leave this project and tend to your other duties. I'll find someone else to fill in."

I should have felt relieved, but my immediate reaction was one of hurt. "You're the boss. You do as you wish. But did you ever stop to think that we've been trying to accomplish the impossible? This country is years behind in securing energy supplies and adapting to energy sources that are more readily available. These solutions needed to be pursued years before you and I were even on the scene."

Kate shrugged. "That's all wishful thinking. Our job is to play the hand that's dealt us. Of course I wish things were done differently years ago. But they weren't, and we have to move on from here. You think I'm being unfair to you?"

"Yes, but I'm sure you're doing what you think is needed to move this project along. Time will tell if it works."

When I returned to my office, I packed up the materials pertaining to Kate's commission and asked my admin assistant to return them. Without them, my desk was pretty bare. I checked my calendar to see if anything was scheduled during the balance of the day. There was one meeting, which I really didn't need to attend. I left a message saying I was gone for the rest of the day.

The next morning, I arrived at the office late, but my absence was not missed. I asked to meet with my assistant Joan. She and I got together at eleven. We reviewed what she was working on, and all her work seemed in order and up to date. In fact, the job she was doing was better than I was then capable of. I told her that I was going to schedule a visit to the Miami regional office. She asked if there was any special problem there. I replied that there was not, but they could use a visit from headquarters.

I went to Miami a week later. As soon as I got off the plane, I knew I had made a mistake. I met with the regional director and asked questions that Leo Frase would have asked me. I made a few meaningless notes. I talked to a few subordinates. We went to lunch. They put on a dog and pony show in the afternoon. I went to the airport and, after a delay to let a thunderstorm pass, the plane returned me to Washington.

The trip accomplished nothing. It wasted my time, other peoples' time, and the country's money. After my return, I was more depressed than before I left.

The next day, I called the office and told my admin assistant that I would not be in until the afternoon, since the trip back from Miami was horrendous and I had been delayed six hours. It was only an exaggeration, not a lie.

But I was learning to lie, and I lied a number of times in each of the following weeks.

Kate never did replace me on the commission. When I heard that she was looking for another assignment for T.T. Basso, I knew that the project in which Kate had put so much hope and faith would die a quiet death.

It takes a while for government to notice that someone is doing nothing. In June, Kate asked me to get evaluated by a staff physician. She thought I was depressed. I could have refused to be examined, but I didn't. I ended up being referred to a psychoanalyst with whom I had three sessions.

When Kate told me, "We think you need a leave of absence," I fully agreed. We worked out a feeble cover story, and a week later I no longer was on active duty with the Federal Energy Department.

I stopped into the office one evening to pack up some personal items. There weren't many. No one was there to interfere or say good-bye. I did not know whether I would ever return.

I had not seen Kate for a week, nor did I see her that evening. But she did call the next day. "I'm sorry you're going away like this. I know it's partly my fault. I know we'll team up again at some better time for both of us."

I said, "I hope so." I did not try to voice my conflicting feelings of hurt and relief. I felt victimized by Kate, and yet I still considered her a friend. I could not make sense of what had happened to me, professionally or personally.

Kate went on to say, "You get the help you need, and I promise to keep in touch."

For some reason I said, "Thank you."

I spent another week in Washington, but I knew I needed to get away. The city reminded me of failure, not only of my own but of the failure of the entire system. I considered visiting my mother, but there I would have had to talk about my situation. That would have been painful.

My assets were paltry. Full pay would continue for six months, and then I would get half pay if I was not fully employed. Probably I could find a cheaper place to live which was more conducive to my recovery. I needed to contemplate a future quite different from the one I had envisioned only a few months earlier. I had always believed that human beings were highly adaptable to changes in circumstances. It was time for me to find out how well I would do.

XXXIII

Savannah, 2063

DURING THE AFTERNOON OF NEW Year's Day, 2063, I sat in the parlor of Mrs. Pinckney's house with my page palette in my lap. I was not reading, although earlier I had downloaded a mystery novel. I was thinking and reflecting.

First I thought about New Year's Eve. I had spent the evening downtown, moving from one bar to the next. At each, I limited myself to one beer. All the revelers seemed to be enjoying themselves immensely—or at least they were doing a masterful job at pretending. Their merriment produced the opposite effect on me. Around eleven o'clock, I headed home. I was in bed before midnight.

Then my thoughts went back to early December when I had finished my latest Washington assignment, babysitting Kate through her surgery and treatments. I made one last visit to Kate's apartment the evening before I left. Kate felt well enough to suggest going out to dinner. We went to the fancier of the two Italian restaurants in her neighborhood.

She had two glasses of wine, a good Barolo, but ate only half the food on her plate. We talked mainly about the work of the F.E.D. I shared some impressions of the status of various projects, which I managed to follow. She accepted my thoughts practically without comment.

We walked the two blocks back to her apartment. The night was cold. Kate leaned hard against me, primarily for warmth. I put my arm around her and could sense how much weight she had lost during her treatments.

She was tired by the time we returned to her home, and did not try to hide the fact from me. After taking off her coat, she sat down on the couch and motioned me to sit next to her. "I have a few things to thank you for, and then I think I better get some rest.

"Thank you for interrupting your life in Georgia and coming here to serve as my aide and companion. Thank you for keeping an eye on the store. I know this wasn't very interesting for you, but as I told you before, you're the only one I can truly trust. I'm sorry I had to drag you into a situation like this. I always seem to find a way to make you uncomfortable. Thanks for being my friend. I deeply appreciate what you've done for me."

Kate's little speech embarrassed me. I thought my two-month sojourn in Washington was a waste of effort. I wasn't able to get involved in the work of the department. "I really didn't do much at all," I mumbled.

"If nothing else, you comforted me."

"Then I consider my time here a success," I replied with excessive gallantry.

On this New Year's Day I also thought about Pat Auriga. We had not spent much time together, but strangely I already missed her. I knew she would be leaving for Florence shortly. She was scheduled to be there for at least a year and possibly for two. I could reach her by phone or email, but I wouldn't be able to be with her.

Why was I thinking about her? We were only friends. Pat had hinted that the relationship could go beyond the platonic stage, but now she was out of reach.

My thoughts were interrupted by Jacqueline stumbling into the parlor. She was wearing sweatpants and a tee shirt. Her feet were bare. Her hair was uncombed. Last night's makeup was smeared over her face.

"Oh, I thought you were Mrs. Pinckney," Jacqueline said dumbly.

"I guess you can see that I'm not."

"Yes, James. Happy New Year."

"Happy New Year, Jacqueline."

"Say, I have a splitting headache. You have anything?"

"Tylenol."

"That will do."

"It's up in my room."

"I'll go with you."

We started to ascend the stairs. Jacqueline wanted to take it slowly. I spoke to her over my shoulder. "Looks like you had a good New Year's Eve."

"Not really. The guy I was with is a jerk. We went to a party in Thunderbolt."

"Where's that?"

"You don't know where Thunderbolt is?"

"If I knew, I wouldn't ask."

"Don't tease me when I feel so lousy. Thunderbolt's out Victory Drive, near the water."

"What water?"

"Oh, please. Don't grill me. I'm in no condition."

We reached my apartment. Jacqueline flopped onto my bed while I looked for the Tylenol in the bathroom. It took a minute to locate the small white bottle under the sink. I hadn't realized that we had left the door open. When I returned with the medicine, Mrs. Pinckney was standing a foot inside the door. "Are y'all alright?"

Jacqueline didn't move. I had to answer. "Jacqueline celebrated a little too much last night. She wants something for her headache."

Mrs. Pinckney looked at us warily. "Well, at least y'all got back here safely."

"I think you misunderstand. We weren't together last night."

"Oh, then I apologize." I assumed Mrs. P. was sorry for having implied that I had abetted Jacqueline's New Year's Eve binge.

"Can I get the friggin' Tylenol?" Jacqueline was still face-down on my bed and, perhaps, oblivious to Mrs. P's presence.

Still somewhat confused by the situation, Mrs. Pinckney said, "I better leave now. Just wanted to let y'all know that I'll be at a friend's house this evening. Feel free to use the kitchen." Mrs. P. departed, but left my door ajar. The action reminded me of old dormitory rules.

I brought Jacqueline the Tylenol and a glass of water. "You're going to have to stand up, or at least sit up, to swallow the pills."

Slowly, Jacqueline rolled over and propped herself up on one elbow. It took two minutes for her to perform the complicated maneuver of putting a pill in her mouth, adding some water from the glass, swallowing, and then repeating the process a second time. The effort evidently exhausted her. She fell back on my pillow.

"Are you going to stay here or go back to your room?" I asked quietly.

Jacqueline did not answer. Perhaps she hadn't heard the question. Somewhat louder I began, "Are you . . ."

"I heard you. Let me think." But if she was thinking, it wasn't apparent. She closed her eyes. I watched her for a few minutes. She had evidently fallen back to sleep. The room was cool. I found my extra blanket and draped it over her limp body. I performed the task slowly. Her midriff was uncovered, and I couldn't help but admire her flat stomach.

I left my room, closed the door, and returned to the parlor. I picked up my page palette, but again I found it difficult to concentrate. I felt guilty about my behavior, even though my violation of the recumbent Jacqueline occurred only with my eyes.

After a while, I began to read the novel, but it didn't particularly interest me. Having gotten four or five chapters into the book, I tried to decide whether to keep on reading or abandon the effort.

Then I watched part of a football game. The two New Year's Day games scheduled were attempts to mimic the bowl games of yesteryear. But with college games limited to local contests, the quality of play suffered. Both offense and defense made numerous errors. After watching two quarters of one game, I returned to the novel, assessing it as the better of my two options.

As five o'clock approached, the parlor was growing darker. I turned on an extra light and considered going upstairs for an extra sweater. Some movement in the house attracted my attention. Since both Mrs. Pinckney and Mrs. Humphreys were out, the noise was caused either by Jacqueline or an intruder. I didn't believe in the many ghosts that allegedly haunted Savannah. A minute later I heard some unsteady steps on the stair treads. Jacqueline gradually appeared, now wearing a heavy sweatshirt along with sweatpants. She had washed her face and brushed her hair. She was attractive again, even without makeup.

"How are you doing?" I asked.

"I'm feeling better. How did I get in your room?"

"You needed something for your headache, and then you passed out on my bed."

"Thanks for fixing me up. What are you doing?"

"Nothing much. Watched some TV and read a bit."

"Sounds exciting." I said nothing. "Anyone else around?"

"No, the youngsters are out."

Jacqueline smiled at my characterization of the two seniors. "If I felt a little better, we could be naughty."

"You were out with someone else last night. Have you no loyalty?"

"He was just a date—and a bad one. I think he slipped something into my drink. I think that's what made me feel so awful. I really didn't drink that much."

Perhaps she wanted me to ask if he date-raped her. But I thought it best not to pursue that topic. She waited for a reply, but when none came, she went on to say, "I think I'm actually getting hungry."

"That's a good sign," I observed.

"I'm going to check the kitchen."

Mrs. P's kitchen arrangement accommodated her tenants to a certain extent. There were two refrigerators, the larger one for her and the smaller for the tenants. Mrs. P. had a large pantry. A small closet was reserved for us. She permitted us to use the stove and cooking implements, as long as we cleaned them promptly and properly—and didn't interfere with her own cooking.

We were supposed to label our food items, so there was no confusion or dispute. In practice, we knew each other's preferences, and there were few conflicts. Generally, Jacqueline kept little food in the house, since she either ate at school or grabbed something at a restaurant where she waited tables. On occasion, she might snatch a slice of bread that belonged to me. She knew I would not complain.

She returned from the kitchen. "Are these crackers yours?" She pushed an unopened package under my face.

"There's a 'J.L.' on the wrapper. That would mean they're mine. You want some?"

"You read my mind." My mindreading feat seemed inconsequential. Jacqueline continued. "I have some peanut butter. I'll make a few crackers for you, if you want."

"Thank you, but I'll pass."

Two minutes later, she returned with four crackers dabbed with peanut butter and a glass of water. "I forgot to buy Coke."

"That's a pretty meager-looking meal."

"Yeah, really sucks. It's New Year's Day, so I can't even go out and get something decent." But her comment didn't prevent her from munching on the crackers.

"I think I have a turkey dinner in the freezer. Maybe we could share." I made a generous offer.

"And I have some old bread."

"The moldy stuff?"

"We can cut the moldy part off."

"I'm not that desperate. We'll find something else."

"In Mrs. Pinckney's fridge?"

"Shame on you, Jacqueline."

"Desperate times call for desperate measures."

"I'm not that desperate."

"I was just kidding, James." But I was not sure that she was. "Can we talk or are you busy?"

She knew I wasn't busy. "What do you want to talk about?"

"I just want to catch up on news. You were away for almost three months. I never heard from you. Then you returned, but we never saw each other. So tell me what you did in Washington."

"I worked."

"No, be more specific."

"My old boss was undergoing surgery and then some follow-up treatments. She wanted me to take care of some things in the office while she was out of commission." Why did I have to use the word "commission?"

"So your old boss is a woman. Is she as old as you imply?"

"Not really."

"Is she an important person in the government?"

"She's Secretary of the Federal Energy Department."

"You don't mean she's the type of secretary who takes notes and arranges meetings?"

"No, she's the head of the department and a member of the president's cabinet."

"Then I think I've seen her on the news. The guys call her the president's scrag."

"I'm not familiar with that term."

"It means a hottie, or maybe something just a bit raunchier. Do you think she sleeps with the president?"

"Definitely not."

"Have you had sex with her?"

"Jacqueline, what sort of question is that?"

"If you don't answer, I'll assume you did."

"No, I never had sex with Kate Hastings." I used Kate's

definition of sex.

"But you know her well enough to tell me that she never had sex with the president."

"Of course, I worked for her for a number of years. I know her ethics." I did not, however, evaluate them for Jacqueline.

"Since you work so closely with her, you must be a big shot, too."

"Would I be rooming in this house if I were?"

"I was."

"What?"

"You said 'I were.' You should have said 'I was.'"

"I said, '*if* I were.' That's the subjunctive."

"What's the subjunctive?"

"It's a part of the English language that has just about disappeared."

"It seems useless. Why hasn't it completely disappeared?"

"I thought we were going to talk. I didn't think I was going to be interrogated."

"Okay. Let me tell you what I've been doing. First, I'm only taking two courses this semester."

"Why?"

"Because that's all I need to graduate in May."

"Great. Do I get to go to your graduation? After all, I was one of your professors."

"But you only gave me an A-minus when I deserved an A."

"To tell you the truth, you really deserved a B-plus."

"Then why did you give me an A-minus?"

"Because you're so cute, I decided to round up."

"That's favoritism. You should be ashamed."

"So what are you doing with all your spare time?"

"Spare time! I'm working at two restaurants. I'm also working again occasionally at the strip bar. And then I'm doing some modeling."

"Well, you have the looks for it."

"Thanks for the compliment. By the way, it's nude modeling for a photographer." A conversation with Jacqueline was rarely dull.

"I'm sure it's very artistic."

"Let me show you." Jacqueline came over to my chair, sat in my lap, took my page palette, and proceeded to access a website. She went through several screens and then up popped a completely nude Jacqueline reclining on a red sofa.

I didn't know how to react. "Yes, that's definitely you."

"See, I'm nicely shaved now."

"Yes, I can see."

"But, reclining like that, I think my tits look too small."

"They're totally fine." I tried to be reassuring, as if Jacqueline needed my reassurance. "Why are you called Natasha?"

"We all use fake names. Some girls have different names on different sites. If you pay a membership fee, you can see all forty-five photos of me."

"And how much is the fee?"

"A hundred dollars for three months."

"That's quite a bit."

"But you'd get access to photos of over two hundred girls."

"I'm sure none of them can compare to you."

"You're so full of crap."

"Why should I look at pictures? It's much better to have you here in my lap."

"Yeah, I could do wonders in your lap. Unfortunately, I'm in no condition, and I'm hardly in the mood after last night. You know that son-of-a-bitch just dumped me off the tram at the Abercorn stop, and I had to stumble home on my own."

"Maybe that's better than having him come up to your room."

Jacqueline pondered my point. "Maybe. You know, the prick might have been as old as you."

"That's old indeed."

"I didn't mean it that way." Then how did she mean it? "Anyway, I didn't like him, but I like you." She gave me a brief kiss on the lips. She tasted of peanut butter and peppermint, and had obviously brushed her teeth before coming downstairs. "Tell me," Jacqueline continued, "did you have a lot of dates in Washington? Do you like Washington women?"

"I don't know what a Washington woman is. They tend to come from elsewhere in the country."

"Did you go out with Kate Habersham?"

"Kate *Hastings* is her name. I joined her for dinner a few times. As I told you, she was recovering from an illness. I kept her company."

"Can you catch the illness?"

"No."

"And who else did you go out with?"

"No one."

"You're lying."

"What makes you say that?"

"I can see it in your eyes."

"Goodness, you're scary."

"See. Don't keep secrets from me. What's her name?"

"The interrogation goes on."

"Just answer that question and I won't ask any more."

"Pat's her name. But she's only a friend, not a girlfriend, if you know what I mean."

"No, she's more than that."

"Why would you think that?"

"Otherwise, you would have told me the truth in the first place."

Jacqueline stood up and began to walk away.

"Are you leaving?" I asked somewhat pathetically.

"No, of course not. I'm starving, and I'm going to make us some dinner."

XXXIV

Nowhere, 2060

AFTER MY DEMISE, I DID not stay long in Washington. Within two weeks, I was on the road searching for a place to settle and start a new life. Had this been the twentieth century, I might have hitchhiked across the country, but now no one could catch a ride on interstates devoid of non-commercial traffic. And, anyway, if I got across the country, where would I find myself? San Francisco? No, that wouldn't have been acceptable.

I might have gone northeast, but that would have been toward my mother and sister. I was not about to slink home to lick my wounds, which could hardly be healed in that environment. Allison had chosen to head in the opposite direction from her estranged husband. I decided that I, too, would head away from the remnants of my family and began a train trip south.

Kate called. I recognized her private phone number, and did not answer. A few days later, when I was in Atlanta, she called again and left a message. I had visited Atlanta a number of times on business and a few times while at the University of Georgia. Atlanta was fine as a business hub. The downtown area did not seem livable. And where could I stay? In some posh area like Buckhead? That was not an option.

I needed to move on. Athens was a logical choice. A light rail service linked Atlanta and Athens. I first verified that the spring term had ended. There would still be students in town during the summer, but not that many.

I found a furnished apartment that had just been vacated and that I could rent by the week. It was within walking distance of the town center, which—rightly or wrongly—I placed at the university arch. The famous arch served as the main entrance to the campus from the downtown stores, restaurants and bars. It loomed large in UGA folklore, but was not so grand when viewed by an impartial observer.

A week passed. I sensed again that I had made a mistake. The Athens economy was based on the university. I was not about to become a student again, nor was I ready to be a professor. The town held few prospects for me.

During the beginning of my second week there, Kate called again. This time I answered.

"James, where the hell are you?"

"Nowhere. I'm lost somewhere in America."

"You can't just drop out."

I didn't see any reason why I couldn't, but I replied in a different fashion. "I'm trying to either find myself or recreate myself."

"You don't need recreating. You just need a little recuperation. I've been trying to reach you."

"Well, you succeeded."

"Seriously, where are you?"

"Athens, Georgia."

"Oh, you've gone back to . . ." She didn't know how to finish the sentence.

"But I'm not going to stay. I'll leave here soon."

"Where to?"

Impetuously I replied, "Savannah."

"Why Savannah?"

"It's pretty."

"Seriously."

"It's a medium-sized city, and it has something of an economy. There's an active port."

"So you've been there before?"

"Oh, sure." I failed to add that my acquaintance was limited to two daytrips from Hilton Head Island when I vacationed with my family years earlier.

"James, wherever you go, I'm going to keep in touch, even if you don't want to hear from me."

"Why?" I asked simply.

"I care about you. I know you feel that I wrecked your career. I don't think I did, but I realize I didn't help you this last time in Washington."

I wanted to say, "No, you screwed me good," but I said nothing, and she continued. "I'll do better by you in the future. We're going to work together again. I just know it."

"I don't see how."

"You feel hurt right now. Maybe it's justified. But we'll both recover."

"I'm the one who needs to recover. You're in fine shape."

"The commission did not work out well."

"A minor blip along your road to stardom."

"We did accomplish one thing. Canada is acceding to a request for more petroleum, and they're going to partner with us to enhance North Dakota shale oil production."

"There are environmental concerns about more production in North Dakota."

"So you might think."

"I haven't seen any of this publicized."

"It hasn't been, and it won't be. But it gives us a little breathing room for a few years."

"I'm so glad to hear that," I said with all the sarcasm I could muster. "And then what do we do?"

"We'll see. There are always options. And that's the way you should view the world. You'll have options. You'll see. By the way, you won't say anything about Canada to anyone?" Kate now seemed anxious about her brief indiscretion.

"There's nothing to say. What do I know? It amounts to nothing."

"That's right. It's nothing. James, do me one favor—when I call again, please answer."

I did not reply but said, "Good-bye, Kate."

"No, instead let's say *au revoir*."

XXXV

WINTER PASSED SLOWLY UNTIL MARCH brought warmer days along with St. Patrick's Day celebrations. On Thursday afternoon, March 15, Jacqueline knocked on my door to ask if I wanted to join her and some of her friends who were going down to River Street the following night. Normally, I would have refused the invitation, not wanting to accompany a bunch of twenty-somethings, who were ten to fifteen years younger than I. I was bound to feel like a chaperon. But the winter had been dull and lonely, and I agreed. Jacqueline seemed happy with my decision. I offered to take her to a restaurant before hitting the bars downtown, but she refused, saying we would get some hotdogs from the vendors along the river.

On Friday evening, we took the tram from the nearby stop on Abercorn to its terminus near Bay Street. The tram was crowded, even though more cars were put in service to accommodate the revelers on this long holiday weekend. We used the ride to catch up on news, since we hadn't spent much time together since New Year's.

My news was scant. I was doing a bit of consulting for the regional energy council, but not nearly enough to satisfy my needs. Jacqueline was naturally busier than I with her remaining studies and a few jobs, although she had given up one wait job at a restaurant where business was slow. She had done two more modeling stints, but she had given that up, too, because she felt the pay she received from the photographer was minuscule in comparison to what he received from the website.

Jacqueline asked about Kate and my other "girlfriend" in Washington. I told her that I hadn't spoken to Kate since late January, and that she seemed okay at the time. My other girlfriend, who was not mentioned by name, was in Florence.

"Florence, Italy?" Jacqueline asked.

"Yes, Florence, Italy. She'll be working there for at least a year."

"Wow, that's extraordinary." Florence seemed to impress Jacqueline more than did Kate's job title. "Imagine, living in Florence for a year. What an unbelievable opportunity."

"That would appeal to you?"

"Of course. I've been studying art for over five years. To see those fantastic renaissance paintings, the sculpture, and the architecture all in one place would be amazing. Wouldn't you jump at such a chance?"

"I guess so," I replied half-heartedly.

We got our wristbands at a gate to River Street. The bands indicated that our IDs had been checked, we were of drinking age, and we had paid our twenty-dollar admittance fee. I bought beers and hotdogs for both of us, and then we began to wander through the growing crowd, trying to spot Jacqueline's friends. Somewhat to my relief, we did not immediately spot them. I realized that, after we joined up, the conversation would turn to SCAD and other topics of interest to those in their twenties. I would serve as their avuncular companion.

We stopped to hear a fife and drum corps perform. As we did so, Jacqueline's friends found us. Three of the friends were students, two women and one man, all in their early twenties. One, Sarah, was an instructor. She might have been in her early thirties and, therefore, closer to my age.

We all went to a bar to get beers. Jacqueline became immersed in a conversation with the other students. Sarah realized that if she didn't talk to me, I would be left out. She asked me what I did. I told her that I did consulting on energy-related issues. Prompted by another question, I had to explain where I obtained my experience. I described my education and, in two minutes, my dozen years at the F.E.D. She declared that she found my vocation "fascinating," but she failed to pursue energy-related topics any further.

I, in turn, inquired what she did. She told me that as a second-year instructor, she had to teach pretty much any course flung at her. Currently, she was teaching one class in drawing and another about Impressionism and Post-Impressionism. I confessed I knew little about the subjects, but asked if she had been to Paris. "If only I could afford to go! But I did get to Washington and New York. There are some nice collections. Here in town, the Telfair does have a Frieseke."

Of course, the name meant nothing to me. Frieseke certainly didn't sound French. To my relief, at the point when Sarah was suggesting I might want to take a summary course in art history, Jacqueline joined us. Perhaps she realized she had abandoned me. She told Sarah that I had a friend who was living in Florence for "several years." That subject carried the conversation for a half hour or so. Even the other friends joined in to gush about how wonderful the experience would be. When I explained she was there for the music rather than the art, they all looked disappointed.

Someone asked why I didn't join my friend, as if I could just pick up and leave. To my way of thinking, the suggestion was preposterous. "Oh, she's busy working there. She doesn't need me hanging around, doing nothing."

Our little group strolled farther along River Street and dropped into another bar. More beers were ordered. For the most part, I stayed on the periphery of the conversation, pretending to listen. Around midnight, Sarah excused herself, saying she needed to do a lot of work over the weekend on some lesson plans and test grading. The others booed her in a teasing fashion.

Fifteen minutes later, Jacqueline asked me if I wanted to leave. Perhaps she had read my mind again.

"Are you sure you don't want to stay longer?"

"Can't you just say 'yes'?"

"No."

We climbed the ramp-like street and then walked a few blocks to the Drayton Street tram stop. A number of other revelers had chosen the same time to leave. We had to wait for the second tram. Fortunately, it filled quickly, so the departure was not delayed.

It was colder than when we had left home. Jacqueline put her arm through mine and cuddled close to me. During the ride, I put my arm around her, and she put her head against my shoulder. For a brief while, I had the illusion that I was back in college and out on a date. But, cruelly, I then reminded myself that I was well past thirty-five, and Jacqueline was barely more than a girl, no matter how appealing she was. I made sure that a dose of shame eclipsed any sense of pleasure I was enjoying. Why did I feel obliged to destroy any tempting fantasies or escapes from reality? Having once or even twice had happiness destroyed, was I now destined to avoid any such emotions in the future?

I squeezed the girl next to me. She was not young enough to be my daughter. But was she old enough to be my lover? Did she even want to be, and did I want her to be? Why did I need to dissect and analyze?

We exited the tram and walked back to the Pinckney house. "Did you have fun?" I asked.

"Yeah," the reply came with no enthusiasm.

"Was I a drag?"

She turned toward me. "No, why did you ask that?"

"You replied 'yeah' to my question about having fun, but it sounded more like 'nah.'"

"Now you're trying to read *my* mind. You shouldn't. You're not as good as I am. My answer should have been 'okay.' It has nothing to do with you. Sometimes I get tired of the barhopping, drinking scene. Maybe I'm outgrowing it. I'm twenty-five now."

"I see."

"You probably think I'm just a kid."

"No, I don't. Sure, you're a lot younger than me, but you're working several jobs, putting yourself through college and—in another few months—you'll have your degree. That's quite an achievement."

"I guess so. You know you said 'younger than me.' Shouldn't it be 'younger than I'?"

"You're probably right."

"It's not the subjunctive, is it?" she asked impishly, crinkling her eyes.

"You've got quite a memory. And you're clever. You'll do just fine after graduation."

"I wish I knew what I'm going to do. There aren't many jobs available for inexperienced graphic artists."

"Just concentrate on getting some interviews. I'm sure you'll impress any number of people."

We were nearing the house. Rather than rush in, we slowed down in order to finish our conversation.

"Maybe I'll attach one of my nude photos to my resume."

"It would definitely attract attention."

"You know I'm kidding."

"Of course."

"Did you ever look at my other photos on the website?"

"No. I prefer Jacqueline in the flesh, or even in a bulky black jacket."

She turned to look directly into my eyes. "I wish we could go upstairs and screw."

"We might wake the older residents."

"Yeah, your room is next to Mrs. Humphreys's and mine is above Mrs. P's. Also, I sometimes scream when I come. Did you ever have sex in the house?"

"No."

"I did once. It was an afternoon when I was sure everyone else was gone. But that was the only time. I might as well live in a nunnery."

"I can't picture you as a nun."

"I know how you picture me." I said nothing. After a pause, she continued. "Come up to my room. I want to give you something."

We tiptoed up to Jacqueline's room, which was one flight up from mine. It was the first time I had been there. The room was small, but neat. There were no dirty clothes strewn around. The double bed was made. She reached into the bottom drawer of her dresser and took out a piece of paper. She handed it to me. It was a large glossy photo of her in a full-frontal nude pose.

"You are very beautiful." In the photo she was extremely attractive and sexy, but I thought the word "beautiful" would be better received.

"It doesn't embarrass you?" she asked.

"Me? Not if doesn't embarrass you."

"I'm cool with it. Otherwise I wouldn't have done it. Well, you can take the photo and look at it when you need a lift."

I knew Jacqueline was thinking of raising more than my spirits. I thanked her, gave her a brief kiss, and headed back to my room. I put the photo in a safe place and began to get ready for bed. The phone rang.

"James, I can't sleep, and I'm naked, and I'm very horny. Get your ass up here quick."

"How can I reject such a gracious invitation?"

XXXVI

Savannah, 2063

ON ST. PATRICK'S DAY, MY phone rang around ten o'clock. It woke me. I had snuck back to my room around five a.m., before anyone else in the house stirred.

"It sounds as if I woke you, James. Goodness, it's ten o'clock. How lazy you've become."

"It's Saturday. And St. Patrick's Day."

"Well, bottom of the morning to you."

"Savannah celebrates St. Patrick's Day."

"And all too well, it seems."

"Did you call to chastise me, Kate?"

She always kept her cool. "I called to give you some news. I'm taking a new job."

"Should I call you Madame President?"

"No, you know I told you I was thinking of returning to the private sector."

"So what's the job?"

"I was getting to that. I'm going to be senior vice president of government relations for Burfack-Gremen."

"They're a big government contractor."

"You got it."

"You should be perfect for the job. There's no conflict with the job you're leaving?"

"No. The F.E.D. has had no dealings with them for the past three years. They've mainly been doing work for the Defense Department."

"Excellent."

"I'm getting a hefty increase in pay."

"I would expect nothing less. That's the main reason you were looking to leave."

Kate hesitated. "Probably true. But I also wasn't getting the job satisfaction I used to. I want to mention something else. I'm not sure my successor will continue your current financial arrangements."

"There are always winners and losers," I commented somewhat bitterly. Kate probably didn't detect my tone.

"Are you doing other consulting?"

"A bit," was the best light I could put on my situation.

"I'll see if I can use you from time to time at Burfack. But, of course, I can't promise."

"Of course not."

"You're angry."

"I'm disappointed. I didn't think our arrangement could continue forever. I'm a realist. Now I'll have to look for some real work."

"Can you do more consulting in Savannah?"

"It's been rather slow since I returned from the latest tour in Washington." I thought I would add to Kate's guilt by reminding her that she dragged me away to keep her company.

She missed the point. "Maybe it will pick up again. The economy is due for a turn."

"Maybe. Tell me, will you be staying in Washington?"

"No. I'm sure I'll be visiting Washington often, but I'll be based in Houston."

"Sorry to hear your bad news."

"No, Houston's fine. I visited a week ago."

"Kate, it's only March. See how you feel in July."

Kate did not appreciate my warning. We exchanged a few innocuous comments and ended the conversation.

For some reason, the call from Kate—perhaps because it

came from Washington—reminded me about Pat Auriga, who, of course, was not currently in Washington. I hadn't spoken to her since she left for Florence. No doubt, she had settled in and was learning how to function in a foreign country. Her experience was of great interest to me. Yet I hesitated before calling. Would I be interrupting? Interfering? She had said her phone was supposed to work in Europe. Would it? What was the time difference? It might be dinnertime in Italy. No, they couldn't be more than five or six hours ahead. But hesitation led to a failure in impetus. I did not call.

On Sunday, I was still thinking of Pat. Furthermore, I was ashamed of my cowardice. With a rush of impetuousness I pressed the numbers that would connect me to Italy.

"*Pronto*."

I couldn't comprehend the greeting. "Pat?"

"Yes."

"It's James." Should I have said, 'James Lendeman'?

Her quick response was reassuring. "James, it's great to hear from you. I've been thinking about you. I meant to call. Really. But I'm glad you took the initiative. There's so much to tell you."

"You just go ahead, because there's not much new on my end."

Pat caught her breath and then began to stream information. She rented a nice one-bedroom apartment six blocks from Santa Maria Novella (not that I knew what "Santa Maria Novella" was). From there, she could walk to the center of the city in less than ten minutes. She had eight voice students, including two Americans. She was also well into her work on the music festival. She found that there were hundreds of American students in the city studying art history, some of whom were also interested in music. Although she mostly had to prepare her meals at home, she had thus far sampled a dozen or more *trattorias*, most of which served very good food. Everywhere she went there was amazing art to be seen. She reeled off a dozen names among which I recognized only the Uffizi gallery. She concluded by telling me that I would love Florence and Italy. I really needed to find a way to get over there. If I came, I could sleep on her couch. She missed me. She really did.

I told her that I missed seeing her, too. I did not comment on her reaction to Florence, but I told her that I was busy with a few projects in Savannah. After ending the call, I was ashamed of myself for telling such a patent lie.

Miraculously, on Monday I was contacted by Joe Porter, who needed work done for the regional energy council. The assignment was fortuitous, because I wanted to increase my rather modest savings, given the expectation that my income from Washington would soon cease. I had managed to put aside some of the pay received for babysitting Kate, but prudence suggested that I should add to that sum.

On Tuesday, I met with Joe and was briefed on a plant expansion I would need to analyze. After an hour spent reading an outline of the project, I figured the task would take more than a hundred billable hours. Just what I needed in my fragile economic state. The work would be part-time over the course of about three months, but perhaps I could find some other endeavor to augment my income.

One thing that did not develop as expected was a relationship with Jacqueline. After spending that Friday night with her, I discovered that she was waiting tables on Saturday and Sunday when extra people were in town for the St. Patrick's Day hoopla. Then she was back into her routine of classes and jobs.

I encountered her at the end of March and asked when we could get together again. She was evasive.

"We could have a real date," I added, thinking that she might have thought I was only suggesting a sexual tryst.

"That would be nice, but I'm so busy right now—work and tests—and I have a paper due."

"Was the sex that bad?"

"No, no. It was fine, great. Just what I wanted. But I'm very busy. I like you a lot, James, and when I have the time, we'll get together. I promise." And, with that, she hurried away.

At the beginning of April, the azaleas bloomed on cue. Some people with time—and the means—went out to Bonaventure Cemetery where the flowering bushes were particularly abundant. If I could have located Jacqueline, I would have suggested we go. But early April passed, along with the azalea blossoms. I was spending more time in Mrs. Pinckney's garden. Jacqueline didn't come to sun herself.

On a Saturday afternoon, our paths crossed as she was leaving the house. "You've been avoiding me."

"No, I haven't. I've been studying, writing papers, taking tests, working two jobs, sometimes three. As a matter of fact, I'm heading to one right now."

"You wait tables in that dress?" It was perhaps the first time I had seen her in a dress. It was green, clinging and low cut.

"I'm now the Saturday evening hostess at the River Grill. You can come down there and check."

"I don't mean to sound suspicious."

"But you are." She could be quick with repartee. "Look, on Monday I have class that ends at noon. I need to stay downtown. But if you want to join me, we can have lunch."

If I had any self-respect, I would have refused such an offer. Our relationship, if we ever had one, was proceeding in a retrograde fashion. We had had sex, and now we were arranging a lunch that would be appropriate for a first date. Getting on the same wavelength with Jacqueline seemed impossible. I tended to be a linear person—I would start at one point and proceed directly to another. Jacqueline would wander all over the place. Yet she showed persistency in pursuing her degree. All other activities were subordinate to that goal. Perhaps I was selling her approach short. At any event I accepted her invitation to meet for lunch.

When I arrived at the café near City Market at twelve fifteen, she was there waiting. We found a table and quickly ordered. She said she had to attend to something before her two o'clock class. I knew not to press her for the reason.

The waiter brought our iced teas. "So, what do you want to talk about?" Jacqueline was obviously not in the mood for small talk.

"You seem to be trying to avoid me."

"I told you, I've been very busy. I'm not *trying* to avoid you." I noticed that there was emphasis on the word "trying." "It just happens. A lot of people probably think I'm avoiding them. I'm going in a dozen different directions."

"Do you think we could go out on a real date?"

"I'd love to."

"How about on Saturday night?"

"You know I work on Saturday nights, and by the time I'm finished, I'm dead tired."

"Then perhaps Friday?"

"Not this Friday. I need to be at the Durango. They're short a girl. One is pregnant. She's in her fifth month. Doesn't make a good impression."

"Might be kinky," I suggested.

"You're kidding. Aren't you?"

"Yeah. I guess I am. So why don't you give me a date?"

Jacqueline looked at her smart phone calendar and frowned. "How about two weeks from Wednesday?"

"That's the best you can do?"

"Yes, I just looked at my calendar."

"How many other guys are you dating?"

"Just one other right now. I've never dated anyone exclusively, at least not since high school. And that was a mistake. So should we get together May ninth?"

"Okay," I acquiesced. "We'll set up a time when we're closer to the date. You know, I don't even have your phone number."

"Are you sure you don't have it? I know I've called you in

the past." She gave me her number and changed the subject from dating, by asking what I had been doing. My reply took only a minute or two. I asked about her two remaining courses. She liked her design course; she didn't like her marketing class. But, all in all, she was looking forward to finishing her classes and moving on to the next phase of her life.

I suggested that she might want to go to graduate school. "Never," was her decisive reply. "Are you going to teach again?"

"Probably not. I haven't been asked."

"You were pretty good at it, especially after the first few classes when you got to feel more comfortable."

"Thank you. You're being too kind." I recollected that Jacqueline had missed nearly half my lectures and perhaps was not the best judge.

A little after one o'clock, she looked at her watch. "I really have to go. How much do you think my share is?"

"I'll take care of it."

"You sure?"

"Yes, absolutely."

"Well, thanks." There was no kiss, no hug, no handshake.

Over the next few days I thought quite a bit about her. I liked her. She was pretty and sexy. I admired her industriousness in balancing a number of jobs and pursuing her degree so diligently over a number of years. Her determination was admirable. On the other hand, she seemed immature and impulsive. Her whim had led to a great night of sex. But was sex all that we had to share? Upon reflection, I realized that we had sex maybe twice, if you threw in the lap dance, but we never had a true, old-fashioned date. Certainly we chatted a score of times in the garden behind Mrs. Pinckney's house. We had drinks on St. Patrick's Day eve, and recently a hurried lunch.

Was it the age difference that bothered me? Nearly fourteen years. I was not old enough to be her father. But looking at it in other ways, fourteen years was a great deal. When I graduated college, she was eight, probably in third grade. I did a quick calculation in my head. I'd have to add another fifty percent to her age to get to mine.

A certain sense of shame came over me. I was romantically attached to a youngster. Yet that youngster was so enticing. And what was I supposed to do? Live like a priest? I had taken no vow of chastity. I was celibate by circumstance.

Each day I came to a different conclusion. I convinced myself that I should stop pursuing Jacqueline. Then I was certain that I could not live without her. But I was sure I was demeaning myself by continuing a relationship with a girl still in college. My next analysis produced the rationalization that I should not deny myself the pleasure of walking arm in arm with her, being an intimate friend, and—all told—there was nothing illegal about our liaisons. She was no longer my student, and she was certainly of an age to make her own decisions. These conflicting impressions and thoughts turned over and over in my mind, producing alternate agony and ecstasy.

On Sunday morning, May sixth, I took to my usual place in the Pinckney garden. I enjoyed the quiet of a Sunday morning. Mrs. Pinckney was invariably at church. Mrs. Humphreys, if she weren't away with family, usually would not stir before eleven. Jacqueline, too, was slow to rise, since she would have to recuperate from her Saturday night job at the River Grill.

I had a large cup of coffee, freshly brewed and never instant on a Sunday, and my page palette accessed the latest news. The day was going to be warm, but it was even a bit cool under the table umbrella. I read a long article on the economy. It must have been nearly eleven when Jacqueline carried a glass of orange juice onto the garden terrace. She wore sweat pants and a tee shirt, her sleeping attire. Her feet were bare.

"What you doing?"

"Catching up on the news."

"Anything particularly earth-shattering?"

"No. What are you doing?"

"Drinking orange juice." What answer did I expect? "Say, can I borrow of piece of bread to make toast?"

"Don't you have bread in the refrigerator?"

"It's moldy."

"I thought you just cut off the mold."

"Too far gone. Even for me."

"Sure. Take a piece. Could you make one for me while you're at it? And put some orange marmalade on it."

She shot me a look implying that she resented being my servant. But she recollected that I was doing her a favor. "My pleasure, mi-lord."

"Where did you get that 'mi-lord' crap from?"

"Some movie, I suspect." With that, she sauntered back to the kitchen.

Two minutes later we were munching on our toast. "Aren't I a good cook?"

"Excellent. But how big is your repertoire?"

"I can also boil eggs and heat frozen dinners. See what a catch I am? You should marry me."

I knew she was pulling my leg. "But you wouldn't want to marry me."

"No. But don't feel rejected. I don't want to marry anyone. I might want to live with a man someday, but I don't want the commitment of marriage."

I returned to my reading without comment. After a minute, Jacqueline broke the silence. "You're not angry with me. Are you?"

"No. Why should I be?"

"You got so quiet."

"I went back to reading."

"Oh. Well, I'm going to make you angry now. I have to cancel our date for Wednesday night."

"Why?"

"Why do you have to know?"

"We had a date and you're cancelling. I think I deserve a reason."

"Something came up."

"What came up?"

"It's personal."

"I see."

"Do you want to reschedule for the following Wednesday?"

"Just to have you cancel?"

"I won't cancel."

"Do I get a guaranty?"

"I promise. I really do."

"Okay. We'll give it one more try."

Jacqueline did not cancel our date, but I probably should have. In the morning I received a message from Washington. It originated in the procurement section of the Federal Energy Department and stated that, in view of the fact that I was no longer providing any consulting services to the department, my retainer would not be paid beyond the end of June.

The plan was for me to meet Jacqueline at seven outside a SCAD building on Bull Street. We were going to get burgers and then go to a bar to listen to some jazz.

To her credit, Jacqueline recognized very quickly that I was unhappy about something. Of course, she did, on occasion, have the ability to read my mind. We had just ordered our burgers from a menu that must have featured twenty or more varieties, all named after people or locations associated with the Savannah area, when she urged, "So tell me, what's the matter?"

"Oh, nothing."

"No, you don't get off that easy. What's bothering you? I know there's something. Remember, I'm a mind reader."

"Well, then you already know what's bothering me."

"I know it's not me. It's something else." She put her hand on mine. "Please tell me. It will help to talk."

"I just got a message from the F.E.D. They're cutting off my pay."

"Can they do that?"

"Yes, I'm pretty sure they can. While Kate was there, she would make sure the arrangement continued, but she left a few months ago."

"Do you know her successor?"

"Yes, I know him."

"But you don't get along with him." Jacqueline was perceptive.

"You got it."

"Can you appeal the decision?"

"I'm not sure. Plus I don't have any real leverage."

"So what will you do?"

"I suppose I'll have to get a job and earn an honest living." I wanted to get away from the subject. "You know, if we could talk about something else, I'd prefer that."

"I understand. What should we talk about?"

"Tell me about yourself. I know about your life in Savannah, but where did you grow up? Do you have brothers and sisters? That sort of stuff."

Jacqueline paused. Perhaps she was trying to figure out how far back to go and how much to tell. "You're going to be bored, but here goes. I grew up just north of Baltimore. I had a mother and a father and a sister and a dog."

"Do your parents still live in that area?"

"Yes, they're still alive and living in the house I grew up in. My sister moved away like I did. Only the dog is dead, and he's the one I liked best. You see, I was the rebellious one in the family. My sister, who is older, was the good child. I was the bad one.

"My father did construction work. He was unemployed half the time. My mother was, and still is, a teacher. She teaches elementary school. She doesn't really like it much, except for teaching art to the kids. But she sticks to it because it's a reliable job.

"I almost left high school before I graduated. I didn't like most of my classes. I wanted to go to New York and learn photography or something like that. My mother talked me into staying and graduating. Then I did go to New York.

"I moved in with my sister who lived in a town in New Jersey called Weehawken. It's right across the river from Manhattan."

"I know it," I broke in.

She continued with barely a pause, wanting to give me the information I requested and get it over as quickly as possible. "But we were like oil and water. I moved out after a month and found a seedy studio in Queens. I worked at menial jobs, but took night courses in art at a college called the New School.

"My jobs convinced me that I needed more of an education to get a job that I would find interesting. I did well in my courses at the New School, and that probably helped me get into SCAD. I borrowed some money from my mother and came to Savannah. You pretty much know the rest. Now it's your turn."

Before I could get started, the waitress arrived with the burgers. "Who ordered the Lucas?"

I raised my hand. Then there was the matter of arranging the lettuce, tomatoes and fried onions, so I could get it into my mouth. After one bite, I was ready to start. I summarized my life's story in about ten minutes. Jacqueline listened politely, but she didn't seem overly interested in my narrative. A few points elicited comments. She was impressed that I had had several dogs when growing up. She was surprised that my father died when I was relatively young.

"Maybe my father will be dead when I reach your age," she observed, almost hopefully. She also noted that I got my graduate degree at UGA, and thus Savannah was my second residence in Georgia.

I asked her if she ever got to see her sister or parents. She had not visited them since moving to Savannah. I told her my situation was much the same.

I asked if her graduation was approaching. "Yes, very quickly. It's Friday."

"Wow. That calls for a celebration."

"Here's the game plan: I collect my degree at three and then I'm at my Friday job by five."

"You're not going to take at least one night off and celebrate with friends?"

"Nope. Still have to pay the bills."

"Do you have any leads for a full-time job?"

"Not yet. I'm working with the placement office. I have a hunch I'll need to relocate. Maybe I'll move back to New York."

"It's not a bad place to live."

"If I move, will you miss me?" It was a strangely emotional question for Jacqueline to ask.

"Of course. Toast just won't be the same without your deft touch." I didn't want to know if she'd miss me.

Our date—perhaps our first true date—was enjoyable. We chatted easily during breaks between jazz sets. Jacqueline found that she liked the music, which nevertheless seemed a bit antiquated. When we got back to our mutual residence, we stopped at the front door and kissed briefly.

In my room, I got ready for bed and then read a book for a while. I did not receive a phone call beckoning me to climb the stairs.

On the day after my date with Jacqueline—my genuine date, not our sexual encounters—I called the person in the procurement section of the F.E.D. who had sent me the mail dispensing with my services. When I mentioned my name and the email I had received, the woman immediately knew what I was referring to. I asked her to whom I could talk about the decision to cancel my consulting agreement. She told me that she was the appropriate person. "In that case," I asked, "please explain the reason behind this action."

She replied that the action was taken with due consideration at a high level within the department. I told her that she was not answering my question. I wanted to know the reason behind the decision, not the level at which it was made. She then stated that, because I had not been performing any consulting duties during the past year, the retainer was being terminated.

I told her in turn that I had been active in the past year, and had in fact spent over two months in Washington during the fall at the behest of the Secretary. That statement brought a halt to the glib ripostes. She thought for a moment, and then told me that she would have to get back to me. Hopefully I would receive a call back the next day.

At ten a.m. on Friday, I received a call from the woman in the procurement section. "I have an answer to the question you posed yesterday."

"Yes."

"You were here in October and November of last year. That is true. But it was not deemed to be a consulting assignment. There was no resultant product, that is, no report such as a consultant would make."

"I was there, working for the Secretary of the F.E.D. I worked directly for her."

"It is felt that such service was as a personal aide and not as a consultant." The procurement section employee had received a careful briefing.

"And who categorized my services as a personal aide? Ms. Hastings?"

"No, she's no longer employed by the department."

"Obviously I know that. So it is the acting secretary who made the decision." Wayne Sickles's involvement was apparent.

"He approved of the decision."

"How can I appeal the decision?"

"There is no appeal process. The decision is final."

The call ended. I knew I would get no consideration from

Wayne Sickles. Perhaps there was an element of spite involved in his decision. He was not named secretary upon Kate's departure, but only acting secretary. Kate had not recommended him as her successor.

After the conversation with the woman in procurement, I felt the need for a walk. I couldn't continue to be cooped up in my room, and wanted to clear my mind. A brisk walk in bracing weather would have been ideal. But such weather is not to be found in Savannah in the middle of May. I dressed lightly and then set a moderate pace west to Habersham, and then south. I ended up at a small shopping center.

One grocery store made sandwiches to go. I ordered one, despite the realization that making my own would have been cheaper. To make matters worse, I entered a wine and liquor shop. I remembered that it was Jacqueline's graduation day. I bought a bottle of champagne. Perhaps we would enjoy it together. Perhaps I would just present it to her as a gift.

I kept the champagne in my room. That night, I listened for Jacqueline's return. I must have dozed off at some point, for around eleven I awoke and heard some noise in the house. At that hour it was unlikely that either of the two older ladies would be up and causing some disturbance. I grabbed the champagne, and headed to Jacqueline's room.

Some additional sounds from her room made me hesitate. There was more than one voice. Then some giggling. Then some murmurs. Finally I heard an exclamation of some sort that was quickly muffled. The sounds were more those of pleasure than danger or hostility. The second voice was a man's. I listened no longer. I crept back to my room, champagne in hand.

The next morning, I arose a bit late and donned some clothes to look respectable enough to go downstairs for breakfast. While I was preparing coffee and cereal, Mrs. Pinckney stuck her head into the kitchen, said hello in a brusque manner, and was quickly gone. I took my cereal, coffee, and page palette out to the garden. I accessed the news and began to read an article about the latest budget problems in Washington.

I was soon interrupted by Mrs. Pinckney entering the garden, followed by Jacqueline, who looked both tired and annoyed. Charlene Pinckney took a seat quite close to me and motioned to Jacqueline to take the other seat at the table.

I looked at Jacqueline. She shrugged in return. But we had no further opportunity for silent communication. Mrs. Pinckney began to speak and command our attention. "I think the three of us need to speak, and we may as well do it right here in the garden. You know, I may be quite old, but I am no fool. My senses of sight and hearing are not particularly keen, but they are not totally impaired.

"You have to understand that I like both of you. You have been respectful tenants here and have caused me little or no trouble. But one thing I cannot permit among tenants is intimate fraternization."

I focused on the term "intimate fraternization," but wasn't quite sure what it meant. Surely, Jacqueline and I were not brothers. Mrs. P. was quick to explain.

"In other words, I can't keep a stable household if romances are in progress. Similarly I rarely rent to married couples."

Mrs. P. looked at both of us. Neither Jacqueline nor I said a word, so Mrs. P. continued. "Jacqueline, I must tell you directly that I heard noises coming from your room last night. There was a man in your room."

"Yes, but it wasn't James," Jacqueline responded quickly.

"That's right," I added.

"But I did see you coming from Jacqueline's floor. You can't deny that."

I paused, trying to find words which would satisfy Mrs. P. and yet not offend Jacqueline. "I was outside her room momentarily. I was bringing her a graduation present, but when I heard some sounds coming from her room, I turned around and went back to mine."

"Hmm." Mrs. P. tried to evaluate my story.

I was angry about the unjust accusation, and also upset by the spying and being treated like an adolescent.

Jacqueline spoke up, again. "There was someone in my room last night, but it wasn't Mr. Lendeman."

This denial did not stop Mrs. P. "Very clever. You say 'Mr. Lendeman,' now, but I've heard you call him 'James' many times."

Jacqueline glared at Mrs. P. "Guilty as charged. I've called him 'James.' What does that prove?"

Mrs. P.'s indignation rose after being challenged. I had never seen her out of control before. "And I suppose I didn't see you two kissing on the front steps a few days ago."

"What are you getting at?" I asked.

"I told you I can't have romances going on here. One of you will have to move out."

Jacqueline and I looked at each other, not quite believing what we had heard. I thought that Mrs. P. was completely overreacting, but if I made such a comment, I was sure she would become apoplectic. After a minute of silence, I said, "I'll move out."

"You're sure you really want to do this?" No doubt Mrs. P. would have preferred to see Jacqueline depart. Her rent was less. She was likely to leave anyway in the next few months. And another student could be found fairly readily to rent the single room.

"Just give me two weeks to find another place." I knew it would not be difficult to locate alternate living arrangements. The ads, offering rooms and small apartments in private homes, were plentiful. The economy had encouraged many homeowners to renovate their quarters to accommodate tenants.

Mrs. P., without saying a word, nodded to demonstrate assent to my request. Jacqueline sensed that the interrogation was over. She rose and went through the garden door, slamming it behind her.

It took only a few days for me to find new living quarters. My accommodations consisted of a large room, which served as both a living room and bedroom, and a bath. Furniture, including a bed, desk, table, armoire, and easy chair, was supplied. There were no formal kitchen privileges, but the owners—Todd and Brenda—told me that I could use the kitchen as long as it didn't interfere with their cooking or eating, and I could keep a hotplate in my room.

My new landlords were in their mid-fifties. Their daughter had married and moved out several years earlier, enabling them to convert her room to separate living quarters for a tenant.

My new home was about a kilometer from Mrs. Pinckney's house. The neighborhood was a bit more downscale. The houses were smaller and less stately in appearance. There were no columns or shady porches, just rectangular boxes. Maintenance appeared to be kept to a minimum.

I rented the room on a month-to-month basis. I hoped my stay would not last too long, and that—in one way or another—I would move on. How this would occur or where I would move next, I had no idea.

It took me only a few hours to pack my clothes and other belongings. I was able to borrow the regional energy council's electrocar. Since the capacity was small, I had to make two trips to shift my stuff from one place to the other. Jacqueline helped me load a few things and insisted on coming with me to my new place. She felt that I was an innocent victim of Mrs. Pinckney's irrational vendetta. I'm sure she viewed her aid as some recompense for my gallantry in volunteering to move out.

"I'm really so sorry you have to do this. It's so unfair," she declared as we drove to my new location.

"It's okay. I kind of wanted to move on."

Perhaps she misconstrued my motivation. "I hope we can remain friends."

"Of course. Why not?"

"I thought you might be mad at me."

"For what?"

"For getting you in trouble."

"You think I'm in trouble?"

"You know what I mean."

Only Brenda was present to watch the process of my carrying suitcases, a number of boxes, and miscellaneous items into my room. I had to introduce Jacqueline to Brenda.

Brenda eyed her carefully. "What a pretty, young girlfriend you have!"

"Thank you," said Jacqueline, hearing the word "pretty." As for me, I thought the emphasis had been placed on the word "young."

After the second trip to my new quarters, Jacqueline sat on the bed as I unpacked some cartons. "James, I want to explain something about the night of my graduation."

"You don't owe me any explanation. You're entitled to your privacy."

"I'd feel better if I told you." I said nothing, as she continued. "The friend who was there is also named James. I probably said his name a few times. That's why Mrs. P. thought it was you in my room."

"Okay. Thanks for the explanation."

"No, I want to tell you something else. We were drinking. We were a bit drunk, and we got a little loud. After all, I was celebrating my graduation. We were playing some electronic games. We weren't having sex."

"You can have sex with whomever you choose. We're not married, we're not engaged, we're not even dating. You owe me no explanations. And if you were having sex with another James, so what?"

"I should have been with you that night. You were the one who was thoughtful enough to buy me a graduation present. If we had been together that night, we would have had sex. I would have wanted that."

"You should have had sex with your other James."

Jacqueline probably sensed a tone of bitterness in my voice. "I wouldn't have had sex with him; rather he wouldn't have wanted to have sex with me. He's gay." Jacqueline got off the bed and wrapped her arms around me. "Kiss me, please. If there's any hard feelings, let's make up."

She kissed me, and I kissed her back. After a few moments, I pushed her away. "Okay, all's forgiven. But I don't want to get thrown out of this place on the day I move in."

"Do you have a prude for a landlord?"

"I don't know, yet."

Jacqueline looked at me slyly. "Well, since you no longer live under Mrs. P.'s roof, we can screw in my room."

The truth was Jacqueline and I did not rush to her room to have sex. In fact, over the next few weeks we didn't see each other at all. We talked on the phone, but one thing or another prevented us from getting together. She was still busy with her part-time jobs, and I didn't want to have another Wednesday lunchtime date. Then she had a job interview in Atlanta. Two weeks after the interview, I received a call from her.

"We need to get together," she declared somewhat breathlessly.

"I've been trying to accomplish that for the past month."

"I know. I'm sorry. But this is important," implying that it hadn't been important for her to see me earlier when I wanted to see her.

We compared schedules and set up a Wednesday night rendezvous.

When we met at a café, it didn't take Jacqueline long to get to the point. "I got a job offer from the company in Atlanta."

"That's good."

"It's good, but it's not great. I want a job as a graphic artist. That's what I've been trained for."

"So what does this job involve?"

"I'll get to do some art work, but initially most of the job will involve office work—word processing, bookkeeping, gal Friday. Should I take it?"

"Hold on a minute. Let me ask a few questions. Did you meet the person you'll be working for?"

"Yes. She interviewed me."

"Did she seem to be honest with you?"

"Yes. I think so. She went into details. Like, initially she expects that the art design work should occupy about one-quarter of my time. They hope to hire another assistant within six months to a year. Then I would get to spend more time on art work."

"And did you discuss pay?"

"Yes. Thirty-six hundred a month to start. It's not a great deal, but I can get by on that until I get an increase. Perhaps I can also do some freelance work."

"Are there dance bars in Atlanta?"

"I'm sure there are." She took my question seriously.

"I think you should take the job. In a fragile economy, you can't afford to be too choosy. This job holds out some hope of progress. I wish you good luck."

Jacqueline squeezed my hand. "We'll get to see each other. Won't we? Atlanta isn't that far. You'll be able to visit."

"I expect so."

In two weeks, she left Savannah. I offered to help her. But a friend named Anthony was able to borrow a natural gas truck to move her possessions. She preferred Anthony's more practical help to mine.

When she settled into a small apartment, Jacqueline called to give me her address. We spoke a few times over the next two months. For the most part she liked her job. And it was natural for her to immerse herself in the life of her new city. She was making new friends, and I, I was sure, would gradually fade from memory.

XXXVII

Savannah, 2063

THE SUMMER OF 2063 WAS hot in Savannah, even hotter than average. I struggled to survive the long period, which generally lasts from May through September. My income had been reduced to near poverty level. I dipped into savings in July to get by. My rent payment to my new landlords was a week late at the beginning of August.

I was not enjoying my new quarters. The air-conditioning was feeble. Nighttime power downs were frequent, adding to the discomfort. Todd and Brenda drank much and argued loudly and regularly. They stinted on pest control, like they stinted on air-conditioning, and palmetto bugs were spied frequently after dark.

I asked Aaron Smith to find out if there were additional projects I could handle for the regional energy council. He said that things were slow given the state of the economy, but he promised to do some checking.

By mid-August, I wondered if I could sink any lower. Of course, I could. I could have been homeless and forced to go to a soup kitchen for food. I could have been suffering from an excruciating illness. I tried to convince myself that I was relatively well off. Yet I realized that, on the ladder of life, I was approaching the bottom, not climbing to the top.

As I was contemplating my lot in life, I received two telephone calls that counteracted my deep pessimism. The first came from Pat Auriga, who was still enjoying Italy. She had managed to get away from Florence for a few days and was calling from a region

known as the Cinque Terre, a rugged area on the Ligurian Coast.
She told me that the scenery was fantastic. The little towns dripped
down from the mountains to the sea like icing on a warm cake.
Whereas in Florence meat was a staple of the diet, everyone in the
Cinque Terre ate fish, and meat was difficult to find. Somehow this
surprised her, even though she was perched on the Mediterranean
Sea.

Always interested in modes of transport, I asked how she
managed to get to such a remote area.

"By train. Although there's no road between the villages in the
region, there's a good rail line. I'm told it was built in the nineteen-
thirties. Amazing, isn't it?

"James, you just have to come to Italy and see this stuff. It's
like a Disneyland of the Renaissance. You can stay in my apartment
for a few weeks or for a month or two—whatever you like."

"Oh, I'm tempted."

"Then do it."

"At the moment my finances are a bit stretched." I minimized
my distress. "But when I put aside some cash, I'm going to take
you up on that offer."

"I'm going to hold you to that promise."

A little later, the phone rang again. It was Kate. She first assured
me that she was enjoying her job, although she didn't like Houston.
"It's over forty degrees and near a hundred percent humidity. You
really can't go outside. It's unbearable. And the air-conditioning
never seems adequate."

"I know the feeling."

"Yes, you're in Savannah."

Kate described her duties, which in truth sounded much less
interesting than being a member of the cabinet. She sensed my
subdued reaction, so she mentioned all the perks she enjoyed,
which seemed no greater than what she had in Washington. Then
she told me her salary and anticipated bonus.

"So you're rolling in dough."

This time she was pleased with my reaction. "So tell me, James, how are you doing?"

"I'm just getting by. It will come as no surprise that Wayne Sickles made sure my retainer was stopped."

Kate paused. "I'm not surprised."

I continued. "Otherwise, work is rather slow. I'm looking to pick up some more consulting work, but the economy is slow here."

"I'm sorry to hear that."

"And I've moved to new, more humble quarters." Since I had started enumerating my woes, I made sure to include each miserable element. "My one good friend in Savannah just took a job in Atlanta. Other than that, my health still is holding up." Perhaps I shouldn't have mentioned the issue of health.

"Well, if you have your health, you have the most important thing in the world. Believe me. I have experience in that area. But, James, with respect to money, I may be able to help you out. We're expanding one of our facilities just south of Houston. We're having some problem getting regional energy council approval. Quite an embarrassment to me. Our CEO thought I could just snap my fingers and the problem would be fixed. I told him we had to comply with regulations, or at least give that impression. I told him I had just the person to do some consulting and solve the problem."

"And that person would be me."

"How wonderfully perceptive."

I asked about pay, and Kate assured me that I'd find it more than satisfactory. We agreed that I would need to travel to Houston to meet with a number of people associated with the project. These would include staff from Burfack-Gremen, Kate's employer, and people at the regional energy council.

Exactly one week later, I was on my way to Houston. I took

the morning flight from Savannah to Atlanta. (I understand that in the past there were five or six flights per day, but now the schedule was down to two.) I waited three hours for the flight from Atlanta to Houston's main airport, which is a ridiculously long distance north of the city. Then I took a shuttle bus to the city's central terminal, where Kate met me.

"Sorry you had to take a shuttle from the airport, but it was more practical than my getting the hybrid car to pick you up. At any event, welcome to Houston. It only hit thirty-six today. Of course, we're expecting torrential thunderstorms later."

"Then we better get going."

Kate looked good, but not great. Her face was drawn and a little more lined. Her eyes, previously deep-set, were now better described as sunken. She was thin, but as elegant as ever.

We had dinner together that evening, but then went in different directions. The facility that was being expanded was in a town called Sugarland, about twenty-five kilometers south of downtown Houston. The project manager was based in that office. Therefore, my hotel room was booked in Sugarland. An electrocar was lent to me for the three days I was expected to spend in the area.

At the end of each day I called Kate and briefed her on the obstacles I perceived in getting approval for the project's completion and the modifications that would probably alleviate the problems. She asked about the timeframes involved. Despite the fact that some of the modifications were minor, she seemed to be interested in the details. So I had to go through a list of my concerns, such as needs for more energy-efficient lighting, including downward-facing fixtures on the exterior; mass transit credits for office staff commuting; a more efficient HVAC system with more advanced electronic controls; a change of exterior access, particularly through the loading dock; and many other things of that ilk. By the time I reached the tenth item, Kate's interest began to lag. "Well, you'll be sending me the report."

My portion of the project would extend over several months,

involving a few hundred hours of work. Much could be done from Savannah. There was no point in staying in Houston, especially since I would likely see Kate infrequently. In fact, on the day I returned to Savannah, she left for a two-week stay in Washington where she would be lobbying for some issues of importance to Burfack-Gremen.

Burfack's position as a government contractor was sometimes complicated by the fact that it was thirty-percent-owned by a German company and another fifteen percent was in the hands of a company that was probably no more than a front for the Chinese government. These complications were one of the reasons that Kate was hired and expected to earn her hefty compensation.

I was happy to return to Savannah, a city of more reasonable scope than Houston, more genteel in its character, and, to my thinking, more sensible in its customs. With my newfound lucre, I could afford to tell Todd and Brenda, that—although I could live with inadequate air-conditioning—they would have to do something about the Palmetto bugs. Otherwise, I would likely move back with Mrs. Pinckney, who was still looking for a tenant for my former quarters. Todd declared that he had no idea that there was more than an occasional offensive critter, but he would get after the exterminator, who—he assured me—was well paid for his services. And as to my comment about the air-conditioning, he was only trying to be a good citizen and not use more than his proper share of energy. He was very conscious of his civic obligations. All of this was, of course, no more than artful bullshit.

I found that I could work more effectively on the Burfack-Gremen project away from the seedy confines of the Todd/Brenda abode. With the economy muddling along, one of the two conference rooms at the regional energy council's office was invariably available. Being a consultant to the council, I felt justified in employing the facility to do regional council-type work, albeit of a "lone star" character. So, for a day here and two days there, I took the tram downtown and walked from the appropriate

Drayton Street stop to the council's office on Martin Luther King Jr. Boulevard.

I kept Kate up-to-date on my progress. At one point, I needed to employ a sub-consultant to conduct an employee commuting survey. This was needed because the office expansion was occurring in a suburban locale with limited mass transit facilities, only a light rail service down the old route fifty-nine corridor. Had they chosen to grow at their headquarters in downtown Houston, this step would not have been needed. Kate did not flinch at spending the extra twenty thousand dollars on the survey. She told me, however, to keep my own bill to under eighty thousand, since she didn't want the total for the consulting to exceed one hundred thousand. If that happened, a higher level of approval would be needed.

At the beginning of October, I was still in the midst of Kate's project. Some change was now apparent in Savannah's weather. I had received my second installment of the consulting fee, and felt more secure with some money in the bank.

I decided to call Pat since I had not spoken to her for a few months. I put in a call in the late afternoon, and from the sound of Pat's voice I must have awakened her. Yet she seemed happy to hear from me.

"Oh, James, no, you didn't really wake me. I had just gotten into bed."

She updated me about her work, which was now mainly centered on voice classes. Only a small amount of her time was now devoted to next summer's festival. I told her about the consulting work for Kate.

"I hope you're saving some money, so you can visit me." I noted that this time she spoke it terms of visiting "her" rather than "Florence."

Without weighing my response, I quickly replied, "I'd love to, but now I need to finish this project. I'm also doing some work for the regional council here in Savannah. Things seem to be picking up a bit."

"Well, that's good, isn't it?"

"Yes, if I want to avoid starvation."

"At least you've now promised to come here when you can get away."

I didn't recall making any such promise, but I did not disabuse Pat of the notion. And I left it at that.

XXXVIII

IN LATE OCTOBER, THE PROJECT reached the point where I needed to return to Houston to meet with the regional energy council and present the plan. I had a quick dinner with Kate on the night I arrived. She was not going to accompany me to the next day's meeting.

The Burfack-Gremen team consisted of the local project manager, Kate's assistant, Lance Thomas, and me. Kate thought it was best not to overwhelm the council with high-powered Burfack-Gremen executives. She didn't want them to know how important the project was to the company. The implication being that if the Sugarland facility could not be expanded, the company could easily expand elsewhere.

The meeting went well. The regional energy council saw the lengths to which Burfack-Gremen was going to satisfy regulations. As expected, they made a few suggestions for rather small modifications, which would accommodate the council and would make it appear that they were conscientiously doing their job.

The company's project manager made the point that they wanted to proceed with finalizing the plan, so construction could start around the beginning of the new year. The council, not wishing to be an obstacle to the creation of more jobs in the area, suggested that if the company would represent that they would make the necessary plan modifications, they could grant conditional approval to begin.

The deal had been struck. I, along with the project manager, simply needed to come back fairly promptly with the additions and changes. Lance Thomas and I reported the results of the meeting to Kate. She was pleased. She knew the executive office of the company would be pleased. Her employment of my services would now appear to have been justified.

The remaining work on the plan took another fifty hours of my time. At least that is what I billed Burfack-Gremen for. In total, I earned a little less than eighty thousand for the entire project. With my living expenses amounting to around five thousand a month, I would be solvent well into 2064, even if I did nothing else. But I was doing a small amount of work for the Savannah council, and at the beginning of December, Kate came up with some additional work for me to do. It didn't amount to anything like the Sugarland project, but it eventually put another twenty thousand in my pocket.

Christmas and New Year's would arrive shortly. The streets and shops were now decorated. Cold weather had arrived, interspersed with warmer days. I left a message for Jacqueline. We had not spoken for three months. She did not return my call promptly. I called Kate. We talked for ten minutes or so, but she seemed preoccupied and sought to end the conversation rather quickly. We concluded by wishing each other a prosperous and healthy new year.

I called Pat. She recognized my voice immediately. "James, I was thinking of calling you. So good to hear your voice."

I asked about Florence, which was still wonderful. I asked about work, which was still rewarding. "So you're totally satisfied," I summed up.

"Well, it is more difficult to be away from home around the holidays. My Italian friends are busy with their families. It makes me realize that however fascinating Italy is, it's not home. It's great. Don't get me wrong. It's like living in the *quattrocento*. I wouldn't give up the experience for the world. When I need to return to the U.S., I will do it with some sorrow and a little reluctance. But I'll be ready to do it."

"And when will you be returning?"

"Not until the fall of next year. I am committed to seeing the summer festival through. I hope to set up some teaching assignments at American for the fall semester. So you have less than nine months to fulfill your promise to visit me. That is, to visit Florence," she added.

I explained that my consulting was still bringing in money. The current assignments should last until March.

"Then you can get here in the spring. It's a lovely time to visit. Better than winter or summer. We'll see every nook and cranny— the churches, the *piazze*, the museums."

"It all sounds wonderful," I broke in. I was not yet willing to commit. "Let's see how things develop. By April, you might have another visitor sleeping on your couch."

"I've had no visitors. Do you think I invite just anyone to share my apartment? I invited you specifically." Her tone implied that I had insulted her.

I didn't see it that way, but I began to apologize. "I didn't mean to suggest . . ." Had I continued, I sensed that I would have been digging a deeper hole. "Pat, you don't know how much I want to visit." I didn't specify whether I would be visiting Florence or Pat. "I'll do everything I can. Believe me, I really want to do this, and I sincerely appreciate the invitation." I knew I sounded too formal and impersonal, but the proper words didn't come to mind.

"Alright. I can understand. Let's hope everything works out for the best."

We exchanged holiday wishes. The phone call ended.

I sat back and thought. I was mad at myself. Why couldn't I make a commitment? A trip to Florence was not like a trip to the moon. Thousands of people managed to go to Florence or Rome or Paris. I had some money saved. The trip would be feasible. Was I afraid of joining Pat in her apartment? No, I thought I would enjoy it. *Then, go*, I told myself. My sense of caution took over. I would wait a few weeks, perhaps a month, and then see how I felt.

On Christmas day, I called my mother. She chided me for calling only two or three times a year and for never visiting. She was in good health, if in bad spirits. She was happy to hear that I was busy with consulting and earning enough to save some money. Since I could now afford it, she suggested that I come and visit her and my sister, if not for the holidays, maybe in the spring when the weather was warmer.

"Perhaps. If I'm not in Florence."

"Florence where?"

"Florence, Italy."

"What's there?"

"Art, architecture."

"Okay, I see. *Who's* there?"

"A friend."

"A girlfriend? You're entitled. Jane is long gone."

"Let's not talk about Jane."

"I don't want to talk about Jane, either. I want to hear about your new girlfriend."

"She's a friend—an old friend."

"Okay, don't tell me."

"I just told you."

"You told me less than you hid."

"Oh, Mom, let's not end on a negative note."

"I love you, Jamie. You know that."

"I love you, too. Merry Christmas and Happy New Year, Mom.

"Merry Christmas to you, too. And I hope the coming year brings you happiness wherever you are. Did you call your sister?"

"I will."

I decided to take a break from consulting during the week between Christmas and New Year's. No deadlines were imminent. And I wanted to reward myself for working reasonably hard over the past few months. I felt the need for a change of pace, even though I had no place to go.

Since a trip to Florence was becoming more likely, I decided to find out more about the city. I spent fifteen dollars to download a small guidebook to my page palette. I did a search for more material, something more of an historical nature. I bypassed several items: Guicciardini's *History of Italy*, which was really focused on a limited period of renaissance history, a book about the Pazzi revolt, Vasari's *Lives of the Artists*, and a biography of Lorenzo the Magnificent. Looking further afield, I came across an early twentieth-century novel, *A Room with a View* by E.M. Forster. I thought I recalled a movie with the same title.

Since it was considered a "classic," I could download the book for less than ten dollars. But with a novel of that age, I had a strange desire to lay my hands on a hardcover version. Kate, who always eschewed the page palette, would have been proud of me.

For the most part, libraries functioned by letting a person download a book for a specific period of time and at a certain fee, generally two or three dollars for a three-week rental. Renewal beyond the initial period was available for another modest fee.

In Savannah, there was one library that still contained real hardcopy books. It was located on Bull Street, not downtown, but about a fifteen minute walk from my quarters. I had used the library on a few occasions to do some research when I was looking into the first gasoline crisis in 1974. Old newspapers were available on-line or in other formats.

I always enjoyed looking at old papers and frequently got side-tracked by the ads offering merchandise that long ago had become obsolete, but was prized at the time. Who today knew of department stores such as Bonwit-Teller, Gimbels, or De Pinna's?

I gave the librarian—a prematurely balding man in his forties—the request for the E.M. Forster book. In five minutes he returned with a slim volume.

"Are you planning to read this?"

"I was really thinking of eating it."

"I should have placed the emphasis on the word 'you.' You might be taking it out for a friend. You don't look like an E.M. Forster fan."

"I'm not. Never read anything by him, if indeed the author was a 'him.' But I'm going to visit Florence." Was my plan now so firm?

"Yes, the author was a 'him,' so to speak. Hope the book doesn't disappoint."

My library card and the book were scanned. I exited the stately old building and began my walk home. Dark clouds were moving in from the west. I picked up the pace. Some rain began to fall about three blocks from the house. I stuffed the book under my jacket, wanting to shelter the old volume from the elements. Unlike a page palette, the book was not waterproof.

Once in my room, I opened a bag of chips and poured a cola. I examined the book more closely. Although the novel was written near the beginning of the twentieth century, this particular volume was printed near the end of the century. It was neither as old nor as valuable as I thought.

I began reading. The action began in Florence. After reading forty pages, I modified my thinking. The *scene* was set in Florence, but the action was minimal. The book focused on Victorian (or was it Edwardian?) manners. Much was made of the slightest nuances in behavior or conversation.

Yet the writing was good, and, therefore, I was prompted to continue reading. However, I realized that I would not get a very complete picture of Florence. A few features were covered—Santa Croce church, the *Piazza Signoria*, the Arno—but Florence was a device, not the centerpiece.

At dinnertime, I put my reading aside. Later, I watched TV instead of opening the book. Around eleven I went to bed, read a few pages and promptly fell asleep.

During the next day of the interval between Christmas and

New Year's, I attended to a few chores, and—despite my prior resolution—I spent some time on a consulting project. It was only in bed that I again picked up *A Room with a View* and found that I was leaving Florence and journeying into the Sussex countryside. The book remained untouched during the next two days.

On New Year's Eve I took the tram downtown, primarily because I couldn't bear to remain in my room, which had no view at all. I started in one bar and then impatiently moved on to another. The beer tasted sour. I wandered into a third bar.

A young woman greeted me as "Mr. Lendeman." I didn't recognize her. She must have noticed the look of confusion on my face. "I was in your class at SCAD."

"Oh, of course."

"Sharon Engblom."

"Yes, Sharon Engblom, how could I forget?" But I had and, in fact, still couldn't recollect her from class. She was a few pounds overweight, but nonetheless an attractive blonde.

"Would you like to join me and some friends?"

Suddenly I didn't feel too social. "I would, except I'm supposed to meet a friend. But I must have the wrong bar." I looked around the dimly lit establishment, feigning a search for an imaginary friend. "No, not here. Have to move on."

"Well, Happy New Year."

"Yes, Happy New Year, Sharon."

I went into the brisk night. A north wind blew across the Savannah River and raked River Street. I ran up the long ramp to Bay Street. It was darker but the moon was a few days short of full. Only the brighter stars were visible. Orion stood out from other constellations. But I could also pick out Auriga, which made me think of Pat and feel lonelier than ever.

On New Year's Day I awoke at nine, a time when most people over the age of twenty-one were trying to sleep off the excesses of the previous night. Not suffering from any excesses, I made myself some coffee and toast. I dressed in jeans and a sweatshirt and began a walk that ended up being no more than a kilometer in length. The weather was chilly; the streets were eerily silent.

Upon returning to my room, I tuned my radio to a station that played soft rock and returned to the E.M. Forster novel. By lunch, I rushed through the task of finishing the book. It was not a bad book, certainly somewhat antiquated, but it did not satisfy my desire to learn about the Tuscan capital.

The book was not about Florence—that was quite clear—it was about love, as, I suppose, most novels are. It portrayed love as a singular, universal emotion. I wondered if this was true.

To my way of thinking, there were different forms of love. There was love for a parent, love for a wife, love for a child. (I wished that I had had the opportunity to develop such a love for Mark.) But, even beyond these differences, there seemed to be a variety of love experiences possible between a man and a woman.

I had loved Jane—in a comfortable, non-intensive sort of way—and then, of course, our love soured, eventually turning to hate. I loved Kate, and probably still did, with a mindless, irrational passion. I was overawed by her beauty and ability to wield power. Even the inappropriateness of our relationship added to the intensity of my feelings, feelings that I was sure were not reciprocated.

Looking at other relationships, I was sure that I had never loved Jacqueline or Allison. My time with Allison was too brief, and even though our feelings were intense, they only served to satisfy our mutual needs at the time. My acquaintance with Jacqueline was long enough to blossom into love, but the ingredients were not there. Jacqueline never would want to fall in love with me and was probably not capable of doing so. We had our few moments of intimacy; we even had a friendly relationship. But it flickered like a feeble fire. Occasionally it could flare up. But the flame would not even last the night.

And then there was Pat. What was she to me? A good friend?

No, I sensed there was more, but the depth of our feelings had never been explored. We moved forward cautiously, almost afraid to reveal our inner feelings. If I took up her invitation, we would either be drawn closer together or split apart. Would I dare to visit—not Florence—but Pat Auriga? If I were to travel to Italy it would be for Pat, not for a foreign city.

I hadn't spoken to Kate for several weeks, but I felt I owed her an update on the consulting project. Since it was a business call, I did not place it until Wednesday, January second.

Her administrative assistant answered the call and told me she needed to determine if Ms. Hastings was available. In a minute a weary voice answered. "Hello, James. Were the holidays good to you?"

"I survived them."

"I know the feeling."

"Do you have a few minutes for me to brief you on the current project?"

"To tell the truth, I'm already late for an appointment. Can you send me an email?"

Something in Kate's voice gave me concern. "Kate, are you feeling okay?"

"I seem to have hurt my back. I'm heading out to visit a chiropractor."

"I hope he fixes you up."

"Thanks. Talk to you soon."

XXXIX

Florence, 2064

ON APRIL 9, I WAS genuinely excited as I started out on my first of three flights that would take me from Savannah to Florence. The route was: Savannah to Atlanta, overnight Atlanta to Paris, and Paris to Florence.

I had a four-hour layover in Atlanta, during which I began to look at a Florence guidebook loaded into my page palette. But, within a few minutes, I was no longer thinking about the upcoming visit to Florence, rather I was reliving the last few months.

By the first week in February I had finished my second project for Burfack-Gremen. Kate declined my offer to go to Houston to present the completed product. She told me to send it along, and she would call with any comments and questions.

As soon as the report was on its way, I called Pat. "Do you still want a visitor?"

"I don't want any old visitor. I want you," she replied promptly and boldly. "Do you really think you can get here?"

"I just finished the project for Kate. I could get a few follow-up issues. Also I have some remaining work to do for the council in Savannah. I guess that should be wrapped up by mid-March or so. You said Florence is wonderful in the spring. How's April?"

"Sounds great. Let me check my calendar." I heard Pat accessing her on-line schedule. "Easter falls on the sixth of April. I'm going to be busy with some church programs during Holy Week. Plus, travel in Italy right around Easter might be challenging— pilgrims and all that. I think it would be better to come several days after Easter."

"Sounds fine to me."

"You're really serious, right?"

"Of course."

"It will be marvelous to see you. I'll clear my calendar as much as possible. How long can you stay?"

"How long can you stand me?"

Pat hesitated. "A long time."

"Is a month too long?" I ventured.

"No, maybe too short. You'll only appreciate Florence if you have time for it to reach into your soul."

"Well, let's shoot for a month, and we'll see how things work out."

There was a moment of silence when both Pat and I, no doubt, thought about the meaning of "things working out." She broke the awkward interlude, "I guess we have a plan."

Yet she felt obliged to double-check once more to be sure that I wasn't simply teasing her. And, again, I had to assure her that I was serious. She concluded with a "*ciao*."

I arranged my departure for April ninth with a tentative return date of May seventh. The ticket gave me flexibility to alter my return with only a modest surcharge.

A few days after my travel arrangements were complete, I called Kate to let her know that I would be unavailable for any follow-up work during the month of April. She took note of my plans and told me that she was envious. She said she would really love to take a vacation; she felt the need to rest and relax. But she never managed to squeeze it in. "Florence is probably very nice, but if I could get to Europe, I'd opt for Paris."

"Not Vienna?" I asked slyly.

"With all deference to our little sojourn, no. Vienna is not *der stadt mein traum. Je rêve de Paris.*"

"*Je comprends*," I replied. "How are you feeling?" I inquired as an afterthought.

"My back is still bothering me. I think the chiropractor has helped a tad, but the pain keeps on returning."

"Maybe you should see a regular doctor."

"Maybe you're right."

In March, I cleaned up the last bit of work for the regional energy council in Savannah. I spoke to Pat several times to finalize arrangements. She told me to take a bus from the airport to the stop outside the Santa Maria Novella station where she would meet me. It was only a five-minute walk from there to her apartment.

By the last week of March, I had plenty of time on my hands. I made sure my clothes were cleaned. Pat told me to bring a raincoat. We were bound to get some cool rainy weather along with some radiantly beautiful days. I possessed no raincoat, so I bought a cheap one at a local shop.

I was happy to see that I still had over fifty thousand in the bank, even after paying for my air ticket. Several times I bothered the bank with questions about accessing funds from Italy. They assured me that my debit card would work fine, and the customer service rep gave me some idea of the transaction charges I would incur.

I paid Todd and Brenda my April and May rent, and gave them my address in Florence. Finally, April ninth arrived. I lugged my suitcases from the house to the tram, and took the tram downtown to pick up a natural gas-powered shuttle bus to Savannah airport. I felt reasonably sure that I had covered all bases. Anyway, I would only be gone for four weeks.

After eating the edible portion of the dinner served on my flight to Paris, I finally managed to read some information in the Florence guidebook. I realized I knew little about the city that I would imminently visit. I hadn't understood that the art patrimony was dispersed throughout the city. The works were deployed in a score of churches, museums, and family palaces. The original of

Michelangelo's *David* was not in front of the Palazzo Vecchio; it was in a building called the Accademia. Donatello's *David* was in the Bargello. Santa Croce contained the tombs of famous Florentines, but Dante's body was elsewhere. Santa Maria del Carmine housed the Masaccio frescoes. The *Birth of Venus* was in the Uffizi.

I suddenly felt tired. The page palette dropped into my lap, and I began to drift into a light sleep, convinced that I would simply put myself into Pat's hands and let her be my tour guide.

The plane flew into the new day's dawn. Somewhat groggy, I looked at a rosy horizon in the distance but, directly below, a carpet of clouds. After going through customs I made my way from the arrival terminal to another where I would board my flight to Florence. My layover in Paris was supposed to be three hours, but it ended up being four. I called Pat to inform her of the delay.

"Yes, I've gotten the update from the airline website. You'll probably get to Santa Maria Novella around four. I'll be there."

And so she was. We exchanged a hug, and then she took the handle of the smaller of my two suitcases. "We can walk to the apartment."

We had not even crossed a street when she pointed to the left. "That's Santa Maria Novella, the Dominican church. We'll visit it on one of our tours." The church's marble façade was geometrically patterned. It gave a square, solid impression, and did not fit my preconceived notion of renaissance architecture. But my notions were not grounded in any formal training.

We walked along streets that combined residential and commercial buildings. They were neither wide nor elegant. Although I did not express it to Pat, my initial feeling was one of disappointment. But, perhaps in some way, she sensed it. "This part of the city is neither Roman nor medieval. It's a working and residential area. You'll get a better taste of what Firenze has to offer later on."

Of course, I didn't want to tour the city just then. I desperately wanted to sleep.

"Here's my building." It was built of the same brownish blocks that fronted many of the edifices I had seen. The apartment was two flights up, with no elevator. We left one suitcase inside the front door, while we collaborated in the effort to get the larger one to her apartment. Then I returned for the second. We pushed them through her door and into a dark hall. It led to a living room that was not much brighter, because it faced a tiny courtyard, which was hemmed in by several four-story buildings. A kitchen was tucked into a corner. Pat's bedroom was on the other side of the living room. And somewhere, although not immediately apparent, a bathroom must exist.

"I emptied a few drawers in that cabinet. You can put clothes in there. There's a clothes tree in the hall with a few hangers. You can use that for slacks and jackets. Behind that is a step leading to the bathroom. We have to share. Do you need a glass of water, some fruit?"

"I'd appreciate the water."

"Then you probably want to take a nap." A good, long sleep is what I really wanted. "But I'm not going to let you sleep more than two hours. Otherwise, you won't be able to sleep tonight, and it will take longer to get over the time zone differential."

The tactic sounded like Kate's prescription when we arrived in Vienna. "Do you want to nap on my bed?"

"No, I better get used to the couch."

"I hope you find it comfortable. I'll try to be quiet. Here's a blanket."

"You thought of everything. I hope you won't find me a nuisance."

"If that's the case, I'll throw you out." The words were harsh, but she tacked a laugh at the end.

The nudge was gentle and accompanied by a soft, musical voice calling my name several times. I was slow to react. Then I realized that I was no longer in my solitary room in Savannah. Pat put her hand on my shoulder, and I intentionally delayed responding.

"James, if you don't wake up, I'm going to tickle you. I think you hear me . . . I'm going to tickle you."

"Well, what's stopping you?"

"Since you're up, I'm not going to satisfy your prurient desires. Besides, we have to go out and get some dinner."

"Okay. Give me a little time to wash away some grime and clear my mind."

"We're going to have a great month together."

"Yes, we will."

We walked south several blocks until we reached the Arno. Then we walked along the river to the Ponte San Trinita. Beyond the first bridge, I spotted the Ponte Vecchio before Pat pointed it out. There were not many lights shining on the ancient bridge, and there was no moon to add its glow. Yet the outlines of arches and shops were clearly visible. No one would call it well designed, but it attested to the heritage of the ancient city. Seeing the famous structure, I began to think that I would come to appreciate Florence.

I thought we would walk on to see the bridge, but Pat said we would soon be turning away from the Arno to get dinner. So we stopped along the embankment to admire the view. "You'll see this plenty of times and at various times of day. We should get to the *trattoria* or else we'll have to wait longer for a table."

Several dining rooms were connected front to back, making the seating capacity well over a hundred, I estimated. Ninety percent of the tables were occupied, but we were led to one reserved for us in the last room. There was a rustic atmosphere to the restaurant.

Pat explained the order of a large Italian meal, but pointed out that one or more of the courses could be skipped, which we quickly agreed to do, and some others might be shared. The waiter conversed with Pat, who had obviously mastered quite a bit of Italian over the past year. I could make out a number of familiar dishes on the menu and could make some pretty good guesses at others, like *insalata*. I asked Pat about some that went beyond my capabilities.

The food was good. The lively atmosphere contrasted with what I had recently experienced in the United States. Probably two-thirds of the diners were Florentine, some others were business visitors and tourists. A small portion was students.

During dinner, Pat did most of the talking. This suited me, since I was still rather groggy from the trip. She outlined what we should visit first and what work commitments she had over the next several days.

After dinner we fought over payment of the bill. Pat had assumed we would share all such costs. I told her that I wanted to pay for one or two dinners a week, since I was not paying for any portion of her rent. She said my presence was not adding to her expenses. I took possession of the bill, and reluctantly she agreed to my paying for one dinner per week. Any grocery bills would be shared.

We walked to the center of the city, to the Piazza Signoria. The Palazzo Vecchio stood in formidable majesty above the square and the loggia enclosing some sculptures. Michelangelo's *David* was outside the palazzo, but from my reading I knew it wasn't the original. Across the broad square were knots of people who came to meet their friends, tourists who wanted to see the lights play on the monuments, and those who were passing through on their way to other destinations within the city. After stopping for a few minutes, we continued on to a broad street full of shops, leading away from the Arno.

We paused at a small, gem-like church, Orsanmichele, which was circled by niches, each containing a statue of a saint. We moved on to arrive at the overwhelming trio of the Duomo, the Baptistery, and Giotto's campanile.

"You'll need to see each of these a dozen times, and each time you'll find new features you've never seen before. And you'll get a lot better view of Brunelleschi's dome. Have you read any account of its construction?"

"Yes, but only in my little guide book."

"Then you know it was an amazing feat of engineering in its day. But I'll get you more information. Do you mind if I give you some reading assignments?"

"I'm in your hands, professor."

"Before we go home," Pat was referring to her apartment rather than the United States, "let's take a walk around the baptistery. We'll need to come when we have sunlight, but look at the panels in these doors. Ghiberti did this side in the early fifteenth century. Of course, they're scenes from the Bible, mostly the Old Testament, I believe. People refer to them as 'The Gates of Paradise.'"

Under the streetlights, the bronze doors lost some of their detail, but I quickly saw that the hundreds of figures were emerging from the background to give almost full form to people and objects. "Amazing," was all I could say.

"And they're over six hundred years old."

"I have to confess my first impression of Florence was not favorable, but I'm beginning to see why you love it."

"Unlike Rome or Paris, it's a city that has to grow on you. But you've really seen only a small part of it this evening."

The next morning, Pat and I started to formulate our routine. Of course, Pat primarily laid it out. While I could be a full-time tourist, she still had work to do. On this first Friday morning, she had a two-hour choir practice, followed by a one-hour private lesson. She gave me a one-page map of Florence and told me to explore at random. "Soak up the smells, sights and sounds." We were to meet at the loggia in the Piazza Signoria around twelve thirty.

I went out onto the street and froze—not literally, for although a bit cool, the sun was brilliant. But I wondered: should I turn left or right? Where was I going to head? I was on my own in a strange city. My guide was gone. Should I wander at random? That was not my style. I decided to start where we had left off the previous night. I employed the map to take me back to the Baptistery. I wanted to see the door panels in a decent light.

At some point in the past, a protective pane of Plexiglas had been placed in front of the irreplaceable doors to prevent vandalism. After all, some maniac had disfigured Michelangelo's great *David* in the last century. The three-dimensional rendering of the hundreds of figures amazed me. They emerged from the panels to give perspective to each scene. My knowledge of art history was not good enough to know how advanced vanishing point perspective was at the time Ghiberti produced the doors.

Obviously, the panels portrayed scenes from the Bible, but limited biblical knowledge prevented me from quickly recognizing any of the characters. Perhaps Mrs. Pinckney, or even Jane, would have done better. Also the scenes reminded me more of classical Greece than the Middle East. The women were in flowing, diaphanous robes. But the sheer beauty of the artistry held my attention and beckoned me to look further.

One of the scenes was that of a battle. In the foreground I spotted a large prostrate figure being decapitated with a sword by a much smaller man. Could this be Goliath and David? But where was the slingshot? Perhaps an object that small would not have been practical to include in a panoramic display.

There were carefully crafted figures in the borders between the panels. But here, again, I had to appreciate the artistry without being able to identify the characters. Yet I could not pull myself away from this art that I could only comprehend on the most basic level. The fact that here it was, out in the middle of a spectacular piazza, available for all pedestrians to see, astounded me. It was nothing like I had experienced in America, Vienna, or, when I was young, in Paris. For an hour or more I stood transfixed by the doors and the general setting. No one bothered me. An art student was sketching some features from a door panel. Some tourists lingered;

some moved on quickly. There were plenty of other things to see
in Florence. But the doors were the first objects I stood before and
admired. I knew I would come back to them again and with more
information at hand. They opened my eyes to Florence and, for
that reason, would hold a unique place in my memory.

After pulling myself away from the north side of the Baptistery,
I poked my head into the Duomo. I quickly decided that it would
take a lot more time than I wanted to devote to it at the moment. I
started down the broad, pedestrian street toward the Arno. I never
managed to memorize the street's difficult name. Why couldn't
it be called something simple like 42nd Street or Bull Street? Of
course, Pennsylvania Avenue might sound difficult to an Italian.

I easily found my way to the Ponte Vecchio. For centuries
there had been shops perched on either side of the pathway. I had
heard that, at some time in the past, most sold jewelry. In the mid-
twenty-first century economy only one still displayed gold. One
dispensed gelato, another peddled upscale souvenirs, a third dealt
in art of various types—some alabaster figurines, a smattering of
Venetian masks.

Not being a shopper, I moved on. It was an easy walk to the Pitti
Palace. I stood outside at the base of the long, sloping courtyard.
This was not the time to attack a museum. My perambulation
would continue. I turned away from the large edifice and soon
found myself looking at the attractive, slightly bucolic square that
fronts the San Spirito church. I decided to get off my feet and relax
with a cup of coffee.

Only a few tables were occupied at the café I chose. Soon I
had my coffee and took a gulp.

An Italian at the next table called over to me from an adjacent
table, "You are American. Right?"

"Yes, I am. Is it so obvious?"

"Clothes. How you drink coffee. But not one of the American
students."

"No, I guess I'm just a tourist."

"But you stop for coffee. Not rushing around."

"I'll be here for a month."

"Good. Not the typical one who stays for three days and thinks he knows Firenze. This city takes a while to appreciate. It, how do say, it has to grow on you. Here by yourself?"

"No. I'm staying with a friend. She's been here for a year."

"*Bene*. Working?"

"Yes, she's a musician."

"Beautiful. *Vissi d'arte*. I visited the United States once. I spent a month in San Francisco with a cousin. It's lovely city. You know San Francisco?"

"Just a little bit." I didn't want to begin a conversation about the city by the bay.

The gentleman rose to leave. He wished me a good visit. "Ah, don't miss the Cappella Brancacci in Santa Maria del Carmine. Just down the street."

I lingered in the café for a while longer. Then I took a leisurely stroll back over the Ponte Vecchio. It was much too early to meet Pat, but I would sit and watch and listen.

Although there were hundreds of people in the piazza, Pat and I spotted each other quickly. She led me to a shop where we got some pizza for lunch. It was much better than the pizza in Washington or Savannah, perhaps on a par with my memories of pizza at a small shop in New Jersey.

After lunch we headed away from the city center and also farther away from Pat's apartment. We reached Santa Croce and went inside. The cavernous, dark interior swallowed us up. But, quickly, large tombs along the periphery emerged. These were the tombs of prominent Florentines, including Galileo and Machiavelli. We spent a half an hour in the chamber, pointing out various details to each other or just observing in silence. We exited by a side door to view a chapel containing Della Robbia ceramics and then pushed further on to view some pre-Renaissance art. Pat made a few observations about the pieces, but I realized I should have had an art history course to appreciate what I was seeing.

I made a comment along these lines to her. She showed no sympathy. "It's not too late to do something about it. You have your computer with you. I'm sure there's a survey course you can download. You'll have time to do the course and see prime examples right here in Firenze. Maybe you'll be able to teach me a few things."

While we were walking back to the apartment, I asked her, "Does the name Cappella, Cappella . . ." I was searching for the rest of the term and Pat looked strangely at me. "Does 'Cappella Brancacci' mean anything to you?"

"Oh, the Brancacci chapel. Of course. It's in Santa Maria del Carmine across the river in the Oltrarno. It has lovely frescoes by Masaccio. I've only visited it once, and I'm sure I missed a lot. We need to go back. And you can teach me more about it from what you study in the art history course."

Over the next week a pattern emerged. Pat was usually busy for half the day. During part of that time, I would study from the art history course that I had downloaded. If the weather cooperated I would do this in a café, if not, in the apartment. The rest of the time, I would stroll on my own. Sometimes the walk would have an objective and at other times it would be at random. I began to cover the same ground, but each time new features would emerge—some art previously unnoticed, a small street previously not employed, a medieval tower house looming over an otherwise ordinary building.

I waited for Pat in order to visit the principal museums and churches—the Uffizi, the Bargello, the Pitti Palace, and the Cappella Brancacci. In the evening, we either ate a simple meal, like pasta, bread and salad, in the apartment; or dined at an inexpensive *trattoria*. We would always find things to talk about. And sometimes I could supply, via my art course, some information that was new to her.

One night, Pat had a performance. We ate lightly a few hours before the concert. Afterward, we joined some of her fellow performers at a reception in the home of one of the organizers. From the outside, the building was not impressive, but—inside— the thirty or so guests could lose themselves in the two adjacent reception rooms. In one, a table was laid with antipasto items, bread, vegetables, and sliced roasted veal. Another table held wine, bottled water, and suitable glasses. A third eventually was used for *dolci* and coffee.

I filled a plate with salami, prosciutto, a few slices of bread, and some sliced artichoke hearts, and grabbed a glass of red wine. Carefully I proceeded to a chair set against an interior wall and tried to eat without creating a mess. A tall brunette came over and sat in an adjacent chair.

"I'm Laura Inglis."

"I know. You're the alto. I'm James Lendeman."

"I know. You're Pat's friend."

"I enjoyed the performance."

"Pat says you don't know much about music."

"I don't, but I know what sounds good to me and what doesn't. I liked this performance." I wanted to get off the subject of music criticism. "You're obviously not Italian. How did you come to join a singing group here?"

"Probably for the same reason that Pat came here. I wanted a change of scene and a bit of adventure. I really wanted to sing in Rome or Milan, but I couldn't find a job in those cities. So Florence was next on my list. I'm getting my fill of Renaissance art as well as *bifsteak fiorentina*."

"Where's home?"

"Sydney, Australia. You didn't detect my accent?"

"No. I didn't."

"You're either deaf or a good liar."

By this point, Laura and I had finished the food and had only wine glasses in our hands.

"So tell me, James Lendeman, are you enjoying Florence, or

just Pat? She told me that you two are platonic friends, but I don't see how you can sleep night after night on that uncomfortable sofa."

"She told you the truth."

"Then you're gay."

"No, I've been married."

"And then you got out of it when you decided you preferred men to women."

"You have quite an imagination. If you don't believe me, believe what you will, but it's not the truth."

Laura was the type of woman who had the habit of placing her hand on a man's arm or thigh while engaging in conversation. Some do it innocently, but Laura was calculating and not innocent. "Maybe I'll just have to determine for myself what your sexual orientation is."

"That's quite an offer."

"Just think of me as an experimenter, employing the scientific method."

I thought it was time to discourage this line of conversation. "You realize I came to this party with another woman."

"But she's only your platonic friend. And what you have to realize about me is that I have a strong sex drive. I'm not being satisfied by these Italian men. Most are half a head shorter than me. Maybe I intimidate them. And you must be horny, too, if you and Pat aren't sharing her bed. I don't intimidate you, do I?"

"Your height doesn't."

"You should work on overcoming your inhibitions. As for me, I've always worked on doing just that."

"And I would think you've achieved your objective." I noticed that Pat was approaching. "I enjoyed chatting with you, Laura. I think I should rejoin Pat."

"Oh, yes, your landlord. Just remember if you want to explore the more illicit side of Florence, I'm your gal."

"I'll remember the invitation." I rose.

Pat was standing next to me. "May I borrow my friend?"

"If 'borrow' is the operative term, I'd love to work out some time-sharing arrangement."

"I'm sure that wouldn't be possible," Pat replied in her brightest tone.

"Selfish girl."

Pat led me away in order to meet other people, less voracious than Laura, including some of our Florentine hosts. I noticed that Pat deftly kept me moving away from Laura for the rest of the evening.

It was not until we were departing that we reencountered Laura, who was parked near the door. "Are you going to let me borrow James from time to time?" she teased Pat.

"James has a limited time in Florence, and he's going to spend it with me."

"But you'll be busy some of the time. I wouldn't want him to get bored."

"He has Firenze to keep him busy."

"But she's an old woman."

"She still has her charms. Good night, Laura. I'll see you at the next rehearsal."

Pat, as usual, put her arm through mine, but drew me closer than normal. We walked a few blocks in silence before she said anything. "What did you think of Laura?"

"She's pretty aggressive."

"Pretty *and* aggressive," Pat played with my words.

I sensed Pat was somewhat miffed at my spending more than two or three minutes with Laura. But I answered her honestly. "She's certainly aggressive, and I think most men would find her attractive."

"So you found her attractive?"

"Yes, a bit, but I think I would be overwhelmed by her."

"Let me tell you something about her. Word has it that she likes women better than men. No doubt, she's had experience with both. Frequently I see women waiting for her after rehearsals."

Pat's approach seemed rather catty. I wanted to see where this defamation of Laura might lead. "Maybe they're students of hers," I suggested.

"I think I can tell the difference between a student and a lover." She paused. "What are you smiling about?"

"Do you really think I'd let Laura intrude on our plans? Anyway, I have a hunch she's more talk than action."

"Don't be so sure. She certainly displays a sense of bravado, but I've also seen mischief and envy in her."

We walked on in silence. I had thought on several occasions in the past that Pat would like our relationship to pass beyond the platonic. This conversation about Laura confirmed it more strongly than any previous incident. I had to admit that I liked the concept. I had known her off and on over a number of years. My feelings had grown, imperceptibly slowly but steadily nevertheless. Were they now at the point where we had to take a bigger step? I would let events take their course.

Pat chose not to talk, but was obviously thinking hard. "A penny for your thoughts," I ventured.

Pat hesitated before replying. "I was thinking about you. I was thinking that I respect you." Perhaps I expected a stronger verb. "I was thinking of the night when Jane, Steve, you, and I were together. Steve got stinking high, which he sometimes did. And when that happens, he can become offensive. He probably would have gone to bed with Jane if he could have."

"He might have been able to. Our marriage was going downhill. Steve was a friend, and I knew him well. He wouldn't have hesitated too long about taking advantage of the situation."

"That's awful. Don't you think so?"

"My love for Jane was waning at that point. Steve probably sensed that."

"And he didn't care that I was present. If Steve wanted to gratify his lust, moral hurdles were very low. Anyway, that night I saw you keep your cool. You prevented any further embarrassment." We were now at the apartment. She unlocked the door. We went into the living room and put the light on. "Do you want a drink? I'm going to have one."

I didn't really want a drink, but I wasn't going to let Pat drink by herself. "Thanks. I'll join you."

"Sambucca or grappa?"

"Sambucca."

"Well, I'm going to have a grappa tonight." She returned quickly with the two drinks and downed a gulp of hers before I could raise mine to my lips. "I wanted to ask you a question." She took a sip this time before continuing. "Did you want to sleep with me that night?"

"The night when Steve wanted to swap partners?"

"Yes."

"I didn't want to hurt Jane."

"I wasn't getting at that. If Steve went off to bed with Jane, would you have wanted to sleep with me?"

"I think you're not asking the question you really want to ask."

"And what's that?"

"You want to know if I would want to sleep with you here and now."

"Well?" She leaned forward to hear my answer.

"Yes, of course. You're a wonderful person. You're talented and good-looking and I like you in so many ways. But I never wanted to risk ruining our friendship."

"Would making love ruin the friendship?"

"Don't you see, I thought you wanted us to stay friends and *only* friends."

"I see. I do want us to remain friends. I enjoy being with you. And I've purposely kept in touch with you through these years." I said nothing. She continued. "Let's make a deal. Let's not be afraid to jeopardize our friendship by seeing how deep our feelings go."

I was not exactly sure what Pat meant, but the statement, in its own way, sounded reasonable. "It makes sense to me."

"You might have said something more romantic," she teased.

"That's not my strongest suit."

"I tell you what. For starters, forget about sleeping on that lumpy couch."

Pat used the bathroom first and I followed. I slipped into the bed with only my briefs on and noticed that she wore a nightgown, which covered her shoulders and probably a good deal more. I left as much room between us as the double bed permitted.

"You may kiss me," Pat said, putting her hand on my face. We kissed with growing fervor. Her nightgown rode up to her hips. For the first time, I felt her body firmly pressed against mine. It was neither flabby nor slim and toned. But it was very appetizing, especially considering that she was no doubt around forty. (I did not know her precise age, and I don't believe she knew mine.) Her legs were not long, but well-muscled, likely profiting from all the walking around Firenze. (I was beginning to think in terms of 'Firenze,' rather than 'Florence.')

Our sexual enthusiasm was growing as we explored each other. Then Pat pulled back. "Would you mind very much if we didn't make love tonight? It was just an hour ago that we decided to change our . . ." She searched for the right word. ". . . our arrangement. We'll be sharing the same bed for another two weeks. We'll have plenty of opportunities. We're just starting the weekend. Could we see how we feel tomorrow? Okay?"

"Sure. If you'd prefer it that way." I was not sure I understood her logic, but I didn't want to make the wrong move and get kicked out of bed.

Probably around four in the morning I went to the bathroom. When I returned, Pat had awakened. "I can't believe what I did a few hours ago. It was insane. We both wanted to make love." Why do women "make love" and men "have sex"? "Are you still in the mood?"

"Can you give me a few minutes to answer that question?"

"Do you always answer a question with another question?"

"Whenever possible."

Slowly we began to pick up where we left off several hours earlier. By dawn we had made love/had sex twice. It was good— good, healthy sex, passionate and mutually fulfilling. At breakfast, she apologized again for what she had done the previous evening.

"Didn't it work out magnificently in the end?" I asked.

"I'll reply with a clear-cut answer: absolutely. I think I am going to end up loving you very deeply, James."

I responded in a similar vein, but without using the word "love." And then, the following day, our lives, which we thought had just been greatly simplified, grew more complicated.

XL

Firenze, 2064

THE CALL CAME AS A complete shock. While in Florence, my phone had only rung a few times, and each time it had been Pat. But Pat was busy in the kitchen only a few meters away.

"James." No additional word was needed for me to know who was calling. "This is Kate."

"Yes. I recognized your voice. Is everything okay? Are you in Houston?"

"I'm in Paris. I've been getting settled for the past two weeks."

"Getting settled. Have you decided to live in Paris?"

"Live. Quite the contrary. I've come here to die."

I was sure that I had heard incorrectly. "What did you say?"

"The cancer has returned. It's in my bones, particularly my spine. The more optimistic doctors hold out some hope. But I'm not deceived. The realistic ones give me a few months, maybe six, probably less."

"I can't believe what you're saying."

"I wouldn't joke about this."

"Are you in pain?"

"Yes. I have better days and poorer ones. Sometimes it's quite tolerable and sometimes it's not. But I have medication of various sorts. Anyway, I didn't want to spend my last days in Houston or Washington. I always wanted to return to Paris."

"I remember your saying so."

"James, I'm going to ask a very big favor of you."

"Name it," I replied, no doubt too quickly.

"I want you to stay with me in Paris. I'll pay all expenses, naturally. I want you to help me pass my last months or weeks, whatever, as agreeably as possible."

By this point, Pat had entered the living room and had begun to follow the conversation as best as she could, based on my comments.

"That is a big favor."

"Do you have a problem helping me out?"

"Yes and no. I certainly want to help. But Pat, the woman I'm staying with in Firenze, is not merely a friend. We love each other." Pat came up to me and kissed me on the cheek. I looked at her and saw the incredible expression of joy written on her face. "We only have another two weeks together before I'm scheduled to go back to the U.S."

"I'm truly happy for you. But you'll be able to spend the rest of your life with Pat; if that's the way you want it. I need your help now. You're not going to be my lover, only my companion and nurse. Hell, we never even had sex when we worked together and I was attractive."

"No, never." I adhered to the party line regarding our nights together.

"I need you to help me and to be my executor. This is a business arrangement, if you like. Even if you're not inclined to help me for altruistic reasons, I'll make it worth your while. I really need you."

There was a panic in Kate's voice that I had never heard before. I hesitated to give a definite reply because I genuinely did not know what to do. I desperately wanted to spend more time with Pat, maybe even extend my stay in Firenze. Yet I also knew that Kate was relying on me in her most desperate days.

Kate knew by the moments of silence that I was thinking hard, wrestling with a difficult decision. "James, if you ever had any feelings for me, you need to help me out now. I'm still in a position to help you, too. You want to build a good life for yourself and your friend, Pat. I'll help you with connections and some money, not a fortune, but some worthwhile money. I'll try not to be a burden. We'll get to explore Paris. I can still get around quite well. After a few weeks, you've probably gotten your fill of Florence . . ."

"I've just started to scratch the surface," I riposted a bit aggressively.

"You can go back to Florence. You have a long life ahead of you." The implication was clear—Kate did not have much time left and I could help her get as much as possible out of her remaining days. She continued, "I've rented a great apartment in a fantastic part of Paris, although all Paris is fantastic. It has two bedrooms and even two baths. You'll be very comfortable here."

"When would you want me to come?" When Pat heard my question, a look of anguish came over her face.

"As soon as possible."

"Let me call you back tomorrow."

"Make it later today." Kate still acted the boss.

After the phone call ended, I sat stupefied. Pat broke the silence. "You're going to go to her."

"How much of the conversation did you pick up?"

"She's in Paris. She's sick." Pat supplied.

"She's dying. Bone cancer. She probably only has a few months to live, and she needs my help."

"Doesn't she have a family?"

"I believe she has two nieces. And she's not particularly close to them."

"I can't believe you're her closest confidant. She's a very important person. She must know hundreds of important people."

"And I'm a nobody."

"That's not what I meant. Certainly there must be other people she can call on."

"For some reason she tends to rely on me."

"Maybe she loves you."

"I'm sure she doesn't. But she trusts me. She knows I don't divulge confidences. And I usually come through for her, not always, but most of the time."

"You're going to go to her." Her sentence was more a statement than a question.

"I suspect so."

"Why does she have to come between us at this point?"

"Do you think she wants to die?"

"You make me feel selfish. But I want you for myself. Were you serious when you told her you love me?"

"Yes, I was telling the truth."

"And I'm sure I love you." There was a tear in her eye. "I don't want to share you with another woman. We need to talk about where we go from here. But you're going to go off to Paris."

"Probably, but even though she'd like me there immediately, I'll delay it a few days. I really don't want to leave you right now."

"But you will return?"

"Why wouldn't I?"

"You answered my question with another question."

"Of course, I'm coming back, and as quickly as possible." As I uttered the last phrase, I realized how awful it was. I would return when Kate died. Did I selfishly want to speed that date? I was ashamed of myself.

Pat climbed into my lap and draped her arms around me. We were silent for a few minutes. When she spoke, it was in a whisper. "Life is strange. I find out that the man I love loves me, and he has to reveal it to another woman."

"Would it have been better if I never said it at all?"

"Another question. When will you make a declarative statement?"

I sensed this was my cue to say something meaningful. "Patricia C. Auriga, I love you, and I'm sure I've loved you for quite a while. I was too stupid not to realize it earlier. But now I promise to love you to the end of my life."

"Wow. What more could a woman ask for?"

"Sorry, no questions."

"Just one more. How did you find out my middle name?"

"I don't know your middle name, only the initial. I must have seen it on something. What does the 'C' stand for anyway?"

"Not now. It's time for a kiss, a long sloppy kiss."

XLI

KATE WANTED ME TO COME to Paris on Monday. I insisted I couldn't leave until Wednesday. She asked why, and I refused to tell her. No doubt she could guess that Pat and I needed a few more days together.

Except for one rehearsal, Pat cleared her calendar. We spent the three days from Sunday through Tuesday in a frenzy of seeing sights I had missed, returning to others that we particularly liked, and enjoying new and deeper intimacies. The Bargello was a return visit, as was the Brancacci Chapel. A trip up to Fiesole via a natural gas-powered bus was a first. Pat made fun of the mental estimates I made of the fuel consumption needed for the bus to climb the hill, as well as my futile search for the spots mentioned in *A Room with a View*. If Fiesole itself was a bit disappointing, the view of Firenze was not. We took pictures on an esplanade overlooking the city. We buttonholed a local to take a picture of the two of us together and then a second one of us kissing. If the gentleman was embarrassed, we were not.

On Tuesday, we had an early dinner in the apartment. Pat cooked while I packed. The meal consisted only of pasta, and not a large portion at that, salad, fresh salt-free Tuscan bread, wine and a light dessert if we got that far. "I don't want you to feel stuffed," she declared, "because we're going to have enough sex to last us both for a while."

This was the first time she talked in the animalistic terms of having sex, rather than making love. "I have a long trip ahead of me tomorrow."

"You'll sleep on the train."

Half of our dinner remained untouched, including the biscotti and *vin santo*.

On Wednesday, April 30, I journeyed from Firenze to the Milano Centrale station, and after an hour and a half wait, during which I fought to stay awake so as not to miss my connection, I boarded a train for the seven-hour trip to Paris. I arrived at the Gare de Lyon in the early evening when most Parisians were sitting down to dinner. Kate told me to take an electro-taxi to her apartment on the rue Jacob. She was not up to meeting me at the train station.

It took only fifteen minutes to get from the train station, near the east end of Paris, across the Seine, and then to Kate's left bank address. The traffic was light, rather different from the visit I made with my parents twenty years earlier. In fact, the trip would have taken even a few minutes less if the driver's GPS had not contained some misinformation regarding the direction of one-way streets in Kate's neighborhood.

At the outside door I found the button labeled "Hastings." A few seconds later I heard Kate's voice through the speaker. "Is that you, James?"

"Yes, it's me."

The buzzer sounded. I dragged my two suitcases through the door before it could shut and then maneuvered them into the small elevator. It was only one flight up to her apartment on the first floor. She was waiting in the doorway about ten steps from the elevator. She held the door while I brought the suitcases past her into a short hall that led to the "salon," as Kate called the living room. Even the small physical act of opening and closing the door seemed to require an effort, which she would have preferred not making.

"You look good, Kate." I lied.

She gave me a slight hug along with a rueful smile. She knew how she looked. "I'll show you something pretty. Look at the courtyard." A large window in the living room/salon overlooked a small garden with a bench and a fountain. The twilight barely granted enough illumination to make out these features. "All my rooms face the courtyard. So much better than the street side. Someone from the French government found the apartment for me. Let me show you your room."

She walked slowly, trying to hide any evidence of disability or pain. She led me past her own bedroom, which I viewed briefly through the open door, to my room. It was an ample size, somewhat larger than the bedroom I had been sharing with Pat. A small window overlooked the courtyard; a door led to a small bathroom; a separate door opened to the toilet. The furnishings were more feminine than I would have chosen. Some, I sensed, were genuine antiques.

"Good enough?" Kate asked.

"Yes, very nice."

"Have you eaten?"

"I had a sandwich a few hours ago on the train."

"You're going to be hungry if we don't get something, even if it's just a snack. There are at least ten cafés and restaurants within three blocks of here. You can unpack later. Paris doesn't stay open as late as she used to."

We walked two blocks. She leaned on my arm. "This is the rue de Buci. As you can see, it's full of cafés and food shops. During the day you can find almost anything you'd want here."

A quintessential Parisian café, named simply "Pauline," had some open tables. I ordered a *baba au rhum*. Kate ordered a cappuccino and a *carafe d'eau*, which I discovered was the method one used for requesting tap water.

"Isn't the coffee going to keep you awake?" I asked.

"I don't sleep anyway. I have some pills if I need them. Sometimes I'll take one or two if I haven't slept for a few nights in a row. I seem to have pills for everything. The medical care is quite good here. A Monsieur Rénard from the foreign office found me a suitable doctor at a clinic here on the left bank. The doctor says he'll cure me; I know better.

"He has me on some chemo pills. I'm supposed to take them for a week, and then skip a week. Sometimes I skip a little more than I should if they make me feel too ill. I'm here to enjoy Paris as much as I can, not to get better. You'll help me get around, won't you, James?" I had no chance to answer. "I want to stroll the streets as long as I can. I don't want to be in a wheelchair, but I will use your arm, if I may. Your girlfriend, what's her name? Pauline?"

"Pat."

"She has nothing to fear. I am past the stage when I can seduce men or would even want to. I will return you to her quite as virginal as you are right now."

"I've been married."

"Ah, yes. Jane. Poor thing. Too bad it ended as it did. A tragedy. But I shouldn't talk like this. I'll make you depressed. How's your *baba*?"

"It's very . . ."

"Let's talk about what we're going to see in Paris." And so she did.

In the morning, Kate was already up when I awoke. I was to learn that she tired easily but slept badly.

"After you dress, please head back to the rue de Buci. You'll find at least three bakeries. And bring back two croissants—I assume you want a croissant—and one baguette."

"I think I can handle that."

"There's ten Euros on the counter.

"I can pay . . ."

"Remember our deal. I pay for everything."

After breakfast, Kate said we would take a walk. She took my arm and led me the two blocks to the Seine. We passed a few *bouquiniste* stalls, and then proceeded onto a footbridge. At the center of the span, Kate stopped.

"This is the Pont des Arts. It's one of the few purely pedestrian bridges. You can see quite a bit of the city right from here. That's the Ile de la Cité. Notre Dame is at the other end of the island. That's the Louvre right in front of us. Huge, isn't it? Those are the Tuileries gardens."

"What's that building?" I asked, pointing to the building to the right of the Louvre.

"I think it's only a department store," Kate dismissed the structure and turned to the left. "Further downstream is the Grand Palais. And, of course, you can recognize the Eiffel Tower."

"Yes, of course."

"Amazing, isn't it?"

"Amazing. And what's that building with the gold dome?" I was looking back in the direction that we had come from.

"I don't know. We'll find out." Kate turned to a man who was walking past. "*Excusez-moi, monsieur. Connaissez-vous . . .*"

"Sorry, ma'am, I don't speak French."

"You're American."

"Sounds like you are, too."

"My friend and I are from Washington," Kate simplified. The man looked at me and then back to Kate, probably trying to assess our relationship. "I don't suppose you know what that building is over there."

"I have no idea. Just arrived in Paris yesterday. I'm here on business."

"Well, thank you anyway. I hope your trip is successful."

"Enjoy your vacation," the man replied, making a reasonable assumption, but missing the mark by far.

Kate turned back to me. "I want to show you two more things before we go back to the apartment." Evidently our excursion was going to be a short one. Kate led me back to the left bank. We crossed the broad street by the *quai* and began to walk along the rue Bonaparte. We walked past some antique shops, and then past a larger building with a gated courtyard. Music emerged from a classroom. A sign read: *Ecole des Beaux Arts.*

"Would this be part of a high school?"

"I don't know. Is it important?" Kate sounded a bit annoyed. She was the guide and she would show me what she chose.

"Just curious."

"I'm sure you'll be able to check it out on your own, if it's important. Let's continue on to something significant."

We turned right on the rue Jacob, away from Kate's apartment. Kate began to look for something on the buildings to our right. "Ah, here it is. How's your French?"

"I managed to get *deux croissants et une baguette* for our breakfast."

"Well, try this." Kate pointed to a brass plaque on the wall. "I think you'll be able to figure most of it out."

I read slowly. The names of famous Americans caught my attention. "What does '*jadis*' mean?"

"Formerly."

I read on. "This is where the Treaty of Paris was signed, ending the Revolutionary War."

"Very good."

"Funny, I figured it would have been signed at a more grandiose location."

"I bet not one American visitor in a thousand sees this plaque, and yet this spot is significant in our history."

"I bet you're right. You'd never notice it from the top of the Eiffel Tower."

"Come," Kate beckoned, "I want to show you a spot I really like." We walked back to the rue Bonaparte and up to the boulevard St. Germain. "This is the St. Germain des Près church. I went inside a week ago. You might want to see it on your own." It was clear that Kate was not inclined to return.

"By the way, that café across the street is quite famous as a gathering point for intellectuals. They charge plenty for drinks. We'll go some time, if you wish. Otherwise, there are cheaper cafés with more genial service."

We turned the corner and walked past a Métro entrance. "Here's what I wanted to show you. It's a little park right alongside the church. It's a great place to stop and rest."

"I can see that." I could also see that Kate was acting like a person who had aged a great deal in the past year. She had always seemed younger than her chronological age. Now, because of her illness, that relationship was irrevocably reversed. A sense of depression suddenly enveloped me. For the next few months I would see Paris, but through the eyes of a dying friend.

On a number of occasions we were to stop at this little park that primarily catered to children and their mothers. Normally we would arrive after having walked a number of blocks. On occasion Kate would fall asleep on a bench, and I would study the peculiar collection of objects—the jungle gym for the children, the statue of a gentleman sporting an outfit from perhaps the seventeenth century and with what appeared to be a giant snail and quartz crystals at his feet, and against the far wall a large, old display commemorating Sevres porcelain. I tried to make out the name of the man on the pedestal, but the letters were mostly worn away.

During the month of May, I learned about Paris and about how to serve Kate. She insisted on taking excursions, but they had to be short. She preferred to use buses rather than taxis. Occasionally, we would take the Métro, but I had to check in advance that any station where we planned to exit had an escalator or an elevator. Métro stations were not always accommodating to those with disabilities. In the first week of May we visited the great monuments—the Arc de Triomphe, the Eiffel Tower (only up to the second level), Notre Dame and les Invalides. We began to tour museums, but only the more modest ones, such as the Orangerie, the Marmottan and the Rodin. Kate said I would do the Louvre some day on my own, admitting she was not up to it.

Once every two weeks I took Kate to the clinic, where they performed blood tests and told her that her progress was satisfactory. At these words, she turned to me and whispered, "Complete bullshit." Kate would complain to the doctor about pain and the inability to sleep. With appropriate warnings about their use, the clinic ordered medications to address these symptoms.

One evening we went to the Comédie Française, not because our French was up to it, but rather because Kate had always wanted to attend a performance. The program consisted of several one-act plays by Molière, interspersed with music by Lully. We understood the wild gesticulations of the actors much more than the words they spoke, although we did manage to get the gist of the plots. In order to fulfill another of her long-standing desires, we went to the Opéra Garnier another evening, although what we saw was a ballet rather than an opera. I think the great and ornate nineteenth-century auditorium with its more modern Chagall ceiling was the attraction, rather than the performance.

In May, we generally had our dinners at restaurants, although Kate's appetite varied depending on the status of her chemo treatments. Most of the restaurants she chose were within six blocks of the apartment.

One she particularly liked was farther away on the rue des Fossées St. Bernard. It required a bus ride to the fifth *arrondissement*. She invariably ordered the *saladier*, which was a portable salad cart containing about a dozen different items from potato salad to tripe to pig's knuckles. It was supposed to be an appetizer, but she made do with that and some bites of a dessert. I ordered a regular dinner, invariably accompanied by the house Brouilly. On our third visit, before Kate could order, the woman who took our order and served—probably the chef/owner's wife—asked, "*Le saladier, madame?*"

"*Oui, merci.*" From then on, as long as Kate was capable, we returned once per week and were considered regulars.

It was on our second or third trip to this particular restaurant that Kate made the open-ended request, "So tell me about Pat."

"She's a musician—a singer and a teacher."

Kate expected me to say more, but I hesitated, so she asked, "How long have you known her?"

"I met her about ten years ago. As a matter of fact, it was at your apartment."

"Really? How bizarre. What was the occasion?"

"It was a soirée. We were both invited."

"I wouldn't assume she crashed. What is her last name?"

"Auriga."

"Pat Auriga." Kate paused to savor the name. "I don't recollect such a person."

"As I recall, you invited her at the urging of someone else. Maybe Brody Stearns."

"Brody Stearns. There's a name from the past. What a bastard."

"I thought he was a good friend of yours."

"He was . . . at one time. But good friends, I find, all too frequently turn into bastards." She stopped and then quickly added. "All except you. You've always been there for me. My faithful friend." She snapped back from her musings. "So is Pat pretty?"

"I think most people would call her attractive, rather than pretty. But I'm biased; to me she's beautiful."

"Is she young?"

"I think about my age."

"But you're not sure. You'll have to find out her birthday. If you miss her birthday, she won't forgive you, even if she says she would."

"I'll have to make a point of finding out."

"I've given you some good advice. By the way, I'll be fifty in August, August thirteenth. I'm a Leo."

"I'll have to make a note of that."

"Don't bother. It will be superfluous information."

"Please, don't say that."

"I always try to be realistic." There was an awkward silence. She stared down at her long fingers, devoid of rings, and spread flat on the tablecloth. To break the silence, she shifted back to Pat. "So we were talking about Pat. Do you love her?"

"I'm pretty sure I do."

"Aren't you absolutely sure?"

"I believe that there are different types of love. Love for a parent or for a child . . ."

"Let's narrow it down to a man's love for a woman."

"Even in that case, I think there are different forms of love. There's the passionate love. There's an intellectual love. There's . . ."

"Oh, you're being too abstract. Did you love Jane?"

"Yes, I did for a while. And then it turned to indifference and eventually to hatred."

"Did you ever feel love for another woman?"

I paused before answering, and then figuring we were long past deceiving each other, I answered. "Yes, I'm sure I loved you."

"How sweet." She squeezed my hand. "You didn't have to say that."

"I'm only being honest."

"I wish I could tell you, James, that I loved you. I respect you for your integrity and intelligence. I'm grateful for your friendship and companionship. But the truth is I've only loved one person in my life. I'm with my love every day, but now my love has grown repulsive.

"Self-love is non-productive, and, I might add, self-destructive. I thought for many years that I could do no wrong. Now I wonder if I ever did anything right. I may have been tilting at windmills all these years. Maybe people like Wayne Sickles are right—I was pursuing the impossible. In the end, I may have done more harm than good. That's a good reason to hate myself."

"Don't say that, Kate. You accomplished more than anyone

else could have."

"Easy to say, tougher to prove." She again switched the subject back to Pat. "You should determine quickly that you really love Pat. And then make sure you tell her. If she feels the same way about you, stay together, work on your life together. Don't live in isolation. A healthy love is a precious thing. Have a child with her. You know I was always afraid to have children. What a fool. That's why I never had sex. Except for one time when I was seventeen and was date-raped. Until I got my period, I was consumed by an excruciating fear that I was pregnant by a boy I detested. I vowed I would never go through that again. Strange how a morbid fear can become ingrained so quickly."

I had always looked on Kate's life with awe and even envy. Now there was only sadness. I was sad for her and sad that my illusions were falling away. Sweet dreams that I could almost fondle and caress were turning to smoke. I realized that she envied me. The world was flipped upside down.

The meal was finished. The waitress/*patronne* came to take the plates, and she asked the normal, concluding question, "*C'était?*"

"*Très bon*," Kate answered for both of us.

"*Déssert?*"

"*Pas ce soir.*"

I paid the bill.

"Let's walk a few blocks," Kate suggested. We did. Then she tired. She seemed incapable of taking another step. We struggled on one more block to the Maubert-Mutualité Métro station and then took the train three stops west to Mabillon. Kate leaned heavily on me as we slowly made our trek of two blocks to the apartment.

I helped her into bed. "Did you take anything for your pain?"

"No, I think I'll be able to sleep."

"No sleeping pill, either?"

"No, I'll be okay."

I stayed in the main room, which I, too, now called the "salon," for a while to read. On occasion I heard her toss and turn and even moan. I wondered for the first time whether I would be able to face, along with Kate, the next few months. I was not, nor am I now, a religious person. But at that moment I sought from an unknowable corner of the universe some assistance to face the coming ordeal.

A few minutes later she emerged from her room. The robe, which only a few weeks earlier clung to her form, now hung loosely. "Did you speak to Pat today?"

"I spoke to her yesterday."

"It's not too late. You can call her now."

"It's almost ten. She has to work tomorrow. She might have gone to bed."

"Don't lose that woman. You may not be sure, but I know you love her. I hope she loves you equally."

"I think she does."

Kate approached me. She put her hands on my shoulders. "I probably will not meet Pat . . . again," she added. "I want to make sure you tell her that I'm sorry to have interrupted your time together. But I give you both my very best wishes for a wonderful, long, loving life together."

I thought this maudlin line of conversation was unbecoming, and it made me feel uneasy. Fortunately she changed the subject. "What is Pat going to do when she's finished with her job in Florence?"

"She's probably going back to Washington to resume teaching at American. She'll do some private voice coaching, too."

"So you'll return to Washington?"

"I suppose so. I've made no plans."

"Tomorrow," her tone became authoritative once again, "we're going to work on those plans." Without saying another word, she turned and walked back to her bedroom more briskly than when she had entered the salon.

XLII

Paris, 2064

THE NEXT MORNING I PERFORMED my usual chore of going to the rue de Buci to buy two croissants and one baguette. Kate had often made the coffee when I was out, but lately she had been leaving that task to me. However, this morning Kate was up and fiddling with the coffee maker when I returned from buying breakfast.

With no preamble she stated, "As soon as we can, we'll call Hazel Dumas. You know she's now acting secretary with Wayne's resignation."

"I heard something to that effect. I guess only career folks are sticking around with a lame duck president in office."

"No matter. Hazel still has authority."

"And what do you propose she do with that power?"

"Come on, you're not that dense. She's going to get you a good civil service position in the department. With your background, that will be no problem. And Hazel owes me a few favors."

"What if I don't want to do that type of work again?"

"Please, don't play games with me. That's what you're trained for. That's what you're good at. You've been doing consulting, even if you haven't been working directly for the department. Do you intend to be unemployed for the next twenty years? And be kept by your wife? Listen to me. I know what's best for you. You need to get back to work, and you need Pat. Both are within your reach."

"If I recall correctly, you urged me to marry Jane, and you set me up with a job in San Francisco to facilitate the process."

"Jane was a good person. She was a good admin assistant. How could I foresee that she'd go a bit crazy?"

I decided not to respond. With a project facing her, Kate seemed to draw new energy. "And you know what else you need to do?" Her question was rhetorical. "You need to call Pat and tell her what we're planning."

"Yes, ma'am."

I put in a call to Pat, but she was evidently busy with work. I left a message. Shortly thereafter, Kate said that she was going to call Hazel Dumas. I had to convince her to wait until after lunch to make the call.

"But Hazel always gets to the office early."

"It's only five a.m. in Washington."

"Okay. I'll wait a little longer."

Once Kate was on a mission, she was difficult to restrain. She watched the clock. A little before noon, she sent me to the rue de Buci to purchase sandwiches for lunch. I took my time. When I returned, she was dozing. I let her sleep.

Just before one, she awoke with a start. "Is it time to make the call?"

"No, it's time to eat."

As was her habit, Kate cut the sandwich in half. She rarely ate even half, and reserved the remainder for "later." The next day she found the hunk of stale baguette with the desiccated filling. This part made it to the *poubelle* rather than her stomach. Another sandwich would be ordered for lunch, and again only a small portion would be eaten.

Kate nibbled on her sandwich, watching the clock, seemingly angry that there had to be a six-hour difference between Paris and Washington time. At a quarter to two, Kate declared, "I'm calling." Then she asked, "James, would you get the number?"

She was proved correct. Hazel was already in the office. Kate began with a few pleasantries. Hazel must have inquired about

Kate's health, because she replied, "Frankly, I'm not feeling that well. I persevere. But, look, I have a favor to ask. In fact, in the end I might be doing you a favor. James Lendeman is going to return to Washington in the fall. I'm sure there are any number of jobs he can do in the department. You know what an asset he can be. He should be put in a high-level civil service job. I don't want him subject to firing when a new administration comes in."

Hazel must have made a few observations. Then Kate replied, "He's helping me right now in Paris. I know he wants the job. He'd be more effective than any grade fifteen you currently have. You know the range of his experience. He's done just about every job in the department."

Kate paused for Hazel's response, and then commented, "He didn't leave the department under a cloud. It was a medical leave. He's been absolutely fine for the past two years or more, doing consulting work. You saw him last year. You know I relied on him."

Again Kate had to do some listening. "I'd really appreciate that, Hazel. I'm sure you'll come through. You'll be extremely happy with your decision."

Another pause. "Oh, I don't know when I'll be back in Washington. I expect I'll be in Paris for a while longer. Have to see how it goes. Have to regain my strength." Pause. "Yeah, life's tough sometimes. I just want to know that you'll do right by James." Pause. "Thanks so much. Hope to hear from you soon." Pause. "Best to you, too."

Kate pressed the button to end the call. "You probably got the gist of the conversation. Hazel is pretty sure she can come up with an appropriate position. You'll need to get to Washington before the election."

"But you might need me here."

"I'll get someone else if I have to. But there's something else we need to discuss." I waited to hear what she was going to say. But all that she said was: "Suddenly I feel very tired.

We'll talk later."

While Kate was dozing or attempting to sleep in her bedroom, Pat returned my telephone call. "*Amore*," was the way she now began phone calls.

After a minute of listening to Pat's recent activities, I broke the news. "We're working on a way for me to return to work in Washington. We spoke to Hazel Dumas today. She's the acting secretary. I think she's pretty well committed to coming up with a good job for me."

"That's nice." I expected more enthusiasm on Pat's part.

"Aren't you happy about that? You do want us to be together?"

"Definitely. It certainly is consistent with our hopes."

"Then why the hesitation?"

"There's no hesitation."

"I think I know you well enough to detect the nuances."

"Oh, it's a stupid woman's thing." She wanted to avoid the issue.

"Please, tell me."

"No, it's petty."

"You can't leave it there."

She hesitated to consider if she should share her thoughts. "Okay. But I'll tell you only because I don't want to start hiding things from you, even the petty thoughts of a silly woman. I just wanted *us* to make our own plans. I suppose it's simply jealousy on my part to resent her taking a role in this. I'm sorry to display my ignoble notion, but there it is."

There was something endearing about her confession. Jane never could have made such an admission. "I'm sorry, too, about not involving you earlier. And it's true I let Kate go ahead and call Hazel on my behalf. But I only had one thought in mind—us. If you weren't heading back to Washington, I wouldn't have wanted to return there. If I fail to keep you involved at every moment, here's a simple thing to keep in mind. From here on in, you're the most important thing in my life. I'll have other obligations that will take me away from you from time to time, but you'll never be out of my thoughts."

"That's a wonderful thing to say. I wish I could have said it first, but it's exactly what I feel, too. And do me a favor. Tell Kate I appreciate what she's doing. I truly do."

"I'll tell her."

"*Ciao, amore.*"

After the call concluded, I thought about what I had said. Had I overstated the point? Was all this declaration of love moving too quickly? It was only a matter of weeks ago that we had decided that we were more than just platonic friends. Now we were committing ourselves to joining our lives and futures. Had I, in this short time, truly determined that I loved Pat? Did I really feel love, or just the need to love and the need to be loved? Even though we had known each other for years, I felt this new phase in our relationship was moving at breakneck speed. Yet it felt exciting and pleasurable, like a surfer riding a huge wave. I would hang on and hope I was going in the right direction.

A half hour after I concluded my conversation with Pat, Kate emerged from her bedroom.

"Did you get some sleep?" I asked solicitously.

"I don't know. I tossed and turned. Maybe I napped for a few minutes."

"I spoke to Pat."

"That's good."

"She sends her thanks."

"For what?"

"For pursuing a job in Washington for me."

"Oh, that's nothing. I owe you a lot more than that."

I expected her to bring up the topic she had postponed in order to take a nap. But she picked up a book and began to read. Evidently, she had forgotten what she had intended to cover. After reading a few pages, her concentration flagged, and she returned to her bedroom. I wished that I could have gotten out of the apartment and strolled through the neighborhood, but I felt I could not leave Kate in her condition. So I stayed, watched some TV, and performed some mundane tasks on the computer.

Sometime around five, Kate called from her bedroom, "James, I need you."

I rushed in. She was trying to get out of bed and was obviously having trouble. "Let's swing your legs around . . . and now give me your hands." In a few seconds, she was on her feet, albeit a bit unstable, but on her feet.

I knew she was embarrassed in having to ask for my help to perform this simple task. "We'll rig something up, so it's easier for you to get out of bed."

"Okay," she acknowledged without enthusiasm and shuffled off to the bathroom.

When she came into the salon, she talked about dinner, something in which she had no interest but recognized I would want. "I don't think I'm up to going out to dinner tonight," she admitted. "Do you mind getting something to take out?"

"Not at all. What would you like?"

"Nothing in particular. You get something for yourself, and I'll share a few bites."

After that evening, not every dinner was take-out. But enough were, for me to make note of nearby establishments advertising food *à emporter*.

The next morning, Kate was scheduled to visit the clinic to have her bi-weekly tests performed. For the first time, she asked to take a taxi. When the doctor returned with the results, there was a look of concern on his face. "It might be best if you entered the hospital for a day or two. More tests would be advisable."

"Why?"

"There we can better assess where your condition stands, and whether we need to adjust your medications."

"You mean strengthen them."

"Perhaps."

"I'd prefer to stay in my apartment. James can take care of me there."

"But he is not a medical professional."

"No. He's a friend. That's more important to me now."

"You know the consequences can be serious."

"I know where my condition is heading. It is quite inevitable."

"Perhaps yes, perhaps no. If you refuse more aggressive steps, we'll try to do the best we can from the clinic."

"That is my desire."

She obtained more pain and sleeping pills. "Let's go, James. There's business to do."

Nothing was said on the return trip to the rue Jacob. But, once inside the door, she said firmly as she turned to head into her bedroom. "I will meet you in the salon in three minutes."

When Kate returned to the salon, she was carrying a manila envelope. She took a seat next to me and extracted a number of papers from the envelope. "James, read this."

The document was titled: "Last will and testament." It took only two or three minutes to digest the key provisions. I was named executor of her estate, and there was a provision for me to be reimbursed for expenses incurred in that role and the settlement of her estate. Two hundred and fifty thousand dollars was allocated to each of four charities. Forty percent of the balance was given to each of Kate's two nieces. The remaining twenty percent was granted to me.

After I read the document, she made sure that I knew to work through the law firm in Washington that drafted the will.

"Kate, do we really have to go through this stuff now?"

"If not now, when?"

I said nothing in return. She was right. Since I was to serve her even after death, we needed to cover these issues while Kate retained all her faculties. But the activity tore at me.

"There's an envelope here with your name on it. It contains money. It's yours. It's not part of my estate. You'll probably have to stay in Paris for a few weeks to take care of arrangements. This money will be your expense money. There's a safe in my room." She made sure I memorized the six-digit number.

"Another envelope here contains some of my final wishes. I'd like to be buried in Paris—in the Père Lachaise cemetery. I wouldn't be the first American cabinet member to be buried there." There was a slight, enigmatic grin at the corners of her mouth. "So you'll take care of that, too."

I said nothing when she finished. She was concerned by my silence. "You are going to take care of all of this? Aren't you?"

"Of course. You can count on me. I just hate thinking and talking about it. I know you want to have everything spelled out in case . . ."

"There's no *in case* about it. I'm dying. We all die. Death, like birth, is part of the life cycle. And my life is coming to an end. I know what's happening to my body. I can feel the pain."

"Maybe you need some better pain medication."

Kate smiled weakly. "Pain is an indication of my problem, not the cause. No, I know the end is coming. Believe me, I would like to live longer.

"On the other hand, even if I could live another twenty years, I wouldn't get back into government. I wouldn't be able to finish what I left undone; I wouldn't be able to correct what I did wrong.

"So I'm reconciled to the inevitable. At this point, I don't fear death. I do fear additional suffering. That will have to be stopped at some point."

I feared the implication of her statement. "What if I can't bring myself to aid you in that?"

"I'll do it for myself. I don't want to compromise you."

Now I pretty well knew what she was planning, and I was

afraid for her and me. "Has it come to this?"

Kate nodded. "It is coming close."

I tried to place my calls to Pat when Kate was asleep. But whether during the night or the day, she slept fitfully, rarely more than an hour or two at a time. I encouraged her to use more pain and sleeping pills. She was reluctant to do so, rationing her intake and guarding her supply like a miser.

Pat was well aware that Kate was getting closer to death. However, she seemed more concerned about me than Kate. Perhaps this was natural. Kate meant little to her, being more of a hindrance than an animate object. I, on the other hand, was the one who loved her, and I was being unfairly tied down, watching another woman die. She worried about the effect this experience would have on me. At times, I suspected that Pat wished for Kate's quick demise. Seeing her suffer, I occasionally wished for the same.

By mid-June, Kate had no thoughts about taking any excursions, no matter how short. She tried to accompany me to the rue de Buci to buy our food. After venturing a block or less from the apartment, she would declare that she couldn't go any further. I would bring her back, make sure she was halfway comfortable in an easy chair, and then do the shopping on my own.

She encouraged me to leave the apartment to get some fresh air and run my errands. However, I felt uneasy about leaving her for even a half hour.

We canceled her clinic appointment for June twenty-third. The doctor called back and more strongly suggested that she enter a hospital. Of course, Kate refused. I told her that we should get her a wheelchair in order for her to go outside. She would not hear of it. "There will be tourists on the streets, some American tourists. I don't want to mingle with them."

She was only partially right about the tourists. Certainly I noticed a few more in June than in prior months, but no city on earth was now filled with visitors. Europe did better than America, where fewer mass transit options existed and distances were greater. There were still a few American tourists to be seen, coming to Paris. But with the chronically muted economy and the cost of a trans-Atlantic flight, the numbers were a fraction of what they had been thirty or forty years earlier.

I told her the streets were readily passable. French was still the most common language heard. "And so if I went outside, what would I do? Skateboard?"

During the third week of June, she placed another call to Hazel Dumas. She wanted an update on how Hazel was coming along with a job for me. Kate still treated her as a subordinate. When Hazel said she was working on something but would have to call back, Kate asked when she could expect the answer. Hazel suggested by the end of the month or early July.

"Please make it this month; otherwise, you might only have James here to talk to."

Kate was using a speakerphone, and I could hear Hazel gasp. "You don't mean . . ."

"Hazel, yes, I do. I'm in agony, and I'm not going to put up with it forever."

Hazel had not seen Kate in over a year. She probably could not visualize how much Kate's appearance and health had deteriorated. "I know I owe you more than one favor. I'll come through for you. I'll call you back."

In fact, Hazel called the next day. She told Kate that there was a level thirteen job in the analytical division that was opening up. She could hold it for me, if I could get back to Washington by October first.

"He'll be there," Kate answered for me. "Thanks. I appreciate what you're doing. But you're getting a good person back. Good-bye."

When the call ended, I told Kate that she shouldn't have committed to my return in September.

"Don't worry about the schedule. The time-frame will be

quite doable."

The next week was pure hell for Kate, and for me, too. She paced her room and the salon. But she couldn't pace for long and she would collapse in bed or on the sofa. But then she would find that uncomfortable, and the cycle would repeat.

She took a pain pill on Sunday. It helped very little. She moaned frequently, beat her hands against the wall, on her mattress, on a table—whatever was handy. She cursed the pain; she cursed life; she cursed herself; and she cursed me.

I tried to get her to eat some food. She took a bite and gagged.

"What day is this?"

"Sunday, June twenty-ninth."

"And the time?"

"About six thirty."

"In the evening?"

"Yes."

"Tomorrow you need to get out. You can't stay with me constantly."

"I have to stay with you. You need my help. That's my job," I asserted.

Kate shook her head. "Not tomorrow. We talked once about your going to the Louvre. Tomorrow you need to go to the Louvre, but I won't be with you."

"A tour of the Louvre takes a long time."

"That's exactly the point."

I still fought her idea. "Anyway, I think it's closed on Mondays."

"No, it's closed on Tuesdays. You go shortly after it opens. Tour the Italian Renaissance section. You need to see *La Giaconda*. It will complement your Florentine experience. Search out the Flemish works, too. There are some Rembrandts. It's a pity, but I hear they're largely ignored. See the *Venus de Milo* and the *Winged Victory*. Go to the Egyptian collection. Take your time. Have lunch there. Save—and this is important—save your receipts."

Kate's plan was quite clear. I knew she was absolutely determined to carry it out. She seemed more composed as she spelled out the steps I should take. I decided not to try to dissuade her. Perhaps it was cowardice. Perhaps it was a matter of taking the path of least resistance. But I made my decision to comply, and consequently I only nodded to show my understanding and acquiescence.

Kate went to her bedroom to sleep, to toss and turn, to try to lessen the pain. I turned the TV on. It took me fifteen minutes to realize that the program was some incomprehensible French game show. I gazed at a book that I had loaded on my page palette, but I couldn't concentrate on that, either. I continued to watch the game show, which made no sense to me—it was probably appropriate that it was so. Nothing was making sense.

Just as I determined to get into my bed, despite the relatively early hour, Kate returned to the salon. "I'd like to be with you for a while. Can we both sit on the sofa?"

I spread my arms to indicate that it was ridiculous to think that I would deny such a simple request. "Would you hold me? I seem to remember being comforted by you in my apartment in Arlington. That was many years ago, and you probably don't remember."

"I remember it distinctly. It was well after midnight, and the moon shone through the window. Your hair looked silver in that light."

"I suppose your memory is better than mine."

I was thinking of reminding Kate about Vienna, but decided it would not be appropriate. She was leaning, really reclining against me. I put my arm around her. What I felt was more a skeleton than a body. The sensuous figure, which used to arouse me more than Jane's, Allison's, or even Pat's, had degraded into something that was now repulsive. I wished I could have extracted myself from this duty, but my obligation to Kate prevailed.

We sat quietly for a few minutes, Kate completely enveloped by my left arm. "Do you believe in life after death?"

I didn't, but I thought it best to be evasive in case she did. "I'm not sure."

"You always hate to take a stand. Well, I don't. We are nothing until a sperm fertilizes an egg. Then, we eventually return to nothingness. I've tried to picture where a heaven or hell could exist. I never could."

"I know how you feel. I used to look through my father's telescope. I looked at planets, moons, nebulas, galaxies. They were mysterious and beautiful. But I couldn't imagine a humanly heaven existing any place up there."

"And I can't envision a god of any sort existing," Kate added. "No, we just become nothing. Our sins or good deeds die with us, maybe a few remain among the living."

"Our atoms live on. Matter is not destroyed."

"Aren't we being scientific? But to put it simply, the atoms are just dust and rot. They're no longer us. No, the only thing we leave behind is what we've done. I've never had a child. Nor wanted one," she added with a slight laugh. "I thought I'd leave behind some accomplishments. Jefferson gave us the *Declaration of Independence*. Darwin gave us evolution." Kate paused. She must have realized that her statement was taking a very egotistical turn. "Well, I never expected to accomplish anything of that sort. But I thought I could make life a little more secure and prosperous for the average American."

"You did," I interjected. "There are dozens of regulations and pieces of legislation you created or influenced."

"Half of them have been rescinded, and a good deal of the remainder might be causing more harm than good. I was hoping to improve the economy by securing a reasonable energy supply. I barely made a dent in that. No, we did our best to adapt to a miserable situation. I believe very few Americans remember my name even now. And that's probably good, because they'd hate me for what I did or what I failed to do. It didn't work out at all like I thought."

"Don't say that, Kate."

"Why? Because it's true. At this point I think it's best to face the truth. If I were a practicing Catholic, I'd make a confession. Instead of a priest, I have you. James, you may not believe this, but I came quite close to loving you. Maybe at some point we should have had sex. That might have turned a great fondness into love. I don't know. Is that the way those things are supposed to work?"

"I don't believe there's a formula for love. If it's meant to happen, it happens," I postulated.

Kate pondered my reply for a few moments. "I suspect you're right. Anyway, I know this, I've never been closer to love in my life than I am at this moment." She took my free hand and guided it to her lips. "Of course, a lot of good it's going to do us now. I'm actually happy you're in love with another woman. You deserve that."

She remained in my embrace for a while longer. Many conflicting thoughts surged through my mind. Kate and I had moved in opposite directions. I had probably loved her once. I was far from loving her now. Even holding her embarrassed me. I was being disloyal to Pat, but I was obligated to Kate. The woman needed my attention. She needed something approaching love. At a minimum she needed my devoted friendship. That, I convinced myself, was what I was providing.

When she said, "I better go to bed now," I was relieved. I went to my bedroom as if seeking a sanctuary. Of course, it was impossible to fall asleep quickly. My mind reviewed scores of interactions I had had with Kate. The majority were pleasant, even enjoyable. In some instances she had treated me badly. Then I returned to the grim realization that, after tomorrow, I would not add to my memories of Kate Hastings; the catalog would be complete.

XLIII

Paris, 2064

ON MONDAY MORNING, JUNE 30, I awoke a bit later than normal, primarily because I had not fallen asleep until the wee hours of the morning. Kate was not stirring, so I took some time to shower and shave. After dressing, I prepared the morning coffee. I was thinking about going to the bakery for croissants when Kate emerged from her room.

"I was heading for the rue de Buci. Do you want anything besides a croissant?"

She pondered the question. "Don't get me a croissant today. I'll have a *pain au chocolat*. Yes, I think that would taste good today."

I went on my errand, wondering why Kate was in a positive frame of mind. Was she looking forward to the day? Was it a sense of relief? Whatever contributed to her mood, I was grateful for it.

At breakfast, she nibbled at her roll. "It's very good. You don't think it will make me fat?" she joked. I made no reply. "What time is it?"

I looked at my watch. "Nine-forty-five."

"You'll be leaving soon." The comment was more a directive than a statement.

"If you wish."

"Yes. We have to get on with it. Let me give you a hug." We shared a brief embrace with no kiss exchanged. Then she added, most inappropriately, "Don't worry. I'll be okay."

The Louvre was almost directly across the Seine from the

apartment. I walked leisurely to the river and across the Pont des Arts. The line at the museum was not long. Under the glass pyramid, the visitors scattered to the automatic ticket machines. I took my ticket along with a small plan of the exhibits. I tried to make sense of the arrows pointing to the various sections. Since I had arrived early, I felt that I had the run of the place. I headed to the Italian Renaissance wing that would, no doubt, be much busier later in the day. Already a small queue had formed waiting to catch a few minutes' look at the *Mona Lisa*, "*La Gioconde*" in French.

Certainly there was a sense of grace and subtleness to the painting. But did it deserve to be the most famous one in the world? It was not large, nor complex like the *Birth of Venus*. I took a quick look and walked on. Perhaps my mind was elsewhere. With my rudimentary art education acquired in Florence I went on to look at works by Raphael, Botticelli, and their predecessor, Giotto.

Every fifteen minutes or so, I checked my watch. Ten forty-five. Eleven. Eleven fifteen. I wandered into the nearby gallery containing French classical and romantic paintings. Delacroix's *Liberty Leading the People* caught my eye. Its chaos and conflict mirrored my own emotions. Revolution and death. In another few hours I would observe death. Would I experience revolution and resolution?

I tried to put Kate in the place of Liberty. However, in no way could the gaunt form I had seen two hours earlier equate with the powerful woman holding aloft the tri-color banner while mounting the eighteen thirty barricade. Nor could I picture myself as any of Liberty's followers, except perhaps the young boy to her left. I was being led, and I knew not where. Yet I was anxious to get the job over with.

I took my time getting to *Venus de Milo*. Why did I try to compare each woman to Kate? Why not to Pat or Jacqueline?

I had not been in a mood to tour the Louvre that day at all. Now it was becoming a burdensome chore. But Kate had warned me about returning to the apartment too early. She had specifically directed me to get lunch (and keep the receipt). I was not hungry.

The plan of the Louvre showed a few dining choices within the museum complex. I chose the self-service cafeteria. Nothing looked appealing. Finally I selected a small salad, a roll that served as bread, and a bottle of water. At the *caisse* I was asked, "*Café?*"

"*Non, merci.*" I found a seat at a bar-like arrangement. I did not want to occupy a table and wondered how long I could manage to dawdle over my Spartan lunch.

One o'clock in the afternoon; *treize heures*, as the French say. I began a slow aimless wandering through Dutch and Northern European art. The Rembrandts made little impression, even though they were easy to view since few visitors got to this wing.

Two-o-five. I felt I could leave now and head back to the apartment. I tried to walk slowly, but as I crossed the Pont des Arts my pace quickened. I no longer wanted to put off the inevitable.

I did not wait for the elevator, but took the steps two at a time. Yet I hesitated by the apartment door. For some reason I knocked, not that Kate would have responded under most circumstances. There was no more reason to delay. The apartment seemed hot and stuffy. An odor, not overwhelming, yet unpleasant, reached my nostrils. She was right there in front of me on the couch. Her head was on a pillow taken from her bedroom. She was in a robe. One leg reached the floor. I was surprised she hadn't fallen. Her mouth was open. A stain had formed on the couch under her buttocks. I did not look long enough to determine its nature. I did not know how to take a pulse. But I touched her arm. She was obviously dead.

For some reason, I sensed that I should not disturb the room, but I needed to open a window because of the heat and smell. I called the person at the French foreign ministry, a Monsieur Rénard, who had helped Kate acquire the apartment. I explained that I had found her dead upon returning to the apartment. He told me he would call a doctor to confirm death and also call the "authorities," whoever they were.

Next, I decided to call the American embassy. I asked to talk to an official regarding the death of an American citizen in Paris. The young man who received the call asked for my number so someone could call back. I urged promptness. He intimated that the return call would likely come later that afternoon.

"Let me explain," I said. "The deceased is Kate Hastings."

"I'm sorry, Mr. Hastings, but your call will be returned as quickly as possible. We're a little short-staffed today."

"First of all, my name is James Lendeman. I was working for Ms. Hastings. Second, she was the former secretary of the Department of Energy."

"We're very sorry about Ms. Hastings's passing, and although she worked for the government . . ."

"No, you don't get it. She was *the* secretary of the department, a cabinet member, someone who reports directly to the president— the president of the United States of America."

Suddenly the supercilious tone was gone. "Oh, I see. Hold on a minute, please."

Another voice came on the line after a few moments. "Sorry for the confusion, Mr. Lendeman. My name is Vance Low. How can I help you?"

I explained that I had found Kate deceased upon my return to the apartment. I was serving as her aide. She had been suffering from terminal cancer and had evidently taken her own life.

"Will you be at the apartment for the next hour or so?" Low asked.

"Yes, I'm waiting for a doctor to verify death."

He took the address, and then added, "I'll be over as promptly as possible."

I wanted to do one thing before the doctor and the police arrived. I went into Kate's bedroom and headed for the safe in the closet. Fortunately, I remembered the combination and pressed it slowly but firmly. The door sprung open. Kate's will was on top of a small pile of envelopes. But that could wait for later. Next I came upon an envelope entitled "Final Requests and Instructions." That I took. I rifled through additional papers. Some were financial records that I put back in the pile. Finally I saw the envelope with my name on it. I could tell there was a lot of cash in it, but before I could assess the contents, the downstairs buzzer sounded. Quickly I stuffed the envelope in my pocket and slammed the safe door.

The person asking for entry was a Doctor Picault, who said he had been summoned by the Quai d'Orsay to provide the death certificate. I assumed "d'Orsay" did not refer to the museum, but to the French ministry, and buzzed him in.

Dr. Picault was short and balding. The remaining hair was black, shiny, and slicked back. He wore steel-rimmed glasses. An untidy blue jacket covered a beige shirt. Both looked like they had seen better days.

"*Monsieur*, my condolences. I apologize, but I do not remember your name."

"James Lendeman. I'm a friend of Ms. Hastings."

"I am Doctor Picault," he stated, perhaps forgetting that he had had to announce himself over the security speaker. "May I see the deceased?"

I led him the few steps to the couch. He observed the body, felt for a pulse, and then dropped Kate's arm. "Obviously deceased. You found her just like this?"

"Yes."

"She was no doubt under a doctor's care. Advanced cancer, I suppose."

I muttered the name of the doctor and clinic she had visited.

"I'm acquainted with it. I'm sure they provided good care."

"But not quite good enough."

"There are limits as to what can be done." He changed the subject. "I understand she was an important person in your government."

"Yes. The secretary of the Department of Energy, equivalent to a minister in your government."

"You can be sure that we will exercise the greatest discretion. However, a police officer will probably be coming to interview you. It cannot . . ."

At that moment my phone rang. I could see it was Pat. "I really need to take this call," I told the doctor. "I will be back in *quelques instants*." I used the French expression, which evidently covered a time period from a minute or two to a quarter of an hour. I went into my bedroom.

"James, is everything alright? You normally call on Monday."

"Kate's dead."

"Oh, my god. I didn't realize it would come this quickly."

"There's a doctor in the other room, examining the body." I lowered my voice. "It was suicide."

"No. How tragic. Are you okay?"

"Yes. I'll be okay, I think. Someone from the embassy is coming. I will probably be questioned by the police."

"Why?"

"I'm not sure. I suspect it's some sort of formality. I have to cooperate."

"Of course. Call me back when you have a chance. I love you."

"Love you, too."

The buzzer was ringing. An Inspector Guicciardi wanted entry. For a second I was confused by the clearly Italian sounding name, but I allowed him in. When he arrived, I was faced with a rather un-Italian looking man. He had sandy hair, perhaps a shade lighter than mine, and blue eyes, and was a centimeter or two taller than me.

"Inspector Guicciardi," he introduced himself again.

"James Lendeman. I'm a friend of Ms. Hastings and was helping her during her illness."

The inspector said nothing, but the look on his face was slightly quizzical. The doctor approached and after introducing themselves, they began a brief conversation in French, but clearly regarding Kate's demise.

The inspector turned back to me. "You've known Ms. Hastings for a long time?"

"Over ten years. I worked for her in the Department of Energy." I thought it best to leave it at that. An old warning given to me when I was coached before a deposition came to mind: "Don't volunteer any information."

"Then you were a good friend. My condolences to you. We will try to be as . . ." The inspector searched for the right word. He didn't find it. ". . . as imperturbable as possible. I understand you found Ms. Hastings when you returned to the apartment."

"Yes."

"About what time?"

"Two . . . *quatorze heures trente*."

"*Ah, vous parlez français.*"

"Not much. Your English is much better than my French. I just thought I'd make it clear that it was in the afternoon."

"I see. Tell me, is everything in the apartment just as you found it?"

I looked around. "Yes, except I opened the window because of the heat and odor."

"*Sans doute.* And everything else is the same?"

"I went into the safe in Kate's, Ms. Hastings's bedroom."

"For what purpose?"

"I wanted to get her letter regarding final requests, such as arrangements for a funeral."

"There will be time to arrange that. Anything else?"

"Pardon?"

"Did you take anything else out of there? Like a will?"

"No, her will is still in there. She showed it to me a few days ago."

"Do you inherit?"

"Only a small amount. The vast majority goes to two nieces

and to charities. I was informed of the percentages but not the total value of the estate." Was I offering too much information?

"Very well. The doctor is not a police examiner, but he thinks death occurred around noon, maybe a little earlier, maybe a bit later. Where were you at that time?"

"At the Louvre."

"*Vraiement.* You were with a friend?"

"No, by myself."

"I see. I will need to look around the apartment."

"Please, be my guest."

The inspector went into the kitchen. In a moment he came out. I noticed he was wearing rubber gloves. "Mr. Lendeman, would you come in here. Do you recognize these?"

I took a step closer to the counter. "Please, do not touch."

"They're Ms. Hastings's medicine."

"What precisely?"

"I need to look at the labels."

The inspector held each bottle up in turn. "Pain medicine. Chemotherapy pills. Sleeping pills."

"I will need to take these with me," he asserted.

"I expect you're just following procedures."

"*Exactement.*"

Before I left the kitchen, I noticed that an opened bottle of Evian was on the counter, along with a glass that contained a small amount of water. There was also a sheet of paper. "Is that a note from Ms. Hastings?"

"I presume so. Please take a look, but don't touch." The inspector held the note in front of me.

> *Life provides no more rewards, only pain. My brief candle has burnt low, and now the pitiful remnants need to be snuffed out. Adieu. K.*

"Is that her writing?"

"Yes."

"My English is not so good, but there seems to be a bit of poetry in it. Very sad." For the first time the inspector's tone softened. Perhaps he now believed that Kate had committed suicide. She had left every bit of evidence she could. "You know, in this country a doctor could have assisted her."

I hadn't known that, and I said nothing in return.

The inspector continued. "I will just take a brief look in the other rooms." He returned to the salon in three minutes. "We need to examine the body at the morgue since we have a matter of suicide to confirm. People will be here soon to attend to that. We will be able to release the body in a day or two. I assume you're the person to call when we're finished with that matter. Just one more thing. When you were at the Louvre, did anyone see you who could confirm your visit there?"

"No. But I have my ticket and the receipt for lunch." I reached into my pocket.

Inspector Guicciardi looked at the two scraps of paper. "Yes. Quite clear. How fortunate you kept these tickets."

"Ms. Hastings told me to." Perhaps I shouldn't have volunteered that information.

After the doctor and the inspector departed, I suddenly felt exhausted. I wanted to sit down and have a drink. There were two comfortable chairs in the salon, but I couldn't sit there and look at Kate's body. I found some white wine in the refrigerator, poured some into a tumbler and took it into my bedroom. I propped a pillow against the wall, leaned back and drained half of the wine. I wanted to rest, but I began to think about what I needed to do.

I grabbed a piece of paper and began to jot down thoughts at random: call lawyer, call nieces, burial at Père Lachaise—who can help?, get apt. cleaned.

The buzzer sounded again. Vance Low was seeking admission. Low had blond hair that many women would envy. He was half a head shorter than I and thin. His eyes were blue and his chin was pointed. His jacket was elegantly cut. He noticed Kate's body and went to stand in front of it. "I never met her in person, but I recognize her. She must have been very ill."

"Yes, she was. Sorry, do you mind if we go into another room?"

"Oh, of course."

We used my bedroom. I sat on the bed, and he used the spare chair. Vance wanted to know where things stood. I told him about the visit of Inspector Guicciardi and Doctor Picault, the questions that the inspector asked and how I answered.

"Do you think that the inspector believes you had a role in Ms. Hastings's suicide?"

"Perhaps he did at first. Then when he realized that Kate made careful preparations for me to be gone and that she left as much evidence as possible pointing to suicide, I think his suspicions subsided. I'm not sure he's ready to drop the idea completely."

"Let's hope he does. Let me know if he persists in the investigation. Do you want a lawyer?"

"I don't know anything about how the French pursue such things." I noted to myself that I really didn't know how Americans would pursue the matter either. "Do you think I should get a lawyer?"

"You probably don't need one at this point, but if the police ask more questions, let me know, and I can recommend one. Does Ms. Hastings have relatives who need to be contacted?"

"She hasn't been speaking to her sister for a while. She was occasionally in contact with her two nieces. They will receive the largest portion of her estate. I've never talked to them, but Kate told me about them. I'll call them unless it's against protocol."

"Are you mentioned in the will?"

"I'll receive a little money and I'm executor."

"If you feel reasonably comfortable calling the nieces, that's probably best. I guess you were a good friend of Ms. Hastings."

"I worked for her for a number of years."

"Then you're in the F.E.D."

"I was." I did not add that I expected to be in the department again.

"Are you going to stay in Paris for a while?"

"I have a number of things to take care of. Kate's body is going to the morgue. It will be released to me in a few days."

"There's someone at the embassy who can help you with procedures for sending the deceased back to the U.S."

"She asked to be buried in Paris—at Père Lachaise."

Low's face exhibited surprise. "Really? Like Jim Morrison."

"I don't suppose you have anyone who can help find a suitable gravesite."

"I'll check."

Low gave me his direct number and the name of his admin assistant. "Give us a call if we can help in any other way."

I sensed Low was making a genuine offer. "I won't hesitate."

"I don't envy what you have to do. At least you can look at the job objectively, having been her subordinate."

Low's final comment was the only one that rankled. "Thanks for the sentiment."

XLIV

Paris, 2064

IT WAS NEARING FIVE O'CLOCK. I might have tried to reach Kate's lawyer or her two nieces, but I had time to do that. I needed to talk to Pat. It was not an obligation, but rather a deep-seated desire to get her support.

She picked up at the first ring. "James, I was waiting for your call. How are you holding up? Can you talk now?"

"I'm doing okay, but I need to talk." I told her about the visits from the inspector, the doctor, and Vance Low.

"Do you think you're suspected of aiding Kate's death?"

"I don't think so, not after the inspector saw the evidence Kate left. But I don't know if I'm totally off the hook. I wouldn't be surprised if there is some follow-up questioning."

"She's . . . she *was* a clever woman. Do you have a lot of things to take care of in Paris?" Pat probably wanted to know when I would be able to return to Florence, but felt it best to avoid the direct question.

"I have to arrange for Kate's burial. She wants to be buried in Paris. I need to get the lawyer started on her estate. I need to contact her nieces."

"Why does all this fall on you?" she asked in an exasperated tone.

"Perhaps I didn't mention it, but I'm executor of her estate."

"Great. And that was meant sarcastically."

"I can tell. Hey, the job comes with some money. We can use that."

"We can use some time together."

"Why don't you come to Paris?"

"Are you serious? I'm up to my neck with the music festival."

"Then if I were in Florence, you couldn't devote time to me."

"I'd find a way."

"Don't worry. We'll have plenty of time together. I'll try to wrap things up and get back to Florence as quickly as possible."

"I'm counting on you. I miss you. I love you."

My desire was to continue to focus my thoughts on Pat, but obligations required my attention elsewhere. I called Kate's lawyer's office. An admin assistant told me that Ms. Claiborne was at lunch. She recognized the name of "Kate Hastings" and expressed shock and regret at her passing. She assured me that the lawyer would return my call that afternoon. I reminded her that I was in Paris and that there was a six-hour time difference. I told her, however, that I would appreciate the call at any time.

I did not recollect which niece was on more friendly terms with Kate. But I had to start someplace. I started with Diane.

"Hello."

"Hello. Is this Diane Fenwick?"

"Yeah."

"My name is James Lendeman. I'm a friend of your aunt, Kate Hastings."

"Yeah, so?" came a disinterested response. I knew which niece I had reached.

"I have to give you the sad news that your aunt passed away today."

"Sorry to hear that. I hope Janet and I don't have to arrange the funeral."

"No, I'm taking care of that. Your aunt has been living in Paris, and she wants to be buried here."

"You're calling from Paris?"

"Yes."

"Well, I can't get to Paris for a funeral."

"I can understand that." I sensed that Diane possessed neither the means nor the desire.

"Let me ask a practical question. Did she leave any money to me?"

"Your aunt's lawyer will have to answer that question."

"But you know. Son-of-a-bitch."

I put in a call to the other niece, Janet. "Hello. My name is James Lendeman. I'm a friend . . ."

"Hold on, let me turn the TV down. Kids, stop fighting. Okay, could you start again?"

"My name is James Lendeman. I worked with your aunt, Kate Hastings."

"Is Aunt Kate okay?"

"I'm very sorry to have to tell you that she passed away today." I found no way to deliver the news in a gentler manner.

"Oh, no. I knew she was sick, but . . . She went to Paris, didn't she?"

"Yes. That's where I'm calling from. You know she was suffering from cancer. She was in a lot of pain. Now she's at peace."

"That's the way I'll have to think about it. Are funeral arrangements being made?"

"Your aunt asked me to do that. She wants to be buried in Paris."

"Oh, my goodness. When will it be?"

"I'm not sure how French procedures work. It could be several days from now."

"What procedures?"

"There will probably be an autopsy."

"Didn't she die from natural causes?"

"It appears that she took her own life."

"Oh, dear."

"She was in a tremendous amount of pain and didn't want to go on with life," was the best way I could put it.

There was hesitation. "I'd like to go to the funeral, but it will be extremely difficult. You will keep me informed?"

"Of course."

"Did you talk to my mother?"

"No."

"I'll let her know. They really didn't get along."

"I understand that."

"I'll call Diane, too."

"I've already spoken to her."

"Good." Janet asked me to repeat my name, including the spelling, and also jotted down my phone number and even the address in Paris.

We said good-bye. I sensed I would like Janet if I ever got to meet her. Obviously, she was the good niece.

I had made all the calls from my bedroom. For a second I forgot why I was there, and then realized that Kate's body was still lying and decaying in the salon. I tried to decide if I should take some action to speed the process of getting the cadaver removed. I looked at my watch. It was now ten after six. Did Inspector Guicciardi forget to have the morgue pick up the body? Did the people from the morgue work this late?

The buzzer rang. A male voice spoke a sentence in French. I was pretty sure I picked up the word "morgue" among the rapidly flowing sentence, distorted even more by the intercom. I pressed the buzzer on the chance that these were the very people I so desperately sought. A minute later my hopes were answered when a man and a hefty looking woman arrived at the apartment door with a gurney in tow.

The man said something, probably about their having come to take the body. He flashed some official-looking identification. I motioned to where Kate was lying. I didn't even watch them do their work. I barely took note as the emaciated body in some sort of plastic sack was wheeled toward the front door and then on through.

When they were gone I noted again the stain, probably urine, on the couch. I took a rag and some household cleaner and tried to eradicate even this evidence of Kate's presence. My cleaning did some good, but did not totally remove the stain. I made a mental note to arrange for the maid to make a special visit.

Two conflicting sensations suddenly came over me. I was both hungry and fatigued. The day, full of emotion and activity, was taking its toll. But the Spartan lunch I had had long ago departed my stomach. I knew I would find little food in the apartment. I looked in the refrigerator anyway to confirm my evaluation. I could not bear to eat the half *pain au chocolat* that Kate had left. A little wine, some milk, orange juice, orange marmalade, butter, and a shriveled apple were all that I found.

As I was bending over to search the bottom shelf of the refrigerator, I felt the envelope that I had stuffed in my pocket. It was the money that Kate had left in the safe for me. I began to count. There were many hundred-euro notes. One thousand, two thousand—when I reached four thousand euros I stopped. There were still some fifties and smaller bills, which I didn't bother to add in. How thoughtful Kate had been, and how anxious I was to get rid of the body. I didn't even properly say good-bye. I would have to do so at the funeral.

I pocketed two hundred euros and returned the balance to the safe. In the rue de Buci I walked among the vendors and bought liberally—a roasted half-chicken, a baguette, some Epoisse (Kate would not allow the smelly cheese in the house but I had developed a taste for it), two tomatoes, and a *mille-feuille* for dessert.

On my way back to the apartment, with my arms full, the phone rang. I rested a bag on a *poubelle* already out for the next day pickup. "Hello."

"Mr. Lendeman, this is Jane Claiborne." Why did her name

have to be 'Jane'? "I'm returning your call. And of course, I was so sorry to hear of Ms. Hastings's passing."

"Thank you. Would you mind if I call you right back? I'm walking in the street and would rather speak from my apartment." Suddenly it was my apartment. "It will only take a few moments."

"Of course."

I rushed back, walked up the stairs, and dropped the food on the kitchen counter. Taking a seat in the salon, but not on the couch, I returned the lawyer's call. Jane Claiborne answered at the first ring.

"Mr. Lendeman, again my condolences. You must have been a very close friend for Kate to name you as executor." I made some indication of acknowledgment. "Do you want me to explain the steps you and I will be taking? Or would you rather wait until the shock has subsided?"

"I think we better go ahead now."

"Okay, the process has been streamlined somewhat in the past twenty years, but it remains a bit complex. First, we need to get you officially named executor by the probate court. To do this I need to present Ms. Hastings's will, which I have. You need to get me a death certificate. While you're at it, you might as well get a half-dozen official copies made. We'll need those for transferring assets from financial institutions to an estate account." Already the process was beginning to sound complicated. "I will file a notice for the deceased database. They used to put a notice in the local newspaper, but since most newspapers have suffered their own demise, a national on-line register was established. This allows someone who thinks he is owed money by the deceased to forward whatever claim he wishes to make to me.

"So, probably within a month, we'll have you named executor and have assets transferred into an estate account. I can notify other inheritors of their interests in the estate, unless you particularly want to do this."

I thought quickly. No doubt having the lawyer do the work would add to the expense, but it would affect my share little, and it would assure that this sensitive contact was done in a suitable way. In addition, I had told Diane that the information would come from the lawyer. "I would appreciate your doing that."

"That's fine. So, to continue, we have to value the estate for court and tax purposes. Ms. Hastings's estate won't exceed the current nine million five hundred thousand dollar exemption for federal and state taxes. By the way, did Ms. Hastings have any bank accounts in France for handling her finances?"

"No, I believe she used her Morgan/American account for her expenses here."

"Well, I'll get the balance on that account from the U.S. I also have details on her investment accounts. She probably had some valuables with her, such as jewelry and cash."

"Kate didn't have a lot of jewelry."

"Whatever she had needs to be inventoried. You can send it to me by insured mail, and I'll get it appraised." Jane Claiborne forged ahead. "Anyway, in three to four months we should be able to disburse all assets to the beneficiaries and close the estate account. You're not a CPA, by any chance?"

"No."

"Then you'll probably want our firm to prepare the estate's tax return and Ms. Hastings's final personal return."

"Of course."

"One or two more things. Get receipts for all expenses you incur on behalf of the estate and forward them to me. This will include burial expenses, shipping the body back to America . . ."

"Kate is going to be buried in Paris."

"Really? You have her request in writing?"

"Yes."

"Best if I have a copy of that, too. Anyway, you'll incur burial expenses in France. Get receipts. By the way, it's fortunate you're in Paris rather than in some remote town."

"Why's that?"

"I'll have a number of papers for you to sign. There's an international facsimile signing facility at American Express, on the rue Scribe, I believe. That will save a lot of expressing of papers back and forth."

"What if I'm in Florence? My fiancée's there." I raised the level of our relationship.

"Florence, Italy?"

"Yes."

"Let me check." A slight pause. "Sorry, no such facility. There's one in Rome and one in Milan. I don't suppose that would do any good. So if you need to be in Florence and papers must be signed, we'll do it the old fashioned way.

"I know I've thrown a lot at you. But I'll lead you through the process step by step as we move along. The first thing is for you to get the death certificates. Assuming they're in French, they can probably provide an English translation. If not, we'll get the translation done here.

"By the way, Ms. Hastings had two life insurance policies in force. I'll file the claims. If you need money quickly, like for the funeral, I can get you an advance against those policies. They total three hundred thousand dollars. So that should more than cover the expenses."

"I would hope so."

"Call me if you have any questions or hit any snags. My admin assistant is excellent. She may be able to answer some of your questions. Is there anything else at the moment?"

"Just one thing I should mention. They think Kate committed suicide."

"Oh." I could sense the wheels turning. "That could delay the death certificates. Let me know if you have any problems. We can get a French lawyer involved if need be."

"Thanks."

"I guess that does it for the present. Good luck."

XLV

Paris, 2064

THE DAY AFTER KATE'S DEATH dawned gray and drizzly. I needed an umbrella as I made my usual trip to the rue de Buci.

"*Bonjour, madame. Un croissant et une baguette.*"

"*Un croissant, monsieur?*" the baker's wife verified, holding up just one finger.

"*Oui, merci.*"

I returned to the apartment, feeling more relaxed as I ate breakfast. Perversely it occurred to me that it appeared that dealing with the deceased Kate would be easier than dealing with the process of her dying. A second after that thought emerged, I felt ashamed.

The morning went by slowly. My list of things to do had been either taken care of or put in other people's hands. I called the woman who performed maid services, and explained in awkward French that I needed a special cleaning because of Ms. Hastings's death. She seemed to understand and said she would be over the next morning around ten o'clock. I thanked her profusely.

Pat called to see how I was coping with Kate's death. I assured her that I was doing fine. In fact, her passing was a bit of a relief, although perhaps the full effect had not yet sunk in. Everything, I told her, was under control. I still had no idea when the funeral would occur.

The rainy weather broke just before noon. I decided to get out of the apartment. I needed a good walk and to have my lunch at a bistro. For weeks I had been burdened with Kate's growing inactivity. I was exhilarated leaving the apartment, heading off in a random direction, and not worrying about the need to return quickly. I crossed the boulevard St. Germain and walked down the rue de Rennes. Then I turned off in the direction of the seventh arrondissement. A number of bistros advertised their *formule* lunches on blackboards. *Entrée et plat ou plat et déssert*—29 euros. They all seemed to want to keep their price under the thirty-euro mark.

I stopped at a place that looked a little quainter and offered a *plat* other than *poulet rôti*. I had grown tired of chicken and knew that a leftover leg still awaited me in the refrigerator. The *boeuf bourguignon* contained more onions and carrots than beef, but it was nicely seasoned. And I enjoyed being served, rather than doing the serving.

After lunch I took a winding route past St. Sulpice church, the Odéon theatre, and a portion of the Luxembourg gardens, and then back to the apartment. I sat down in an armchair and pulled out the 'to do' list that I had made the previous day. Did I need to add any items? I couldn't think of any. Should I start following up on any? Probably. When would Kate's body be released? Was the embassy making any progress on the burial site at Père Lachaise?

I called Inspector Guicciardi. He was not available. I left a message asking for the status of progress at the morgue. I called Vance Low at the embassy. Again I needed to leave a message.

With nothing else to do, I turned to the TV and flipped through the channels. A news program was covering a demonstration around the Place de la République. A few thousand people were protesting something. I heard the word *grève* (which I knew meant "strike") mentioned. Paris had seemed so calm in the sixth arrondissement, whereas a few kilometers away in the third, the streets were teeming with activity. Students, workers, teachers were chanting slogans. After another few moments, I flicked on the text option because it was easier for me to follow French in written rather than spoken form. The report said that ninety percent of the Métro trains were running and overall only fifteen percent of the municipal workers were participating in the one-day strike. Evidently vacation time for younger workers was one of the key issues, and the unions wanted to make their point before the prime vacation period began.

I suddenly remembered that I needed to do something else, although I had failed to put it on my list. Kate's jewelry needed to be sent off to the lawyer. First, I needed to find it.

She never wore a lot of jewelry, but she always wore earrings. (I hadn't noticed if she went to the morgue wearing a pair.) I didn't recall seeing any jewelry in the safe when I was rummaging around, so I was relatively certain that I would find some items elsewhere in her bedroom. Quite frankly I was uncomfortable about poking around in Kate's clothes and undergarments. Too bad Pat wasn't around to help me out, but she was busy a thousand kilometers away.

With grim determination I headed into the bedroom. I hadn't previously noticed that a pair of her slacks was draped over the chair. I just left them there. There was no jewelry on the dresser. I looked in the top left drawer, and there was only underwear. In the top right drawer I found a small leather box. I found three pairs of earrings, including a pair of gold knots that Kate wore frequently. I left the small box on top of the dresser and continued my search.

Lower down in the dresser I mainly encountered clothes: blouses, sweaters, pajamas. Behind a bulky sweater, I found another, somewhat larger box. It contained two bracelets—one plain gold and another set with red gemstones. I checked another small chest of drawers, but there was no more jewelry to be found. I went back to the safe. In the back, there was a small box I had previously not noticed. The first thing I saw was a note. "James, please give this to Pat. I hope she likes it."

The locket accompanying the note was a gold oval about three by two centimeters. The face was set with small diamonds forming a fleur-de-lys. I could not remember seeing Kate wear the locket. Perhaps she had bought it in Paris.

I looked for more jewelry. There was no more in the safe. Did she have a secret hiding place? I had begun to look elsewhere in the closet when my phone rang.

It was Inspector Guicciardi. "Hello, Mr. Lendeman. I know you are interested in when Ms. Hastings's body can be released. Unfortunately, there's a bit of a complication. Perhaps you've heard of our little strike. Two technicians had to represent the morgue at the demonstration. Therefore, we couldn't finish all the tests and reports."

"Then can I expect your work will be done tomorrow?" I decided to set the target myself.

"*Normalement*," the inspector began in French and then caught himself. "If things go as expected, it is probable."

"Then I can expect a call tomorrow."

"I would say 'yes.'" I didn't understand this conditional phraseology. Nor did I understand why technicians had to represent the morgue at a demonstration, as if it were a sanctioned event. Guicciardi continued, "Mr. Lendeman, you're staying in Paris for a little while?"

"I need to make the arrangements for the funeral at Père Lachaise."

"*Vraiement*? We have so few funerals there anymore. The only available graves are in old family . . . how do you say?"

"Plots."

"Yes. Very few. This is Ms. Hastings's request?"

"Yes. She was specific in her written instructions."

"I suppose she's heard about Jim Morrison."

"I don't think that's her motivation."

"*Pardon*?"

"I don't think that's her reason."

"Whatever. You might check in the columbarium."

Now it was my turn to seek clarification. "*Pardon*?"

"She would be cremated and then her ashes placed in the columbarium at Père Lachaise. Did she object to cremation?"

"She never said so, but she did mention burial."

"Then you will have to determine if cremation would be permitted by the family."

"That's good advice. But tell me, why did you ask if I'm leaving Paris?"

"I need to finish my report and my boss needs to accept it. He might want me to ask you more questions. You know how these things are."

I was not at all sure about how those things were. "I think that I'll be in Paris for another week or ten days."

"I'm sure you want to return to the United States."

Again I sensed the inspector was fishing, but I decided to be forthcoming. "Actually, I'll probably go to Florence. My fiancée is working there."

"Ah, Florence. A lovely city. Not as impressive as Paris, but quite marvelous in its own way.

We ended the conversation by agreeing that Florence was well worth a visit. I wondered if the Guicciardis originally came from that part of Italy.

Talk of Florence reminded me to call Pat. "You doing okay?" she asked.

"I can use your help with something."

"What's that?" she sounded a bit wary.

"I'm going to have to sort through Kate's clothes. A woman could do better than I."

"So you want me to come to Paris and do that?" Her voice implied a conflict between wanting to help me and the difficulty of making such arrangements. "You know I'm in the midst of the festival season. I'm up to my neck."

"You don't get a break in the next few weeks?"

"Let me check my schedule." There was silence for a few moments. "There's a break around the third week of July. But won't you be back by then?"

"I doubt it. My inspector friend asked me to stay around until he completes his report. And the lawyer needs me here to sign papers. Evidently Paris has some special signing machine that Florence doesn't."

"Is the inspector treating you as a suspect?"

"I don't think so. I think he's just being careful. There seem to be a lot of arcane procedures to follow."

"I'll try to keep a few days around the twenty-second open."

I thanked her profusely, and we told each other that we loved one another.

A bit later I received a call from the embassy. Vance Low's assistant confirmed that there were no available gravesites at Père Lachaise. She suggested two or three other cemeteries in the suburbs. I told her that I didn't think that would do, but I asked if she could determine whether a spot in the columbarium at Père Lachaise could be found. I had to explain what the columbarium was, and the assistant promised to check.

That evening I decided to speak to Janet, the good niece. There were several points that I needed to discuss with a member of Kate's family. First, I explained that her aunt had wanted to be buried in Père Lachaise cemetery; however, no plots were available. There was a possibility of having Kate cremated and placing the ashes in a memorial vault at Père Lachaise. Kate and I had never discussed the possibility of cremation. Did Janet know about her aunt's attitude on the subject?

Janet had never discussed any such thing with Kate. She reminded me that she and her sister had had no contact with their aunt since her illness took a turn for the worst. Janet asked for my opinion, which I was prepared to give her. "Kate had expressly wanted to be buried at Père Lachaise. We had no discussion about cremation. I had never heard Kate voice an opinion on the subject. Since she wanted to rest at Père Lachaise, the only way to accomplish this is to place her ashes there."

Janet agreed with my logic. But she wanted to check with her sister.

Next I asked if she or Diane would want any of Kate's jewelry. "I don't remember any I would want. Her earrings were rather plain. Did she have much?"

"No, several pairs of earrings, two bracelets."

"What happens to the jewelry if Diane and I don't take it?"

"It gets sold, and the money becomes part of the estate."

"Unless I get back to you, assume Diane and I don't want any of the items. I'll mention this to Diane, too." Janet seemed to correctly sense that I preferred to deal with her rather than her sister.

"Third question," I continued. "Would you or Diane want any of your aunt's clothing?"

Janet giggled. "You've never met us. I'm ten centimeters shorter than Aunt Kate, and Diane is ten kilos heavier. No, we couldn't wear her clothes. What will you do with them?"

"Maybe give them to charity."

"I can't imagine any poor woman feeling comfortable in those clothes. But she's welcome to it."

I told Janet that I would keep in touch, especially when I had the funeral arrangements made. She again said that it would be difficult for either her sister or her to attend, but she would appreciate knowing when the internment would occur.

The next few days were a mixture of boredom interrupted by a few spurts of activity. A spot for Kate's ashes was found in the newer columbarium. Inspector Guicciardi told me on Wednesday that Kate's body would be released the next day. I asked him if this meant that the investigation was concluded.

"Not exactly," he replied. "My boss still has to approve the findings. So I hope you will stay in Paris for a while longer."

"I expect to stay another two weeks."

"I see you have formed a strong attraction for the city."

"I have barely seen Paris. I've been taking care of Ms. Hastings."

"Then you need to make up for lost time. Invite your Florentine girlfriend to join you."

"She's American. She's only working in Florence."

"American, all the better. She'll have a nice vacation here. I think Americans appreciate France more than the Italians do."

"Weren't your ancestors Italians?"

"No, not at all. They were from Nice. I am as French as Jeanne d'Arc. Some French names sound Italian, but really aren't. You never heard of Gambetta and Gallieni?"

"Perhaps I need to study French history."

"Not a bad idea."

The inspector gave me the location where the funeral home would be able to claim Kate's body. Our conversation concluded with him wishing me an enjoyable stay in Paris. I sensed he didn't expect to talk to me again. If that were to be the case, it would be fine with me.

I wanted to get Kate's ashes into Père Lachaise as soon as possible. From my prior conversations with Janet it seemed impossible for her or her sister to attend. So with the weekend approaching I felt justified in moving quickly. I called Janet to give her an update, but she was not available and I could only leave a message.

I had fallen asleep when a phone call awakened me. It was Janet, and she immediately sensed that I had been sleeping. "Sorry, isn't it ten thirty there?"

"No, it's eleven thirty."

"I can call back in the morning."

"I'm awake now, so let's talk."

"Okay, but I'm really sorry. Well, I spoke with Diane, and just like you suggested, we both agree that Aunt Kate should be cremated and her ashes placed in that cemetery she picked out." I sensed that expediency and cost influenced the decision making process. "And we definitely have no interest in her clothes. Do with them as you see fit." Was the pun intended?

"Okay. And the jewelry?"

"Are you planning to sell it there?"

"No, I'll send it to the lawyer. She'll have it appraised and sold."

"Could you send me some sort of description of the pieces, just in case Diane and I want some remembrance?"

"Sure."

"By the way, could you give me the name and phone number of Aunt Kate's lawyer?"

I was a bit surprised that the lawyer had not yet contacted Janet. I gave her the information. I also gave her the news that her aunt's body was being released on the following day.

"You know, Diane and I can't possibly attend the service."

"I realize that. I'm going to try to accomplish it on Friday. I'm sure your aunt would consider that appropriate."

For a moment, Janet didn't get my point. Then she understood. "July fourth. Yes, above all, Kate was an American, even if for some reason she wanted to be buried in France."

"She was a patriot. She always tried to figure out what was best for America."

"Yes, the news programs generally pointed that out."

For the first time it struck me that Kate's death had been news in the United States, even if it was just a matter of details and procedures in Paris. *Kate*, I asked myself, *why did you want to stay here?* Of course, the question would never get an answer.

XLVI

Paris, 2064

I RECEIVED KATE'S ASHES FROM the funeral home in the late morning of July fourth and took a taxi to the northeast gate of the cemetery. An administrator met me and took me to one of the two three-story edifices that possessed all the charm of self-storage units. The spot for Kate was in an inconspicuous corner of the third floor of the newer unit. No wonder it was available.

The administrator and I climbed the stairs, and I placed the urn with Kate's ashes into the compartment, where they were promptly locked away. I think my companion asked if I wanted to take a moment and pray.

"*Pour quelques instants.*" The indefinite phrase had become one of my favorites.

"*Oui, monsieur.*" She moved a few steps away and waited.

I didn't pray. Kate wouldn't have expected that. But I told her good-bye, that I would miss her, and that I would never forget her.

The administrator handed me some papers. I looked quickly and was pleased to see that an English translation was provided.

For the next week or so, I had little to do. I went twice to the office on the rue Scribe, where I electronically signed documents sent by Jane Claiborne. In addition to this, Jane told me that she had been in touch with both nieces, who were anxious to find out the provisions of the will. They seemed disappointed that a certain significant portion of the estate was going to charities. But Jane didn't think they would contest their aunt's will. "After all, they will each get about a million and a half dollars. It's certainly not a fortune in today's money but, nonetheless, a tidy sum."

It took me a moment to realize that the sum mentioned for the nieces meant I would receive something in the range of three-quarters of a million. For someone who had been struggling over the past several years to make ends meet, it represented a tidy sum, indeed. When I thought about it some more, I realized that the estate in total amounted to around five million—quite a large amount by some reckoning. Yet not that large a sum when one considered the positions Kate had held in both government and the private sector.

I hated to think of Kate in such pecuniary terms. Another financial matter related to her concerned me. What should I do with the nearly five thousand euros she had given me as a gift? The bulk of it was still resting in the safe. Would some authority think I had stolen it? Would they think it was really her money and should be part of the estate? I knew better, but I had no proof.

Of course, I needed some of the money for living expenses. But the apartment—and even the cleaning woman—had been paid in advance.

I decided that I was being neurotic about the issue and began putting some of the money into my own account a bit at a time. Some I would give to Pat for her trip to Paris. I would need a few hundred euros to entertain her properly during her short visit.

That week, with Kate having been placed, if not interred, at Père Lachaise, with most of my administrative duties delegated to the lawyer and with no further contact from Inspector Guicciardi, I became a tourist. I visited one museum a day: the d'Orsay, the Orangerie, the Rodin. All were within walking distance. Then I went farther afield: the Marmottan, Jacquemart-André and Nissim do Comondo. Later I returned to some closer to home: Cluny, Carnavalet and Centre Pompidou. I figured if I went to one museum a day, it would take me about three months to visit them all. Of course, I had no intention of staying that long in Paris.

I spoke with Pat, on average, every other day. Now instead of talk about dying, burial, and sorting through a dead woman's belongings, I spoke about my museum tours.

"Hey, save some for me," she joked.

"But you've only arranged to spend two days here."

"Let me see if I can stretch it to three." And this she managed to do.

In order to make the most of her time, she flew rather than taking a train. There was an early morning flight from Florence to Orly, where she took a non-stop bus to the Montparnasse station. That is where we met and kissed quite passionately right on the sidewalk. The passersby took no note. After all, we were in Paris.

"How far is the apartment?"

"Maybe a kilometer."

"It's a beautiful day. Let's walk."

I took the handle of Pat's suitcase, and we started down the rue de Rennes. The two-century-old straight street was not very interesting. Many shops sold lesser quality merchandise, not very attractively displayed, and with *soldes* signs in the windows, promoting perpetual sales.

"Is this your neighborhood?" she asked.

"No, it will change in another few blocks." And it did when we came to the boulevard St. Germain. I pointed out the church of St. Germain des Près and the Deux Magots café.

"Do you need a drink?"

"Is the apartment far?"

"No, only two blocks."

"To the apartment, please."

Two short blocks down the rue Napoléon and then a few steps along the rue Jacob brought us to the apartment's front door.

"Now, this is what I expected Paris to be."

I showed Pat around the apartment. "I'm glad your bed is a double. I wouldn't want to sleep in Kate's."

We sat on the sofa, which now showed no evidence of Kate's demise. I let Pat assume that Kate had died in her own bedroom. Pat had a Vittel water and I poured myself a glass of orange juice. We chatted. We kissed again. Despite the hour, the kisses led to "love making"—as she would say.

"Aren't we naughty?" Pat asked, looking at the sunlight streaming in the window. "We can't even wait for nightfall."

"Why wait? Any time is appropriate."

"Even in the middle of the Champs-Elysées?"

"I said any *time*, not any place."

"Now I see where you draw the line."

It was good to be with Pat again. I held her tight. After a few more minutes of kissing, she said, "Enough of this. I want to see Paris." I must have looked a bit taken aback. "Don't look so glum. I'm not rejecting you. There's always tonight and then the rest of our lives. Let's take a shower—together, if you like."

We walked to the Pont des Arts. We stopped in the middle, just as Kate and I had. I pointed out the key monuments and buildings that could be seen from that vantage point. I had learned that the gold-domed building, which Kate could not identify, was the Institut de France. It housed the academy, the guardians of French language and culture.

"This is such a great spot to start a tour," she observed. "I want a kiss. Right here. Right now."

"Yes, madame."

"Aren't I a mademoiselle?"

I didn't want to tell her that all women of a certain age are *mesdames* whether married or not. "As you wish. But let's move on. We have lots to see."

A Métro ride from the Louvre stop to Franklin D. Roosevelt took us to the point where we began our stroll up the Champs-Elysées. A ride back along the same line took us to the Palais Royal. We sat in the garden for twenty minutes and kissed some more. Upon leaving, Pat took note of the Comédie Française. "Was that

Molière's hangout?"

"I doubt if the building was there at that time, but he was the founder."

We walked a short distance through the arcades of the rue de Rivoli.

"Who's the golden guy on the horse?"

"Not a guy. It's Jeanne d'Arc. Or 'Joanie on the pony,' as I heard someone describe the statue."

"Sorry, Joan."

We walked back across the Seine via the Pont Royal. The rue du Bac took us to the rue de l'Université, which becomes the rue Jacob. I suddenly realized that it was well past two o'clock, and we hadn't had lunch. "You must be starving."

"I really didn't notice. Being with you has satisfied my hunger." Pat looked at me and then laughed. "That was corny. Yes, I could use a snack. But only something light. I'm counting on a great meal tonight."

"You got it. There's a café at the end of the next block. But first I want to show you something."

Right after the rue de l'Université becomes the rue Jacob, I pointed out, as Kate had shown me, the spot where the Treaty of Paris was signed. Pat was not impressed. "They used this little building. Why not some palace? Why not the Louvre?"

I shrugged. My historical knowledge was inadequate, and I could not answer her question. We moved on to the café at the corner of the rue Napoléon. We had drinks and shared a *salade niçoise*.

By the end of our excursion and the snack, we realized that we were tired. At the apartment we took our clothes off, stretched out on the bed, and held each other. I was dozing off as I heard Pat whisper, "I do love you so."

When I awoke, the sun was still high in the sky. I checked my watch. It was six thirty. Thirty years earlier Parisians had eaten dinner after eight and frequently not before nine. Now it was more

typical to dine at seven thirty or even as early as seven because
the last Métro train made its final run at eleven Sunday through
Thursday.

There was a restaurant near the Pompidou Center that Kate
and I had wanted to try, but never managed to. She could not get up
the energy to travel to a place where she wouldn't have an appetite
to eat the copious portions. I called and made a reservation for
eight o'clock.

By the time we freshened up it was seven thirty. Pat was
ravenously hungry. I told her that was good because her capacity
would be tested. "I'm sorry, but I need to put something in my
stomach. What's in the apartment?"

"Not much. Some bread from this morning. Some cherries. A
bit of cheese."

"A little cheese on some bread sounds good."

I took a hunk of Epoisse out of the refrigerator. "This is from
Burgundy," I informed her, as I unwrapped the half-empty little
box.

"Whew." Pat screwed up her nose. "Was it trucked here from
Burgundy or did it come through the sewer system?"

"It's strong, but the taste is sublime."

"I think I'll pass." Pat broke off a piece of bread and poured a
half glass of water. That allegedly satisfied her.

We took the Métro line from St. Germain-des-Prés toward the
Porte de Clignancourt. A lot of youngsters exited at Les Halles,
and then we exited at the next stop. I got my bearing and found the
rue aux Ours. Then another block led us to the restaurant. It was
rustic inside. We were led to a table across from the entrance to the
downstairs dining room.

We were handed menus. We asked about the contents of the
copper pot that was on a low flame burner. "That's our specialty—
aligot. It's a potato puree whipped with Cantal cheese. It's served
with several of the *plats*." The maitre d' asked if we wanted English
menus, which we declined. He smiled and left us to dope out the

meaning of the French descriptions.

Pat leaned over to me and said sotto-voce, "He thinks we're married. *Ma no hai une bague.*"

"I think, my sweet, that you're mixing Italian into your French or vice versa. But you had the word for ring right. How did you pick that up?"

"Last act of Carmen. I'm a mezzo, lest you forget. Probably all the French I need can be found in that opera. '*Sur la place chacun passe, chacun vient, chacun va.*'"

"Excellent. If you need to talk about people coming and going in the square, you've got it made."

Before the night was over, we ate too much. The aligot would have been filling enough. With a lentil salad, duck breast for Pat, a sausage for me, and a shared bottle of wine, it was all too much.

Pat insisted that we walk a bit before getting on the Métro, which we eventually boarded at Châtelet. From our own stop we took a circuitous route back to the apartment, and we still felt full.

We sat up for a while and planned. The next morning she would start going through Kate's personal items. In the afternoon, we would go to the Musée d'Orsay. Pat had seen plenty of Italian Renaissance art in Florence. She was hungry for the impressionists.

For her last day in Paris, Pat suggested that she finish off any remaining work on Kate's possessions in the morning. In the afternoon we could take a boat ride on the Seine. I pointed out that the fleet of *bateaux mouches* had been greatly reduced over the years. For fuel conservation purposes, they had switched from diesel to natural gas forty years earlier. Then around twenty-forty an accident occurred in which a poorly engineered boat hit a bridge and exploded, killing ten and seriously injuring another thirty people. The boats were put into dry dock. Eventually, four were reconfigured and put back in service. It was thought that reduced river traffic would improve safety. This was a case I had studied in graduate school. My professors felt that there were lessons to be learned about hasty conversions from one type of fuel to another.

"Okay, we'll skip the boat ride. But if we visit the Eiffel Tower, do you think it will be in imminent danger of toppling over?" she chided.

"We could take a chance."

"My brave hero."

We went to bed and shared a long kiss before falling asleep. In the middle of the night, I felt her hand on my chest. She noticed that I had produced a firm erection in my sleep. "Were you dreaming of me?" she asked when she sensed my eyes were open.

"Absolutely." I lied.

"Well, let's not waste it."

"You know you woke me from a sound sleep."

"Nonsense."

"Yes, you did. I should give you a good tongue lashing."

"Sounds exquisite." She spread her legs.

In the morning, I was back to my routine of *deux croissants et une baguette*. The baker's wife probably figured that my wandering wife or mistress had returned.

After breakfast, Pat began to look through Kate's clothes. She held a pair of glittering black slacks against her own body. "Who else but Kate could wear these?"

I had an idea. I called the woman who cleaned the apartment. In hesitating French I asked if the clothes that belonged to Madame Hastings could be given to any person or organization.

She replied that they were inappropriate for poor people. In addition, there were few tall and thin people who would want such clothing. Models could afford their own outfits. Put them in the garbage, she suggested.

I thought it was a shame but, reluctantly, came to the same conclusion. A few minutes later, the maid called back. She said that before we threw the sweaters and blouses in the *poubelle*, she would take a look at them and see if they were suitable for a friend.

I readily agreed. Pat and I began the sorting process.

"Looky here," Pat exclaimed after reaching the bottom of a drawer. "An envelope with 'For James' written on it. Guess you're the only James in the room." She handed it to me.

"It's Kate's writing." I could tell by the distinctive "J." Inside the envelope were a short note and a smaller brown envelope. The note read: "The treasure is yours, if you can find it." Instead of a signature, the note concluded with Kate's simple but large letter "K." The smaller envelope was made of heavier stock and was about six by four centimeters in size. On the front it read, "Meridian Temple Bank." Inside was a key that was the type used for a safe deposit box.

Pat was looking over my shoulder. "This should be a snap. We just need to find the office Kate dealt with. It probably was near her apartment."

"I bet the Meridian Temple Bank doesn't exist anymore. There have been so many bank consolidations over the past twenty years. But still we can probably do some research via the multinet."

"I wonder what we'll find in the box. Diamonds, I hope."

"Who knows? Let's see where the trail leads us." While chatting, I was doing research. "Here it is. Meridian Temple Bank was bought by Potomac River Bank in forty-five. Potomac River became part of Morgan/American in twenty fifty-three. I bet Kate used Meridian Temple during her first tour in Washington. We'll see if there's a branch near the Arlington apartment."

"We met at that apartment," Pat interjected.

"Yes, I opened the door for you."

"I didn't make an impression then."

"Yes, you did."

"We had a date or two, as I recall. Then you passed me on to Steve."

"I got pressure from Jane to date her exclusively. But let's put that aside. Eventually we sorted things out."

"It took a dozen years."

"What can I say? We can't turn back the clock. We can only move ahead."

"You're right. Give me a kiss, and I'll get back to work."

As we looked through the remaining drawers, we found only more clothing. Nothing matched the safe deposit box key in interest. In the closet were more clothes. Blouses and sweaters went on one pile for the maid to sort through. The other items went into the garbage.

In the afternoon, we followed through on our plan to visit the Musée d'Orsay. Pat said she was too tired to view the whole collection, so we concentrated on the impressionists and their offspring. She thought she would appreciate the works of Degas and Monet the most, but she became captivated by the Van Goghs.

"Poor man. He never sold anything during his tormented life. Finally, discouraged and deranged, he took his own life." She looked at my face. "That was insensitive. I'm sorry."

"No, that's okay. People turn to suicide as a last resort to bring an end to real problems and anxieties of various sorts. For many it might be the best way out. I think Kate had a very sound reason to do what she did. I will never second-guess her actions." I wanted to drop the topic and abruptly said, "Let's check out the Cézannes."

"Yes, let's do that," Pat responded all too enthusiastically.

Victorine, the woman who provided maid services, stopped by the next morning. She brought a wheeled shopping basket and a few plastic bags. Obviously she had decided that she would salvage a number of Kate's belongings for "a friend."

I introduced her to Pat. She greeted Pat and looked at me with a wry smile, no doubt figuring that I was a fast mover, acquiring a new girlfriend when the other was barely dead.

One by one, she examined the items we had put aside. She put a sweater against her own chest and looked in the mirror, and then explained lamely that her friend was approximately her own size. Victorine worked her way through the pile, accepting about two-thirds and rejecting the balance. As she said good-bye to Pat, I offered to help her with the clothes—at least as far as the *rez de chausée*. While descending to the ground floor, I tried to explain that Kate had been my boss and not my girlfriend. Pat was my fiancée.

We managed to pile the various bags in the shopping cart. Victorine headed toward the St. Germain-des-Près Métro stop.

"I think that woman is shrewd," Pat observed upon my return. "Or at least she thinks she is."

"She does a good job cleaning, and I've found her to be honest. That suffices."

With our afternoon free and with the weather again beautiful, we went up to Montmartre, strolled around Sacré Coeur and the Place du Tertre, and then went down the long flight of steps to Pigalle. From there, we took the Métro to the Marais and sat in the Place des Vosges while eating ice cream cones.

"What are you going to do about the safe deposit box?" Pat asked between licks of the cone.

"I've been thinking about that. I think it would be fairly easy to find the right bank, assuming it still exists."

"It must still exist. Otherwise, they would have to have switched Kate's belongings to another location and given her a new key."

"There's no bank name on the key, only on the envelope. Maybe she kept an old envelope and put a new key in it."

"That isn't logical."

"People aren't always logical," I suggested.

"But Kate was."

"Yes, generally. But there's another problem. How do I gain access to the box? I think I need the lawyer's help."

"If you go through the lawyer, she's going to tell you you're only entitled to twenty percent of the treasure. I bet her opinion will be that the contents are part of the estate. The nieces will get eighty percent, per the will. I bet Kate's note doesn't carry much weight relative to the will." Now Pat was being shrewd.

"For a musician, you have a pretty good legal mind. Maybe I can negotiate a larger share since Kate indicated the contents of the box are meant for me."

"Perhaps the good niece would agree, but will the other?"

I stopped to think. "I can't figure how to avoid going through the lawyer. But I think I should go to Washington in person to meet with her and protect my interest."

"Good!" exclaimed Pat.

"You want me to go to Washington?"

"Just for a few days or a week. You can kill a few birds with one stone. You can visit the lawyer, locate the treasure, and find an apartment for us."

"Sounds like a snap."

"You do want us to live together when we're both in Washington?"

"If you want to."

"Of course. Do you have doubts?"

I could tell Pat did not like the sound of my indecision. I needed to sound positive. "I have no doubts. I'm just reluctant to take on the responsibility of finding an apartment for both of us. Women have such definite likes and needs."

"The way I was thinking, we'd get a furnished apartment for a few months. Then we could look for more permanent housing together. And at the same time we can see if we can stand each other."

Obviously her thinking was way ahead of mine. "I guess I can do it, if you give me some guidelines."

"Do you remember my old apartment? It wasn't that great, but it worked. Something along those lines would be fine. Just make sure it has a good sized bed with a mattress that can take a good workout."

Sometimes her suggestive chatter reminded me of Jacqueline. Beyond that, there were few similarities. Age, figure, hair, eyes—

all were different. Jacqueline wasn't stupid, but she didn't possess Pat's culture and savoir-faire. Yet Jacqueline, too, was an artist, and their temperaments were not totally different.

"Are you listening?" she broke into my analytical reverie.

"Sorry."

"I was just saying that I tried to live with a guy when I was in my early twenties. It lasted about two months. I never lived with Steve, you know, except in China."

"Do you expect it to last this time?"

"I think so. I'm a lot more mature. I know that compromises are necessary. And then there's the matter of love. I didn't love Gary, and I didn't love Steve. Maybe I thought I did at the time."

"But you think you love me?"

"Better than that. I *know* it." Had she asked me in turn, I might have been totally honest and said that I was almost a hundred percent sure. But she didn't ask.

It was time to move on. I asked Pat if she wanted to see the Opéra Garnier. "It would be frustrating to only see the building and not hear the music."

"You know, it's mostly used for ballets now."

"Really?"

We returned to the Left Bank. Pat wanted to see the unicorn tapestries at the Musée Cluny. From there it was an easy walk back to the apartment. We rested for a while. Then we went out for an early and light dinner. This would be our last night together for several weeks. We wanted to make good use of the time, and dining was not our foremost priority.

XLVII

I CALLED KATE'S LAWYER, JANE Claiborne, on the day that Pat left Paris and told her about the note and the safe deposit box key I had found. My thought, I went on to say, was to come to Washington to track down the location of the bank.

"How do you propose to get into the box once you find the bank?"

"I'm executor of Kate's estate. I have a paper attesting to that."

"True, but we need to make proper application to the bank. Do you want my advice?"

"Sure. That's the reason I called."

"First, there's a database that's available to trace the safe deposit box through Kate's name. That will be a lot faster than having you hit the pavement. Second, the note you found does not have the same legal standing as the will. Even though Kate wanted you to have what is in the box—and presumably it's something valuable—her nieces have a claim to their share in accordance with Kate's will. Third, together we can get into the box easier than you can alone. Of course, you could retain your own lawyer to advance your claim."

"But you don't think I'd be successful."

"No."

"You realize Kate wanted me to have one hundred percent of the contents of the box."

"She very well might have, but she didn't state it in her will.

You could try to have the nieces renounce their claim to a share. Do you think they would? You know them better than I."

"One might agree, but I know the other wouldn't." I hesitated before suggesting something that I had been considering. "Is it possible to negotiate some compromise?"

"It's possible, but I don't think you would want to force the nieces to get their own lawyer to protect their interests."

"I was thinking I could take one half, and the nieces could share the other half. Could you present that?"

"I could try, but remember I represent the estate, not you personally. This could make it dicey. But if you could negotiate some settlement, I could draw up the agreement."

Jane, like any good lawyer, seemed to be adept at avoiding the dirty work, while taking on duties that added to billable hours. I took note of the tactic for use in any future consulting work.

"So," I thought it time to conclude, "when can we get into the safe deposit box?"

"First, we have to find it."

"I'm sure it's in Arlington, Virginia."

"I'll note that, but we'll use our own methods."

"As far as timing goes, can I come over to Washington next week?"

"I'm on vacation next week. Let me check my schedule for the following week." After a few seconds of silence, the phone revived, "Why don't we plan to get together on August sixth. Say ten o'clock. In the meantime you can work on getting an agreement with the two nieces, and we'll locate the box. You might want to check with my admin assistant at the end of next week to make sure we've been successful. And by the way, send me a scan of Ms. Hastings's note to you."

Most of the next week was devoted to sightseeing in Paris. A few things were accomplished before I took the flight to Washington. I spoke to Janet.

"I have some news regarding your aunt. I found something of hers. It was an envelope containing a note and a key. The note was to me, saying that if I found what Kate called a treasure, I could have it. I'll send you a scan of the note. You'll see it's in your aunt's handwriting."

"Well, good for you. What's the key for?"

"Probably a safe deposit box. Look, I know your aunt seemed to want me to get what's in the box. But I'm not totally comfortable with that. Here's what I propose. If I find anything of value, I'll give you and your sister half and I'll retain the other half. What do you think?"

There was hesitation. "I don't know what to say. I'll have to discuss it with Diane."

"Of course."

"Will you get back to me tomorrow or the next day? I plan to head to Washington soon to find out what surprise your aunt prepared."

The next day, Janet called back. She said that Diane figured they were entitled to eighty percent of contents of the safe deposit box, and I was only entitled to twenty. The stuff in the box, like all other assets, was part of the estate, even though their Aunt Kate had written the note.

"You can make that claim," I replied, somewhat deflated. Either Diane had good legal instincts, or she was being coached.

Janet had not concluded. "Here's what Diane and I propose. We'll split whatever you find in the safe deposit box three ways, one-third for each of us. I realize you might think you deserve a lot more, but we think we deserve the lion's share. After all, that's the way Kate wrote her will."

I had thought there was a possibility that the nieces would seek some compromise. My reaction was mixed. On one hand, I wouldn't get the whole treasure as Kate's note stipulated; on the other hand, I could end up with only twenty percent if I tried to oppose them. And I would be spending my own money fighting a losing battle.

"James, are you still there?"

"Yes, I was just pondering your offer. Look, I don't really want to get into a legal battle with the two of you. We'll all end up paying lawyers needlessly. Do you think Diane will sign something agreeing to the three equal share approach?"

"I'm sure she will."

I found myself in Washington travelling on the metro from my reasonably priced hotel near American University to the lawyer's office on K Street. Jane Claiborne's assistant told me an hour earlier that Janet and Diane had signed the agreement to divide the contents of the safe deposit box in thirds. The law firm had located the box itself in a bank in Arlington, Virginia, as I had expected. Jane and I were scheduled to travel to the bank after meeting in her office. Assuming we found something of value, Janet was scheduled to meet with us the next day to review the contents. Diane, who lived near Philadelphia, would not make the trip, but would join us via the Quisters on-line meeting facility.

Jane Claiborne was about fifty years of age. As we spoke, a number of strands of dark blond hair fell across her eyeglasses. Her features were regular, but she was not particularly good looking. She wore a plain white blouse and a straight black skirt. Although a lawyer, she could have passed for a waitress.

She offered me coffee, which I declined. We exchanged some pleasantries about my flight, and she asked if I had had any trouble finding my way to her office. I reminded her that I had worked in Washington for a number of years. She told me an assistant, Tim George, would be taking me to the bank in Arlington. He and I would do a quick inventory of the box and then bring its contents back to the office, unless we thought the value of the contents ran into the millions of dollars.

Almost miraculously, Tim appeared just after she mentioned him. A few minutes later we were heading to Arlington in an electrocar owned by the law firm. Tim brought along an oversized briefcase that, he was sure, would be large enough to hold the contents of all but the largest safe deposit box.

On the trip he tried to engage me in a conversation about baseball. I explained that I had been out of the country all spring and summer and, consequently, was not following U.S. sports. In order to rectify my deficiency, he proceeded to update me on the standings and how the top players were performing. I was happy to let him talk while I daydreamed about the potential riches I'd find in the next hour.

The bank's branch vice president was waiting for us. He reviewed the papers that Tim produced, made a copy, and then returned for the key that was still in my possession. Tim and I accompanied him to the vault where the proper box was quickly located. The bank's key was inserted in one side of the lock and mine was put in the other. I held my breath, but the door opened promptly. The bank's officer slid the box from its compartment.

"Kind of heavy," he commented, as he passed it over to Tim. He led us to a small room where Tim and I would have privacy in order to review the contents. "Take your time," he suggested as he left us alone.

Tim put the box on the table. "I suppose you'd like to take the first peek?" he asked.

"Indeed I would."

"Just remember, I have to account for everything we find."

I nodded and sat down in front of the box that was about two-thirds of a meter long, thirty centimeters wide and twenty deep. I slid the box closer and sensed its heft. Carefully I opened the lid, almost expecting something from within to attack me. Instead what I saw were three silver boxes, each tied with a red ribbon.

"Merry Christmas," Tim exclaimed. "Go ahead. Open your first present."

I lifted one box out and undid the ribbon. Inside were plastic envelopes, and inside each was a gold coin. Tim was at my side and immediately saw what I saw. "Gold. Looks like about twenty, maybe thirty coins."

"I guess they're somewhat valuable," I ventured.

"Oh, yes. Let's look at a few." He checked them rather quickly. "It looks like these are half-ounce coins from earlier this century and the end of the last. They were minted for investors. Since gold is selling for over three thousand an ounce, they're worth at least fifteen hundred a piece. They look genuine enough. But we need an expert evaluation."

"Understood."

"Gold is a damned good present. Let's hope you find more than frankincense and myrrh in the other two boxes."

"Wrong season," I replied, picking up the next box. "Plus this box is even heavier." I undid the ribbon. "More gold coins. Bigger ones."

My sidekick with the two first names took a closer look. "These are called double eagles. They were minted in the early twentieth and late nineteenth centuries. I think those from the twentieth century are Saint Gaudens. Some people consider them to be the most beautiful coins ever minted in the U.S. Their pattern was used in the other younger coins we saw in the first box."

"They certainly look good to me. And they're heavier than the others."

"Yeah. Each one is an ounce."

I started to do some math and was somewhat repelled by my own greed. Then I acknowledged to myself that it was precisely greed that brought me from Paris to Washington.

The third box weighed about the same as the first. Inside were many smaller gold coins. "These look French," I commented to my sidekick. Almost all were marked twenty francs, although a few were larger. Many had a rooster on the front; some had a standing figure; and others, the older ones, had profiles of kings or Napoleon.

Tim saw what I saw. "Some of these are over two hundred

years old. I have no idea if they have some extra value for collectors beyond the gold content."

"I guess we'll find out."

"I'll make a few notes. Then we'll pack the stuff up and take it back to the office. It's probably worth quite a bit, but not in the millions. I don't think we need an armored car."

It was around noon when we arrived at the law office. Tim ordered some sandwiches brought in. We would eat while we worked on an accurate inventory. Before we started the inventory, I called Janet.

"What did you find?" she asked a bit breathlessly.

"Gold coins. It looks like your aunt was accumulating them as the ultimate safe haven for some of her money."

"Do you think they're worth much?"

"I really haven't made any calculations, but they have to be worth over a hundred thousand dollars." I thought it best to lowball the estimate.

"In total? Or for each of us?" Janet exhibited a touch of greed that's implanted in practically all of us.

"I shouldn't speculate. We haven't even started on the count."

"But there's enough there to warrant my making the trip tomorrow?"

"There has to be at least a hundred coins. Of course, some are kind of small, although some weigh an ounce each."

"They still use ounces?"

"All of the coins are over fifty years old."

"I see. I'll be there. One thirty. Right?"

"Right."

"I'm looking forward to meeting you."

"Same here."

By two thirty, an inventory was complete. It read:

2 – 40-franc gold coins
59 – 20-franc gold coins
42 – half-ounce American eagle gold coins
33 – Double Eagle gold coins

I asked to have all the French coins that were from the reign of Napoleon the Third and earlier to be listed by date. This took another twenty minutes.

While waiting for modifications to be made to the list, I called Pat.

"I was hoping you'd call before I went to bed. Was there really a treasure?"

"Yes and no. It wasn't diamonds."

"Rubies?"

"Not even rubies. Gold."

"Well, that's not so bad. Do you think it's worth a lot?"

"Not a fortune. But it's a nice little stash. By this time tomorrow, I hope to have some decent estimate of the value."

"*Buona fortuna.*" The Italian seemed to contain a double entendre.

"I miss you."

"I miss you, too, *amore.*"

Jane Claiborne returned with my copy of the inventory. "We'll see you tomorrow."

"You bet. Oh, I have something for you." I handed her a few printed pages.

"What's this?"

"My airfare. It's chargeable to the estate's expenses."

At one-fifteen the next day, I was back at the law office. I was early and was asked to wait in the outer office. Five minutes later a woman, who appeared to be in her thirties, arrived. She was shorter than Kate. Her face was rounder, her figure plumper. Her hair was short and light brown. Yet there was a certain resemblance around the eyes and nose.

"Janet?" I ventured.

"Yes. You must be James. Good to meet you after all our conversations."

While we waited, we talked about her aunt. Janet told me that she could understand her taking her own life. Kate only wanted to think of herself as young and vibrant. Janet felt that she wouldn't have wanted to live if she couldn't come close to that image. I agreed, but I did not tell Janet how bad her aunt looked in the final few months.

Janet appreciated my taking care of all the arrangements in Paris, including the burial at Père Lachaise. She asked about how she could find Kate's resting place if she ever went to Paris. I told her that I would send her detailed information.

At precisely one thirty we were ushered into a conference room next to Jane Claiborne's office. Accompanying Jane was a man, but it wasn't Tim George. Jane was introduced to Janet, and both of us were introduced to Buford Hanley, two last names to balance Tim George's circumstance. Jane simply described Buford as a qualified appraiser. Tim George entered and activated the Quisters hook-up.

For the first time, I got a view of Diane. She looked a bit like her sister, except the corners of her mouth turned down, probably from wearing a perpetual frown. It turned out that Janet's husband, Larry, also joined us, since Quisters had the capability of including up to a dozen people in the conference.

Once everyone was online, Buford Hanley took over. "You have a nice little trove of coins here. Primarily their value is based upon their gold content, not their numismatic value. Let me divide my analysis into a few parts. First of all, we have forty-two half-ounce American eagle coins. They're going to bring slightly more than the melt value of the gold. In other words, this group of coins is worth about sixty-five thousand dollars. By the way, I'll talk in terms of Troy ounces for the American coins. A Troy ounce is a little over thirty grams.

"Second, the thirty-three double eagles are going to be worth a little more vis-à-vis their melt value. Many are on the borderline between uncirculated and almost uncirculated in quality. I didn't spot any rare dates. Yet each has a bit of extra value for the coin collector who wants to own gold. Therefore, I estimate the value at between one hundred ten and one hundred fifteen thousand for this lot, totaling thirty-three ounces.

"Lastly, we have the French coins. There are fifty-nine twenty-franc pieces, dating from eighteen-seventeen to nineteen-twelve. Most are of the angel and rooster varieties. Many of these are in almost uncirculated condition. Yet they sell for prices only slightly above the value of the gold content. They were minted as a savings device for the conservative bourgeoisie who trusted gold more than banks. Perhaps not such a bad idea at that. There are fourteen twenty-franc pieces from the reigns of Louis the Eighteenth, Louis Philippe, and Napoleon the Third. Except for two from the period of Napoleon the Third, all are in very fine or extra fine condition. The Louis Napoleon coins are uncirculated. But, still, the value of these coins barely exceeds their gold content value.

"The two forty-franc pieces are somewhat rarer. The Napoleon Premier Consul dates from year eleven . . ."

"Year what?" Janet interrupted.

"Year eleven. It's dated by the French revolutionary calendar. I believe year eleven would be equivalent to eighteen-oh-three."

"Does that make it very valuable?"

"Not tremendously so. Some collectors may be interested, and it could bring thirty to fifty percent over melt value. Please understand that even this coin can be found quite readily on the market. Similarly the eighteen-twenty-four Louis the Eighteenth forty-franc coin may be sold for twenty percent above gold content, since it's in almost uncirculated condition.

"So what's the bottom line on all this?" Jane Claiborne's patience was waning.

"The total value of the French coins is around forty thousand. Therefore, if you add the French gold to the American, the grand total comes in at around two hundred fifteen thousand dollars."

"Is it relatively easy for the estate to dispose of the coins?" Jane asked.

"Yes. We can find dealers who specialize in bullion coins to bid on the whole lot. We might not quite realize the figure I mentioned. But it could be done very expeditiously."

"I have a question," I interjected. "If Janet, Diane or I want to own one or more of these coins, in remembrance of Kate, rather than having it sold, is that possible?"

Jane took responsibility for the reply. "I suppose so. We'd have to have a good appraisal of that particular coin, and then that value would be subtracted from the proceeds you'd otherwise receive from the estate. Do you want a specific coin?"

"Yes, the forty-franc Napoleon from year eleven."

"Janet, do you want any of the coins?" Jane asked.

"No, I don't think so."

"Diane, how about you?"

Diane's face came to life on the computer screen. "No, I want the money. But how do we make sure James isn't getting a special deal on the coin he's taking?"

"I'll get the appraisal and communicate it to all of you." Jane replied. She went on to make a few concluding comments.

I exited with Janet. "I wish I could stay, and we could chat. But I have a baby-sitter waiting for me." Janet and I shook hands.

"Thank you for your help," I added.

Janet laughed. "You're the one who did all the work. Good-bye. Good luck to you and your fiancée. Is the Napoleon coin for her?"

"You're quite perceptive."

XLVIII

Florence, etc., 2064

I RETURNED TO FLORENCE BY way of Paris, where I surrendered possession of Kate's apartment. The landlord was gracious, saying he would arrange to have the unwanted items removed. He probably realized that I was not going to attempt to claim the unearned portion of Kate's rent. Only two days were required to wrap up business in Paris. I took a last leisurely walk around the quarter where I had spent a few long, agonizing months. My feelings were mixed. One part of me hated to leave the city. Another said good riddance. In the two days I found no opportunity to visit Père Lachaise and Kate's vault.

On my last walk, after a final three-course meal, I stopped at the café opposite the St. Germain-des-Près church, and plunked down my twenty-five euros for a cognac. It was ten o'clock. Yet there was still a bit of ambient light in the sky. I watched the people coming and going. Sometimes I spotted a foreigner. I wondered what they were doing in Paris—probably just tourists. They did not have the same sort of mission that brought me here.

Tomorrow I would be going. I assumed I would never return.

The next evening, I arrived at the Santa Maria Novella station in Florence. Pat, as she had four months earlier, met me at the station. The greeting, of course, was different. The kiss was long; the embrace was tight.

We returned to our apartment. Pat prepared a quick dinner of pasta and salad. We opened a bottle of wine.

"Tell me more about the coins." Pat said, after we were into the meal.

"They were a bunch of gold coins, mostly American, the rest French. None is terribly valuable by itself. But when you add them all together you get maybe sixty ounces of gold. So with gold these days at three thousand dollars an ounce, we're talking about two hundred thousand in total."

"I thought, at one point, gold sold for more than fifty thousand an ounce."

"I think you're right. But that was before the revaluation of the dollar in the twenty-thirties. If that hadn't happened, gold would be above two hundred thousand an ounce now. Of course, a loaf of bread would cost two hundred dollars."

"I forgot you know so much about economics."

"I even taught a course at one point." I made a mental note to add that experience to my résumé.

"And the nieces agreed that you'll get one-third of the two hundred thousand? Are you going to get the actual coins or cash?"

"The coins are part of the estate. They'll be sold and the proceeds divided up . . . with one exception." I reached into my pocket. "Here. For you."

Pat took a careful look at the coin, which was still in a plastic sleeve. "Wow. Napoleon. So how old is it? There's no date."

"Actually there is." I pointed to "An XI." "Year eleven."

"That can't be B.C. or A.D."

"No, it's a year in the French revolutionary calendar," I replied authoritatively.

"I didn't know they used a different calendar during the revolution."

"So they tell me."

"Then this coin is from around eighteen hundred."

"Give or take a few years."

Pat started to hand the coin back to me, but I stopped her.

"No, it's for you."

"Really? Why?"

"Do I need to count the ways? Because I love you. Because you found the note and the safe deposit box key. Because you've had to put up with my absence while I spent a few months with another woman . . ."

"A dying woman."

"And because I thought you'd like it."

"Oh, I do. It makes me think of Beethoven."

"The consummate musician. I give you a coin with Napoleon's portrait on it, and you think of a German composer."

"Did I ever tell you about the dedication of the *Eroica Symphony?*" For the next five minutes Pat expanded my scant knowledge of musicology. Then she came to a screeching halt. "But I don't want to talk about music."

"What do you want to talk about?"

"I want to talk about plans. I made some plans for us."

The phrase "plans for us" somehow made me envision a discussion about marriage, something I perceived as premature. To my relief, Pat headed elsewhere. "Before we leave Italy, I thought we should spend a few days in the Cinque Terre. It's a rugged coastal area, maybe a hundred kilometers from here. It consists of five small towns. I made a reservation for three nights at a *pensione* in Monterosso.

"I passed through there with a girlfriend last summer. But it would be so much better to spend a few days there with you. And on the way we can stop in Lucca and see Puccini's home."

"I thought music would come into the picture at some point. How about Beethoven's home?"

"We'll have to wait until we get to Vienna."

"If we get to Vienna, I'll show you around."

"You've been to Vienna?"

"Yes. Some F.E.D. project." And I left it at that.

For the balance of the month of August, Pat was busy with the last few performances in the festival series as well as accounting for money due artists and income and pledges that were still being received. I was reminded that a person working at a small festival needs to be a jack-of-all-trades.

I spent most days exploring churches that I had not yet visited and returning to places that had impressed me the first time around. Sometimes I went to a vantage point like the Piazzale Michelangelo or Fiesole and took in the view. But it wasn't the same without Pat. The weather was invariably hot. I moved slowly and sought shady paths. At cafés, umbrella-covered tables were quickly taken.

Some of Pat's evenings were occupied, as well, with concerts or dinners with visiting artists. Occasionally I was invited to a dinner, but mostly not. Several times she managed to come up with an extra concert ticket for me. I was able to go backstage and meet the musicians. Most were young artists from other countries, including the United States. The Florence festival was not prominent, but a good place for a musician with talent but limited experience to gain a foothold. No performance involved a large orchestra. A chamber orchestra performed on occasion, but more often it was a trio, a quartet, or a soloist.

I gained more experience with live music. I found that I liked Bach more than Mozart; Chopin more than Schubert. I began to offer my evaluations to Pat. Sometimes she agreed; sometimes she thought I was entirely off the mark. Then she made sure to tell me why I was wrong. I didn't mind, although frequently I retained my own opinion.

There were many things I wanted to discuss with her concerning our return to the United States. I had left a deposit with an agent with the understanding that we'd pick one of two apartments. Pat barely had time to look at the photos I had taken of each. She said either would be satisfactory for a few months. "You decide." Her mind was still focused on wrapping things up in Italy. To her, the United States was a long way off. In fact, we were to return in just a few weeks.

We did manage to book our flights for the trip back to Washington. Pat required a few days after our planned sojourn to the Cinque Terre to finish her remaining duties. Yet she needed to be back at American University by September fifteenth. I decided to return a few days earlier to make sure the apartment was clean and ready for our occupancy. Beyond picking our return dates, Pat wanted to put everything else off. If need be, she said, we could discuss the details while on the beach at Monterosso.

The last performance in the concert series was on Sunday, September first. The featured work was César Franck's sonata for violin and piano. I was able to stand in the wings with Pat.

"That was great," I commented when the last notes were played.

"Very good, I'd say," she corrected.

"Well, I liked it a lot."

"I'm glad you did, dear."

We went to a small reception afterward. The pianist was Korean. She spoke practically no Italian and only a smattering of English. The violinist was Russian. He had studied at Julliard and spoke excellent English, albeit with a heavy accent. He told us his ambition was to be concertmaster of the New York Philharmonic someday. Pat told me later that she didn't think he would achieve his goal.

On September fourth we departed by train for the Cinque Terre. As Pat had planned, we made a several-hour stop in Lucca. We quickly toured San Marino cathedral and the elliptical Piazza San Michele. She was anxious to get to Giacomo Puccini's apartment. But when we got there, it had closed for lunch. Nearby, we found a spot to get some pasta and a half bottle of wine.

When we did get into the apartment, she spent a good hour looking at the furnishings and memorabilia. She would have loved to play some notes on the piano, but she didn't dare. We knew we needed to catch the next train for Monterosso, so Pat dragged herself away. As we exited, she noticed that there were reproductions of posters, done in the art nouveau style of the period, advertising the composer's operas. "Don't you think we should get one or two? They'd look great in the apartment."

"You haven't seen the apartment."

"Okay, they'll look great in *any* apartment. Which ones do you like?"

"No, Pat, you pick. This is a musical decision."

Pat looked them over with some care but rather quickly because we were pressed for time. "Let's get *Tosca*. My father's favorite aria is *E Lucevan le Stelle*. Do you like her?"

"Yes, she looks a bit like you."

"You think so? You're just saying that. Funny, I always thought Tosca should be a dark brunette. This one has medium brown hair."

"Maybe she had it dyed."

"James!" she scolded. "Come on, you pick one, and then we'll go."

"You have the musical taste."

"This is not, my dear, music. This is decorating. Come on, pick."

"How about the *La Bohème*?"

"Good choice. It still must be the most-performed opera, even to this day."

"I just like the cascade of figures tumbling from top to bottom. The red really stands out, too."

"Great. So it's *Tosca* and *La Bohème*. You know, they're not very expensive. We'll never get back here. Let's get one more."

"You didn't like my choice of *La Bohème*?"

"No, I think it's excellent. But I like *Turandot*, too. It's so exotic."

"Fine, we're up to three. Any more?"

"No, that's enough. We have to catch our train."

I thought that we would see many outstanding vistas from the train ride along the coast. For the most part, we saw tunnels, along with a few glimpses of the Mediterranean. After traveling through the other four villages of the Cinque Terre, we arrived at the most northerly—Monterosso al Mare.

There were two electrotaxis parked at the station. We managed to take possession of the second one and asked to be driven to Pensione Amelia. The driver nodded his head to show recognition. The ride was short. We arrived in a small square. The driver proceeded to unload our two small pieces of baggage.

"*Dov'è Pensione Amelia?*" Pat asked.

"*Su.*" The driver pointed upwards.

"*Su?*"

"*Sì. La scala.*"

The driver began to drive away. "I guess this is as close as we can get," Pat deduced.

"From here we climb." I grabbed the heavier suitcase.

"At least I won't forget the spot where our steps are. Rossini."

I looked around and saw nothing that said "Rossini." "Rossini?"

"The store," she answered quickly. "Come on, let's get started."

About sixty steps up, we came to the Pensione Amelia. We were greeted warmly. The manager carried the heavier bag up one flight to our room. Too bad he hadn't provided the same service from street level.

We unpacked quickly. Pat wanted to explore the town a bit before we took showers and had dinner.

"Remember, we'll have to climb the steps again."

"You're talking like an old man. What is it? The equivalent of about three flights?"

"How about five."

"So what?"

"You're right. What are a few steps? *Andiamo*." I used one of my hundred words of Italian.

The town consisted of two parts linked by a tunnel. Both parts had shops and restaurants. Our side had the beach, the jetty where tourist boats docked, and two churches. We found out that in addition to the train, boat service connected the five villages, plus the somewhat larger town of Portovenere to the south. One could also walk on the mountainside paths between the villages. Some legs of the walk were easier than others. An English tourist advised us to try the via dell'Amore first, the easiest stretch between Rio Maggiore and Manarola.

"Via dell'Amore. That sounds like a winner." Pat winked at me.

At dinner, we found that seafood and pasta were the staples of the area. Meat was not featured. After dinner, we strolled around town again. There were hundreds of people out doing much the same as we—taking their evening *passagiatta*. Many, of course, were not Italians. English, Scandinavians and Germans were present in large numbers. A few even sported their walking sticks in the evening.

Around ten o'clock Pat said, "Let's go back up." She grabbed my hand and brought it to her lips.

"I know what you have in mind. I love aggressive women."

"You know many of them?"

I covered my mistake. "I know one, and she's the one for me. Let's find Rossini."

"Yes. *La Gazza Ladra*—the store by the steps. Strange name for a shop."

"Of course." I made a mental note to look up the name on the multinet.

In our room we undressed, turned the lights off, and opened the window that looked out toward the town. There was a string of faint lights about fifty meters away. Farther below, lights from bars and restaurants shone more brightly. There were houses above us, but they were mainly dark.

We didn't think people could see into our darkened room. But there was something erotic about thinking they might be able to. Even after making love we still left the window open. Pat lay on top of me and said she wanted to fall asleep that way.

The next morning, Friday, we took the boat to Portovenere. Pat observed, "You're being unusually quiet."

"I'm trying to work out the economics of the boat transportation. They didn't charge that much. It's obviously diesel. Still the fuel has to cost a fortune. I bet the government subsidizes the transportation along the coast."

"You always have to be thinking about energy usage."

"And you never think about music? Let's me guess. You're looking at the water—must be Handel's water music."

"That's silly. I'm looking at the sea, so obviously I have Debussy's *La Mer* going through my brain."

We explored the town, which Lord Byron had allegedly enjoyed. A little cove bore his name. We climbed steps up to the castle and a church that was perched precariously on a point of land. Back in town we explored some shops, which struck me as quite similar to the ones in Monterosso.

We caught the boat again for the short trip to Riomaggiore. Here, people—younger than us—swam from the rocks because there was no sand beach. We ate pizza on the patio of a restaurant on the town square. Then we attacked the via dell'Amore, which proved to be more of a stroll than a hike. When we arrived in Manarola, clouds were beginning to roll in. We took a quick look around the town and then took the train to Monterosso. Rain was threatening when we arrived. Before going up to our room, we bought a bottle of wine, some cheese and bread.

Rain began to splatter on the terraces and roofs as we ran up the last twenty steps to the *pensione*. We were wet and out of breath when we reached our room. Pat took her clothes off and wrapped a bath towel around her torso. The coverage was not totally complete, which was fine with me.

She reclined on the bed. I stripped to my underwear and joined her. I reached inside the v-shaped opening left by the towel. I put my hand on a firm thigh that always seemed so inviting.

"I appreciate the sentiment, but what I really want to do is talk."

"We can talk this way."

"I want you to concentrate on what I'm *saying*." Her tone seemed forbidding, but soon I realized it was her business voice.

I removed my hand. "Why don't we lie side by side?" she suggested in a friendlier vein.

"Better yet, let me open the wine, and we'll each have a glass."

"Good idea, but I still want to talk."

I began to open the wine. "What do you want to talk about?"

"Us."

I handed Pat a glass. "*Cin cin.*"

"*Salute.*"

We each took a sip of the fruity red. "Okay, you wanted to talk."

"Yes, I think we need to discuss several things. First I want to talk about the temporary apartment and what we have to do to make it habitable." Although the apartment was furnished, we would need to supply linens, dishes, pots, pans, and utensils. She speculated on whether she could get most of these things out of storage.

Then we talked about finances. We agreed to split the rent and ongoing expenses associated with the apartment—utilities, food, etc. We both had jobs waiting for us, so we figured we could comfortably handle these bills, while leaving an ample amount for personal expenses and savings. All this was reassuring.

There was one thing bothering Pat, and that was our schedules. Pat had to teach two evening classes in the upcoming term. In addition, she would have evening rehearsals and the occasional performance. Would we have enough time together? Would we be able to nurture our relationship? I was willing to see how things developed. Pat looked at the potential pitfalls and barriers.

The discussion continued. Half the bottle of wine had been consumed. She realized she needed to put something else in her stomach. We began to nibble on the bread and cheese. The glasses were filled again.

The rain made the evening cooler. Pat put on a sweatshirt, but left her bottom bare, perhaps to be provocative. "James, this might be an awkward topic."

"That's okay. I'm ready for it." Now on my third glass of wine I was ready for almost anything.

She ploughed ahead. "Let's assume we live together for a long time. Perhaps we'll even get married at some point."

"Why not?"

"Well, let's make sure of our feelings before committing," she counseled.

"As you wish."

"Okay, here's the issue we've never discussed. Do you think you want to have a child again?"

I thought for a minute or so. "It's not important to me. If that's what you want, it would be fine with me."

"It might matter to you some day. You shouldn't treat the matter so lightly."

I didn't think I had reacted cavalierly to her question. I genuinely felt I would be equally satisfied with or without a child. I had had a son, and for a short time he provided some pride and pleasure—and then there was longer-term agony. "You know I have some experience in this area. It's not that I don't have feelings about the matter, but they're genuinely mixed."

Pat laid a hand on mine. "I'm sorry. That was insensitive on my part. But here's the issue. In another few months I'll turn forty-two. Perhaps I'm too old to have a baby."

"If it's important to you, we could always adopt."

"That's a possibility. Although I'm not sure I have enough maternal instincts to raise a child that wasn't my own."

"Then we can have a dog." As soon as the words left my mouth, I regretted the statement.

She looked askance at me. "That's not the same."

"I was just thinking of companionship."

"I like dogs, but they're not my own flesh and blood. They're not going to care for me when I'm old and feeble."

Perhaps Kate's death had led Pat to focus on care during a final illness. "There are always ways to obtain help when you need it."

Pat shook her head. "First, I might not be able to afford someone to care for me. Second, it's still not like having a family member helping you. I have a father, who is reaching the end of his own life. I have no brothers or sisters. I have two cousins who I never see and with whom I have nothing in common."

"Kate had a sister and two nieces. But I was the one who cared for her, and I'm also the executor of her estate. Family can be overrated."

"You did a good job for Kate."

"Let me say one more thing before we drop we subject. What makes you think I won't be around for you? Now let's talk about something more pleasant. We came here to enjoy ourselves." I kissed her on the forehead.

"You're right. I just need to find out one more thing. When you say you might be around for me, are you younger than me?"

"You're going to turn forty-two?" Suddenly I realized I didn't know Pat's birthday, and she didn't know mine.

"Yes, on Christmas Eve."

"You poor kid. You probably had combination birthday and Christmas presents."

"Generally. But don't avoid my question. How old are you?"

"I just turned forty."

"When?"

"Two days ago."

"You bastard. And you never told me that September third is your birthday. Why didn't you tell me?"

"We never discussed birthdays until now. And it's something I don't dwell on."

"Come on. Let's get our clothes on and go out and celebrate."

"We could take our clothes *off* and celebrate."

"We'll do that later. Let's go out, get something to eat and get totally smashed."

"We have a pretty good start on that."

"Let's finish the job."

It was nine o'clock. The air was cool and fresh. The rain had stopped at some point during our long discussion. We worked our way down the wet steps to street level and only had to walk a short distance before we found a bar where we could get some snacks and more wine.

We discovered a white semi-sweet wine from the region. It was called "Sciacchetra," a name even harder to spell than to pronounce. The liquid went down quickly and easily. We started on a second bottle, and then took the balance up to our room.

I had barely entered the room when Pat pushed me onto the bed. "Did you ever hear of a woman raping a man?"

"No, but it sounds intriguing."

"I'm going to give you a sample of everything you could ever dream of, and then you let me know what you like best."

After our smorgasbord of sex, we drank some more wine and then fell asleep. In the middle of the night we both threw up. It was a memorable fortieth birthday party.

The next morning we awoke late but basically in good spirits. The nocturnal purging of our stomachs probably saved us the agony of morning hangovers. We arrived for breakfast just as the owner's daughter was about to remove the coffee and *cornetti*. We—rather

Pat—asked if the weather would be good. "Yes, definitely. Perfect for the beach."

"That's sounds great, just to loll on the beach. But we also have to get you a birthday present. What would you want?"

"You're my only desire."

Pat groaned. "And I always come cheap."

"That's exactly what I can afford."

"But it's your birthday, so I buy the present."

It was nearly eleven when we arrived at the beach. We staked out a prime spot and rented our chaises. The air was warming nicely.

I helped Pat apply sunscreen to her back. I considered her back one of her best features. It was firm and narrow, like a younger woman's. Like Jacqueline's, perhaps. Despite Jacqueline's sexiness, there were many things about Pat that I preferred. And the antics of the prior night showed she did not lack her own sexuality. If only one could piece together the ideal woman, I daydreamed. Then I told myself that I really needed to rid my mind of such fantasies. But, then again, a beach was a wonderful place to let the mind wander and indulge in fantasies.

Around one, we decided to go to one of the nearby trattorias for a light lunch. We shared a *panini* and only drank mineral water. Then Pat dragged me along one of the small shopping streets looking for a present.

"How about a print of a Cinque Terre village?"

"You bought Puccini posters."

"We can get you a piece of art, too."

"Then I think I'll pick Botticelli's *Birth of Venus*."

"We'll get you a print when we get back to Firenze."

"If I can't have the original, I won't consider a substitute."

"Well, I checked at the Uffizi, and it's slightly out of my price range. We'll have to come up with something else."

We passed additional shops. She kept urging me to get one thing or another. Obviously her need to grant a present was greater than my desire to acquire one. Finally, at a souvenir shop, I picked out a tee shirt with a Sciacchetra label pictured on the front.

"That's what you want?" Pat asked a bit incredulously.

"Absolutely."

"You won't throw up each time you wear it?"

"No. I think I've recovered. I probably will even have some more wine tonight."

We found the right size. Pat paid the forty euros and handed me the package. "Happy birthday, *amore*."

We stayed on the beach all afternoon. In the evening, we had a light seafood dinner. Pat had shrimp with pasta. I chose the *fritto misto di mare*—a fried mixed seafood dish, which wasn't as heavy as what you would find in Savannah. It also contained a small fish, fried whole and with its head on. Something that wouldn't pass muster on the other side of the Atlantic.

At around nine thirty we climbed the steps to the *pensione* and began to pack. Since we hadn't brought much, we were soon finished. We set our alarm for seven and got in bed. The window was open, as it had been on our first night in Monterosso. A band began to play in the square near the waterfront. It struck up a dance tune, and we could hear shoes tapping to the rhythm.

"This is Saturday night. What are we doing in bed at ten?" We dressed again and followed a path to the music.

We tried a local dance but weren't too successful. While we were sitting out the next number, a townsman, who must have been around sixty, asked Pat to dance. She looked at me with raised eyebrows, indicating that she was obliging so as not to cause an incident. She mastered the dance quite quickly. Unfortunately, she then proved to be a popular partner, and I was left on the sidelines. After four or five more dances, she finally refused the next one, claiming exhaustion.

I pulled her off to the side. "You look like you need a Sciacchetra."

"*Si, Signore.*"

We went back to the bar where we drank our first Sciacchetra. This time we ordered by the glass. We drank slowly and talked.

At first we talked about our experiences during the past three days. Then she changed the subject. "Someday I hope we can get an apartment that really suits our needs, maybe with an extra room to use as a study, maybe a living room big enough for a piano. Maybe we could even afford a condo at some point."

"We might. Probably by year end I'll be getting my share of Kate's estate."

"Will it amount to much?" This was the first time she tried to quantify my inheritance.

"A few hundred thousand." I low-balled the figure. "It would give us a nice down payment on a decent apartment."

"Do you really want to use the money for that?"

"What better use could I make of it? An apartment is a necessity, plus it could be a good investment."

"You realize I couldn't contribute anything like that amount. I have about a hundred and eighty thousand in my university retirement plan, but I wouldn't want to touch retirement money. Aside from that, I've saved about a hundred thousand as an emergency fund."

"We'll use the money from Kate as a down payment," I asserted.

"Maybe I should sign something acknowledging that the money going into the condo is yours."

"Wow. We're really getting legalistic. No, you won't sign any such thing. I trust you." I thought briefly how I once trusted Jane. Maybe I should be more careful this time. But with the passage of time, I thought I had become better at evaluating people.

She reached over to clasp my hand. "You can trust me. I'll never let you down." Had she read my thoughts?

We were finishing our second round of wine. The waiter told us that if we wanted another glass, we should get one because the bar would soon close. We declined the offer. At the same time, we noticed that the crowd had dispersed. Only a few couples and some solitary workers were on the streets and in the squares.

"We should go up to our room," I suggested. "In the morning we need to get up early."

"Maybe we could just enjoy this getaway a little longer. We can always sleep on the train. Let's take one last look at Monterosso as it goes to bed. Let's walk out on the jetty where we boarded the boat. It's a great view from there."

Slowly we strolled along the walkway leading to the boat dock. No other romantics chose to do the same. The lights in town were sparse. There was no moon. We were careful where we stepped, in order to avoid falling into the sea.

We sat down at the very tip of the boat dock. Pat looked at the village. "So quiet and peaceful. Almost everyone has gone to bed. I bet it's very late."

"It must be well after midnight." I looked at the sky. "*Lucevan le stelle.*"

"You remembered."

"I have a good teacher." I turned away from town and looked out above the Mediterranean. "There's the summer triangle out over the sea."

She immediately knew what I was talking about. "I forgot. That's something we share. Our fathers were both stargazers. And what's that overhead?"

"The great square in Pegasus," I replied confidently. It was coming back. For the past twenty years I had lived in or near cities—Washington, New York, San Francisco, Savannah. Even with reduced lighting to save energy, the night sky was not an attraction. I now remembered how beautiful it was.

We were both sitting, but I suggested we recline. I asked to put my head on Pat's stomach so I could look up.

"And what else do you have in mind?"

"No, I really want to take a good look at the sky." I stayed that way for ten or fifteen minutes. I saw the Milky Way, which I hadn't spied since I was a youngster.

"What are you thinking?" she asked.

"I was only thinking how wonderful the sky is, how wonderful you are. Now, it's your turn."

We switched positions. Pat looked up. I saw the direction where she was gazing. "Somewhere between the corner of the Great Square and Cassiopeia is the Andromeda Galaxy. It was one of the first things I saw through my father's telescope when I was a boy. I thought it looked like the end of a cotton swab."

Now it was Pat's turn to recollect. "I don't remember many things that my dad and I looked at. But he had a photo of something—I think it was called the dumbbell something or other . . ."

"The Dumbbell Planetary Nebula."

"That's it. I thought it looked more like a bow tie or a piece of bow tie pasta. Anyway, it was in a room that Dad used as a study, and it doubled as a spare room for guests. If he didn't like the visitor, he would say that so-and-so was in the right place—the dumbbell room."

Pat lay with her head in my lap for a good while. The world was very still. Only the lapping of water against the jetty broke the silence.

She finally stood up. "I need to stretch."

I got to my feet as well. It was time to return to our room. We faced the town again. I pointed to the elongated pentagonal formation of stars coming up in the east. "That's your constellation—Auriga." I chuckled.

"Don't laugh. One can't choose one's surname."

"No. I suppose not. Nor can you choose your own first and middle names. It's done for you before you can possibly object. You know, I finally figured out what the 'C' stands for."

"Sea as in ocean?" Pat interjected all too quickly.

"No, you know what I'm getting at. The 'C' in your middle

name."

"Okay, genius, you figured it out. Now let's forget about it." She sounded genuinely annoyed.

"But it's a pretty name, even musical in nature."

"I suppose so. But that was not my father's intent. It was a prank my father pulled on me. Can we get away from my middle name? You know, I don't even know yours. I hope it's something outrageous like mine."

"Sorry to disappoint, but I don't have one."

"Everyone has a middle name."

"Not me."

"I'll give you one. Let's see. Ichabod? Japetto? Amadeus?"

"You can't give me a middle name. I have all sorts of documents with none listed. My parents had to register it, and they didn't. They were satisfied with just James."

"Was a relative named James?"

"No, the story I heard was that my mother adored the movie star James Stewart. She was a fan of old movies."

"Then you should be James Stewart Lendeman. That's very distinguished, unless I start calling you 'Stew.'"

"My parents thought that James Lendeman was quite enough, and that's what I'll stick with."

"Poor us. Your parents short-changed you by one name, and I have a middle name I don't want."

"I guess we can only conclude that the fault, dear Pat, lies not in ourselves but in our stars."

"Oh, that's bad. I get it, but I wish I hadn't. Have we seen enough of the stars, the sea and the town?"

"I suppose so. 'Let us go then, you and I' . . ." I could have added the next line but chose not to.

XLIX

Washington, 2064...

PAT AND I MOVED INTO our rental apartment near American University in September of two thousand sixty-four. It was apparent from the outset that she was not thrilled with my choice. Fortunately we were only required to stay there three months and could give a month's notice after that.

We found that we needed to make some adjustments and compromises living together. Because of our schedules, we were frequently preparing meals for only one, and that proved to be impractical. Therefore, we came up with a number of recipes for dishes that could be reheated. I learned to make an acceptable chicken cutlet in a Dijon mustard sauce, and a portion could be reserved for Pat when she needed a quick meal. She made various salads that could be kept a day.

I had to learn to clean up sufficiently to meet her standards. She learned to shop for grocery items that would satisfy me, both in taste and quantity.

We had some arguments, but we learned to talk through our differences and work them out. Unlike my experience with Jane, we did not let problems fester. And we were reasonably well-off financially.

I was working steadily again at my job in the F.E.D. My pay grade put my wages roughly on a par with what Pat earned from teaching, performing, and giving private lessons. We established our own "rainy day" fund.

In January, Kate's estate was settled. I received a payment

of about seven hundred thousand dollars. I showed Pat the accounting statement that was sent by the law office. "I'd be crazy to lose you. You're such a rich man. Rich and handsome—what more could I want?"

Of course that sum of money did not make us wealthy. It amounted to about what Pat and I earned on a gross basis in a year and a half. However, it arrived in one lump sum and was free of taxes. We felt rich.

Sometime after I received the money from Kate's estate, we began to seriously discuss getting married. Pat must have assured me in a dozen different ways that she was not marrying me for the money. I believed her. With the added money, we could buy a condominium. Somehow the combination of two incomes, a permanent home, and marriage meant security for us.

There was one complication. I confessed to Pat that a divorce from Jane was never finalized, partly because Jane was never located. Perhaps she was even dead.

Pat was shocked by this revelation. "Well, hadn't you better find out if she really did die? I wouldn't want to get into any legal trouble."

"No. You're right. I'll see if that lawyer I used in San Francisco still exists." What I didn't divulge to her was that I stopped pursuing the divorce because I could not afford any more payments to the lawyer. And at that time, a divorce was not my highest priority.

It took a day to track down the lawyer. He vaguely remembered me and the situation with Jane. He asked me when he last worked on my case. I figured it was probably in fifty-eight.

"The trail is probably cold. We'll need a private investigator. It will probably take a few weeks of his time to start making progress. If we're lucky, we'll find she's dead. That would be cheapest for you. Some work for the P.I.; almost no work for me. That way it might only cost ten thousand or so. Otherwise, we could be talking twenty, thirty thou . . . Who knows? What was your wife's name?"

"Jane."

"Yeh. If she's alive, let's hope Jane doesn't want to contest the divorce. Of course, she walked out on you. You got that in your favor. Anyway, we could be getting into some serious money. You got it?" Perhaps he remembered my difficult financial circumstances.

I told him that I was prepared to pay. The lawyer asked me to transfer ten thousand to his account to get the investigation started.

A few days later I received an email from the lawyer indicating that a search of databases revealed no death certificate for either a Jane Lendeman or a Jane Sorel. They would proceed to a more detailed investigation. The last line read: "Send another ten thousand so we can go ahead."

Pat was a bit concerned by the mounting cost and additional expense to come. But she wanted the divorce as much as I did.

Two weeks later the lawyer wrote: "Making progress. Jane left the Humboldt County compound in 2058 after son's death. Went to live in a religious community in Arizona. Police records show her there in 2059. Compound raided for suspected child abuse activities. No charges filed against Jane. She left the compound after that. Following through. Send another $10000."

I showed the note to Pat. "I guess this is the first confirmation you've gotten about your son."

"Yes."

"I'm so sorry."

"It doesn't surprise me."

"But it still must hurt."

"I don't think I've processed the information."

"I see the lawyer's after more money."

"Naturally."

"We won't run out?"

"No, we'll be fine."

Another two weeks went by, and I was tempted to call the lawyer. But miraculously he called first. "Bingo, James, we hit the jackpot. Jane is very much alive. She's living on a ranch near a town called Boise City, Oklahoma. And are you ready for this? She's married to a rancher. Calls herself 'Mrs. Kegler.' And they have a three-year-old daughter.

"Evidently she never told her husband she was married. He's hopping mad. He wants to get this divorce done even more than you do. He's using a lawyer in Oklahoma City. Apparently Boise City is a pretty small place, despite being called a city.

"Look, I want to pay off the P.I. now. So send another six thou. Don't worry; you'll get an itemized bill. I hope we can wrap this all up in a month or so. After all, you two haven't been together for years. They're going to want to avoid bigamy charges against Mrs. K. But that's not our problem, although it plays in our favor. So that covers it. Bye."

I never had a chance to ask a question, but he seemed to cover all the bases.

When I told Pat, she was happy to hear that the divorce could be concluded quickly. She had one question: "What's Jane's daughter's name?"

"It wasn't mentioned. I'm not really interested. She's not my child."

"Right."

In early July, Pat and I, accompanied by her father and two of her friends to act as witnesses, went to a justice's office in Rockville, Maryland. The ceremony took only a few minutes, and I remember it none too well. I do recall Pat smiling slightly, almost mischievously, and saying: "I, Patricia Capella Auriga, take thee, James Lendeman, to be my lawfully wedded husband."

My mother and sister decided not to attend. My mother declared rather tactlessly that a second marriage was not as important as the first.

After the morning ceremony, the five of us present returned by metro to downtown Washington and went to lunch. Then Pat's two friends returned to work. Pat and I accompanied her father to Union Station where he took the train back to Philadelphia.

We returned to the apartment and somewhat later, at our leisure, consummated the marriage.

In August, we moved into our condo, which was in Maryland a few stops up the metro line from American University. We put down four hundred thousand in cash and obtained a fifteen-year mortgage for the remaining four hundred thousand. It wasn't the home of our dreams, but it was ample in size, had a spare room to use as a study, and was convenient to transportation into the city.

How quickly additional years passed. I worked with two secretaries of energy, as well as a score of deputy secretaries and assistant secretaries, over the next five years. Generally they appreciated my experience, knowledge and abilities. None of them, in my opinion, were nearly as perceptive, inventive or audacious as Kate. As time went on, her rough edges and unfairness disappeared. She became a paragon of the great executive. And I don't think I was at all influenced by her final generous act.

The work of the department was no longer exciting. We were performing caretaker functions. No grand initiatives were pursued. Rather, we tinkered with rules and tried to eke out more efficiencies to extend our limited energy resources. Nighttime power downs became more common, even in the largest cities. We still debated, and we still needed to defend our policies before government committees. But there was no zeal in any attacks; there was no glory to be gained in tearing the rump department down any further. And, within the F.E.D., there was no hope of accomplishing anything significant. The statisticians became more important than the policy tinkerers.

L

IN MID-SEVENTY-TWO I was offered—and accepted—an assistant secretary position in the department. Perhaps it was a stupid thing to do. This was near the end of Charles Denkman's second term as president. Many of his first-term appointees had left for private sector jobs. Many political appointees would lose their jobs when a new administration took office in seventy-three.

The lure of the title and position outweighed the safety net of a civil service rank. Pat knew I wanted the job and encouraged me to take it. "It will set you up for a better position outside of government when the time comes."

My appointment to assistant secretary had to be approved by the Senate. I appeared before a sub-committee to answer questions about my qualifications. The questions sounded probing, in case constituents or the media were present. But the media was not there. They didn't care and neither did the senators. A new administration would soon be in charge and would sweep the vast majority of appointees away. I was quickly confirmed.

Along with my title, I was assigned a new office. It was the office Kate had occupied when she first interviewed me for a job. The workstation where Jane had labored was still outside the door. I knew that moving into the office was a mistake, but I could not reject the honor.

Working late on fall and winter evenings, I felt, on a few occasions, bony fingers on my shoulder and strands of wispy hair against my cheek. One night I was revising a report, making an unpalatable truth sound less alarming. A soft, female voice whispered in my ear: "bullshit." But this was Washington, not Savannah. No ghosts were supposed to haunt these halls, and—at any event—I didn't believe in them. Nonetheless, I jacked up the lighting level, contrary to conservation guidelines, to discourage the apparition's return.

My departure from the F.E.D. came quickly in March of seventy-three when a whole new crop of appointees eased out the old. But this, in a way, ended up being fortuitous.

Pat applied for, and was chosen to fill, a high level administrative position at the Metropolitan Opera in New York. She was the assistant to one of the three associate directors at the Met. We sold our condo in Maryland and put the proceeds into another one on West End Avenue in Manhattan, a little over a kilometer from Lincoln Center.

By the time we moved to New York we knew we would never have children. When Pat had turned forty-five, she had thought we should take some tests to determine if a surprise pregnancy was possible this late in life. The tests showed that my sperm count was adequate to do the job, but she had a hormonal imbalance that was hindering conception. The fertility specialist told us that the condition could probably be treated successfully. We said we would think about it.

We discussed the pros and cons over the course of a month. Ultimately we agreed that we were too old to start a family. Plus, the risk of an abnormal birth was too great.

In the year that we made our decision to remain childless, Pat's father passed away, and my mother died the following year. Suddenly, our only immediate relative was my sister, who lived in New Jersey.

After we moved to New York, Pat insisted that we invite my sister, her husband, Tony, and Tony's son by his first marriage, to dinner. Caroline, at first, looked for an excuse to decline, but Pat's persistence along with Tony's genuine desire to visit us won the day.

Tony and Pat, surprisingly, hit it off well. On the surface, they had little in common. Tony was a butcher. He had a high school education and his musical knowledge was negligible. His interest in sports was lost on Pat. But Pat made sure he knew that she was of Italian extraction. He rose to the bait and told her that his family was originally from Sicily.

"Some of your family no doubt came from Puglia, hence your surname—Pugliese." Pat employed her knowledge of Italy in order to make this assertion.

Tony seemed unaware that any area in Italy was called Puglia. In New Jersey, most Italians thought they came from Sicily originally. It seemed to be a matter of pride. Who knows why?

Tony's son, Vincent, kept busy with electronic games while the adults talked. Even when we ate, he gobbled down his food and quickly returned to the games. Tony was a lot more interested in Pat's job than was Caroline.

Caroline bent my ear about how much she missed our mother; how life was boring; how she disliked teaching second graders; how she thought Vincent would amount to no more than a butcher like his father; how Tony went to too many sporting events and she didn't enjoy them; how difficult it was to make ends meet even with two wage earners; how they wished they could afford a vacation; what a hardship it was living in a suburb, even an inner suburb like Dumont, and doing without a car.

I told her that I never in my entire life had owned a car. She had never owned one either, she countered, although up to ten years ago, she and Mom had shared an electrocar. I thought that this amounted to ownership, but I did not dispute her point. "It's a bleak existence," Caroline concluded.

After my sister, her husband, and stepchild departed, Pat observed, "Now that was fun. Wasn't it?" I shrugged my shoulders. "I liked your sister."

"You were talking to Tony most of the time."

"Well, I thought you'd want to catch up on family matters."

"There's Caroline and me. That's the whole family."

"That's more than I have."

In New York, there were fewer opportunities for me to do consulting than I would have expected. Manufacturing was only found in the fringes of the city. Few new structures—whether factories, office buildings, or warehouses—were being constructed. My assistant secretary title got me on the board of directors of a medium-sized corporation. I had to do some reading, attend six meetings a year, and listen in on an occasional conference call. For this I was paid fifty thousand a year.

At one point, I did consulting for an engineering firm that was based in Jersey City. The commute was easy, requiring a short subway ride and a twenty-minute trip on a PATH train. After six months, the company's business began to decline. Several of their bids on decent-sized projects were rejected. My consulting contract was not renewed.

I had much time on my hands. In nice weather, I enjoyed walking along Broadway and Amsterdam Avenue, and into Central Park. I did some window shopping but bought little aside from groceries. Even tempting ethnic delicacies were avoided.

Pat, on the other hand, always seemed to be busy. Her job at the Metropolitan Opera was a yearlong endeavor, despite the fact that the season had been shortened twenty years earlier. Booking artists, attending to details of new productions, issues involving union contracts could be active at any point in the year. Beyond this, she squeezed in some time to help with a summer music festival and even did some coaching for several off-Broadway productions.

Pat eventually supplied the majority of our income. That seemed to be sufficient because we didn't need to dip into savings. Of course, we spent modestly.

Occasionally, Pat would come up with an unsold ticket to a Met performance. Although notice came at the last minute, I was invariably available. So, for only the cost of a subway ride (or in nice weather a bit of shoe leather), I managed to see operas such as: *Ariadne auf Naxos, Rienzi, Il due Foscari*, and *The Ballad of Baby Doe*. Never did a ticket come my way for *La Bohème, Carmen*, or the double bill of *Cav and Pag*—in other words, the most popular in the repertory. But at each performance I found something to enjoy and gradually increased my musical knowledge. Frequently I was able to go backstage after the performance and meet some of the singers, although rarely the top stars, who wanted their privacy.

An annual pattern developed. It started with the new opera season in the fall. Pat was frantically busy from early September on, making sure all was ready for opening night, which usually occurred in early October. The fall season concluded with the holidays, so we had little time to celebrate her birthday, Christmas or New Year's. But I made sure she received at least one present on her birthday and one on Christmas. No more would she be disadvantaged by having been born on December twenty-fourth.

January provided a slight hiatus with a five-week break in the opera schedule. Of course, Pat had things to attend to for the second half of the season. Unless some unforeseen circumstance occurred, this part of the season tended to be slightly more relaxed, perhaps because a pattern had been established in the first half. On occasion, we entertained a visiting performer at a good restaurant— never at home. I indulged at these times because the bill was picked up by the Met.

On occasion Tony, my brother-in-law, would spend a night at our apartment after attending a college basketball game at Madison Square Garden. The quality of competition in the New York area was not exceptional, but the best could be found at the Garden. Sometimes Tony would bring us a little gift, almost always related to his profession—veal cutlets, lamb chops—the highest quality that was available. Occasionally, we had a late dinner centered on his offering. My sister never accompanied him, despite being invited.

May brought the summer recess. But Pat always had some work to do for the following season and for the summer concerts where she assisted. Spring also brought my longer walks.

The summer festival lasted only three weekends. Then we were generally able to get away for a week to a beach on Long Island or the New Jersey shore. Train service was available to either location. We also tried to visit my sister and Tony at least once each summer for a barbeque. We would sit on the deck, drink beer or white wine, and talk. Tony's subjects were his job, baseball, and the glories of Italian cuisine. Caroline found much to criticize and little to praise. One year, Vincent decided that he wanted to be a chef and was fortunate to find a summer job working in a restaurant's kitchen.

And then we were back to autumn.

After a few such cycles, Pat made a suggestion. "Since you haven't found much consulting work, why don't you do some work for yourself?"

"What do you mean?"

"You've been a part of something very important over the years—the attempt to get this country out of its energy predicament."

"Of course, we weren't very successful."

"Yet you and others like Kate tried. You struggled with this in ways that most people don't realize. Few have had your experience, knowledge, and perspective. Why don't you write about what you've seen and done?"

"To what purpose? No one wants to hear about the energy shortages over the last fifty years. It's a depressing saga."

Pat threw up her hands. "At a minimum it would give you something to do. But obviously it's up to you. Do it; don't do it. Sit around the apartment doing nothing if you prefer."

Her words stung. I remembered my criticism of Jane when she vegetated in our San Francisco apartment and couldn't even bother to cook a decent dinner.

A few weeks later, Pat looked over my shoulder while I was composing something on the computer. "What are you working on?"

"Nothing much."

But she had focused on the screen. "You're writing about working with Kate. That's good."

"You haven't read enough to determine if it's good or bad."

"You know what I mean. It's good that you're jotting down your recollections."

"I've barely begun. I have no idea how far I'll get."

"Do as much as you wish." I could tell that she didn't want to push me too hard.

LI

New York, 2084

ADDITIONAL YEARS SLID BY. THEY were rarely marked by milestones or memorable events.

One winter we—rather Pat—had the opportunity to go to Paris. She was going to attend a few performances at the Opéra Bastille in order to hear some emerging talents who had not yet crossed the Atlantic. In addition, she had contracts to finalize for the following two seasons. She encouraged me to join her, since my airfare and meals would represent the only added expense.

"You want to visit Kate's resting place. Don't you?"

"I think Kate's now back in Washington. Her ghost could not stay away."

Pat's eyes opened very wide. "You really believe that?"

"No. I'm just kidding."

"I'll go along with you to Père Lachaise."

"And while we're there you can see the graves of Bizet, Debussy, Chopin, and the like."

"Well, we wouldn't want to miss those, would we? And for lovers like us, there's Abelard and Heloise."

But Pat came down with the flu, and someone else went in her place.

Pat had keener ways to keep track of the passing years than I. She could recall the various great performances and the more egregious mishaps. I judged the passage of time by the accumulating centimeters on my waistline or by finding that two kilometers now represented a long walk.

The year after our aborted trip to Paris, I sensed that the normal aging process had speeded up. I seemed to have more aches and pains. Pat said I wasn't looking my "normal self," whatever that meant.

I advanced my annual check-up. Some blood analysis came back abnormal. My primary care physician referred me to a hematologist. She admitted me to a clinic for more tests. In two days they came back. I had something called "myeloma." I knew that most times when "oma" was the end of a medical term, it meant cancer. The doctor gave Pat and me an explanation of the disease. Pat concentrated on each of the doctor's points more than I did.

"Okay, so what do we do about it?"

"First of all, you need to understand that we can slow the disease. In fact, we can just about bring it to a halt. But we can't provide a total cure; at least, not at this point. There are different types of medicine we use—chemotherapy of various strengths. We can try the type that generally is well tolerated and won't cause too many side effects."

"So how long do I have?"

The doctor forced a chuckle. "At this point, there's a wide range of possibilities. We haven't even started on your treatment and gauged your body's reaction. If things go well, it could be quite a number of years."

"If not?" I asked. Pat was too afraid to ask the question.

"A shorter period of time." She changed to a more upbeat tone. "You're fortunate to live in New York. We have some of the best treatment centers here." She gave me the name of a specialist, who would also be working on my case. She turned to Pat. "Mrs. Lendeman, do you have any questions?"

Pat shook her head no, and she didn't even bother to tell the doctor that she was still known to the world as "Ms. Auriga."

"I have one more question," I interjected. "What causes this thing?"

"As with a number of cancers, we suspect that some environmental factors could be involved. We know that people who have had exposure to certain toxins have a higher risk. But we don't know for sure."

"I've always been an office worker and not exposed to any unusual environmental factors."

"But the pollution and radiation pumped into the environment over the past hundred years or more put everyone at risk to a certain extent. Individuals will react differently to the same set of factors."

None of us said anything for a few moments. I knew Pat was thinking of me and perhaps of being without me. I thought about a child I never got to know.

The doctor knew our meeting was over. She rose. We all shook hands. Pat and I emerged from the office into a brilliant autumn day.

"Lovely day," I observed.

"It sucks," Pat replied.

My treatments began the next week. At first, the medicine didn't have any significant side effects, and I thought that I would have any easy time of it. Then, after perhaps two weeks I began to feel some nausea after taking a dose. But I had medicine to counteract nausea, and this helped quite a bit. It became apparent that I would have a few good days, followed by several poor ones.

Besides being on a pill schedule, I put myself on a writing schedule. Over the past three years I had accumulated a hundred or so pages of notes, observations, anecdotes and episodes forming a loose amalgam of my experiences inside and outside the Federal Energy Department. I told myself that I needed to establish a routine to piece all of it together, add missing material, and turn the whole into a meaningful narrative. I promised myself—and in doing so I was really promising Pat—to put in at least three hours each day to meld paper notes and computer documents into something readable. I figured this would be my final gift to my wife.

Several months passed. As happens so frequently in life, patterns were formed. There were times to take pills; times to feel good and to feel bad; times to eat; times to go to the bathroom; times to go to the doctor. At one visit, I asked the doctor, "How long will this go on?"

"The treatments?"

"The treatments. My illness. Whatever you can answer."

The doctor thought a minute. "Look, you're doing well. We've just about stopped the progress of the myeloma. You can go on for years. We have cases where the disease is stopped for ten years. Ten years of life—wouldn't that be worthwhile?"

"But it could be five or three or two?"

"That could be true, but as long as you respond well . . . Well, we just keep going on. Right?"

LII

SIX MONTHS HAVE GONE BY since my first treatment. I go to the clinic every two weeks. Each month they do an extensive analysis of my condition. At the conclusion of the last one, the doctor in charge of my case told us that I was doing very well. My treatments would continue along the same lines.

Pat has managed to accompany me to each clinic visit. Her boss has been understanding and accommodating.

Pat's emotions have changed from day to day. She has been hopeful. She has been depressed. Most of all she has been fearful.

She tries to maintain a close relationship with my sister, brother-in-law, and my sister's stepson. But Vincent, having gone through his chef's training, did some work in New York restaurants and then decided to take a job in Los Angeles.

Even Tony's visits have slacked off. He's sixty-five and within three years of retirement. Both he and Caroline have realized that their savings are insufficient to fund their retirement plans. Tony's contribution to a revised financial plan involves attending fewer sporting events and joining his buddies less often for beers after work.

Pat dotes on me even more. When I am feeling well she cooks my favorite dishes. When I feel up to it, we go out to restaurants, which are varied and abundant in our neighborhood. She avoids the after-work discussions that I know she enjoys. I tell her that she needs to keep up her friendships and professional relationships.

When I pass away, those people will form her support group.

She doesn't want to hear this line of talk. "James, you can never be replaced. You're the only man I ever loved. You are the whole world to me. If you die, I won't be far behind."

"You mustn't talk like that." And I add, "If you're alone, you should consider remarrying if you find the right person. That would not dishonor my memory."

Pat merely smiles a sad, ironic smile. "Let's not talk about my life without you."

Secretly I wish that she were more like me. Somehow I managed to move on from one woman to another. Two or three I loved. Some were just passing fancies, but enticing nonetheless. I am less critical, less committed.

I notice that Pat is interested in the pain control and sleep aid medicine that's prescribed for me. She makes sure that the prescriptions are refilled, even before I use all the pills. The behavior seems similar to Kate's; perhaps she is even emulating Kate.

After observing her adding to the cache one night, I commented, "You know, we needn't save all that stuff. If my pain becomes too great and my situation is terminal, physician-assisted suicide is permitted now in New York."

Pat replied tersely, "Permitted for *you*."

The next morning as we passed through the hall preparatory to taking a short walk on the bright June day, Pat stopped short of the door. "I think we're missing something."

"We have our keys. I have my wallet."

"No, the wall is missing something." The wall displayed the three posters we purchased in Lucca: *Tosca, Turandot,* and *La Bohème.* "We can fit in one more."

"As you wish." We left the apartment, got into the elevator, and from the lobby stepped into an early summer day awash in sunshine.

"A glorious day. It's good to be alive. I think I'll have no trouble making it to the park and back."

"Then let's give it a try." Her voice sounded more cheerful.

Our anniversary is almost here. It will be our twentieth. I want to get something special, but have no idea what Pat would want. I ask her.

"I have everything I need. If you're feeling well, why don't we go to a really good restaurant?"

"A fancy French restaurant sounds perfect. Perhaps André."

"Italian might be more appropriate for our anniversary," she counters. "We fell in love in Italy."

"You're right, my angel. You're always right."

Fortunately I'm not on my medication when we dine at Trattoria Gobbi on the East Side. I'm feeling well. We order too much—antipasto, veal chops, zabaglione for dessert. Of course, we can't finish it all, and the waiter chides us.

After taking a taxi home across Central Park, I sit down in the living room, a bit tired from the outing and feeling too full.

Pat says, "I have a confession to make. I bought a present for both of us. It's not expensive," she adds defensively. "I'll be right back."

She returns with a fairly flat, rectangular package, about five centimeters thick and a little over forty centimeters on its longer side. I suspect I know the contents. Pat urges, "Open it."

I tear the paper away. And there she is: Cio-Cio-San sitting in her room, looking away longingly toward a bird alighting on its nest among cherry tree branches. "Madama Butterfly. She'll go well, right next to Tosca."

By this point in my opera education, I know the outline of many libretti. I observe, "Too bad Puccini created so many unfortunate heroines—Cio-Cio-San, Tosca, Mimi."

"I guess that's what we can expect from life," Pat says mordantly.

"Pat, you're spoiling a great evening."

"I'm sorry. At least we have Turandot on the wall. Things worked out well for her when she found love."

"Yes, a sad beginning but a joyous conclusion. Think of me as Calaf. I'm clever; I can solve all the riddles."

"The answer to the first riddle is 'hope,'" Pat supplies quickly.

"Then, also remember my promise."

"Which is . . ."

"*Vincerò. Vincerò.*"

She kisses me and smiles. "You will win and beat this thing, won't you?"

"I'm trying."

Acknowledgements

AN AUTHOR MAY CREATE A novel, but it doesn't come to life without the help and guidance of others. I want to thank all those at Two Harbors Press for their contributions to the complicated process of publishing a book. In particular, Robert, my editor, provided valuable input and suggestions, along with his careful review of the text. Wendy's skill and creativity were evident in the excellent cover and overall design of the book. Thanks, too, to Hannah, who answered so many of my questions, and to the entire team at Two Harbors Press, which provided consistent support throughout each and every step.

About the Author

B. R. FREEMONT WAS BORN in New York and has lived in the Savannah area for over a decade. He holds a B.A. and an M.A. from northeastern universities.

During his career in business, he filled a variety of management assignments and had brief stints working for government entities. Over the years, his interests have included: astronomy, domestic and foreign travel, dog breed club administration, wine tasting, and avidly reading both fiction and non-fiction.

He is married and has a son and two daughters.